PERSONAL
REASONS

MICHAEL BOTZ

For distribution information contact End of the Road Publications – 1350 East Flamingo Road, Suite 508, Las Vegas, NV 89119 - endoftheroadrpublications@gmail.com

Library of Congress in Publications Data is available upon request.
ISBN: 978-0-578-25528-6

ALSO BY MICHAEL BOTZ

FICTION

Author of the Storms

Chatsworth Royalty

For Joe Mannix who made me who I am…
and for Mr. Kato, Lola, Heidi and L.W.

1

Detective Leonard Diggs grimaced at the bleeding paper cut inflicted by Jesse Huszer's murder book and presumed it had something to do with cosmic payback. Mr. Huszer's bullet-ridden body had been found in a dumpster twenty-three years before, and due to some of the most atrocious investigative work Diggs had ever come across, whoever stole Huszer's life remained a mystery.

For most of the morning, Diggs had tried to keep his focus on the contents of the brittle and stained pages, but with each instance of uninspired police work, he grew more irritated. After a parade of loud sighs and angry groans, he said to the opened notebook at the center of his cluttered desk, "Buddy, you deserved a lot better."

Seated in a cubicle behind Diggs was his partner of nineteen weeks, Detective John Stall. A paper plate holding a third of a microwaved meatball sandwich lay on his desk, and an opened newspaper blocked his face.

Stall lowered the newspaper. "Did you say something, boss?"

Diggs answered with a surly grunt Stall understood all too well. He went back to the newspaper without another word.

Pages blotched with coffee and food stains Diggs could live with. Poorly constructed investigations left him exasperated and the Jesse Huszer case was a doozy of ineptitude. Diggs rubbed his temples at the endless incompetence. Each bush-league step made by Detective Desmond and Detective Green felt like the tap of a hammer against his skull.

If Desmond and Green's shoddy work didn't make it clear that they couldn't have cared less about finding Jesse Huszer's killer, the painfully skinny murder book drove the point home. Twenty-four pages—not much longer than a comic book.

A murder book compiled by competent detectives typically ran hundreds, often thousands of pages. It was supposed to be the all-encompassing document of the crime. It was not supposed to include dozens of misspellings and careless typos. It was not supposed to look like a family of five ate lunch on it. It was not supposed to be twenty-four pages of abysmal, lazy, and bewildering police work. The Huszer murder book was a joke and an embarrassment.

Diggs closed his eyes and turned to a page at random. He pressed his fingertip on the center of page and opened his eyes. "Ex-wife said she was unaware of husband's insurance policy at the time of his death."

Diggs recognized the sentence as a perfect opportunity to throw Stall a confidence-boosting softball. In the four-plus months they had been partnered, Stall had been useless on his best days and a disaster on most of the others. The week before had been particularly rough.

Outside a masseuse parlor, they spotted one Harvey Smith, a witness to a park shooting who had been dodging the police for weeks. Smith recognized Diggs' unmarked car for what it was and immediately ran. Diggs pursued in the car while Stall chased on foot. A block up, Diggs turned sharply into an alley and suddenly Stall was bouncing across the hood of the car. He rolled up the windshield, over the roof, down to the trunk, and onto the pavement. Had Stall been a soapy sponge, the car's exterior would have been its cleanest in months. Diggs slammed the brakes and for a moment lost control, narrowly missing a row of propane tanks stacked four high. The pursuit ceased and Smith got away.

Diggs called out over his shoulder, "Stall, listen up. Got a quiz for you." Diggs read the sentence his finger had chosen.

Stall laid the newspaper on his lap. Eagerly he said, "Okay. Insurance policy. Ex-wife. Got it."

"Add this fact. According to Huszer's cousin, Huszer had every intention of writing his ex-wife out. In fact, he was going to change the policy the week he was murdered. Since he never got that chance, she cashed out. If you were the detective investigating Huszer's murder, would this interest you?"

Diggs swiveled his chair. Stall was squinting at the overhead fluorescent lights.

"Twenty-five thousand. Would this make you suspicious?"

Stall became fidgety. He leaned forward, placing an elbow on a chair arm. His index finger touched a spot between his upper lip and nose. After thirty seconds, Diggs grew impatient. A simple question with an obvious answer had turned into a think tank.

The day before, the week before, the month before, Diggs would have given up. He kind of liked Stall. Nice guy. Friendly. Respectful. He'd be a neighbor you'd trust to grab your mail when you were on vacation. But this was business, and Stall wasn't in the Juvenile Crimes division anymore. He needed to pick up the pace and learn to be a much better detective than he was.

Stall's body language didn't offer any promise. He scanned the floor as if Diggs had taped the answer to his shoe. He hemmed and hawed for a few moments.

Finally, he said, "Did I tell you Angry Joe was looking for you?"

"She found me. Yesterday."

"Have you heard anything new on the Glen Palmer case?"

"He's still missing. Now answer my question."

"Wouldn't I have to examine all of the evidence? Like you always say, boss. Not everything is always as it seems."

Diggs told Stall to go back to his lunch and turned his attention to the Huszer murder book. Not much more than a minute later, he threw up his hands. "Why did these idiots even bother to come to work?"

Stall swept a grease-stained paper plate and an empty can of Mountain Dew into a trash can.

"Boss, I get the sense that something's wrong."

"Desmond and Green's abysmally awful investigation is what's wrong. This case never had a chance. No follow-up interviews. Alibis that don't make any sense. His ex-wife cashes out. They talk to her only once, outside of a strip club, and believe every word she says. Less than a week after the murder, the ex-wife's new boyfriend packs up everything he owns and leaves town. Nobody brings him back. Nobody tries to interview him. In twenty-three years!"

Stall nodded in agreement. "That's crazy. How many years has this one been open?" He wheeled his chair closer to Diggs, attempting to read over his shoulder.

"Twenty-three, and get away from me."

Stall wheeled himself backward to his desk. "Who were the original investigators?"

Diggs let out a long and drawn-out sigh that he didn't attempt to hide. He pressed his fingertips against his temples. "Like I said five seconds ago, Desmond and Green."

"And you said the case has been open for twenty-three years?"

Diggs lifted his head and looked past Stall to his nearly barren workspace. "Stall, why is your desk so clean? You could rent it out for ballroom dance lessons."

"You haven't given me anything to do."

Diggs started to remind Stall that he wasn't his babysitter but no longer saw any point. That sentiment had been expressed several times already in every way he could think of. Whether he lectured patiently with a smile or sharply through an angry grimace or somewhere in-between, it had become a worn-out speech, as ineffective as an old cat sleeping on a driveway.

"Assertiveness, Stall. Every real detective has it." He pointed at the Huszer murder book. "You don't want to end up dead weight like Desmond and Green, do you?"

"I will, boss. I'll start being more assertive. Count on it. It's just I'm new at this and I don't want to screw up." Meekly, he added, "Everyone knows you're the best and I want you to be happy with me."

In what Diggs hoped would pass as gentle fatherly advice, he said, "I understand, Stall, but doing is learning. I'll never get angry at an honest effort."

Diggs told Stall to finish his lunch and turned his attention back to the Huszer murder book. On the last page was an envelope labelled "Pics." Diggs cleared a spot on his desk and laid the photos out in front of him. In the prehistoric Polaroid days, the quantity and quality of crime-scene shots were often badly lacking. Usually, the shots were barely in focus and poorly framed, taken by cops who had no business holding any kind of camera.

For the most part, the Huszer photos fit that bill. The one exception stood out like a stallion amongst a herd of donkeys. The photo was in sharp focus and the framing couldn't have been more perfect. Considering the inadequacy of the twenty-three other shots, Diggs couldn't explain it other than blind luck.

Thirty-four-year-old Jesse Huszer lay face up and shirtless behind a dumpster in a convenience store parking lot. Two bullet holes were in his chest, one in each thigh, and two in his upper right arm. His head was bent severely to one side with his chin touching the top of his shoulder, and his arms were spread apart in a crucifixion position. Across the dead man's chest like a going-out-of-business banner across a storefront, a tattoo read: *Kill or Be Killed.*

Diggs never met Huszer but as a kid vaguely knew of him. Huszer's mother sold Avon products that Diggs' mother purchased on multiple occasions. Every time Huszer's mother saw Diggs, she told him that he looked like Jesse when he was a boy. Huszer's body had been discovered near a fish taco stand that Diggs regularly frequented. Huszer was an unlucky thirteen years older than Diggs and they shared the same birthday. Diggs stumbled upon Huszer's murder book the day after he had been partnered with Stall.

Diggs wasn't as superstitious as a lot of cops he knew, but the dead man's chest screamed dire premonition. The time to request a new partner had come. Diggs hadn't griped to his boss Al Swenson about anything in almost a month, and complaining about Stall wasn't really complaining any more than protesting global warming was complaining.

Stall said, "Huh, that's interesting."

Diggs barely heard him.

"The father was bludgeoned and the mother was strangled. It doesn't say how the daughter died."

Stall pulled his head out of the paper and looked at Diggs. "I bet you could solve this one in five minutes, boss."

"What are you talking about?"

"A family was murdered in Mojave Creek."

"In Nevada?"

Stall nodded thoughtfully. "Yep."

"My sister lives in Mojave Creek."

Stall's eyes widened. "No kidding? You think she knows who did it?"

"Correction. I'm not sure if she lives there anymore."

Astonished, Stall said, "You don't know where your own sister lives?"

"We're not close." He turned to face Stall. "What'd you say the cause of death was?"

Stall read from a line in the article, "Police said that Mr. Geist likely died from blunt force trauma and his wife was strangled." He shook his head. "Odd, huh? The daughter's cause of death isn't mentioned." Stall frowned. "I bet the father was involved with drugs. So much for legalizing pot."

"When you're finished with that, pass it over here."

Stall grabbed a spool of dental floss from a desk drawer. "In a few minutes. I'm going to the can."

Stall headed to the restroom and Diggs accessed the *San*

Diego Union-Tribune website. The same story Stall had read from was posted. A photo beside the article showed an attractive family. William Geist was a handsome man with a solid build. His daughter Julia's pretty face and large, expressive blue eyes no doubt made her the focus of countless high school fantasies. Farrah Geist's short blonde hair, trim figure, and especially her bright enthusiastic smile reminded Diggs of his mother, and like Farrah Geist, she had been murdered by strangulation.

The way the story read, the motive was wide open, but Diggs couldn't help believing that Stall had called it right and drugs had been a factor.

Diggs turned away from the screen, tapping his lips with a fingertip while he thought about how he would present his case to Swenson. He would have to be convincing and knowing that Swenson had an abnormally short attention span, he would have to be brief.

He called upon the marketing minor he had earned at Arizona State University. Simple, effective taglines could mold opinions and instigate action. The Few, The Proud, The Marines inspired his best friend growing up to enlist. As a high school athlete, Diggs so thoroughly bought into the Wheaties, the Breakfast of Champions mystique that he ate a cereal he could barely stand every morning for a year. What Los Angeles cop or defense attorney would ever forget, "If it doesn't fit, you must acquit"?

The phrase on Huszer's chest—kill or be killed—was both concise and memorable. It could prove to be a difference maker in convincing Swenson that if he and Stall continued as partners, someone would die. It might be Diggs. It might be Stall or, god forbid, Stall's incompetence might get a civilian killed.

Diggs thanked Mr. Huszer's chest for its wisdom and returned the photos to the envelope.

*   *   *

On his way to grab a quick lunch at the Baja Fresh across the street, Diggs took a shortcut though a police corridor. A tall, skinny old man was being escorted by a burly uniformed officer. The old guy reminded Diggs of a walking mountain peak. He wore a white button-down shirt, white jeans, and black boots. A pointed white cowboy hat hung awkwardly over one eye and snow-white hair flowed to his shoulders.

They were six feet apart when the old man stopped dead in his tracks. He stared directly at Diggs and began to shake in a rage. As he growled guttural sounds, his hat fell to the ground. He lifted his handcuffed wrists and thrust out two middle fingers.

The surprised officer looked at Diggs. "You know this guy?"

Confused at the old man's behavior, Diggs said, "I don't think so."

The officer picked up the hat and grabbed the old man by the shoulder. "Be polite, old timer."

The old man mouthed Diggs a vulgarity.

Back at his desk, Diggs couldn't get the strange actions of the old man out of his head. He sought out the arresting officer and after three transfers found him.

"This is Leonard Diggs in Homicide. I just saw you bring in a tall old guy."

The officer said, "You mean the weirdo in the white safari outfit?"

"What's his story?"

9

"A security guard caught him shoplifting at a Dick's Sporting Goods. The criminal mastermind tried to steal two Cokes. He was carrying hollow-point bullets and a knife with an eight-inch blade."

"What's his name?"

"His driver's license said Richard Miller. It's a fake and not a very good one. Even the security guard wasn't fooled, which was another reason he called us."

"He's in a holding cell now?"

"Yes, sir. Over in Robbery. Probably not for long though."

Diggs hung up and hurried to the Robbery division.

He asked the desk sergeant, "Has anyone interviewed the shoplifter?"

Through a smirk, the sergeant asked, "Why would Homicide be interested in him? We're not even interested in him."

Diggs' aggravated impatience was impossible to misinterpret. The sergeant said, "Sure, whatever, be my guest. We don't have time for shoplifters today. I'll have him brought to interrogation room number three."

Diggs made his way to the second floor and into the stuffy interrogation room. Ten minutes later, the door opened and in came the old man. His eyes practically popped out of his skull when he saw Diggs waiting for him. He stopped and turned to the officer nudging him forward. "Take me back to my cell."

The officer ignored the old man's plea and handcuffed his wrist to an iron ring attached to a metal rectangular table. The old man edged himself as far back against his chair as his handcuffed wrist would allow.

Through a lopsided grin Diggs said, "You know you're hurting my feelings."

The old man was breathing hard. Droplets of perspiration

owned his face. Diggs raised his palms in the air in a calm-down gesture. "Mr. Miller, I'm not here to hurt you. Would you like me to get you some water, a soft drink?"

The old man mumbled, "No."

"How about something to eat? A candy bar, a bag of chips?"

"No."

"Can I at least take off the handcuff?"

"I'm fine as I am."

Diggs continued the Mr. Congeniality act, which felt as bogus to him as a reading from a carnival psychic. "Mr. Miller, I really am a nice guy. I've offered you food. I've offered you something to drink. Nevertheless, you seem to be afraid of me. A half hour ago, you were downright hostile."

The old man stared into his lap.

"Look at me, Mr. Miller. Have we met before?"

The man lifted his head. Barely above a whisper, he said, "No, sir. I don't think so."

"Why were you so angry with me?"

"I wasn't angry with you."

Diggs nodded. "I think you were, Mr. Miller."

"No, no. I wasn't."

Diggs grinned. "Okay, then. What's your real name? Don't tell me Richard Miller. Your ID is one of the worst fakes I've ever seen."

"Brian."

"Brian what?"

"Harper."

Diggs narrowed his eyes suspiciously. Brian Harper was as common a name as Richard Miller and as easy to make up.

"Are you sure?"

The man nodded. Remorsefully, he added, "I have no more reason to lie."

Diggs suspected he was probably telling the truth, although he wouldn't have bet more than five dollars on it. Regardless, the name Brian Harper meant nothing to him.

Diggs tried to picture Harper clean shaven. He tried to picture him with shorter hair. He tried to picture him as a much younger man. He tried to remember anyone who had his similar gravelly voice or the jagged scars beneath both eyes that appeared to be botched cosmetic surgery. Diggs looked at the old man's veiny hands and long fingers. Nothing rang a bell. Diggs had no idea who Brian Harper was. He was virtually certain they had never met. He concluded that he was wasting his time. Harper was simply an old nutcase.

Diggs stood. "Mr. Harper, you got anything to say to me before you go back to your cell?"

"Why am I going back? I was going to pay for those Cokes. That security guard arrested me before I had a chance. I'm really sorry for the misunderstanding. I have money. I'll pay." On the verge of tears, he begged, "I just want to go home."

His pathetic pleas would have been heartbreaking if Diggs hadn't been exposed to so many situations a million times worse. Harper wasn't going to be in a cell for long. He'd likely be home before dinner time. The San Diego Police were not interested in elderly shoplifters.

"I'm curious why you had hollow-point bullets. You know, they're illegal in California."

"They are? I didn't know."

"Where did you get them?"

Harper looked away. "I don't know. I might have found them in a dumpster."

"Do you have access to a gun?"

"Um…no. I don't like guns."

"How about knives. You like knives?"

"No, I don't like knives either."

Diggs spoke in a gentle tone that he'd use with a small child. "You were carrying one. A large one. Big enough to hurt somebody badly."

The old man dipped his head. "I found that this morning. I was going to throw it away."

"Good luck to you, Mr. Harper."

The old man raised his head. Urgently, he asked, "Can I please have that soft drink you promised? My mouth is so dry."

On his way to the vending machine, Diggs stopped at a computer and searched for Brian Harper in San Diego County. If that was his real name, there were no outstanding warrants or any arrest history.

When Diggs returned, Harper's palms were together and his eyes were closed. He whispered a pleading mumble.

Diggs placed the opened soft drink can on the table and interrupted, "Everything alright, Mr. Harper?"

Harper ended his muttering with, "So sorry, my little amigo," before reaching for the can. He smiled weakly and said, "Thank you and God bless."

When Harper opened his mouth to drink, Diggs saw a white capsule with a red cross on the tip of the old man's tongue. With the full force of his open palm, Diggs slapped Harper across the face.

2

Diggs' index and forefinger burrowed under Harper's tongue while the crux of his left elbow held Harper's head in a tight lock. The old man's lanky body thrashed, and his gagging reverberated throughout the room. His free arm swung wildly while his handcuffed wrist rattled against the iron ring connected to the metal table. Blood from his wrist dripped onto the floor, drool poured from his mouth. The stale smell of his sweat was overpowering. Diggs gritted his teeth while his fingers were being chewed apart.

A day before, Diggs had read a bulletin warning that white heptagonal-shaped cyanide capsules stamped with a red cross had been smuggled from Mexico onto the streets of San Diego. Three were already dead and more were expected. One way or another, Diggs was not going to allow Harper to end his life in that sweaty closet of a room.

Diggs shouted in the old man's ear, "Spit it out! Goddammit, spit it out!"

More than once, Diggs had a moment's control of the tablet soaking under Harper's tongue, but each time, Harper yanked his head just enough to allow it to slip away. Diggs was well aware that he was running out of chances. Once the tablet broke apart and particles washed down Harper's throat, he would be dead before Diggs could count to five.

In one motion, Diggs released his arm from Harper's neck and got a firm grip on his long wiry hair. He wrapped it around his fist and yanked it forward while at the same time, pulled his mashed-up fingers from Harper's throat. With a fist, he attempted to pound on the back of Harper's skull, hoping that the impact of the blow would unencumber the tablet and allow gravity to do its part. As Diggs brought his fist down, the old man roughly pulled his head to the side, causing Diggs to graze the target.

That was the moment Diggs knew Harper had won the war. He heard a sickening crunch and in seconds the old man's eyes rolled to the back of his head. White foam soaked his lips, his body began to shake violently, and in full death throes, he slid off his chair. His handcuffed wrist kept his buttocks hanging awkwardly three inches off the floor.

Diggs pushed past several officers who had gathered outside. Questions were hurled at him that were all background noise as far as Diggs was concerned. A captain in Robbery whom Diggs recognized but barely knew rushed toward him. She made a stop gesture with her palm and Diggs stood still for a moment.

"He killed himself. A red-crossed cyanide tablet."

Diggs led the captain to a computer at an empty desk. He pulled up the recent bulletin from the Narcotics division and pointed at the screen. "I gave him a soda. I saw that in his mouth. I tried to get it out. I couldn't."

The captain had more to say, but Diggs was jacked. Full investigative mode had taken over. Nothing about the tall old man made any sense. He hurried to the first-floor property room. A uniformed cop was reading a magazine behind a counter.

Diggs rapped his knuckles on the counter. "I want all items taken from Richard Miller. He was arrested for shoplifting about an hour ago. He was carrying a knife and hollow-point bullets."

The officer showed a bemused grin. "Since when do we arrest anyone for shoplifting?"

Diggs turned his palms to the ceiling. The officer nodded. "Okay, I get it. You're in a hurry." He lifted himself out of his seat and went into a backroom. While Diggs waited, he called Stall and told him to meet him at their car.

The officer returned with a legal-sized manila envelope. Diggs snatched it from the officer's hand and ripped it open. He pawed through a key chain with three keys, thirty dollars in cash, less than fifty cents worth of spare change, the bullets, the knife, and a McDonald's gift card.

"No wallet?"

The officer held out a clipboard. "What you see is what you get. Sign on the bottom line."

Diggs' signature wasn't much more than a smear on the page. He jogged to the car while at the same time examining the keys. One was an old-fashioned car key issued by Honda, nothing fancy—no buttons, no keyless entry, nothing computerized. The other two keys could have been for anything.

Stall was staring out the passenger window when Diggs threw himself into the driver's seat.

"What's the hurry, boss?"

Diggs didn't answer. Stall began to talk about Netflix.

Ten minutes later, they were at an outdoor shopping mall,

parked in front of Dick's Sporting Goods. Rows of automobiles surrounded them.

"I should write a letter, or maybe an e-mail. Which do you think they'd…?"

Diggs turned toward Stall and glared. The intensity stamped on his face immediately quieted him. "Listen closely. Get out and start looking for older-model Hondas. Nothing after say 2015. Forget any cars with a keyless entry. We're only interested in old Hondas that take an old-fashioned key. It'll be a less expensive model. Take photos of every Honda that fits and make note of its location. Got it?"

Stall nodded. "Got it."

Diggs pointed toward the driver's side door. "I'll take this side, you take that side."

Stall nodded. "Got it."

Diggs moved swiftly, searching for older-model Hondas. When one fit the bill, he stuck Harper's key in the lock. If it didn't open, he moved on. Within minutes, he found the winner. Eight rows over and three rows back. A rusted 2005 Civic with Nevada plates.

Inside the glove compartment, a wallet. Inside the wallet, a Discover card, three lottery tickets, and two ten-dollar bills. The credit card indicated that Brian Harper was the old man's name.

Diggs dialed the customer service number on the back of the Discover card. He spoke to a friendly representative in a confused voice. "Hello, my name is Brian Harper. I haven't gotten a statement from you guys in a while. I did some checking and I just found out you're still sending stuff to my old address. I'm a little worried. I've heard the new tenants are kind of shady."

The representative asked for Diggs' card number. Diggs read it off and made up a Nevada address.

A moment later the representative said, "I found your account. It's attached to a California address, not Nevada."

"In San Diego?"

"Yes."

Diggs chose a street name near his home. "On West Grand?"

"No, I have 3215 San Marcos Boulevard."

"That's my brother-in-law's address. Let me find out what's going on. I'll call you back."

He hung up and called Stall's cell.

"Meet me at the car."

Stall sounded out of breath. "You found the Honda?"

Diggs told him he had.

He could hear Stall's relief. "Am I glad to hear that. I took photos like you asked, but I forgot to make note of the locations. I had to…"

Diggs hung up and ran to his car.

*   *   *

Brian Harper's address was an off-color white Spanish-style home on a high traffic, two-lane street. A sunny-side-up realtor would sell it as a fixer-upper with lots of light and loads of potential. A more experienced agent would pitch it as wonderful investment property. A casual observer with no ties to the real estate market would call it what it was—a rundown shack.

On the filthy front porch, broken chairs lay on a grimy old sofa blocking the main front window. Two other windows were partially blocked with busted horizontal blinds. Diggs guessed the home had been a rental to countless tenants, none of whom gave any kind of shit. Its future, an out-of-its-misery teardown. He parked along the curb two houses over.

"Stall, when we hit the property, keep your weapon discrete but out."

Stall immediately pulled out his gun and waved it like a flashlight in a cave.

Diggs exited the car and Stall followed. A cold wave that had started in the Pacific Ocean gusted chilly air across San Marcos Boulevard. They walked briskly against the wind to the edge of the property, Diggs in front, Stall two steps behind. Diggs abruptly stopped and grabbed Stall by the shoulder.

"Front porch. I'll take the doorknob side."

Stall nodded that he understood.

They stepped over hard dirt and trekked through patches of dead grass across a rectangular front yard. Once they were in position, Diggs pounded on the door. No answer. He listened carefully and could hear no stirring within the house. He pounded again.

"Police. Open the door."

Still, he heard no discernable movement. Diggs stuck one of Harper's keys into the lock and heard the deadbolt release.

He turned the handle and nudged the door open with his foot. No return engagement was waiting. He pushed the door further with his palm. He looked inside and saw no one. His gun drawn, he entered. Stall followed.

The living room amounted to a scavenger room. A ratty brown sofa positioned against a wall, two unmatched rickety chairs side by side in a corner. A cathode tube television hulked on a dusty black plasterboard stand. A DVD player balanced on the top of the TV. On the floor, a cardboard box, its flaps hiding the contents. Diggs saw nothing that couldn't have been picked up off a curb.

Beyond the living room was a small kitchen. Crowded together on a chipped ceramic countertop was an opened box of Cap'n Crunch cereal, two paper plates, and two dirty drinking glasses. Diggs turned toward Stall and made a peace sign. He mouthed, "Two of them."

To their right was a darkened hallway with three opened doors—two on the right, one on the left. A fourth room with its closed door waited in shadow at the end of the hallway.

Diggs whispered, "Head on a swivel, Stall. Watch for any movement." He could feel Stall's breath on his neck. Diggs turned his head. They were close enough to kiss.

"And back up."

They stepped into the narrow hallway, passing an empty bathroom with a grungy, red linoleum floor, dripping faucet, and a missing shower curtain.

Across from the bathroom, a completely empty room. No furniture. No storage. Not anything but dirt and dust and a tan carpet so threadbare that Diggs guessed it had been laid when the house was built.

Two rooms remained. Diggs stepped into the last room on the right. A beaten-up dresser stood against a wall. On top of a folding table, a small lamp, a spiral notebook, and a pen. In an opened closet hung four white shirts on hangers. A futon lay on the floor beside a brown-stained white pillow missing its case.

Diggs stepped backwards out of the room. Stall stood in the hallway staring at the door at the end of the hall with an odd look on his face. Diggs wasn't sure what it meant, if it meant anything at all. He stepped past Stall and headed toward the closed door.

Diggs leaned against a wall and Stall did the same to the opposite wall. His ear pressed up to the door, Diggs took several moments to listen carefully. He thought he heard slow, labored breathing.

Diggs whispered to Stall, "Can you hear that?"

Stall shook his head. "Hear what?"

Diggs reached for the doorknob and gently turned the handle.

He mouthed to Stall, "Locked."

Diggs dug in his pocket for Harper's key chain. One key had worked on Harper's car. Another had worked on his front door. Diggs suspected the third key would open the door in front of them.

He fingered his way through coins, a tube of ChapStick, and several sheets of tissue paper before he had the keychain in his grasp. Suddenly and without warning, a hand on his shoulder roughly pulled him away. Diggs eyes widened with disbelief. He flung an arm toward Stall and shouted, "No!"

3

Shards of the fractured wood flared through the cramped hallway. The overpowering scent of gunpowder seared his nostrils, two deafening blasts had his ears ringing and his head throbbing. Instinctively, Diggs touched his face feeling for blood and felt none. Through a hazy cloud of smoke, he saw the door open and Stall inside the room.

"Boss, look!"

On a futon lay an unconscious boy. A ratty gray blanket covered most of his small body, but his age, his full head of bushy red hair, and the small star-shaped birthmark on his neck instantly revealed who he was.

As he raced to the boy, Diggs shouted for Stall to call the paramedics. While Stall dialed from his cell, Diggs bent to a knee and felt for the boy's carotid artery. His pulse beat steadily and he was breathing. He spoke into the boy's ear. "Glen, can you hear me?"

The boy offered no verbal response and his eyes remained closed.

Stall knelt beside Diggs. "Is he going to be alright?"

"I think so. Pulse is strong, breathing is steady."

"Are you thinking what I'm thinking?"

Diggs gently pulled the blanket away from the boy's chest to lay it at his knees. "A Star Wars t-shirt, red hair, the birthmark. It's him alright. Glen Palmer."

It took less than five minutes for the blaring siren of the EMT to screech to the front of the house. Stall directed them to the room where Diggs waited with the still unconscious boy.

Throughout his career, Diggs had been in the presence of EMTs more times than he could remember. He had seen the successes and he had watched hearts stop beating and pulses fade to nothing. It had been a long time since he was drawn to watch them in action, but Glen Palmer was special.

The Glen Palmer missing persons case and the overwhelming city-wide grief that followed felt different from anything Diggs had ever witnessed. Glen Palmer's baffling disappearance from a local park with his mother ten feet away became a mystery that had taken on a life of its own.

Thousands upon thousands of volunteers had scoured hills and fields. Tens of thousands of flyers had been handed out. Glen Palmer could be seen on billboards and storefront signs. A committed staff of social media volunteers created websites and Facebook pages that attracted thousands of tips. Churches across the city prayed for Glen's safe return. Candlelight vigils that drew thousands had become almost a weekly occurrence. A GoFundMe campaign had raised over three hundred thousand dollars in reward money for anyone who could lead the police to Glen Palmer. The crusade of an entire city to find the missing boy had been an ongoing drama for nearly a month. Watching Glen's parents Mack, a high school football coach, and Katie, a teacher for special needs children, plead daily for their son's return broke the hearts of the San Diego community.

One week passed into two and then three and four. Official statements from the police had gradually changed from bringing Glen back home alive to just bringing Glen home. If or when Glen Palmer was found, most assumed it would be by hikers stumbling upon human bones.

But now, Diggs knew for certain that Glen Palmer's fate would be much different. Diggs had felt Glen's pulse. He had heard him breathing. Glenn was in the hands of trained medical professionals. Glen Palmer was going to make it and it was a miracle.

Always wary that a happy ending could be snatched away without a moment's notice, a cautious Diggs asked, "He's going to be alright?"

The paramedics' expansive grins gave the answer away.

"He looks to be in good shape. He likely has a sedative in him. The docs at Palomar should know soon enough."

While Glen Palmer was rushed to Palomar Medical Center, Diggs spoke over the phone with his supervisor Captain Al Swenson. Diggs had never heard Swenson as excited. The news had him nearly hyperventilating.

"Diggs, before I call the chief, I need to be absolutely, one thousand percent certain that the boy in the ambulance is Glen Palmer."

Standing on a cracked driveway in front of Harper's house, under blue skies on a bright and chilly afternoon, Diggs watched the ambulance carrying Glenn Palmer rapidly shrink to the size of a postage stamp.

"Zero doubt, Captain. It's Palmer. He's on his way to Palomar."

Swenson exhaled deeply as if the weight of an entire city had been lifted off his shoulders. He uttered a brisk congratulations and abruptly hung up. Diggs walked to Stall, who was leaning against their car with his hands in his pockets. A private smile hinted at his thoughts.

"I never thought he'd be found alive."

Stall answered, "Really? I knew he would."

"He's been missing a month."

"I know, but I knew."

Diggs could hear a deluge of sirens heading their way.

"They're coming, Stall. Any minute, it's going to be a zoo."

Diggs noticed a dimness pass over Stall's face. Stall had a multiple-choice kind of demeanor that often made it a challenge to know what he was thinking. As a default, Diggs mostly assumed he wasn't thinking of anything at all.

"Something wrong, Stall?"

"They're coming. Glenn's going. Out of the womb and into the light."

"I don't follow, Stall."

"That ambulance is Glenn's womb. He's safe there. Once he's out, it's going to be a lot different for him. He's going to get attention that he won't want. He's suffered too much already. It's a shame."

Diggs thought he kind of understood what Stall was getting at, but with Stall one never knew, and the first wave of marked squad cars had pulled up to the front of the house. Stall's cryptic utterance slipped away without further comment and five seconds later, Diggs had forgotten about it altogether.

Soon detectives began to arrive in unmarked cars. Uniformed officers were already setting up crowd control barriers to keep at bay the onslaught of descending TV news crews and civilian lookie-loos.

Two detectives from the Robbery division approached. Under their purview came kidnappings for financial gain. Diggs hadn't been made privy to all the aspects of the Palmer investigation, but as far as knew, no ransom had ever been demanded.

At the detective's request, Diggs summarized the arrest and suicide of Brian Harper. Diggs detailed each step that led him and Stall to 3215 San Marcos Boulevard. As Diggs explained, the detectives couldn't keep the smiles off their faces. When he was finished, compliments were exchanged and hands were shaken. Finding Glen Palmer alive felt like as big a feel-good win for law enforcement as anyone could remember.

After the robbery detectives moved on, Lieutenant Graver from the Sex Crimes unit approached and introduced herself. Graver had been working in Sex Crimes longer than Diggs had been with the department.

Her lined face showed no signs of joy and Diggs got it. She had one of the toughest jobs in the department, one he wouldn't have taken for triple his pay. She asked, "Did you see anything sexual in nature inside the house? Lube, porn, anything like that?"

The imagery made Diggs queasy, but her questions were important and necessary. If there had been no ransom demand, it was fair to assume that Palmer had been kidnapped for deviant sexual purposes.

Diggs answered, "Nothing that I saw. He was fully clothed when we found him. It appeared that he had his own room and Harper had is. There's a DVD player in there. A box is beside it. Maybe there's something in there. I don't know."

Graver thanked him and headed toward Harper's house. Diggs recognized a representative from the FBI speaking with the detectives from Robbery. After the second week, Chief of Police Francis Jackett had requested the FBI's assistance.

Like a whale breaching water, a super-sized SUV slowly maneuvered through the assorted police cruisers and news vans, parking near the burgeoning throng of reporters. Mayor Randy Pelton stepped out, followed by Chief Jackett and Swenson, who quickly noticed Diggs and Stall separated from the pack. He waved and spoke a few words into the chief's ear. The chief nodded and Swenson hurried over.

His hand extended, Swenson said, "Congratulations, boys. You made my year."

While Diggs shook, he asked, "We needed here any longer?"

"No, you can go. Have your report on my desk before you go home."

Ever since Stall had blown apart the door's lock, Diggs wondered what he'd been thinking. Now that they were in a quiet car, away from the commotion, he asked, "Stall, what happened back there? I had the key. Why'd you fire your weapon?"

Stall hiked his shoulders. "You told me to be assertive, and I thought that was really good advice. You're not mad at me, are you?"

Diggs considered Stall's question. On any other day, he would have responded with a stern lecture, but the sun was shining, the sky was as blue as the water on La Jolla beach, and Glen Palmer was alive. The bottom line was that a ten-year-old boy had escaped a predator.

Stall had made a colossal mistake, and the number of potentially disastrous scenarios made Diggs shudder, but for once, a nightmare had a happy ending. Nothing could alter the euphoria Diggs felt at that moment.

He spoke through a grin. "Well, despite the fact that you could have blown off my hand, or a ricochet could have killed us both, I'm not too upset. The boy is out of Harper's house and he's going home to his parents. Right now, that's all that matters."

4

Two hours after the EMTs delivered Glen Palmer to the Palomar hospital, the mayor and the chief of police held a joint press conference. When the mayor proudly reported that little Glen Palmer had been found alive and was at a hospital for observation, the assorted press broke out in spontaneous cheering.

A day later, Glen Palmer was released to his parents. A waiting audience of several hundred well-wishers greeted him outside the hospital entrance. Thirty miles away, Diggs was summoned into the office of Captain Al Swenson.

Diggs viewed Swenson as a man gluttonous with power, as self-interested as a wannabe A-list actor trying to claw his way to the top and as fair-minded as a ten-year-old in charge of the Halloween candy.

Diggs stood outside Swenson's door reluctant to enter. So many times, Swenson's office had been an incubator of stupid requests and frustrating orders. It was where Swenson would grumble over the tardiness of an unnecessary report. It was where Diggs had been ordered to cooperate with a TV crime show that was filming an episode on the Sidewalk Ghoul, a thrill killer Diggs had chased for over eight months before a gun fight in a smack house left the Ghoul dead.

Not much more than two weeks after killing the Ghoul, Diggs schlepped a TV host with movie-star teeth around the city, revisiting crime scenes he badly wanted to forget. Swenson's office was where Diggs learned that he would be partnering with Stall.

Diggs inhaled, exhaled, and tentatively stepped inside. Swenson was leaning back in his chair fiddling with a Rubik's Cube. His feet were propped on his desk and a frustrated grimace formed unhealthy lines across his fleshy face. When he saw Diggs, he dropped the cube into an opened drawer and put his feet on the floor. He pointed to a chair in front of his desk. "Have a seat, Diggs."

After Diggs followed his order, Swenson said, "Your work on the Palmer case has made City Hall really take notice."

"That's great, Captain. Thank you for letting me know."

Diggs started to stand and Swenson let out a rollicking laugh, which wasn't uncommon. Swenson laughed more than anyone Diggs knew.

"You're a funny man, Diggs. Not as funny as your partner though. Have you seen Stall's invisible cat routine?"

Diggs said he had, but Swenson felt the need to explain it anyway. "He has this dog collar that's starched. It's stiff as a board. He pretends that he's walking a cat." His grin expanded from cheek to cheek. He began to laugh uproariously.

"I've seen it, Captain."

Swenson continued. "He has this whole bit. The cat sees a dog, stops for a second, and yanks Stall's arm in the opposite direction. Then the cat sees a squirrel and starts to track him ever so slowly. Bam! He pounces! Sometimes Stall pretends he has a little shit kitten and other times it's as big as a tiger. It's hilarious because it's a cat, not a dog. You get it? Cats have minds of their own. They're harder to control than a dog and when is the last time you saw a cat on a leash? It's a very inventive bit. It's Chaplinesque. You like pantomime, Diggs?"

"Not my cup of tea."

"You don't like pantomime? You don't like Chaplin?"

Diggs didn't believe Stall's walking-cat routine was quite on the same level as *City Lights,* but rather than argue the point, he shrugged. "To each his own, Captain."

Swenson ran a hand through his thick, dyed brown hair. "I feel sorry for a man who doesn't appreciate pantomime."

Diggs sat silently waiting for the inevitable piece of bad news.

"Well anyway, I read your report. Terrific work. It really was. I doubt that any of our other fine detectives would have taken the initiative you did, and Stall, what can I say? Shooting off that lock, kicking down that door. A regular T.J. Hooker. Never would have guessed he had it in him."

Diggs saw the opening and took advantage. "Speaking of Stall, I've been meaning to talk to you about him. As you probably know, I'm serious by nature. I like to focus on the work. I don't like distractions. To be honest, I'm not sure Stall and I are right for each other."

Swenson's eyes narrowed disbelievingly. "Not right for each other? Are you kidding? You two found the Palmer boy. It seems to me that you are perfectly right for each other, and Stall tells me he's very happy working with you. That makes me happy. Against all odds, I found someone who doesn't despise you. Sarducci had a nervous breakdown because of you. Delvin loathed you. Half the department calls you Mr.

Hyde behind your back, and no one ever calls you Jekyll. Stall is the only guy who has ever been enthusiastic about working with you, and you want me to swap him out? No comprende and no can do."

"Captain, I appreciate that Stall doesn't hate me, but I honestly think Stall would be better off with a different partner and maybe even a different unit."

"Great idea, Diggs. Let's move Stall to back to Juvenile Crimes. That wouldn't make the department look too incompetent."

"Captain, the Palmer case was a missing persons case and a kidnapping. Transferring Stall to Missing Persons would be a slick PR move. The detective who found Glen Palmer is the newest member in Missing Persons. Everyone would buy into that."

Swenson glanced at his watch. Dismissively, he said, "The chief wouldn't."

"Sir, it's kill or be killed."

Swenson glared at Diggs dumbfounded. "Huh, kill or be killed? I have no idea what you're talking about. Stall isn't going anywhere. Who are you voting for? Pelton or Wackerly?"

"Why?"

"Because I want you to report to Mayor Pelton's office. ASAP."

"Can you tell me why?"

"Just do it, Diggs."

"Just do it?"

"Right, Diggs. Quit bellyaching. Just do it. Go. Now."

Diggs trudged out of Swenson's office. It never failed. Always bad news.

*   *   *

Stall was leaning back in his chair and rubbing his chin. The Huszer murder book was open and resting on his lap. Diggs had made it his and Stall's number one cold-case priority.

On first appearance, Stall was reading its contents carefully, but Diggs knew better. It had been on his lap for a half hour, and it was still open at page two. He was daydreaming about something that had nothing to do with the Huszer case. His landscaper. The two for six-dollar meal deal at Arby's. An after-work trip to Jiffy Lube.

"Stall, I have to run over to City Hall. I don't want it to take long. Call me in twenty minutes."

Stall twitched with surprise. He jerked his head up. His eyes held a faraway gaze. "Say that again, boss."

Diggs repeated himself.

Stall nodded. "You got it, boss. Glad to help."

Diggs had seen this movie at least a hundred times before. Stall had heard him but hadn't listened. "You'll call my cell in twenty minutes, right?"

Stall's index finger bounced over his watch. "Twenty minutes. Got it."

Diggs left police headquarters and walked toward City Hall along C street feeling like he had an appointment with a firing squad. He stopped at a crosswalk and stood under a gently swaying palm tree. A few feet away, the heavenly aroma of baking bread wafted from a croissant sandwich shop. The cold spell had been replaced by a warm, refreshing breeze blowing off the Pacific. Fluffy white clouds shaded most of the street. In the last year, he had cracked the biggest case of his life and days earlier he reunited a kidnapped boy with his family. What exactly was the problem? What exactly was he worried about?

No matter how pessimistically Diggs thought, no situation he could conjure up would be more than a mild annoyance. He guessed that Pelton wanted to bolster his sagging campaign with a dose of positive publicity. A handshake in front of a photographer. Maybe he'd be asked to accept a stupid award. Assuming it didn't take too long, he'd play along.

If nothing else, meeting Mayor Pelton before he was voted out of office would probably be kind of interesting. He'd seen him on television hundreds of times. At heart, Pelton was like most successful politicians—a gifted blowhard who could figure out what you wanted and make you believe he wanted the same thing. Diggs hadn't voted for Pelton the first time around, and he had no plans to vote for his reelection.

Diggs entered the Thomas C. Carter building and rode the elevator to the top floor. A receptionist politely asked him to sit in a waiting room covered with plush black carpeting. Diggs was parked on an overstuffed leather chair for barely a minute when a woman with flowing red hair and beautiful porcelain skin approached.

With a smile as flashy as a string of diamonds, she said, "You chose my favorite chair. Don't you just love its old-world charm?" Before he could answer, she reached out her long, slender fingers. "Thrilled to meet you, Detective Diggs. My name is Samantha. I'm Mayor Pelton's administrative assistant. Please come with me."

A side door led them to a corridor with a bright white marble floor. Diggs walked alongside her, listening to her high heels clack against the marble and appreciating the San Diego-themed photos that adorned the walls. When they passed a black and white shot of Croce's restaurant, he said, "Shame they were forced to close down."

Without a glance, she cheerfully agreed.

She led Diggs into a large open room with cherry wood-grained walls and a showroom full of ostentatious furniture. At a corner office, she tapped on the open door. From inside the room came an enthusiastic, "Come in."

Samantha stepped aside and motioned for Diggs to enter. Pelton's office breathed excess—antique furniture, a ten-foot Persian rug, a mahogany desk as long as a Las Vegas buffet table. Floor to ceiling windows large enough for a commercial airplane to fly through wrapped around two sides of the office.

Samantha rested the palm of her hand on the square of Diggs' back. "Detective Diggs, meet Mayor Pelton."

Pelton hurried toward Diggs with his arm extended. Pelton was thinner than he appeared on television. Without TV makeup, his facial complexion showed a weary dullness. Diggs noticed more than a few gray strands in his two-hundred-dollar haircut. Regardless of any imperfections, Pelton was a handsome man, even distinguished, although not so much so to obscure his smarminess. As they shook hands, he took hold of Diggs' shoulder and like a baton in a relay race, snatched him away from Samantha.

"Detective Diggs, it is an absolute pleasure to meet you. Awesome work on the Palmer case."

Diggs offered a thank you, but less for the compliment and more because Pelton had finally let go of his shoulder.

"My wife doesn't call you by name. She calls you 'hero' and who can blame her? She wants me to nominate you as San Diego Man of the Year." Through a shy grin, he added, "I told her I'd have to speak to you about that first."

Pelton crowded Diggs to a leather chair that faced his desk. "Please have a seat, Detective."

Diggs sat and glanced at his watch. Twelve minutes had passed.

"I am very proud of the work you did on the Palmer case. You saved a young boy's life. If San Diego had a police force with even ten detectives as outstanding as you, San Diego would be America's finest city and America's safest city."

Diggs sat patiently counting away the seconds and making odds that Stall would call him before Pelton ever got to the point of their meeting.

"Detective, I won't beat around the bush."

Diggs was pleasantly surprised. Less so when Pelton added, "I need your help."

Diggs responded with a cautious, "How so?"

"Captain Swenson tells me that you have the best clearance rate in Homicide. He says that's been true for the past six years. That tells me that you're San Diego's best detective. Your excellent work on that serial killer case and now the Palmer case proves that beyond all doubt."

For several long moments, Pelton went silent. Whether to gather his thoughts or simply for a dramatic pause, Diggs didn't care. He added nothing and glanced at his watch. Fourteen minutes had passed.

Pelton's lanky body ambled to a floor to ceiling window. The fluffy clouds that earlier blocked the sun had departed. The Symphony Towers glowed spectacularly under a shiny bright blue sky. The ocean was dotted with ships that looked like toys in a bathtub.

He turned away from the window. "Detective Diggs, I want you to join my reelection team."

Before Diggs could answer, "Over my dead body," Pelton added through an enthusiastic smile, "With the election ten days away, I'll admit that it's going to be a little hectic, but it will also be exhilarating. Have you ever been part of a political campaign?"

"No."

"Maybe it's time, Detective. You're obviously a man who craves adventure and let me tell you, there is nothing more exciting than the final days of a campaign. When the rubber meets the road, and all the marbles are at stake. When the future of an entire city hangs in the balance."

Diggs shook his head and grinned affably. "I'm sure that's all true, but I'm working sixty-hour weeks as it is. I'm sorry, I don't have the time."

Pelton carried on as if Diggs were a muted television commercial.

"Detective, I believe that when it comes to the future of San Diego, we both share the same vision. A clean and safe environment for our children. Growth for our economy. Compassion for all of our citizens. Chief Jackett is a long-time friend. He tells me that the department desperately needs money for essential technological advances. A new fleet of cruisers. Increased manpower. He says the department could use another helicopter. Once I am elected to my second term, my main focus will be to make the San Diego police department the envy of the country."

Rather than ask why he hadn't achieved any of that during his first term, Diggs said, "I'm all for it, Mayor. Good luck." He leaned forward in his chair and started to stand.

"Well, before you turn me down..."

Diggs thought he already had.

"Please hear me out. By campaign I mean attend a few rallies. Meet the citizens of San Diego. Let them tell you how much they appreciate all the tireless work you put in every day. Let them meet a real-life hero. All I'm asking for is ten days. I've spoken with your superiors—Captain Swenson, Chief Jackett—of course. They're both fully onboard."

Diggs tried to arrange his thoughts into words that wouldn't sound too unnecessarily harsh. He didn't like or dislike Pelton personally. He got the sense that he had tried to be a good mayor. Although everybody accused him of gross financial mismanagement, no one ever accused him of corruption. In Diggs' opinion, Pelton was simply overmatched. Running a city the size of San Diego was hard. Pelton hadn't been up to the challenge. Simple as that.

Diggs smiled kindly. "Mayor Pelton, with all due respect, I am well aware that you just got a bump in the polls, likely because of Glen Palmer. I think you're searching for something Glen Palmer related to help you build even more momentum. The problem is that I don't want to be involved with politics. I know you can find other ways to make yourself more appealing to the voters. Don't rely on the Palmer case. Instead, use it as a steppingstone."

Pelton immediately launched his counterattack. "What you say is not entirely incorrect. Any campaign would want to boast about the Palmer success. It's something to be proud of. However, it's not as self-serving as you seem to believe. The truth of the matter is that I have the best interests of the city at heart. Let me explain."

Pelton boasted that he was a humble man but also hardworking and a dedicated servant to the people of San Diego. He had no plans to use the office to climb any political ladders.

He wasn't eyeing the governorship; he didn't want to be a state senator. His sole interest, his only desire, was to make San Diego as great as it deserved to be. If the voters would allow him four more years, he was certain he could build on all the positive achievements his office had accomplished.

He pleaded, "As lackluster as the previous administration was, it's going to take two terms to clean up all the messes and completely implement my vision."

Pelton raised his palms to the sky. "Electing that idiot Wackerly makes no sense. He doesn't have any experience. All the progress we've made will come to a grinding halt. Is Wackerly worth taking that kind of chance on? I don't think so. Is he Winston Churchill? Is he Abe Lincoln? I mean, who the hell needs him?"

Diggs looked at the Rolex on Pelton's wrist, cursed Stall under his breath, and begrudged the twenty-eight minutes of his life he had lost. Through the most authentic fake enthusiasm he could muster, he said, "I have a suggestion that I think will work out very well for you."

Pelton's voice perked up. "I'm all ears."

"As you probably know, Detective Stall is my partner. We found Palmer together. If I'm a hero, he is too. Stall is the man you should consider."

Diggs ignored Pelton's empty expression and forged ahead. "I think Stall is far better suited for what you're looking for. He's funny and engaging. He's a handsome guy. He's younger than me. He was a high school football player and remember the Palmer boy's father is a high school football coach. That's million-dollar symmetry. The public will latch on to that. Of course, Stall is a tremendous asset but to help you out, I wouldn't make a fuss if Stall joined your campaign."

Pelton responded with an annoyed shake of the head. "I'm aware of Detective Stall. Apparently, he's a little dense. I don't need a guy with CTE, I need someone quick on their feet. Someone who is nearly my equal. Do me one favor, Detective. Meet my campaign manager, David Flores. Have a chat over coffee. At most, he'll only take twenty minutes of your time. Any concerns you may have about me, ask him. I promise that he'll be brutally honest. That's why he works for me. Ass-kissers need not apply, which is why I need you. Please, speak with David. Grant me this one favor. It's all I'll ask of you."

The desperation in Pelton's voice made Diggs wary. Pelton would sell him to death if that's what it took to get him to change his mind, and unless he acquiesced, gave at least a little ground, Pelton's disappointment might fester to bitterness. Diggs didn't need a powerful adversary at City Hall with a contact list full of ruthless friends well versed in the art of payback.

Diggs got out of his chair with a constipated grimace. "You sure you can't use Stall? I promise you he'd be a lot better than me."

Pelton tightened his lips and shook his head. "No, sorry. Not interested."

"I'll wait for Flores' call."

A winning grin covered Pelton's face. "Thank you, Detective. Trust me on this. I'm certain that we're going to have a very bright future together."

5

Diggs stepped out of the Thomas C. Carter building to a shining sun and the smooth breeze that hadn't gone anywhere. As he racked his brain for a plan, his phone rang. Like any expert salesman, Pelton wasn't going to let the customer off the lot until the sale had been made. Diggs picked up to a youthful and energetic voice.

"Detective Diggs, my name is David Flores. I'm Mayor Pelton's campaign manager. If you have a few minutes, let's shoot the shit. You can get a handle on me, and I'll do the same with you. Wanna meet in five minutes? I'm heading over to the Starbucks in the Bellinger building this very moment." He added, after a blunt laugh, "You know how it is. I'm like a damn crack whore. Gotta get my fix."

Flores' word choices caught Diggs' attention. He didn't think Flores would utter casual obscenities during a first meeting with a wealthy campaign donor. When the governor visited San Diego the week before, Diggs doubted that Flores referenced crack whores. Flores was revealing expectations. In his mind, Diggs was the stuff of tough-guy crime novels and over the top cable TV dramas. A telling insight, and one that could be exploited. Flores had handed Diggs his angle. A get-out-of-jail-free scheme began to emerge.

Smiling into the phone, Diggs said, "Of course. See you in five."

He entered a barely half-full Starbucks. At a table next to a wall, a clean-cut, impeccably dressed, thirty-something man with longish black hair waved to him.

An opened laptop and a yellow legal pad were on the table, and a closed briefcase was propped on the seat beside him. As Diggs approached, Flores shut the laptop and stood. His posture was relaxed and his handshake firm. Flores took his seat and Diggs sat on a hardback chair directly across from him.

"Thanks a ton for agreeing to get together on such short notice. By the way, congratulations on Palmer. F-ing amazing work."

Diggs didn't believe Flores would record him without his consent, but he had to be absolutely, positively sure. He scanned the general area for any potential recording devices and saw nothing alarming.

With an indifferent shrug, Diggs said, "Nice the kid was found alive but to be honest, I lost ten Franklins on him."

Flores made a face. "I'm sorry?"

"I bet on the shallow grave. Good for the kid, shit for me."

Flores' eyes widened, but he quickly recomposed himself and spoke through a thin smile. "I see, that's very interesting. I won't waste your time, Detective. Let me start off by telling you a bit about myself."

For nearly five minutes, Flores did so in great detail. He was a third-generation Hispanic and a San Diego native with a bachelor's in political science from San Diego State. A law degree came from Berkley six years before. Married with two children: one six years old, the other nine. Flores claimed that his mother insisted that he study, study, and then study some more. Her dream was for him to become a doctor and his sister to be an attorney.

He laughed. "Actually, happened the other way. I'm an attorney and my sister is at Stanford. She's studying to be an audiologist."

While Flores mused, Diggs glared back with narrowed eyes and what he hoped was a noticeable sneer—his angry man in a mugshot face.

"I think sisters are the greatest gift a boy can have. She's a few years younger than me but I'd always seek her advice about girls. She actually introduced me to my wife. Met her at a Three Tenors concert. After ten minutes we knew that we were going to spend the rest of our lives together."

Diggs growled, "How precious."

Flores let the boorishness slide pass and asked enthusiastically, "So, Detective, who is Detective Leonard Diggs?"

Diggs could have told Flores that he became a homicide detective because the inadequate investigation of his mother's murder and the railroading of his father shaped his life. He never wanted anybody to feel as shorted by the police as he had and still did.

Diggs could have told Flores that tearing up his knee and losing his chance at a professional baseball career was his greatest disappointment. His greatest accomplishment, capturing the Sidewalk Ghoul. His most exhilarating, finding Glen Palmer.

Diggs could have told Flores that his best friend was the manager of Long Beach State Dirtbags baseball team. During the spring and early summer months, he could often be found at Blair Field, offering a tip to a struggling hitter, throwing batting practice, dissecting a scouting video, or just hanging around enjoying the unique ambience of a college ballpark.

Diggs could have told Flores that he was an unapologetic smooth jazz fan, or that he had a weakness for local carnivals.

Diggs could have revealed the essence of his personality. He was not a self-effacing individual; he was a driven, arrogant person who held himself and everyone around him to incredibly high standards.

Instead, Diggs answered, "I'm the chump that keeps the goddamn sewer from overflowing."

Flores let out a nervous chuckle. "Oh, come on, Detective. I have a feeling you're a fascinating fellow. Your family from around here?"

"My parents are dead. My sister and I haven't spoken in twenty years. I've never been married. I have no kids now, nor do I expect to ever have any, and to tell you the truth, I'm fine with all of that. I have no interest in a greedy sleep-around wife or children too busy ogling their phones to learn how to string a sentence together." Diggs chuckled. "No, thanks. I'll take the dark alley with a shank in my heart or a spent .38 in my skull." Flashing a toothy smile, he added, "As long as I get to kill them too."

Flores jotted something on his legal pad and placed it on his lap.

"Well, let's get down to business. As the mayor likely told you, he has a ton of exciting plans that will make the San Diego police department the envy of California."

Diggs furrowed his eyebrows. "California? The mayor told me his force was going to be the envy of the entire country. Being the envy of California is like being the sweetest smell in a slaughterhouse. Los Angeles is corrupt as hell. San Francisco is a joke. Does anyone anywhere ever enthuse about the greatness of the Sacramento police department? If you're going to brag that San Diego is going to be the envy of California, you might as well say it's going to be better than Fresno."

Flores maneuvered effortlessly. "If Mayor Pelton is shooting for the best police department in the country, I have no doubt it will happen. In your opinion, what does the mayor have to do to make that happen?"

"You do want an honest answer, correct?"

"Absolutely, Detective. Say whatever is on your mind."

Moving in a few inches closer to Flores, speaking just above a whisper, Diggs said, "The first thing the mayor needs to do is kick all the goddamn numskulls out of the department. A lot of them aren't any more skilled than a convenience store security guard."

Flores edged his chair against the wall. "Frankly, that surprises me."

Diggs took several moments to glance around the Starbucks, pretending to hunt for eavesdroppers. In a low voice, he said, "Don't get me wrong. Some of them try but for the most part, they're hopelessly incompetent. Quite a few are corrupt."

"Corrupt, really?"

"Maybe not as corrupt as LA. An LA cop expects a payoff; a San Diego cop will settle for a bag of bagels. I've only heard of a few dozen hardcore shakedowns but," Diggs smiled gleefully, "give our boys time. We'll get there."

Flores stared, part mesmerized, part appalled, and very much scared to death. Diggs was enjoying himself but it was getting late, and leaving Stall alone for too long would likely end up increasing his workload.

"David, let me relate a couple of personal experiences. One of my previous partners had problems in his marriage.

He constantly bitched that his wife refused to put out. Every time we were anywhere near one of the hooker hangouts, he'd scope the talent and set something up for himself."

Flores spoke incredulously. "He'd pay prostitutes while on the job?"

"Of course not. He never expected to pay."

"That's absolutely appalling."

"Another partner usually came on duty drunk and if he didn't come in drunk, he left drunk." That was Sarducci and that was true. "You know, David, I'm working on a book that I hope the mayor will let me plug at his rallies. You know, since he expects me to work for free. It's a memoir about my experiences on the force. How does *Drunken, Lazy Stalkers: My Years with the San Diego Police* grab you?"

Flores smiled stiffly. "There's always going to be a few bad apples. The mayor will work diligently to get rid of them all."

"Well, to be honest, it's gotten a lot worse under Pelton. The crime stats bear that out. As I'm sure you know, Wackerly hammers that home in every speech. If he knew the backstories, how bad it really is…" Diggs chuckled. "Kaboom, David. Kaboom."

Flores flicked his pen shut and turned away. He opened his briefcase and dropped the pen and the legal pad inside. He slid his phone into a jacket pocket.

Hastily, he said, "I'll talk to the mayor about our conversation and one of us will get back to you." Abruptly he stood and offered Diggs a feeble handshake before pushing past the table.

As Diggs watched Flores cross the street with his phone to his ear, he ordered a cup of coffee and a vanilla muffin before moving to an outdoor table. The breeze caressed the back of neck and lightly tussled his hair. He dallied with his afternoon snack and smiled at his best lines.

6

Diggs read the scrawled message on a yellow Post-it clinging to the edge of his desk: *My office, pronto!* He crumpled it in a fist before dropping it into the wastepaper basket and headed over to Swenson's office.

Swenson was sitting behind his desk, his fingertips digging into the back of his neck.

"You wanted to see me?"

Swenson made a sucking sound with his teeth and dropped his hands onto his desk. "I'm rubbing my neck, but I should be rubbing my ass. You know why?"

Diggs could have seen the punch line from the coast of Japan, but out of respect for the office, he took the stale gibe in stride.

"No, sir, I don't why you should be rubbing your ass."

"Because you're a pain in the ass and I have to deal with you."

"Sir, I don't…"

Swenson interrupted. "Save it, Diggs. I got good news for you. You're going on vacation."

Diggs eyed him suspiciously. "What are you talking about?"

Swenson lifted a white legal-sized envelope out of a drawer and tossed it at Diggs. It slid across his desk and toppled onto the floor.

Diggs was lifting the envelope off the carpet when Swenson said, "A ten-day stay in sunny Las Vegas. You can leave tonight or tomorrow morning. Your choice. No point in arguing. It comes from upstairs."

Diggs held the envelope in front of him. "Oh, I get it. Flores didn't like what I had to say so he whined to Pelton and now Pelton wants me out of town until after the election is over."

He had the urge to tear the envelope in half, but that was too dramatic for his taste, and premature anyway. Diggs wasn't crazy about Swenson, but he could be reasonable and if pushed, there was a better than average chance he'd take the coward's way out. Diggs dropped the envelope on Swenson's desk. "The last I checked, Pelton has no say over my vacation time. All I have to do is complain to the union. They'll back me up and everything the mayor is worried about will get worse."

Swenson leaned back in his chair. Warily, he said, "What is the mayor worried about, Diggs? What happened between you two?"

"A bunch of nonsense. It's not important."

"Apparently it is."

"I don't want to go on vacation, and I certainly don't want to go to Las Vegas."

A rush of air blew from Swenson's lips. "Look, Diggs. You're getting a free paid vacation. Let me restate that. It's free. It's not coming out of any accumulated vacation time or any days off you have coming. It's a bonus. Why is that so horrible?"

"It's the sneakiness of it. Pelton is afraid I'll talk to Wackerly. I don't like Wackerly any more than I like him."

For several moments, Swenson stared silently while Diggs waited patiently, understanding exactly how the wheels in Swenson's head grinded. Swenson was calculating whether he'd be better off knowing what happened or staying out of it. He was playing politics like he always did. Finally, Swenson let out a sigh and said, "Take my advice, Diggs, and go. Pelton and the chief are close, and I know from personal experience that the chief can be a spiteful bastard."

"Captain, I just started working on a cold case. The poor guy has been dead twenty-three years. By the time I get back, something else will have come up and then something else after that. Before you know it, it will be another twenty years and then it will be pointless."

"Why do you care about a twenty-three-year-old case?"

"Because his mother sold my mother face soap and because it's twenty-three years old. Justice delayed…"

Swenson interrupted. "Oh, who cares about your mother's soap? Did you hear me when I told you that Pelton and the chief are close? Do I need to remind you again that Jackett can be a spiteful bastard?"

Diggs mumbled, "I heard you."

"You're probably feeling a little cocky because you found the Palmer kid. Remember, Diggs, heroes have a short shelf life. When was the last time anyone congratulated you on the Sidewalk Ghoul case?" He folded his arms across his chest.

"Pelton did, just this morning."

Swenson scoffed. "Was that before or after he asked for something? Do as you're told. Go to Vegas. Enjoy yourself."

Diggs lifted the envelope off Swenson's desk and tore it

open. Inside was a sheet of white paper that included an itinerary and two twenty-dollar bills. Diggs scanned the itinerary.

"The Bugsy, never heard of it."

"From what I understand, it's not quite Caesar's Palace."

Diggs held out the twenties by their edges.

"What's this for?"

"Expense money."

"Forty dollars?"

"I'm sure your gambling expertise will parley it into a vast fortune."

He shoved the money into the envelope. "Plane ticket?"

"Sorry, no can do."

"Pelton wants me gone so badly, but he isn't willing to spring for an eighty-dollar Southwest flight?"

"That's with a couple weeks' notice. It's a lot more expensive when you book at the last minute. Besides, I've read that Southwest bought a whole fleet of 737 Max's. You're better off driving."

"Can I pass on the trip and stay home?"

"It seems abundantly clear to me that they want you in Vegas. Go to Vegas, Diggs."

"Can I at least stay where I want?"

"They want you where they want you. Quit fighting this, Diggs. Try to enjoy the benefits of a paid vacation."

"You know, this is ridiculous. I should take this to the union or leak it to the press and let the chips fall where they may."

Swenson shrugged. "I can't prevent you killing your career if that's what you want. Always remember, Diggs, the union can keep a job for you. Which job is an entirely different matter."

That was checkmate. Hero or not, Jackett could bury him at the evidence room counter or give him Stall's old job working a desk in Juvenile Crimes and he'd have no recourse.

Diggs stuffed the itinerary and the forty dollars into the torn envelope. He was halfway out the door when Swenson called out, "The way I understand it, the Bugsy isn't in the best neighborhood. You might want to pack a weapon."

*   *   *

The sun had already set when Diggs stopped for Mexican takeout near his Del Mar condo. He ate in his living room on a worn but comfortable sofa and watched the final Padres game of the season.

After the final pitch, Diggs entered his home office and slid though the half-opened sliding glass door that led to a balcony. The air was still and warm. Mars and most of the constellations were obvious. The parking lot at the shopping complex across the street wasn't quite a quarter full. He could see no ships on the sliver of ocean visible from his balcony. After a few minutes of gazing out at nothing he hadn't seen countless times before, he stepped back inside and sat at his desk. He nudged the mouse with his knuckles and waited for the computer screen to light up.

Diggs logged into his secret e-mail account where he was known as Malcolm. Eight weeks had passed since he first made contact with the collector who called himself Billy T. For forty-seven consecutive days, Diggs had religiously checked for a response and with each passing day and no return message, his once high hopes had crumbled. After a month and a half of edge-of-his-seat waiting, he took it for granted that Billy

T. was another dead end. The latest failure. A cold streak that refused to warm. It stung more than the others because had Billy T. delivered what he claimed to own, it would have been a difference maker.

When Diggs saw the message sitting between an insurance ad and a refinance offer, he wanted to kick himself. Billy T. had made contact three days previous. Diggs could feel his nerves tingling when he clicked open the message.

> *Hey Malcolm! Sorry it took me so long to get back to you. Personal issues that really suck have been holding me back, but thankfully those are behind me now.*
>
> *I still have all of the Silk Degrees magazines, along with a few boxes of VHS tapes. I am certain that I have everything Silk Degrees ever produced, and I'm probably the only guy in the world who can say that (LOL!).*
>
> *I'm thinking $2,000 for everything would be fair. Remember, this includes at least six hundred magazines, and dozens of movies. Naturally, you'll have to pay for shipping, which will be another several hundred. They'll be coming from Chandler, Arizona.*
>
> *I really hope we can make this work. I'm getting older and this stuff takes up a storage locker. Let me know how you'd like to proceed.*
>
> *Billy T.*

Fearful that he had blown the chance of a lifetime, Diggs quickly typed out a response.

Billy T., very sorry for the late response. If you have all the material produced by Silk Degrees, two thousand is reasonable. Traveling to Arizona is not an issue. I would like to see the magazines before any deal is consummated, and I agree with you. The sooner the better. I have time off this week if you are available. Let me know.

Malcolm

He read through the message twice. Satisfied, he clicked the send button and sat back in his chair, praying to the heavens that he wasn't too late.

Diggs was certain that the magazines would prove to be as crucial as they had been elusive. As one year blended into the next, it had become more and more clear that the magazines were his last and only chance to discover who was responsible for leaving his mother dead in a ditch.

7

Under a bright morning sun, Diggs tossed a suitcase into the back of his Prius. No longer grumbling over his banishment, a message from Billy T. had been waiting for him when he awoke. He had no issue meeting in person and provided Diggs the address to a storage facility in Chandler, Arizona. He wrote that Friday at noon would be best for him and Diggs wrote back confirming that he'd be there.

Diggs couldn't believe his luck. All the unjustifiable nonsense had become a timely and welcomed opportunity. Las Vegas to Chandler was a hardly draconian 325-mile drive. A day at the Bugsy to establish himself sounded about right and then he'd slip away to visit his alma mater. After a few days of visiting friends, he'd head off to Chandler, pick up the magazines, and return to San Diego.

Once Diggs escaped San Diego, proper traffic quickly thinned, and he was left with a boring desert drive with only satellite radio to keep him company. The empty time allowed him to once again chronicle the events that had been his lifelong scourge.

Over the years, Diggs had written a movie in his head of

those first days of the investigation. He compiled his script from the case notes he'd read from the murder book, a single audio cassette of the initial interview with his father, and the homicide investigators he managed to speak with before one after another passed away.

*　　*　　*

Sylvia Wright's body was discovered at 2:14 p.m. on a cool, gloomy June 24th Tuesday. By the time Detective Scotty Dixon arrived, the crime scene had been secured. Sylvia Wright lay in a hole three feet deep. Her pink blouse and her dark-colored jeans were buttoned and clean. Diggs remembered it as the same clothing she wore when she drove him to school that morning. Her watch hadn't left her wrist and her wedding ring remained on her finger. Her neck showed bruising that pointed to strangulation.

The date and time written on the cassette indicated that Detective Dixon and his partner Chuck Pace spoke with Diggs' father Nathen an hour and eight minutes after the discovery of his wife's body. Dixon rode Nathen Wright hard, skillfully keeping Wright off balance with threats and lies, while his partner Pace barely spoke a word. His father's plaintive sobs and the tear-soaked pleas made Diggs want to cry. When the tape ended, Diggs felt grimy and sad.

Diggs had always been encouraged that the rough treatment never changed his father's story. Except for a forty-five-minute lunch break, his father vehemently claimed to have been at work all day. When Dixon sharply pointed out that forty-five minutes gave him plenty of time to kill his wife, his father's tearful response was he had no reason to kill his wife and he would never hurt his wife.

The lack of motive was a complication that Dixon and Pace must have struggled over. The history of Nathen Wright provided nothing that would point to a potential murderer. Before he married, he worked as a pastor at a small Christian church in Carlsbad. He volunteered on a suicide hotline. No arrest or domestic violence history existed. The detectives found no hints of an extramarital affair. They found no significant life insurance policy. Nobody Dixon and Pace interviewed spoke a bad word about Nathen Wright. No juicy gossip materialized that would explain why a soft-spoken, seemingly happily married man would brutally murder his wife. Dixon and Pace allowed Wright to go home after that first interview and the case notes indicated that they believed his denials were convincing.

Two days later, Dixon received an anonymous tip that would lead to the discovery of a magazine that immediately launched a brand new bombshell theory and a serious reevaluation of Nathen Wright.

*   *   *

Diggs looked out the window at endless sandy plains and lonely dark hills gliding past him at seventy-five miles per hour. In a resigned voice, he said, "The magazine. It always comes back to the magazine."

The magazine was a forty-eight-page fetish porn rag meant for men with peculiar sexual tastes. It featured mostly black and white photos and included almost no text.

Dixon and Pace scoured the local sex shops searching for a copy of the magazine. Neither detective fully believed it existed until they found it in a seedy Oceanside adult bookstore wrapped tightly in cellophane. On its cover, a young woman dressed only in a bra and panties lay hogtied on a bare mattress. As the tipster reported, the magazine was titled *Bondage Adventures*.

Inside the magazine, the detectives found a six-page photo spread featuring a model identified as Jennifer Page, but who closely resembled Sylvia Wright. With the magazine in their possession, Dixon and Pace hurried back to headquarters. Dixon made contact with the magazine's distributor, an outfit out of Van Nuys called Gold Distributors. Ran by the former cellmate of an organized crime figure, Gold supplied adult bookstores nationwide with soft-core fetish magazines.

Gold Distributors may have swum in some dingy waters, but they went out of their way to be cooperative. They provided Dixon with the address and phone number to the publisher of *Bondage Adventures*—a company called Silk Degrees, based out of North Hollywood.

Dixon made contact with the owner of Silk Degrees, a character who went by the name Silk Hemmingway. He confirmed that Jennifer Page and Silvia Wright were one and the same and produced a signed model release form dated March 4th, 1986. Hemmingway claimed that the photo shoot had taken place at his office in North Hollywood. In a one-sentence paragraph, Dixon wrote that Hemmingway's alibi had checked out.

Nathen Wright was brought in for a second round of questioning. If an audio cassette existed, Diggs hadn't found it, but he knew the pressure exerted on his father would have been ferocious, and it had not resulted in a confession.

The notes stated that Dixon showed the magazine to Nathen Wright and although Wright became visibly agitated, he claimed to have known about his wife's bondage modeling but didn't think it was important. Beside that notation, Dixon had written a smiley face and an explanation point.

Two days later, a press conference was held. Diggs could almost recite Dixon's words by memory. He had retrieved a beta copy from the vaults of a San Diego television station and copied it onto a DVD. Over the years, he had screened it dozens of times.

Barrel-chested with a neatly trimmed black goatee, blue fedora, and a dark three-piece suit, Dixon gave off a flashy and intimidating aura. His partner Pace stood two steps behind wearing an off-the-rack jacket that hung large and loose.

Dixon did all of the talking and he spoke cheerlessly with his words often punctuated with sighs.

"Some of the facts of Sylvia Wright's life are shocking, and I don't take any pleasure in revealing any of it. But she was brutally murdered, and the public is rightfully concerned. I will reveal a few pertinent facts, but out of respect to the Wright children, I won't go into detail about the more titillating aspects of Mrs. Wright's secret life.

"Ms. Wright sidelined as a model in the sex industry. I won't reveal the name of the company she worked for or the name of any publications, but the content was disturbing. Barely clothed women tied in ropes. Photos that only men with violent and deranged minds could ever find sexually stimulating. Unfortunately, this kind of material is legal to produce, and it's legal to own. I don't know why Ms. Wright decided to work for this operation. In the end, it doesn't matter. She was murdered and she deserves justice."

Dixon took a few questions and revealed that the distributor of the magazine had agreed to destroy all copies in its possession and would insist that all issues that were already in stores be returned immediately, where they would then be destroyed.

When a reporter asked if there were any strong suspects, Dixon replied, "Yes, absolutely."

With a hint of a smile, Dixon concluded the press conference by saying, "Mrs. Wright's killer won't be free for long. I can promise you that."

*　　*　　*

The morning after the press conference, Nathen Wright was found dead in his garage, with a gunshot wound to his head and a blood-alcohol count twice the legal limit. The coroner ruled the death a suicide and the investigation was promptly closed.

Leonard and his sister Claire were placed in the permanent custody of his grandmother in San Diego, the surname Wright legally changed to Sylvia Wright's maiden name—Diggs.

Since his first day out of the academy, Diggs made it his mission to find the truth behind his mother's murder. He promised himself that if the evidence proved his father's guilt, he would find a way to accept it. Until then, he worked under the premise that his father had been railroaded into a suicide.

Although the Sylvia Wright murder book offered a multitude of insights, it wasn't complete. The magazine was missing. Contact information was gone. No audio existed with Hemmingway or anyone associated with Gold Distributors or Silk Degrees.

Gold Distributors ceased business operations in 1989. Silk Degrees stopped publishing eleven months after Sylvia's

Wright's death. Silk Hemmingway disappeared into the wind and Diggs knew not a thing about him. He had never seen a photo of Silk Hemmingway and countless internet searches and social media hunts led nowhere.

Following the belief that those associated with the pornography business normally worked under an alias, Diggs suspected that Hemmingway was more than a guy who made his living selling smut. Silk Hemmingway's name appeared on the masthead of every Silk Degrees publication Diggs had ever seen, and the murder book, the official document of his mother's murder, identified Silk Hemmingway as Silk Hemmingway. If Silk Hemmingway was his real name, why couldn't Diggs find anything on him, and if Silk Hemmingway was an alias, why didn't the murder book reveal his real name? Diggs suspected that Silk either had significant wealth, or high-level connections within the police department or at City Hall, or all of the above.

Scotty Dixon would be of no help. He died in an automobile accident in 1994. Dixon's partner, Detective Pace, succumbed to a heart attack the year before.

An alternative San Diego newspaper, the *San Diego Reader,* provided Diggs with his most compelling clue. In the fall of 1991, the *San Diego Reader* ran a two-page quicky story on the Sylvia Wright murder.

Dressed in denim shorts and a white t-shirt, a woman identified as Jennifer Page/Sylvia Wright sat securely tied to a chair with several strips of duct tape pasted over her mouth. Standing over her wearing black lingerie and a perplexed grin was a tall black-haired woman. The caption under the photo read: *Sylvia Wright's kinky secret led to her death.*

It was the first and only time Diggs saw an example of

his mother's fetish modeling, but it was the tall dark-haired woman that captured his attention. On a June morning in 1986, they had met, only weeks before his mother was killed.

On his way to baseball practice, twelve-year-old Leonard Wright saw a bright red Mustang parked a few doors away from his house. A woman wearing a tight black dress and green high heels got out of the car. Her type didn't belong in his boring middle-class neighborhood. She belonged in a Whitesnake music video sprawled over the hood of a corvette.

She was a warrior princess—at least six feet tall, sturdy, and toned. A thin face with high cheekbones. Expressive black eyes, full red lips, and legs as long as a water slide. Hands down, she was the most beautiful woman the young Leonard Wright had ever laid eyes on. They were barely three feet apart when she looked directly at him and winked. In a soft southern voice that belied her physical presence, she said, "Morning, sunshine."

Leonard watched enthralled as the goddess walked up his driveway and rang the front bell. He mother opened the door and smiled up at her. They hugged and his mother let her inside.

That night, Diggs asked his mother about the woman. Her response, a quick and terse, "Just a friend."

Years later, the internet supercharged Diggs' investigation. He scoured sites that sold old pornography. Ebay became a daily habit. He initiated dialog with bondage enthusiasts and learned that the beautiful dark-haired woman modeled under the name Libby Grace.

Finding Libby Grace became his obsession. The hug he witnessed at his front door had been warm, the embrace of two friends. How had Libby Grace met his mother? What brought her to his house?

Diggs' father claimed his wife's modeling hadn't been an issue. Dixon and Pace were convinced it was a motive for murder. What did Libby Grace believe? The car his mother drove was too unreliable to make an Oceanside to Los Angeles roundtrip trek. Diggs believed that Libby Grace had been the driver, which meant she and his mother sat side by side for at least five hours. Diggs needed to know what Libby Grace and his mother had talked about. He needed to understand his mother's mindset in the weeks before her death. Diggs needed to find the one woman who could answer questions no one alive could.

Diggs was certain the Silk Degrees inventory would lead to more Libby Grace content. He hoped it would lead to other models who shot with her. Diggs would begin searching for them too. Link to link to link. A spider-web approach.

If the magazines led nowhere, the spider web would droop and dangle into a final dead end that might bring his lifelong investigation to a screeching and likely permanent halt.

8

Thousands of tiny red and blue bulbs flashed under a rainbow of glittery yellow lights: *The World-Famous Bugsy*. Diggs parked in a shaded spot under a thirty-foot-high billboard of pancakes and sausage links and tugged his suitcase through sweltering heat. Beyond a thick glass entrance door, he was greeted with a thirty-degree temperature drop and the smell of a million Pall Mall cigarettes.

A middle-aged man at the front desk offered an indifferent welcome while a maintenance worker plastered a hole in the wall as large as a man's foot. As the clerk asked the usual check-in questions, he lifted his head from the computer screen and gazed past Diggs' shoulder. His hollow expression immediately turned tense. Diggs followed his eyes to a couple of drunk guys wearing different colored Tom Brady jerseys, shoving each other while a garishly dressed woman holding a half-filled drink watched on with bored indifference.

The clerk quickly finished up and handed Diggs the card key before stepping away and reaching for a phone. Diggs made his way through a quarter-filled gaming room with the usual row after row of noisy, glittering slot machines to his first-floor room directly across from the elevator bank.

Inside a stuffy cave of a room, Diggs quickly turned on the window air conditioning unit and opened the curtains. A foot in front of him was a gas station's air and water machine.

He closed the curtains and pulled down his bedspread, suspecting to find several generations of bugs laying on their backs, peacefully deceased. There were none, which up to that point was his Las Vegas highlight. Diggs lay on the bed and closed his eyes. The early rise and the long drive had taken its toll. Within minutes, he was napping.

The blaring of police sirens roused Diggs from sleep. The room was nearly pitch black and the red glow of a clock on the nightstand read 12:34 p.m., but even in a sleep-driven daze that didn't seem right. Diggs pawed around the nightstand for his phone. It read 7:19 p.m. and he remembered exactly where he was.

Outside his window, harsh demands laced with a dozen different obscenities raised Diggs out of bed. At the first gun-shot, he dropped to his hands and knees and crawled to the window.

Ten feet beyond the water and air machine, five policemen had their weapons drawn. Two men were lying face down on the greasy pavement with their arms and legs spread in an X. A third man lay against a pump, gripping his chest with two hands, trying to keep his heart from dropping onto his lap while slowly sinking into a pool of his own blood.

Diggs' cell phone rang. On its face was a Nevada number he didn't recognize. He assumed it was someone from the Bugsy imploring him to leave his room immediately. Gladly, he thought, and then he'd never come back.

The voice on the line was smooth and disc jockey-deep. The woman said, "Lenny, is that you? It's Claire."

After the initial surprise came wariness. The history of Leonard Diggs and his sister Claire was one of indifference. As children they never had a close relationship, and after the deaths of their parents, they grew even further apart. Calling him out of the blue was a first, at least Diggs thought so. The truth was he couldn't remember the last time she called him, or he called her.

"This is a surprise."

She laughed. "A little enthusiasm, Lenny. I'm here to suck up now that you're famous."

"What are you talking about?"

"What do you think? The kidnapped kid case. I've been following it. As you might remember, I'm a true crime junkie. All the podcasts are covering it. Even Greta Van Susteren talked about it on her show."

"I'm not famous, Claire. You'd be surprised how little this case has gotten me."

"Always the cynic, Lenny. What was he like?"

"Who? Harper or the boy?"

"Duh, Harper. The boy is boring."

"I was only with him ten minutes."

"Even so, he must have been incredibly interesting."

Diggs looked at the scar on his index finger. "More painful than interesting. Are you still living in Mojave Creek?"

She laughed merrily. "I sure am, and I'm engaged."

"Congratulations. That's fantastic."

Diggs could hear the pride in her voice. "He's a great guy. Smart, sophisticated. Just a really, really great guy."

Diggs again offered his congratulations and told her he was happy for her.

"Thanks, I'm very lucky. Are you still with that blonde? I'm sorry, her name escapes me."

"Laurie?"

"I don't remember. Big smile. Played Scottish bagpipes."

"I haven't seen her since I moved back to San Diego. I'm pretty sure she's married with a couple of kids."

"No kidding. Time flies. So, what about Harper? I don't mean to be so nosy, but true crime fascinates me."

"Totally forgettable."

"That's a weird way to describe him."

"Claire, the truth is that most criminals aren't memorable in the slightest. They're usually dumbasses and I didn't get the sense that Harper was any genius. The smart ones run Fortune 500 companies and I haven't crossed paths with any of them yet."

She burst out laughing. "I suppose you're right. You think he had help?"

"There is no evidence of that. It's not my case, so I don't know exactly what's going on."

"It's not?" Diggs could hear her disappointment.

"No, I work homicides. The Palmer case was a kidnapping."

"Oh, okay. No known motive?"

"As far as I know, nothing certain. Only speculation."

"What do you think?"

"I don't know. All I can tell you is that he was a weird old guy. His likely motive I can guess at, but I hope I'm wrong."

"Mm, I see what you mean. We had a big murder down here not too long ago."

"I heard. The Geist family. Have the police made any progress?"

"Ha, yeah, right. A bunch of boneheads over here. If you want to commit a crime and get away with it, this is the place."

"Hopefully, something will…"

She interrupted. "Are you driving in a tunnel? You sound like you're six feet underground."

Diggs moved to the opposite end of the room. "Must be a bad connection. I'm in Las Vegas."

"Vegas? Unless you've changed, Lenny, Vegas definitely isn't your kind of town. What are you doing there?"

"Long story. I won't be here for more than a day and then I'm heading down to Arizona. I'll be passing by Mojave Creek."

"I'd keep right on going if I were you. I used to think San Diego was dull but compared to this place, it's midnight at Mardi Gras." She laughed. "I admit, I'm being a little facetious. Really, I love it here. No way I'm ever leaving."

Later, Diggs would tell himself that Claire's cheerfulness and the sarcastic sense of humor they shared convinced him that he had been cheating himself from something exceedingly worthwhile. The words rolled out of his mouth and they felt right.

"If you're free tomorrow or the next day, we should get together for lunch." With a sinister edge, he added, "I'll tell you all about the sordid underbelly of San Diego."

Claire let out a child-like giggle that made Diggs smile. "That would be fun. I would love that. Let me talk to my fiancé. We have some family commitments. If it doesn't work out this time, hopefully I'll see you at my wedding."

"I wouldn't miss it."

"Okay, great. It was really nice hearing your voice again, Lenny."

After the call ended, Diggs sat in the dark on a lumpy chair listening to the purring white noise of cars traveling along Maryland Parkway, thinking about the only sibling he had and the tragedy they shared. How Claire dealt with it, he had no way of knowing. She sounded happy and content. She was getting married. She was living in the present and looking forward to the future. It appeared that she had done a better job of adjusting than he had.

Diggs opened the curtains a few inches. The police and the ambulances were gone and the blood on the pavement had been washed away. A guy in short pants and a button-down shirt pumped gas into his out-of-state Ford Explorer while sipping a slushie. His wife sat in the passenger seat drinking from a bottle of water and two kids in the back were eating out of white bags. The essence of Las Vegas unfolded in front of his eyes—quash the troublemakers, keep the tourists unaware, happy and spending. Diggs closed the curtains and got dressed.

Fifteen dollars of his forty-dollar stipend was spent on dinner at the Bugsy Bistro. He placed a twenty-dollar bet on the Astros to lose and the last five dollars bought him a margarita at the Bugsy Bar. The burger and fries were decent if not memorable. The Astros won by ten runs, and the margarita was mostly ice. In a little over three hours, he had blown his entire forty-dollar stipend and he guessed he had done pretty well.

He slipped furtively into the warm Vegas night with suitcase in hand. He packed it into the trunk of his car and drove to a Denny's across the street. A leisurely stroll back to the hotel followed. Along the way he made sure to be captured by as many Bugsy security cameras as possible. Once in his room, he undressed and brushed his teeth before crawling into bed. His mind drifted to pleasant thoughts of a reunion with his only sibling.

The constant chattering outside his door didn't upset him. The screaming man tumbling out of a window above him was only a momentary distraction. His night was spent in a sound and peaceful sleep.

9

Diggs felt no reason to flaunt his escape and it made no sense to underestimate Pelton. The moment the elevator doors opened, Diggs ducked from his room and mixed into the steel box with a group of somber pre-dawn Bugsy guests. After a sluggish ascent to the second floor, Diggs exited into a dim hallway and casually walked to a stairwell, down a flight of stairs, and onto the street. He crossed the street to the Denny's and got into his car. Through his rearview mirror, he watched the *World-Famous Bugsy* recede into a brown desert haze.

A few miles outside of the Las Vegas city limits, Diggs stopped for gas. As his tank filled, he drank coffee from a Styrofoam cup, with a sticky muffin on a pile of napkins beside him. His phone on his thigh, he used a clean finger to pluck over to the *San Diego Union-Tribune* website.

Meet Detective John Stall—San Diego's Super Cop.

An accompanying black and white photo showed a close-up of a blank-faced Stall. Over the past six weeks, Diggs had seen that same expression on Stall's face several times a day. On Stall's right, Glen Palmer's black and white face stared out with the same blank expression. The empty stares, the choice of black and white, the tight cropping from the chin up, the title—*Meet Detective John Stall*—were all distinctly familiar. Diggs took a sip of coffee and swallowed before he figured it out. The headline and the photos were meant to mimic the Beatles' first album cover.

Diggs couldn't discount that he was hallucinating inside his Bugsy room. The gunfire at the gas station had been brief but fierce. A wayward bullet could have shattered his window and grazed his skull. He could be lying on the floor suffering through a psychotic stupor, or he could be in a Las Vegas hospital room under heavy medication, his neocortex irreparably damaged, his mind running wildly amok with frightening delusions. He pinched himself. Once. Twice. Three times. There were no grim-faced doctors standing over him and no nurses reading his vitals. He began to read the article.

Detective John Stall knew he wanted to help people since he was five years old. Bringing in the trashcans for the handicapped man across the street. Walking the neighbor's dog at no charge. Every Sunday, getting up at 6:00 a.m. to wash his grandmother's car before she went to church. "Doing the right thing has always given me a high," Stall says today, without a hint of burden or self-congratulation.

"Detective Stall isn't only a do-gooder by nature, he's a hell of a cop," says Captain Al Swenson, Stall's supervisor and a highly decorated officer in his own right.

"John's an extraordinary police officer and a hero," adds Chief Francis Jackett. "There wasn't a man or woman in San Diego not searching for Glen Palmer and John was the one who found him. It doesn't get any better than that."

Stall's keen instincts led him to a dilapidated home near a warehouse district. It was there he found Glen Palmer lying unconscious on a dirty futon. The rest as they say is history and, in this case, magnificent, marvelous history.

Leaning back in his chair at police headquarters, Detective Stall's eyes are serious, his expression tense. "It was a stressful moment," Stall recalls. "The door was locked, and I wasn't sure what was on the other side. But the situation felt immediate. I'm not sure how to explain it. Gut instinct, I guess. I just felt like something had to be done at that very moment. Not a minute later or even a second later." He stresses with a burrowed brow. "At that very moment..." Detective John Stall stares with the eyes of a tiger. "I aimed my weapon at the lock and shot it off. Then I kicked down the door." His face relaxes. His smile soothes. He is remembering the life that was saved. "That's when I found Glen."

Stall wipes a tear from his eye. Detective Stall's compassion is both authentic and heartwarming. He is a gentle hero. His bravery is unquestioned. There is no doubt that Detective John Stall would have singlehandedly challenged the Red Army to get Glen back to his loving parents. Don't ever bet against John Stall's determination. He is a man who will find a way to get things done.

There is a glimmer in the detective's eye. John Stall is a cross between Bradley Cooper and Gary Cooper. Six-foot-one with a beefcake body, jet black hair, the chiseled features of a Hollywood leading man, and a disarming smile that could charm the Taliban. If Stall wasn't a real-life hero, he could be a movie action hero.

Stall chuckles heartily. It's the laugh of a leader. "My mom wanted me to grow up to be Clint Eastwood. My dad wanted me to be Dan Fouts. My wife tells me that I fell somewhere between that."

Diggs let out the laugh of a lunatic. He closed his eyes and took in a deep breath. Slowly, he inhaled and exhaled and then repeated the process. He counted to a leisurely ten and finished the remaining twelve paragraphs of comically overblown idolatry that bordered on performance art.

Diggs didn't remember calling in sick the day Glen Palmer was rescued, but from the first paragraph to the last, his name was MIA. The author of the article was a name Diggs didn't recognize.

The sun had climbed forty-five degrees over the horizon. The ocean of sand surrounding Diggs would be scorching within a few hours. A sharp glare bounced off the rear of his car. His seat was heating up and his backside had produced the first traces of perspiration. He rolled up the windows and turned on the air conditioning. With cynical admiration mixed with a healthy dose of awe, he said, "Shrewd bastards."

Up to that point, Diggs was certain Pelton had banished him to Vegas in a ham-handed attempt to prevent the possibility that he'd contact Wackerly's people, but the problem with that strategy was that he owned a telephone and he assumed Wackerly did as well. Now he understood that he had badly underestimated the mayor. His expulsion had nothing to do with defense; it was a bold, offensive maneuver.

Now that he was out of the way, a new Glen Palmer narrative, one that promoted Stall as the star and left Diggs relegated to the cutting room floor, could be advanced with limited interference.

Diggs tried to call Stall and predictably got his voicemail. Diggs guessed that Stall was instructed to ignore any of his phone calls, and Stall would have no choice but to follow orders. Diggs left a brief message to return his call, fully expecting to be ignored.

The highway held little traffic and nothing interesting enough to take the time to notice. Soon, Diggs put Stall, Pelton, Palmer, Flores, and the Beatles behind him and reflected on the surprisingly pleasant phone call from his sister.

Claire had been funny and charming, and he felt humbled that he expected so much less. He began to blame himself for their non-existent relationship. When Claire moved to Mojave Creek, he never gave it a second thought. Never had he called to see how she was doing. Never had he asked to visit. For most of his life, he had been chronically self-involved, his sole focus on whatever was important to him at the time. His excuse had always been drive and commitment. Selfishness had a lot of euphemisms.

Diggs remembered Claire as a bright and happy child and somewhat of a prankster. Water balloons at the top of doors. Silly phone calls to businesses. An imaginative kid who enjoyed afternoon game shows, jigsaw puzzles, and Nancy Drew, and who had a healthy circle of friends.

A year or so before both of their lives were torn apart, Claire had tried to get the family on a game show. She claimed that she had devised a system that would guarantee a win. Diggs didn't quite recall the system, but to his ten-year-old brain, it was much too complex for him to fully grasp. She sent letters to the producers of the show seeking an audition, but for whatever reason nothing ever came of it.

Claire would become valedictorian of her high school graduating class, but for reasons Diggs never learned, she decided not to enroll in college.

Diggs wondered if her engagement would result in her first marriage. He wondered if she had children from past marriages. Diggs felt embarrassed that he knew as much about his sister as he would a sixth cousin.

The remembrances of Claire made his drive pass quickly. The exit that led to Mojave Creek neared. A choice he would have never considered twenty-four hours before had become an easy one to make.

Two miles later, Diggs was in the dusty little town of Mojave Creek, population twenty-two thousand. At the first fast-food place he saw, he stopped for lunch. He sat in a booth and considered the positives and negatives of presumptuousness. Claire hadn't called him back, but there was no law that said he couldn't drop by to say hello.

Diggs finished his lunch and sat in his car, still uncertain about what he should do. He reminded himself that timidness had never gotten him anywhere and dialed her phone number. After six rings came a harsh buzz with no opportunity to leave a voice message. Diggs tried the number again with the same result. The buzz and the lack of a voice recording stoked Diggs' investigative instincts. He opened a reverse directory app from his phone and typed in Claire's number. Her number was attached to 2235 Ocotillo Road, Mojave Creek. He punched the address into his navigation. Ocotillo Road was barely three miles away.

Diggs drove past older homes dotted between small

businesses—Murry's Air Conditioning Repair, Cactus Trail Mopeds, Driscoll's Garden Gifts—mixed with the occasional chain restaurant—Coco's, MacDonald's, Kum and Go. Not surprisingly, Mojave Creek appeared to be a town supported by service jobs.

That alone made it hard for Diggs to understand Mojave Creek's appeal. Opportunity seemed lacking, while heat and the sand were more than plentiful. On the other hand, the land was probably cheap. Drug abuse and crime no doubt existed, but not anywhere near big city levels. Sunrises and sunsets were likely beautiful, and the internet brought everything to your phone, all of which could be delivered to your home.

As Cactus Trail merged onto Ocotillo, Diggs passed a bar-restaurant called the Sleeping Volcano. After that came a trailer park and for the next quarter mile, old rundown ranch houses with dirt front yards. As far as Diggs could tell, Claire's socio-economic state didn't appear to be much above lower middle-class.

In the distance, Diggs saw a large brown mailbox with the numbers 2235 painted in white. He eased the accelerator and cruised toward the box. Behind the mailbox were the remains of a fire-gutted home. He made an abrupt stop and placed his car in park at the edge of the two-lane road.

Diggs quickly exited and approached Claire's home. It had been a one-story ranch with a red tiled roof and a two-car garage. He stepped over burned boxes and charred wood. He walked around two badly burned chairs and an overturned pair of stereo speakers.

He entered the frame of the house where the front door used to be and into what was once the living room. A water-damaged red sofa lay on its side on scorched gray carpet. Three broken bar stools lay in a loose pile. In the kitchen, the refrigerator had partially melted. Diggs placed his palm on its surface; it was warm to the touch.

In a bedroom, a king-sized mattress almost completely black with soot hung over a metal frame and nearly touched the floor. The remains of a red painted dresser lay blistered and broken in a corner of the room.

As Diggs roamed, he sniffed around for accelerants—gasoline, kerosene, paint thinner—but the wind was gusting and he couldn't pick up any scents that offered any hints.

He meandered into the backyard. Two black metal chairs were overturned. A few feet away, four metal stakes pounded in the ground made a five-foot square. Tied to one of the stakes, a short strand of shredded rope. Diggs again called Claire's number, with the same result—six rings and a harsh buzz.

An internet search revealed a hospital eight miles away. A woman identifying herself as a nurse picked up his call.

Diggs identified himself. "I'm on Ocotillo Road at a house that recently burned down. Can you tell me if a Claire Diggs has been admitted?"

He could hear her fingers clicking a keyboard. After several moments of silence, she said, "No."

"How about Claire Wright?"

"I'm sorry. No one by that name either."

"Over the past twenty-four hours, has anyone been admitted with burns or smoke inhalation?"

"No."

"Is there another hospital near Mojave Creek?"

"The nearest is St. Joseph's in Pierce Junction. It's fifty miles away."

Diggs felt the muscles in his stomach tighten. Anyone present during a house fire would have at least been taken in for observation. That is, unless no one survived.

Diggs ended the call and drifted around the property, taking photos of the wreckage. As he kicked through the damage, he tried texting Claire's number. Almost immediately, a failure to deliver notice appeared on his screen.

Diggs returned to his car and looked up the address to the local sheriff's department. Before he contacted the morgue, he wanted to reach out to the helping hand of law enforcement.

10

Perched on a ridge that overlooked the interstate, the Mojave Creek Sheriff's Department was housed in a khaki-painted building with a flat roof that resembled a shoe box. Diggs parked on a black tar lot amongst a half-dozen police cruisers and exited his car to the mild scent of exhaust fumes from whooshing vehicles twenty yards below.

Diggs was nearing the entrance when a man in a brown policeman's uniform holding a Styrofoam cup backed his way out. When he noticed Diggs, he abruptly stopped and kept the door ajar with his foot.

He was a tall man, only an inch or so shorter than Diggs. Minus a slight paunch, he was lean and his posture rail straight. Anyone who saw him from a distance would see the body language of a serious and focused man, perhaps ex-military. Up close, his wavy dark hair needed a cut. Half-moons draped heavy under his eyes. His unhealthy pallor would concern any doctor. Diggs guessed him to be in his mid to late forties, but he looked ten years older than that. Diggs understood all too well. When he'd tracked the Sidewalk Ghoul, he'd fallen into the same tattered state, had the same dark circles under his eyes, and had even neglected trimming his beard until he looked in the mirror and was aghast to see Ted Kaczynski staring back at him. In the biggest cases, the ones that would never be forgotten, there was never enough time. Diggs guessed that the Geist murder case had taken over this man's life.

Their eyes locked and through a frosty smile, the policeman said, "Good afternoon, may I help you?"

"I hope so. Do you know who's investigating the fire on Ocotillo Road?"

He stepped away from the door, letting it shut behind him. "It might be me. Depending on what the fire marshal reports. And may I ask who you are?"

Diggs felt a sudden rush of relief. Had anyone perished in the fire, it would already have been a police matter. Diggs offered his name and opened his wallet, showing the policeman his badge and identification.

"Welcome to Mojave Creek, Detective. I'm Greg Potter. I'm the sheriff around here. May I ask your interest?"

"My sister Claire lives at that address. I haven't been able to get in touch with her."

He nodded. "Oh, I see. I'm sorry for her loss." Potter perceptively picked up on Diggs' body language and understood his worries. "I'm happy to report that nobody was home at the time of the fire."

A rush of relief blew from Diggs' lips.

"We haven't heard from anyone either. My guess is that she hasn't found out yet. I feel awful for her. She's in for quite a shock."

"Who reported the fire?"

"At the moment, I don't know. Maybe someone driving by. There's a trailer park not too far away. If the fire turns out to be arson, and the chances are it won't, I'll send someone over to ask around. Of course, I'll start an investigation and I'll need to talk with her."

"When was the fire reported?"

"A little after 1:00 a.m."

Diggs was about to ask the sex of the caller when Potter interrupted. "My apologies. I'm in the middle of something right now. Pleasure speaking with you, though. If you want to leave your contact information inside, I'll keep you updated."

Diggs pulled a business card from his wallet and held it out. "How about if I give you my card?"

Potter pulled the card from Diggs' fingers.

"How is the Geist case coming along?"

Potter slipped the card into his back pocket. "Well, the press has moved on, which means a big nuisance won't be taking up any more of my time. It helps when there aren't any five-star hotels within fifty miles."

"Probably moved on to the Barkley case in St. Louis. It's become quite a national phenomenon."

"Well, sorry for St. Louis, but good riddance to them."

"If the Geist case is solved, they'll be back. Five-star hotels or not."

Potter took a sip from his Styrofoam cup. "No ifs. The Geist case will be solved. I can promise you that."

"You're close?"

"We are. I'll be in touch if I hear from your sister. Sorry, gotta go."

The sheriff brushed past Diggs and hopped into the police cruiser closest to the front entrance. The motor gunned and the car sped out of the lot.

Diggs sat in his air-conditioned Prius considering his next

move. Two things were for certain: he wasn't going to leave Mojave Creek until he found Claire, and he had no intention of waiting around for Potter's updates.

Normally, the first step of an investigation was canvassing with the hopes of finding someone who saw something. On Ocotillo Road, the homes were spread far apart. Claire's nearest neighbor was at least twenty yards away, and the fire had started in the early morning hours. Diggs doubted that canvassing would be effective, but the saloon he had passed, the Sleeping Volcano, held ample promise. Establishments like the Sleeping Volcano were invented for socializing, and it was near Claire's home. Diggs reasoned that a destructive fire might encourage opinions and gossip.

Diggs drove into the Sleeping Volcano parking lot with diminished optimism. Counting his vehicle, there were seven in a lot that probably held a hundred. Returning later when the crowd would likely be thicker crossed his mind, but he was there and he had to start somewhere. He reasoned that a small number of patrons might not be terrible. It improved his chances of a leisurely talk with a bartender, a manager, a waiter, a regular, or all of the above.

From the outside, the Sleeping Volcano felt safe and uninspired. Something devised by a twelve-person committee with years of experience creating boring themed restaurants. Its faux-wood exterior was intentionally faded in some places, less so in others, and a steeply pitched faux-tin roof was intentionally dented in several areas. Near an outdoor seating area, a murky pond was filled with plastic algae. The usual neon beer signs stained the windows, while dinosaur rock played from overhead speakers. Above the entrance, a plastic sign treated to look like faded barn wood read: *Welcome Mojave Creek Nation!*

After Diggs pushed through saloon doors, the sudden dimness momentarily wreaked havoc on his eyes. Once he regained focus, he discovered that Mojave Creek Nation consisted of an older man wearing a cowboy hat chatting it up with a heavy-set bartender and two guys playing pool.

Diggs walked over a purple tiled floor past empty chairs pressed against unoccupied tables to a barstool. Behind the bar, a purple and black neon volcano spewed green neon lava. Surrounding the splashy sign were long black shelves that held the usual array of imported beers, wines, and harder alternatives.

In a conversational voice, the bartender asked Diggs what he was drinking. Diggs asked for a Heineken and as he sipped from a bottle, took in his surroundings.

The pool table sat twenty feet to his right. A man the size of an NFL linebacker was smashing the balls around the table without any attempt to land them in the pockets. Watching the big man's foolishness was a short skinny kid wearing a Pearl Jam t-shirt.

While Diggs scanned the room, he listened to the bartender and the man in the cowboy hat chit chat about the Phoenix Suns. The NBA wasn't Diggs' sport, but he knew enough that he believed he could find a way to casually interject himself into the conversation.

A raspy voice sneered, "You little shit-stain."

Like everyone else, Diggs turned toward the voice. The skinny kid's feet were a foot off the floor. The monster had slung him into a suffocating headlock.

The kid screeched, "I was only kidding! I was only kidding!"

The bartender called out, "Hey, Remy. Knock it off."

The man in the cowboy hat said, "I don't know why you let him in here."

The kid continued to squirm frantically. Through gasps, he cried out, "Come on, Remy. You're killing me."

The bartender yelled, "Goddammit Remy, leave him alone." He muttered in Diggs' direction, "Remy is a tough guy as long as he's four times as big."

Remy turned toward the three men with the kid tucked under his arm. A cocky "What are you going to do about it?" grin polluted his pudgy face. As the kid thrashed and begged, Remy glowered at him with disdain.

Diggs thought once, then he thought twice. He knew that practically speaking, it wasn't his greatest idea, but as a teenager with severe acne, he had suffered through bullying himself and rather than forgive and forget, he used the memories as motivation to dish out an occasional teaching moment.

He called out, "Hey."

Remy looked up just as a glass ashtray ricocheted off his forehead. He fell to his knees howling like a wounded animal, while covering a gash that was bleeding through his fingers, along his forearm, and onto his shirt.

The bartender and the man in the cowboy hat stared on speechlessly. The kid darted out the front entrance while Diggs took another sip from his bottle. He anticipated that Remy would curse at him and make a threat or two before slinking out.

The bartender shouted, "Remy, don't."

Diggs glanced over in Remy's direction. He stood in a semi-crouched position. His left eye had begun to swell, and he had bizarrely smeared his blood across his face. Remy was weighing his odds and every advantage appeared to be his. He stood at least four inches taller than Diggs and had to be at least fifty pounds heavier. Diggs was obviously years older, and he was dressed like a community college English professor. The longer the behemoth eyed him, the more Diggs realized that Remy was liking his chances.

Remy's counterattack commenced without a word being spoken. He lumbered towards Diggs like a charging bull. The man in the cowboy hat hopped from his bar stool and ran. The panicked bartender called out, "Remy, stop!"

Diggs kept calm. His breathing was steady—he was the patient batter waiting for the ball to curve over the center of the plate.

Remy was eight feet away when Diggs slid off the stool. One step backwards gave him all the space he needed. Grabbing the bar stool by its legs, he took a quick but ferocious swing directly into Remy's ribs, shattering the stool into three separate pieces. Remy crumpled to the ground like a discarded piece of tissue paper. His face bloody and his eyes teary, he wailed barely coherent threats laced with obscenities meant to save face.

Pleased that his vision and accuracy hadn't deteriorated over the years, Diggs dropped what was left of the stool and slapped a twenty-dollar bill on the bar counter. He stepped around Remy and headed toward the exit.

Diggs' body language was nonchalant, and his paces had no hurry in them, but he couldn't wait to get into his car and onto the road. In front of three witnesses, he had committed assault and battery. In California, that usually meant automatic jail time. In San Diego, cops arrested and charged with serious crimes were terminated without exception. The kid was standing at the edge of the outdoor patio. He trotted toward Diggs.

"That was a heck of a throw. You should pitch for the Diamondbacks."

Out in the light, Diggs got a better look at him. The top of his head barely reached Diggs' chest. Through a brown crew cut that had grown out unevenly, Diggs saw an ugly two-inch scar on the left side of his scalp. His face was round like a panda and his eyes brown like a UPS truck. His arms were deeply tanned and painfully skinny. The bar's dim lighting had fooled Diggs. The kid was a young adult rather than a teenager and probably about the same age as Remy.

Diggs' steps had progressively gotten quicker. As the young man tried to keep up, Diggs noticed that his left leg limped slightly.

"That was once my plan."

"You played in the majors?"

"Gave it my best shot. Came up short."

"I like baseball. I like football better."

"Football is fun to watch. Not as fun to play."

Diggs slid inside his car.

"Not many people pick fights with Remy. Thanks for helping me out."

Diggs had one eye watching the Sleeping Volcano and the other on the road hoping not to see any police cruisers pulling into the lot.

"At some point, everyone gets what they deserve. What's your name?"

"Rusty. What's yours?"

"Call me Malcolm."

"Thanks again, Malcolm."

"Rusty, let me ask you a question. You wouldn't know anybody named Claire, would you? She's a Caucasian woman. She'd be in her mid-forties. She lives on Ocotillo at the burned down house."

"No, sir. Sorry."

Diggs thanked him and closed the door. As he started the engine, Rusty tapped on the driver's side window. Diggs rolled it down halfway.

"I know someone who might know her. Ever hear of Petey White? He's a famous actor."

Diggs recognized the name although Petey White hadn't been famous for decades, and even at his most famous, he wasn't that famous.

"I've heard of him."

"Mr. White knows everybody. There's going to be a party at his ranch later tonight. Lots of people will be there. Maybe Claire will be there too."

"What time is the party?"

"Midnight."

"Why so late?"

Rusty grimaced as if Diggs asked the date of Christmas Eve. "Mr. White's parties always start at midnight."

"Are they always on Wednesday?"

Rusty nodded. "Uh-huh."

"Where's his ranch?"

"Off Iguana Road. I'll take you if you want. You probably won't be able to get in if Mr. White doesn't recognize you."

With no hesitation, Diggs answered, "Okay, Rusty. I'll take you up on your offer."

"I might leave before you do. Is that okay?"

"That's fine with me."

"Then I'll see you tonight. Meet me here at 11:45. I don't have a car. You'll have to drive."

"I'll be here."

Diggs jerked his head in the direction of the Sleeping Volcano. "You going to be alright?"

Rusty smiled. "I'm not stupid. I'm not going back in there."

The quirky young man began to walk backwards. At five paces, he playfully called out, "Don't be late."

11

The Western Jewel appeared to be a better than the average small-town motel. An eight-foot-tall lizard sculpture in a grassy area near the courtyard had an interesting retro appeal. Two attractive palm trees crossed in an X over the front entrance reminded Diggs of something he'd see at a resort-style hotel. Management still seemed to care and that was enough for Diggs to give it a chance.

A chime announced his entrance into a small, sparsely furnished lobby. Several feet behind the front desk, a middle-aged woman sat on a brown lounge chair in a tiny room, laughing uproariously as she knitted something on her lap. The television wasn't visible from where Diggs stood, but the audio was loud and clear. He didn't mind standing unnoticed for a few seconds, but he had no intention of waiting until the commercial break. He counted to ten in his head. At eleven, he tapped the front desk bell several times.

She kept her eyes on the television while casually raising an index finger. Another five seconds passed before she lifted herself out of the lounge chair and sluggishly approached the front desk.

The back of her hair was matted, presumably from watching too much afternoon TV. A white plastic, rectangular nametag read: *Esther*.

"You have a reservation?"

Her face was distrustful, and the tone of her voice announced permanent displeasure.

"Do I need one?"

"One hundred and twenty-five a night."

Diggs frowned. "One twenty-five? No wonder the parking lot looks like a cemetery."

"I don't remember forcing you to come here. If you can't afford us, there's a dump a few miles down the road. All the bugs you want and plenty of noise. The way I understand it, they don't charge extra for either."

Through an annoyed edge, Diggs said, "Whatever, I'll take a room."

"Just tonight?"

"Probably."

"Well, let me know as soon as possible. We book up fast."

Diggs had no interest in jostling with a surly motel clerk, but she had placed the ball on a T and taking a swing was too irresistible to pass up. Through a subversive grin, he said, "By the half hour or hour?"

She scrunched her face, which allowed her glasses to slide to the tip of her nose. "Don't get smart. There's no law says I have to rent to you."

Actually, there were several federal laws and probably a state law or two that would argue the contrary, and although Diggs had an urge to reference a few of them, he reminded himself that he didn't want to waste his time arguing with a surly motel clerk.

She adjusted her glasses and began to painstakingly write down Diggs' credit card information onto a manual card imprinter. After the charge was approved, she flicked a key card across the counter with a forefinger. "You're in sixteen."

Diggs walked across a concrete courtyard radiating scorching heat that felt combustible. He slid the card into the lock and stepped into a room that appeared clean and easily livable for one night. The desk was an adequate size. The small refrigerator would be useful. The mattress was firm, and the tiny bathroom good enough. The air conditioner rattled but didn't skimp on cold air. As long as the wi-fi wasn't slow, Diggs would have no complaints.

After washing up, Diggs sat at the desk and concentrated on finding his sister. He started with social media—a great tool, a godsend in more cases than he could remember, but without basic information, it was useless.

Diggs didn't even know the name he was searching for. Claire Diggs or Claire Wright, or was it something else? For all he knew, Claire had been married and divorced five times.

Facebook got him nowhere, but there were plenty of other platforms out there and Diggs tried the ones he was familiar with. Two hours later and nothing but dead-ends, Diggs gave up on social media and turned his attention to Petey White, the famous actor who hadn't been famous since the mid-1970s when he co-starred on a clichéd cop show called *Rev and Roll*. Diggs remembered it as an uninspired amalgamation of the hit police dramas of the era. Mismatched buddy-cop nonsense seemingly produced for halfwits.

White woodenly played Howard Roll, the strait-laced, tight-assed pair of the investigative duo. Roll's partner was Rev Davis, Vietnam vet, crazy man, and ladies' man. He was portrayed by an actor named Ricky Racine who Diggs hadn't seen on anything since *Rev and Roll*. He did recall reading something somewhere that Racine had handed over all his money to a religious cult in Northern California.

With his safe, clean-cut good looks, White was the destitute man's Robert Stack. For the sixty-five plus female viewer, he was eye candy. The quintessential sexy-to-grandma actor.

As a teenager, Diggs would sometimes watch *Rev and Roll* reruns on cable, but only if it was raining in buckets or he was too sick to change the channel, or he felt like laughing at something that was beneath the intelligence of a ten-year-old.

White's IMDB page showed a face that was the color of an old penny with more lines than a Rick James afterparty. A mass of flowing gray hair fell to his shoulders and his studded leather jacket made him look like an ancient prog-rocker at the Rock and Roll Hall of Fame induction ceremony.

White's acting credits began in the late 1960s and ended in 1999. He appeared in several guest roles on popular series—*Police Woman, Mannix, Barnaby Jones, Kojak*—but his only starring role was *Rev and Roll*, which ran on ABC from 1975 to 1979. After *Rev and Roll* ended its run, White settled into roles at the bottom of the cast list in a smattering of theatrical movies that Diggs had never heard of and at the bottom of the cast list in a few made-for-TV movies that Diggs never heard of.

According to his bio, White had won the 1977 Best Lead Actor Emmy Award for *Rev and Roll*. Diggs cross-checked the Emmy Award website and miraculously it was true.

Diggs clicked over to the *Rev and Roll* IMDB page. He found no series gossip or behind-the-scenes facts that shed light on anything that held any interest, at least he didn't think so. Diggs wasn't really sure what he was looking for or why he was spending so much time looking.

Diggs skimmed the comments section. Most were positive, no surprise there. Only diehard fans would ever bother to visit the *Rev and Roll* IMDB page. A commenter's headline read: *One of the Great Upsets in Emmy History!*

Diggs mouthed to the screen, "No kidding."

After IMDB, Diggs opened Google and into the search field, he typed: *Petey White party Mojave Creek*. He found no information on any past or future parties held by the legendary Petey White, which struck Diggs as surprising. Rusty implied that White's parties were common and the way he enthused made Diggs believe they were a big deal.

A natural suspicion began to kick in. Diggs considered the possibility that Rusty hadn't been as grateful as he let on. Every cop knew of cases where the abused couldn't stop falling over themselves to protect their abuser. Whether a similar dynamic was in play between Rusty and Remy, Diggs had no idea, but a late-night, middle-of-the-desert ambush began to sound like a possibility. Diggs dug his Glock from under a pile of clothing and laid it on top of his wallet. Moments later, his phone began to ring. He read the caller ID and picked up immediately.

"Stall, thanks for calling back."

"Sorry it too me so long, boss. They have me running around over here like a crazy man."

Diggs told him that he read the article in the *Union-Tribune*. Before Diggs could go any further, Stall blurted, "I'm really sorry. Believe me, I gave you full credit. I don't know why she wrote the story like that."

Diggs believed him. "Understood, Stall. Don't worry, I'm

not mad. I think it's great for you. How many people ever get to read a story like that about themselves?"

Stall's voice brightened. "Phoebe is really happy. She bought every copy at the 7-Eleven by our house. She's sending them to everyone she knows."

Diggs smiled into the phone. "As she should. Have her save one for me. Did David Flores set up the interview?"

"He did. It was in Pelton's office. Pelton congratulated me and told me he wanted me to campaign with him. It seemed like an order more than a request. I told him I'd have to check with my wife, but I also wanted to clear it with you."

"You don't have to clear anything with me, Stall. If you want to do it and Phoebe is okay with it, go ahead and do it. A chance like this may never come again."

"Thanks, boss. I appreciate this. By the time you get back from vacation, everything should be back to normal."

Stall thanked him again and it sounded so heartfelt that Diggs could almost convince himself that he wouldn't complain about him anymore.

"Oh, in case you're interested, I've been talking with Detective Stokely. He's working on Glen's case. We met him outside Harper's house."

Diggs said he remembered.

"He told me that Harper had another driver's license with a different name. That's three! How many names does a guy need?"

"What is it?"

"Richard Reed. I think I like that one best. Sounds like an Old West sheriff." Stall started to mimic John Wayne. "Richard Reed, US Marshall to the rescue. Stay seated there, pilgrim…"

Diggs rubbed the back of his neck and grimaced as if

he were in excruciating pain. He interrupted. "Reed's his real name?"

Still speaking in his John Wayne voice, Stall said, "I don't know. I can ask if you want, pilgrim."

Diggs told him it wasn't necessary. It wasn't his case and even if the old man's real name was Harper or Reed, it didn't matter anymore. They were both dead.

"Did you want something, boss?"

Diggs told him it was nothing. They ended the call and Diggs took a shower before changing into shorts and a t-shirt. He crawled under the covers feeling decidedly uncertain about the night ahead, but he hadn't found Claire. He'd take his chances.

Other than a thin ray of sunlight lasering past a quarter-sized opening between the front window curtains, the room was dark. Diggs' eyes followed the beam to the Glock .357 lit up like the star of a Broadway show. Diggs got out of bed and adjusted the curtain. When he returned to bed, he pulled the sheets to his shoulders and hoped that the Glock would be nothing more than an unnecessary standby.

12

An eight-foot-high chain-link fence stood no more than five inches from the driver-side window. The rear bumper was nearly touching a dumpster. The headlights were off and the motor silently idled. Burrowed in a crevice in the Sleeping Volcano's moonlit parking lot, Diggs felt as unobtrusive as a spider at the edge of a ceiling.

Any cars entering the lot, Diggs would see before they saw him. Anyone on foot had to approach from the front or from the passenger side. The loaded Glock on the seat beside him completed the final layer of precaution. As long as he remained observant, an ambush was impossible.

Diggs kept the radio off and the moonroof open. What he couldn't see, he hoped he'd hear. Except for the distant sound of a rare vehicle humming past the Volcano, there wasn't much of anything to hear.

11:45 p.m. came and went. At midnight, Diggs was ready to pack it in. At 12:03 a.m., he heard the rustling of kicked gravel. His eyes seesawed as the stirring got closer, but nothing was presenting itself. He lifted the Glock. At the hood of the car, a dot of light glowed.

A voice whispered, "Malcolm?"

Diggs rolled his window down a crack. "Yeah, it's me."

He approached wearing a black t-shirt and a dark-colored baseball cap. Crouching at the passenger window with a cigarette dangling between his lips, he took a moment to scan the inside of Diggs' car.

He pulled the cigarette from his lips. "It took me a while to see you back here. Ready to go?"

Diggs jerked his head toward the passenger seat. In a clipped voice, he answered, "Get in and no smoking."

Rusty let the cigarette drop. As he crushed it with his foot, Diggs slipped the gun under the seat.

"Where to?"

"Take a left out of the parking lot, then a right at Mason."

Diggs followed orders. At Mason, Diggs asked Rusty if he had had any problems with Remy. Rusty grunted, "No," before lowering his window all the way.

At fifty miles per hour, the air from the window roared through the cabin. Diggs glanced at his passenger. His shoulder was propped against the door, his face stared out his window. He was a hard one to figure out. Earlier in the day, he had been a friendly motormouth. Diggs wondered if something had changed.

Diggs approached the Highway 55 entrance ramp.

"East or west?"

"West. Could you close the roof?"

"Sure, can you roll up your window?"

Diggs closed the moonroof and without saying a word, Rusty raised his window. Without the illumination from the sky full of stars, the cabin darkened noticeably.

For several minutes, they sped through the blackness in

eerie silence. Diggs made another attempt at engagement with the mystery man he didn't entirely trust.

"Rusty, how old are you?"

"Twenty-two. Why?"

"You look younger than that."

"How old are you?"

"Forty-four."

"You look older than that."

Diggs grinned in the darkness. "It's the beard."

Rusty grunted. "It's the way you dress. The car you drive. The way you talk."

"You should be a detective."

Rusty turned his head toward Diggs. "Are you?"

"Why would you think that?"

"The way you dress. The car you drive. How you're trying to size me up. The way you handled Remy. The gun under the seat. The way you dodge my questions. You're either a cop or a bounty hunter. Are you investigating the Geist murders?"

"I'm not investigating the Geist case. I'm not a bounty hunter. I'm not with the Mojave Creek police, the Nevada State police, or the FBI or the CIA, or for that matter, any black ops. I'm in Mojave Creek for personal reasons only."

"Personal reasons. What does that mean?"

"I want to locate my sister. Her house burned down. I can't find her."

Rusty turned his head and stared out the window.

"Did you know the Geists?"

Talking into the glass he said, "No, I heard Julia was nice."

"I'm curious why Petey White throws his parties on a Wednesday? Why not Friday or Saturday?"

"He has his reasons. They're kind of stupid if you ask me. A lot of people go so I guess he knows what he's doing."

"What are his reasons?"

"His TV show used to air on Wednesday nights. He thinks Wednesday is his lucky day."

"Sounds like he might be living in the past just a little bit."

"If you're smart, you won't say that to Mr. White or Jerad."

A massive truck that Diggs never saw coming flashed past, startling him. Watching the truck's taillights fade to pinpricks, Diggs spoke out of the side of his mouth. "Who's Jerad?"

"Do you always have so many questions?"

"Just want to know what to expect."

"If you're having second thoughts, we can turn around. Doesn't matter to me."

"Not a chance. I'm looking forward to the party. Tell me about Remy."

"He won't be there. Mr. White doesn't like him."

"Why not?"

"Ask Mr. White."

"You like Remy, right?"

"He's a friend."

"Didn't appear that way."

"He likes to show off."

"He's not going to blame you for what happened?"

"He's probably forgotten about it by now."

Diggs found that hard to swallow. The gash over Remy's eye and the scar that would follow were going to be constant reminders of an embarrassing humiliation. If Remy was like most of the low self-esteem losers Diggs had the misfortune of encountering, he would need to build himself back up. Someone would need to take a beating. It might be a stranger at a bar or someone who looked at him the wrong way, but it would be someone that he could handle easily. Someone like Rusty.

Rusty opened the passenger side window as Diggs was saying, "Be careful."

The cabin filled with ear-splitting white noise. For the next several miles, it was conversation over.

Out of nowhere, a light-colored vehicle sped past. Less than a minute later, an SUV did the same and then a BMW and then a pickup truck. Diggs guessed that all had to be going at least ninety miles an hour.

Rusty rolled up his window. His tone was playfully scornful. "You drive like an old lady. They're all flying by you."

Diggs pressed the accelerator. As his speed approached eighty, he said, "This more to your liking?"

"It's going to be hard to impress me with a Prius."

Diggs glanced at Rusty and thought he saw a grin.

"Start watching for the Iguana Road exit. It's still a way away but the sign is hard to see. Sometimes people don't see it until the last second and they try to make a sharp turn. Last year some foreign guy got decapitated." After a moment of silence, he added, "I don't know about you, but I'm too young."

Diggs grunted a laugh and through a smile said, "Thanks for the warning, but this car has the suspension of a finely tuned Jaguar."

"Uh-huh, right."

Moments later, darkness was fractured by speckles of lights in the distance.

"Iguana isn't too far away. When we get there, take a right. Half a mile up is White Way. Take a left there. You can park on the side of the road. It's a little bit of a walk but if you decide to leave early, it will be a lot easier."

Six minutes later, Diggs had exited the freeway and made the right at Iguana. A minute later they were on White Way. Fifty feet in front of him was a pickup truck. Diggs pointed. "How about behind him?"

"If you don't mind the walk."

Diggs parked and was out of the car, standing on a dirt embankment, and Rusty hadn't exited. He was about to ask if something was wrong when Rusty finally dragged himself out. With a scowl across his face, he unenthusiastically pushed the door shut. His shoulders were slumped, and his eyes stared at the ground.

Diggs called out, "You okay?"

His chin nearly touching his chest, he muttered, "Yeah."

In the distance, a dozen points of light made a loose square. As Diggs' pace quickened, he could feel his energy blossoming. With each step, his strides were getting longer and his concentration becoming more focused. Rusty was ten feet behind, limping along languidly. Diggs stopped and waited impatiently as steady streams of vehicles slowly passed, searching for a spot to land. Partygoers were piling out of cars, excitedly rushing toward the lights as if White had issued an attendance limit.

For the most part, everyone dressed in the typical cowboy regalia—blue jeans, boots, cowboy hats—although some were more ostentatious. A woman with bleach-blonde hair wore a garish cowgirl outfit that would have been more apropos at a Halloween party. Her date wore typical cowboy clothing along with a white hat and a black mask across his eyes.

Several couples were holding hands. Women danced as they walked. Laughter echoed with regularity. Diggs was impressed. Anyone who could attract this many happy people to the middle of nowhere on a Wednesday at midnight had to be offering something unique and doing it right. Any thoughts Diggs had of an ambush had melted away.

As Diggs waited for Rusty to catch up, he gave a few discreet moments of visual attention to every female who appeared older than forty. It didn't take long to realize the folly of that idea. The crowd moved too fast, and the only illumination was the flash of a phone or the beams of headlights brushing past. He'd have to wait.

A slumping Rusty, his hands shoved deep in his pockets, finally caught up. After two minutes of walking in silence, they joined a growing single-file line tailing outside of an open eight-foot-high wrought-iron gate. Above the gate under an arch, a circular emblem as large as a truck tire read: *The P.W. Ranch.*

A square sign zip-tied to the gate and written in bright red lettering read: *CAMERAS FORBIDDEN! NO PHONE PICTURES OR VIDEO PLEASE! VIOLATERS WILL BE IMMEDIATELY REMOVED AND WILL NOT BE WELCOMED BACK!*

Diggs noticed that White had no neighbors. His plot of land was a sandy island, and to drive that point home, eight-foot-tall iron fencing not only ran across the front of the house, it also stretched along both sides of the house seemingly deep into the desert, blocking White's property from three directions.

The slow trudge forward took several minutes before they passed through the gate and were standing on Petey White's property. A short, thick Hispanic man sat on a large decorative rock, wearing an expansive happy smile, smoking a cigar, watching the line plod by. He appeared as thrilled to see the party's attendees as they were to be there. Many he greeted by name. He regularly tipped his hat to the ladies.

Diggs and Rusty were fifteen feet away when the man noticed them. He waved trying to attract Rusty's attention. When Rusty didn't respond, he called out in a cheerful voice, "Hey, Rusty." Rusty made eye contact but rather than smile, he shrunk.

The Hispanic man lifted himself off the rock and ambled toward them. As if he and Rusty were old friends he said, "Rusty, my man. I'm glad you could make it. Where have you been?"

Rusty grimaced. "Around. I've been kind of busy."

He nodded like he understood and said, "Who's your friend?"

"My uncle Malcolm. He's cool."

The man grinned at Diggs and then Rusty. "You sure he's not your science teacher?"

Diggs supposed he was dressed like a science teacher. Brown slacks, white shirt, and a brown sports coat. When he departed San Diego, he never expected a honkytonk party in his future.

Diggs smiled, taking the ribbing with good humor. He lied, "I used to teach high school chemistry, in Phoenix."

"Well, teach, I hope you have a great time tonight."

Rusty touched his stomach. He said to the Hispanic man, "I feel like crap. I'm going home soon. If Mr. White asks, can you tell him that Malcolm is cool?"

Rusty's announcement was a surprise, but it also kind of explained his odd behavior, but not entirely. Diggs looked on skeptically.

"Sure, Rusty. No problem at all. Hope you feel better soon, buddy."

The line continued to snake up to a modest ranch home

adorned with tiny white bulbs. Diggs was surprised at the size of the house. It couldn't have been more than twenty-five hundred square feet. Seeing all the partygoers and the line growing every minute, Diggs was reminded of a clown car in reverse. Where were all of these people going to fit?

The Hispanic man was several feet behind amiably chatting with another partygoer. Diggs asked, "Was that Jerad?"

Rusty said, "No, that was Johnny. He's a fucking piece-of-shit asshole."

Diggs squinted with surprise. "What makes you say that?"

Rusty's reclusive face held a frown. "Don't worry about it."

As they got closer to the front entrance, Diggs heard country music from generations past blaring from behind eight-foot-tall black vinyl fencing that adjoined the house and the iron gate, blocking off the back of the house. Diggs' question to himself had been answered. White's party was going to be an outdoor affair, but if that was so, why did everyone have to go through the house?

The line was moving and when the music stopped, Diggs heard the faint echo of a barking dog. All the while, he kept an eye on Rusty. His pained expressions were constant, but they never appeared authentic. He would clutch his stomach for a few seconds and afterwards he'd reach up and place his hand over his heart. Every minute or so, without fail, in that order. It reminded Diggs of a Fred Sanford heart attack.

Rusty began to cough and not entirely convincingly. Diggs turned to him. "Rusty, why didn't you tell me you were sick?"

"I promised I'd bring you here. Now that I have, I'm going home."

Diggs didn't understand why the theatrics were necessary, but to ask was to likely hear a non-answer or a lie.

"You have a way to get home?"

"I can Uber."

Calling for an Uber after midnight in the middle of the Mojave Desert didn't seem like the most palatable plan.

"You sure?"

"Yeah, Noah's working."

"He's a friend?"

"He's my uncle."

"Your uncle is an Uber driver?"

"Noah has a lot of jobs."

Diggs pulled a twenty from his wallet and held it out.

"Here, let me pay for your ride."

Rusty made no attempt to reach for the bill. "That's okay. Thanks anyway." His face turned sad and in a voice that sounded mournful, he added, "Good luck, Malcolm."

Diggs wasn't sure how to respond and he didn't have much of a chance anyway. Rusty's back was turned and he was walking away. He weaved through the incoming crowd and stopped at the gate to take a moment to speak to Johnny. The friendly Hispanic man that Rusty despised crushed his cigar with his foot and minus his affable grin, said something back.

Rusty walked through the gate onto the road. As the desert night soaked up the strange little misfit, Diggs wished he hadn't left his gun under the front seat of his car.

13

The line trudged in long fits and shorter starts. Nearly ten minutes after Diggs watched Rusty disappear into the darkness, he was stepping into a hallway. Resting on a tripod greeting White's guests was a life-sized color photo of a gleaming Petey White, standing triumphant on a stage, his arm wrapped around the waist of a vivacious Suzanne Somers. He held his Emmy Award high in the air, seemingly toasting the unseen audience.

A cowboy couple in front of Diggs oohed and ahhed the photo with an adoration that seemed a few miles over the top, but Diggs had to admit the image was impressive. A treatment had been applied that added extra levels of sharpness and vibrancy, making Petey White and Suzanne Somers virtually jump off the wall. Diggs almost felt like he was watching at the 1977 Emmys from the front row.

As the line edged forward, Diggs could feel a euphoria that was intensifying. Voices were becoming louder and more animated. The line fidgeted with excitement. The electric buzz of anticipation felt like the moments before a heavyweight championship prize fight.

Further up the line, a man with a booming voice conversed with a much younger man. Both were dressed in pretty much the same cowboy regalia as everyone else.

The older said to the younger, "I promise you it's Hell on Earth in the middle of those fires."

The younger didn't appear too interested. He ignored the man's words of wisdom and complained that he hadn't eaten all day. Diggs took two steps sideways and got a good look at the man who spoke about fires. His face was deeply tanned and pockmarked. He wore a large, shiny silver ring on the fourth finger of his right hand. Once inside the party, Diggs planned to seek him out.

The hallway opened into a large room that was part Western themed and very much Petey White themed. The chairs were made of brown cowhide. The lamps on two coffee tables rested in the center of thick-roped lassos. Above a fireplace was a Warhol-inspired montage of Petey White's mug in blues, greens, and bright yellows. In front of the fireplace was a rug decorated with Native American tribal designs.

On every wall hung framed photographs of White at different stages of his career: a young Petey on set, leaning against a vintage Mustang, drinking from a coffee cup while conversing with a gorgeous starlet in black capri pants; White partially hidden behind a bush, his eyes steely, a cowboy hat on his head, a pretty ingenue crouching beside him; White donning a black leather jacket imitating James Dean, roaming Times Square alone on a dreary winter day.

Below two giant deer antlers sat a hairy-faced, skinny old man on a black leather sofa. His stringy gray hair touched his shoulders, and a well-trimmed beard hid most of his face. Peering through the mounds of hair were large and alert ocean blue eyes. From a distance, Petey White looked a lot like his IMDB photo. What the photo didn't capture was the strange energy that radiated from him.

Diggs believed that every last partygoer was aware that White was the definition of a has-been. He could only imagine how many wanted to roll their eyes at White's self-indulgent photos or chuckle at his monstrously oversized ego. What was abundantly clear was that everyone adored the man. White's remarkable energy was undeniably positive and it was clearly infecting everyone. Diggs felt like he was in a room full of newly minted Lotto winners and White was the man in charge of handing out the oversized checks.

Sitting beside White was a much younger man with a serious weightlifter physique. His massive biceps swelled against an ultra-tight, black short-sleeved t-shirt. His head was shaved and his black eyebrows cut a line as straight as the edge of a credit card. On the sofa between him and White was a body building magazine. The hulking man didn't seem to want to be there. Rather than speaking to or even acknowledging the partygoers, he casually cleaned a cowboy gun.

Petey was relishing his role as a wealthy museum piece. He'd listen graciously and smile agreeably as a hurricane of compliments showered over him. Many of his guests he'd welcome by first name.

"Billy, so glad you could make it."

"Sharon, how's little Missy."

"Phillip, my friend. I made sure to have those barbequed baked beans you like so much."

A tall man with a Marlboro Man presence asked, "What was Telly Savalas like?"

White smiled. "Wonderful man. We once went bowling together."

Grown men stood tall and straight when in White's presence, and all hats were off. The women tended toward meekness, usually saying little and often, smiling nervously. It all struck Diggs as rather cult-like. He started to feel like he was at a late-night campfire at the Spahn Ranch listening to Charlie play guitar and sing to his most loyal family members.

The woman with the Marlboro Man said, "It sure is beautiful. What an achievement."

White replied, "I'm very proud of it."

A woman with braided red hair and a huge smile chimed in. "I know you don't want anybody to touch it, but I wish I could hold it."

As the line pushed on and Diggs got closer to White, it became clear what the red-haired woman wanted to hold. On a side table next to White was his Emmy Award glistening under golden track lighting.

A man with most of his button-down shirt hanging sloppily over his belt said, "*Rev and Roll* is my all-time favorite TV show." He pointed to the Emmy. "You deserved to win ten of those." He grinned at a guy with a nervous smile standing beside him.

White responded with a tight smile and a thank you.

The bootlicker continued to gush. "I've practically worn out my DVD set." Chuckling, he added, "Told my sister to get me another copy for my birthday."

The bootlicker's buddy tried to nudge him forward, but White held up a palm and the two men stopped as if they'd been paused with a remote control.

"What's your name, friend?"

The bootlicker said, "Toby Neal, sir."

White smiled pleasantly. "Toby, I'm so happy you enjoy *Rev and Roll*. What was your favorite episode?"

Toby paused for a moment. Everyone in the room could see the wheels in his head grinding. "The episode you won the Emmy for."

White gently rubbed his hands together while his lips formed a dissatisfied frown. "Toby, you don't win an Emmy for Best Actor in a Dramatic Series for one episode. One episode could be a fluke. Perhaps the result of a particularly well written teleplay or a perfectly directed episode, or maybe there was a unique chemistry with a guest star that brought out the actor's best work. A best actor award from the Television Academy is not judged on one episode. An Emmy for Best Actor in a Dramatic Series is won for an entire season's worth of episodes."

Diggs could feel a room-wide cringe. The eyes of the weightlifter had left the revolver and were squarely on Toby Neal.

Toby's tone was soggy with defeat. "I guess all I can say is that they were all great."

With unsparing eyes, White nodded. "Toby, we agree on that, but I'll confess, my memory is slipping a bit. What was the name of my archenemy, my ex-Korean war buddy who became a kidnapper and a bank robber? He threw acid in my face, blinding me for an episode. In our highest rated episode ever, he tried to extort Peter Frampton. You should remember his name, Toby. He guest-starred on five separate episodes. I'll give you a hint. He was played by the wonderful actor Clu Gulager."

Toby exhaled a pitiful chuckle that was clearly a cry for

help. "I'm sorry, Mr. White. I'm nervous and I guess my memory is slipping a little bit too."

White's unforgiving frown felt as long as an afternoon at the DMV. He clapped his palms together. "Toby, it just came to me. Clu portrayed Sergeant Milton Montgomery."

Toby had nothing more to say. He stood with his head bowed like a sacrificial virgin. White glared at him like he would a poop stain on his carpet. Toby's friend watched on, shaken and scared. They were naked men standing in front of a hostile dictator surrounded by his most ardent followers.

"Jerad, please show Toby the exit." Jerad took Toby by the arm and led him out of the room.

"I assume you're with Mr. Neal?"

The nervous smile answered submissively that he was.

"And your name is?"

"Jerry. I work at your diner. I'm a cook."

Through a warm smile, Petey said, "Very happy to meet you, Jerry. Do you enjoy working there?"

"Yes, sir. I do."

"Are you a fan of *Rev and Roll*?"

His face was flushed and sweat had formed at his temples. "To be honest, Mr. White, I've only seen a couple of episodes." He smiled awkwardly before adding, "The theme song is kind of cool. I thought the actress who played the rookie officer was really cute."

White let out a crazy boisterous laugh. The room followed his lead and in moments, everyone was in hysterics. Diggs followed the flow and pretended to laugh along.

White patted his chest with his palm and through gasps for air, said, "Indeed, she was, Jerry. Indeed, she was. You're more than welcome to stay if you wish."

Jerry thanked White and promptly moved on. Four attendees later, Diggs passed in front of Petey White. His plan was to smile, nod politely, and never stop moving.

With a kind smile, White said, "Welcome, Uncle Malcolm. A pleasure to meet you."

Diggs stopped and faced him. "Likewise, Mr. White. I'm very happy to be here."

"Please enjoy yourself. If you need anything, I offer my humble assistance."

Diggs bowed politely and thanked him. Depending on how the night went, White's offer might prove exceedingly helpful.

Diggs moved on and the line quickly picked up speed. Soon, he was in a room with an open sliding glass door that led into the backyard. An old man wearing a yellow cowboy hat stood at the door. Every few seconds, he said, "You enjoy yourself, you hear."

Diggs followed the line out of the house and onto a large plot of land filled with happy commotion. Tin buckets filled with beer and beverages were spread about the grounds like Easter eggs. Two men in white cowboy hats stood behind four large outdoor grills busily preparing hamburgers and hotdogs. On four separate folding tables were stainless steel vats, paper plates, and plastic utensils. The vats were labelled: *Chili (HOT)*, *Chili (Mild)*, *Baked Beans*, *Potato Salad*. At numerous spots around the grounds, signs read: NO PHOTOGRAPHS! NO VIDEO! VIOLATORS WILL BE ASKED TO LEAVE AND WILL NOT BE WELCOMED BACK!

Diggs saw the pockmarked man from the line helping himself to a hamburger. He waited for him at the condiment table. As the man squeezed ketchup onto his burger, Diggs approached. "Excuse me, I overheard you in the line talking about fires. Were you referring to the fire on Ocotillo Road in Mojave Creek?"

The man placed the top bun on the burger. "No, sir. The wildfires going on in California. I used to be a fireman and have some dear friends working it."

Diggs asked if he knew if any of the firemen at the Ocotillo fire were at the party.

He thought for a moment. "Hm, Robby was probably at that fire." He added, knowingly, "If he's not here now, he will be eventually. If you like, I'll keep a lookout for him."

Diggs told the man that he'd check back later and watched him blend into the crowd before moving over to a palm tree adorned with white lights. Diggs stayed there for several minutes keeping an eye out for any woman who might be his sister. With no one catching his eye, he meandered through the party, watching faces and eavesdropping on conversation after conversation.

He strode past a dirt dance floor and for a few moments stopped to admire several women and three brave men show off their dirty-dancing skills. At one of several card tables, he looked on as four men and four women played a round of Texas Hold'em.

Somewhere between the dance floor and the card tables, Diggs got a sense that he was being followed or, at the very least, watched, but he could never single out a particular suspect. Everyone seemed fully engaged with drinking, dancing, gambling, eating, and socializing.

A hard tap on Diggs' shoulder startled him. He turned to see the ex-fireman holding a bottle of Budweiser.

"Just wanted to let you know, I haven't seen Robby, but I

hear he's out there." He lifted his arm near the top of his head and pointed beyond the party. Fifty yards away, flames from two separate bonfires soared toward the sky.

"What's Robby look like?"

"He's a lot younger than me and a hell of a lot more handsome." He grinned. "He'll be the one surrounded by pretty girls."

Beneath a bowl of sky deluged with millions of shimmering stars, Diggs departed the party for the bonfires. At the first, a woman and a man danced wildly to a Taylor Swift song on a small rechargeable speaker. Diggs moved in closer, trying to get a better look at the woman. Her height was right, and her age was close. Her hair looked to be Claire's natural dark brown. She reminded him of the Claire he would have recognized a generation ago.

A twentyish guy with a goatee sat on a blanket with a joint between his fingers. A girl was curled in a ball with her head on his lap. Between puffs, the young man and Diggs met eyes.

"Are you Robby?"

He flashed Diggs a toothy smile. "Sorry, I'm not, but I wish I were. I hate it when I disappoint."

Diggs nodded over to the woman doing the crazy dancing. "Is her name Claire?"

"That's Suzie. Who's Claire?"

"My sister. I'm looking for her."

His toothy smile returned. "You don't recognize your sister? That's tragic, my condolences, and before you ask, the only Claire I know is my stepmom's parrot, and you wouldn't like my stepmom's parrot. She's almost as annoying as my stepmom." He started to giggle.

About fifty feet away, further into the desert, stood a

wooden structure. Flat and maybe five feet off the ground. It reminded Diggs of a backyard patio deck.

Diggs pointed to it. "What's that?"

The goatee took a puff from his joint. "A stage. That's where the great Petey and the Gumshoes play their versions of the country classics, mixed in with an original or two. Don't miss it. Petey wouldn't like that." Again, he giggled.

"No good?"

He ran his fingers through the girl's hair. "Babycakes." She looked up at him with tired and dreamy eyes. "He wants to know if Petey and the Gumshoes are any good."

She spoke into the goatee's chest. "God no, they're awful. Can we leave before they start?"

Her hand disappeared under his shirt, and he went back to his joint. Diggs headed toward the second firepit. A group of kids young enough to be Claire's children, if she had any, were taking turns snorting white powder off of a torn flap of an Amazon Prime box while a few others conversed excitedly and laughed often. Diggs' attention was drawn to the clean-cut, well-built one who appeared a few years older than the rest of them. He was playing spin the bottle with two teenage girls.

"Excuse me. Sorry to interrupt the game. Are you Robby?"

The three of them smiled up at Diggs. The man said, "No worries. I'm Robby. What's up?"

"Were you working the fire over on Ocotillo Road last night?"

He nodded. "Uh-huh, sure was."

"Did you see the homeowner?"

"No, but the memory of that fire will forever be singed in my head—it was the stuff of nightmares, man." After he spoke, he performed a dramatic shiver.

Diggs asked him what happened.

"It was right around one in the morning. I was the first one there. The fire had already gotten real bad. Flames shooting into the sky, out the windows. It looked like Satan's lair. A car was parked in the driveway, but I didn't see anyone waiting outside the house. My first instinct was that someone was trapped inside. I ran around the house searching for an entry point that wouldn't be a total suicide mission. At the back of the house, I found a door that was clear enough that it wasn't certain death, so I took my chances."

One of the girls lightly touched his cheek. "Baby, you're so brave."

He kissed her fingers before looking up at Diggs. "You ever smell burning flesh?"

Diggs had several times but decided against raining on Robby's parade.

"No."

"Pray to Jesus that you never do. It has a real distinct smell. It's disgusting and once it's in your head, it will stay with you forever."

That much was true. Diggs asked, "You smelled burning flesh?"

"I sure did. It was faint, but it was there. I searched around for as long as I could before the fire got too hot and the smoke too thick. Didn't find anyone. After I got out, I went back to the front of the house to wait for reinforcements and the car was gone."

"What was the make and model?"

"I don't know, man. I had other things on my mind."

"You tell the police all of this?"

"I told my boss. Whether he told the cops, I don't know."

"You didn't find any bodies?"

"No, and we looked long and hard."

According to the hospital nurse, no burn victims had checked themselves in. Images of Claire slumped dead in her car, rapidly decaying under the desert's stifling heat stuck in Diggs' head like a moth captured in a spider web. He needed quiet to consider a plan of action. He thanked Robby and walked until he reached the small stage. Two guitars were laid on two folding chairs, a small piano sat beside the chair. At the rear, a drum set. In a Western font, *Petey and the Gumshoes* was stenciled on its face.

The barking Diggs had heard at the front of White's house had grown significantly louder. Mixed with angry barking were anguished howls and it was clearly coming from more than one dog. With the lights from the heart of the party a hundred yards behind him, Diggs stared ahead into the sandy abyss. A dark curiosity compelled Diggs to follow the empty cries.

14

Diggs trekked over mounds of sand and shallow holes dug by nocturnal creatures. After stumbling over a tumbleweed and nearly colliding into a four-foot-tall cactus, Diggs pulled his phone from his pocket, turned on the flashlight, and pointed it into the darkness.

Thirty feet in front of him, a structure blended neatly into the night. Twenty steps closer, he saw that it was a barn. As Diggs approached, he listened carefully. The barking had for the most part ceased. A thin border of light seeped from around the frame of the door. He stood outside and listened for voices inside. Hearing none, he opened the door a crack, saw no one, and slipped inside.

Fifteen feet away, two lanterns hung over a ten-foot square patch of dirt. An eight-foot-tall chain-link fence surrounded the patch. A dozen folding chairs were loosely placed around the fence.

At the far end of the barn was a row of eight cages. In each cage was a large, powerful dog. A growling Rottweiler paced. A Doberman with ice-cold eyes sat in a trance-like state. A seventy-pound Pit Bull with teeth as sharp as razors snarled at nothing. Diggs recognized it for what it was—a row of gladiators waiting to fight to the death for the pleasure of contemptable men.

Diggs began to back out when he heard whimpering followed by scratching noises. He stood for a moment and listened. For several beats, he heard nothing and then the whimpering and the scratching started again. He followed the noise to a stack of tires. On the ground, a blue blanket was draped over something small and rectangular shaped. Diggs pulled the blanket away. Inside a metal crate was a handsome little dog with a large muzzle, thick folds of skin, small brown eyes, and turned up ears. His tail stuck out of one end of the cage and his nose pressed against the other. His eyes pleaded as he panted. He was scared to death.

Diggs didn't think the dog was much older than a year, and he definitely didn't appear to be any kind of fighter. He was trying to soothe the dog when ferocious barking broke out. A shadow moved in behind him. Standing over Diggs was the friendly man at the front gate whom Rusty despised. He looked at Diggs with a surprised smile.

"Hey, teach, what are you doing here?"

Diggs wiped the sand off his trousers as he stood. "I heard about the games and I wanted to evaluate the talent."

Johnny grinned, betraying no suspicion. "I wouldn't have guessed you'd be interested in this type of thing."

Diggs shrugged. "I'm more of a competition junkie." He raised his eyebrows for emphasis and added, "Any kind of competition. When does the action start?"

"Not until after Petey finishes his set."

Diggs pointed to the cage at their feet. "This one isn't going to be fighting, is he?"

Johnny snorted a laugh. "He'd be a lot better off if he could fight. He's the warm-up."

Diggs asked him what that meant.

"Before the main action begins." He pointed to the cages across the barn. "He'll be pitted against one of those beasts."

Diggs could hear his voice turning hostile. "What's the point?"

"It's just a dog, don't get so bent out of shape."

"It'll be a massacre. He won't stand a chance."

Johnny eyed Diggs suspiciously. He pulled his phone from his back pocket and began to scroll through his contacts list. "Sorry, teach. I'm going to have to let Jerad know I found you here."

Diggs said, "Sure, whatever you have to do," before sucker-jabbing Johnny in the center of his throat. Johnny tumbled backwards against the stack of tires, gripping his neck and gasping for air.

Diggs snatched Johnny's phone off the ground and hurled it toward the far end of the barn. He glanced down at the cage. It was too bulky to lug through the dark desert over thick, bumpy sand. A jog to his car with a frightened and thrashing thirty-pound dog in his arms wasn't going to be the answer either.

Diggs glanced at Johnny. His breathing had gotten steadier. He wasn't going to lay helpless on the ground forever. The dog had a collar. If he could find a piece of rope to tie it to, a successful escape seemed possible.

Diggs stepped out of the shadows. The barn was deluged with aggressive barking. He scanned the barn for rope. His eyes widened when he saw several leashes hanging on nails attached to a post a few feet from the row of cages.

A stranger bolting at them put the dogs in a savagely agitated state. The crescendo of snarling and howling was as ear splitting as an airport runway. As Diggs yanked a leash off a hook, he saw Johnny trotting toward him with a claw hammer raised high in the air.

At two feet, Johnny took a wild swing that Diggs dodged easily. While his arm was in full backswing, Diggs rammed his shoulder into Johnny's upper body. Rather than splash to the ground as Diggs had hoped, Johnny only stumbled backwards with the hammer still firmly in his hand.

Diggs was confident that unless Johnny got very lucky, it was only a matter of time. Diggs was six inches taller, fairly muscular, and lean. Johnny looked like he ate at Wienerschnitzel every other day. Johnny's chances to prevail seemed slim, but with a deadly weapon, not impossible. As Johnny aggressively surged forward, Diggs bluffed a retreat, taking two quick steps backwards. As Johnny lumbered forward, Diggs pushed hard off his back foot and charged. He grabbed hold of Johnny's wrist while bulldozing him against the post that held the leashes. Protruding nails drilled into the top of Johnny's back, collapsing him to the dirt as he howled in pain.

The dogs were like rioting prisoners banging against their cages. Diggs scanned his surroundings, searching for anyone else who might have heard the commotion. The barn door was closed, and no one had revealed themselves.

Out of the corner of his eye, Diggs saw Johnny on his stomach, fiddling with the lock on a cage that held a razor-toothed Pit Bull. Diggs took three quick steps and grabbed Johnny by the ankle. As Johnny wildly kicked at him, Diggs roughly yanked him away from the cages. He fell to his knees straddling Johnny's thick chest, and with his left hand, pinned

Johnny by the throat and with his right, delivered four hard blows to his face.

With Johnny unconscious, Diggs dashed to the dog with a leash in his hand. He opened the cage and clipped the leash onto the collar. The dog offered no resistance. Together they ran out of the barn.

Diggs' goal was to get back to his car and he figured he had three viable options. He could traipse through the desert beyond the gate. It would avoid running into anybody, but it would be a long, clumsy, and unpredictable journey.

He could wait for Petey and the Gumshoes to begin their set. He assumed most of the party would congregate there, which would offer minimal obstacles, but he had no idea when the concert would start, and Johnny wasn't going to be unconscious forever.

The most expedient option was also the most immediately perilous, but considering the circumstances, it was the way to go. He and the dog headed toward the party, searching for an exit that would lead to the street.

For the first several minutes, it was smooth sailing. To avoid human contact, Diggs took a path that cut between the firepits. Once he was in the midst of the party, he moved briskly along the vinyl gate, avoiding any eye contact.

While he had been away, the crowd had gotten larger and louder, and it was to Diggs' advantage. A man wearing a sports jacket, walking a dog at a midnight party might look somewhat odd, but everyone was enjoying themselves too much to take any interest.

With each step, Diggs' confidence grew, and the dog helped to feed that confidence. Never once did he bark, nor did he stop to sniff at anything, and no bathroom breaks were necessary. He was as cooperative an escape partner as Diggs could have hoped. Diggs guessed that the dog wanted to get out of there as badly as he did.

As they weaved through an increasingly boisterous crowd, Diggs wasn't finding any exits along the fencing that would take him off the property and onto the street.

He came across a couple of twenty-somethings sharing a lounge chair. Her fingers were caressing his face. He stared into her eyes while his hands roamed her upper body.

"Excuse me. Where's the exit?"

He scowled up at Diggs. She began to blow lightly into his ear.

He pointed in the direction that Diggs had come from. "Over there."

"I didn't see an exit."

"Trust me, it's there."

"I don't think so. I would have seen it."

Her eyes were closed, and her voice peeved. "Maybe it hasn't been opened yet."

The man began to nibble on the girl's earlobe.

"You know of any other exits?"

Through a gasp of ecstasy, she answered, "Can't you just leave the way you came in?"

Minutes later, Diggs and the dog entered through the same sliding glass door that led into the party. The old man in the yellow cowboy hat was gone and the line had completely dissipated.

They turned the corner into the room where Petey White had been holding court. Petey was nowhere to be seen, but Jerad was on the sofa talking quietly into his phone as he leafed through the body building magazine. The Emmy hadn't gone anywhere; it continued to sparkle under golden track lighting.

Diggs' on-the-fly plan was to pass by quickly, make no eye contact, say nothing, and hope that Jerad was too engrossed in his phone conversation to notice or care. Barely three steps in, Jerad spoke into his phone. "I'll call you back."

He lifted his large body off the sofa. "Where are you going with our dog?"

Diggs spoke with urgency. "He's been throwing up. Johnny told me to take him for a walk. I'll bring him back in a few minutes."

"Bullshit. That's Johnny's job and if he were puking, he damn sure wouldn't tell you to bring him into the house. Who are you?"

"I'm a friend of Johnny's, and it's true. One of the Pit Bull's got out of his cage. Johnny is dealing with that. I guess I wasn't thinking. I'd better get this guy outside before he pukes again."

"You're a liar." He lifted his gun from the sofa and pointed it at Diggs' chest. He punched a button on his phone and turned on the speaker while Diggs eyed a poker beside the fireplace. The phone rang four times before going to voicemail.

"Unless you want some really bad shit to happen, you're going give me back our dog."

Petey White stepped into the room. His attire had changed to tight black jeans, black leather boots, and a glittery black denim jacket—a poor man's Johnny Cash with a touch of Vegas.

White gazed at the two men. He spoke softly and patiently. "Son, what's going on here?"

With a touch of panic in his voice, Jerad said, "Dad, he's stealing our dog."

Petey glanced at the dog and then looked kindly at Diggs. "Uncle Malcolm, is that true?"

"He's sick, Mr. White. He needs to be taken outside."

Jerad sneered, "How dare you lie to my father." He turned to White and spoke pleadingly. "I tried to call Johnny. He's not answering his phone."

Jerad cocked the hammer back and turned to Diggs. "Last chance, asshole. Hand me the leash."

Diggs' eyes dropped to the gun barrel. The chamber and the cylinders were empty. Jerad was bluffing—the gun was unloaded—but Diggs chose not to let on. A brawl made no sense. Although Jerad wasn't as large as Remy, he looked like he could fight, and this time Diggs had no advantageous element of surprise and no convenient weapon at his fingertips. A physical confrontation with Jerad meant hand-to-hand combat and Diggs didn't have any confidence he'd win that battle. He turned his attention to Petey White. His gentle smile hadn't left his face.

"Mr. White, you're throwing such a wonderful party. Everyone is waiting for you and the Gumshoes to perform. Ask yourself if you really need this disruption right now." Diggs looked toward Jerad. "And Jerad, before you do anything you'll regret, you need to know that I'm a cop."

Jerad kept the gun pointed at Diggs' chest. As White spoke, his eyes turned steely.

"I'm a principled man, Uncle Malcolm, and if I believed the dog belonged to you, I'd tell my son to let you and the dog go. But he is my son and I'll always take the word of my son over a stranger. If Jerad says the dog is his, then I believe the dog is his. And since I do believe him, you need to give that dog back now."

His smile strained. He added, "And, whether you are a police officer or not, you have no right to steal from us."

Diggs nodded. "Okay, Mr. White, if that's your decision." He began to hand the leash to Jerad. As Jerad reached to accept, Diggs took the route he had hoped to avoid. With the sole of his shoe, he clubbed Jerad's kneecap. As Jerad collapsed to the floor, Diggs hurried around him and snatched the poker from beside the fireplace. Slowly, he approached the Emmy.

"Which is more important, Mr. White, the dog or the Emmy? Make up your mind, now."

White let out a disappointed sigh. "You and the dog can go. Your negative energy is going to affect my singing voice. Go, leave. Take the dog with you. Enjoy your evening, Uncle Malcolm. We'll see each other again."

"Thank you, Mr. White."

"Before you do go, let me tell you that winning my Emmy Award was like winning the Super Bowl, the World Series, the Daytona Cup. It was like being the first man on the moon. Had you damaged it, you would have never left my home alive. Any resulting consequences would have been worth it."

Diggs and the dog began to edge out of the room. "Understood, Mr. White. I'm sorry it came to this."

"Against my better judgment, I allowed you into my party. Needless to say, I made a mistake. Go before I make a decision that you'll no doubt regret."

Diggs and the dog backed out of the house. White watched with a patient stare. Jerad lifted himself to his feet, his eyes glaring enmity.

Once they were out the front door, Diggs dropped the poker and they ran. At the car, Diggs yanked open the passenger door and the dog leapt inside. Diggs slammed the door shut, raced over to the driver's side, and piled his sweating body inside. The engine revved and Diggs hauled away from the P.W. Ranch fast and recklessly. Once they were safely on the freeway, Diggs opened the moonroof to a sky crowded with stars.

He pressed the accelerator. The open road never felt so safe and so fine. He flicked on the radio to a bouncy little lounge number and cranked the volume as the dog gazed though the moonroof with his tail swaying.

Diggs looked into the rearview mirror and saw nothing but blackness. He turned his head toward the dog and saw possibly the happiest eyes he had ever seen staring up at him. Diggs let loose a subversive grin and hollered over the wind. "We made it. Hallelujah, we made it."

15

A cold, wet, and spongy something was dabbing Diggs' cheek. Through early morning grogginess, he saw two tannish, mushroom-shaped nostrils sniffing his beard. Behind the nostrils was a brown muzzle shaped like an upside-down heart. Peering over the muzzle were two curious tan-colored eyes.

Diggs took a moment and allowed the dog's nose to roam his face. Gently he pushed the dog away and fumbled for his phone on the nightstand. He swept the phone's flashlight across the floor. The water in the coffee mug was nearly empty. The paper wrapping that once held the Wendy's hamburger was nothing but a stain of grease. He could find no accidents on the floor and a couple of deep inhales uncovered no alarming scents.

Diggs sat up on the bed while the dog stood awkwardly, looking at him like a stumped contestant on a game show. Diggs reached out and scratched behind the dog's ear and kicked away the bedcover. At that, the dog jumped onto the floor.

Diggs slipped into a sweatshirt and jeans. He bent to a knee and snapped the leash onto the collar. Enthusiastically, he said, "Let's go outside."

They stepped into a beautiful seventy-degree morning. The sun was picking its way through a mass of thick purple and gray clouds. Blackbirds were squawking and the wind blew steadily across the seemingly endless sandy planes.

Diggs had parked behind the Western Jewel, out of sight from any passing vehicles, and was glad he did. He had no idea if White's crew had made his car, but with only three SUVs parked in the lot, his Prius would have been as conspicuous as a shining red light in a closet.

While the dog was practically yanking Diggs' arm out of his socket investigating scraggly bushes and chasing every smell in his path, Diggs phoned the local police. He asked for Sheriff Potter and was transferred to an answering machine. Diggs left a message stating what the volunteer fireman had told him.

Diggs exhorted, "Have your officers keep a lookout for Claire's car. It will likely be somewhere between her home and the hospital. Maybe even in the hospital parking lot. You'll need to check with the DMV for the make and model." Before ending the call, Diggs added, "I drove the path between Claire's house and the hospital last night. I didn't see any cars parked alongside the road that seemed unusual, but it was dark and I didn't know what I was looking for. Once you know the make and model, it's going to need another look. I'll be happy to help."

While the dog was having the time of his life, Diggs wished the circumstances with Petey White could had been different. A potentially valuable connection had been exchanged for a powerful enemy. Despite the White setback, Diggs felt confident that either he or the local police would find Claire. Whether she'd be found alive, there was only hope, but at that moment Diggs couldn't help thinking that his sister might need a Glen Palmer miracle of her own.

Diggs' other worry was Rusty, and he had maybe even less confidence that Rusty would be alright than he did Claire. It was Rusty who brought him to the party, and it was Rusty who vouched for him. One way or another, at some point soon, Diggs would be in the wind and Rusty would remain settled in Mojave Creek. If either Petey White or Jerad or Johnny had retribution on their minds, it was Rusty who would bear the brunt.

Diggs watched the dog joyfully sniffing at sand and couldn't help but grin at the dog's unabashed delight. He was a handsome dog, seemed healthy, appeared to be well trained. Under normal circumstances, Diggs would have dropped the dog off at a shelter. It wouldn't take long for someone to fall in love with his body full of wrinkles, keen eyes, and Jimmy Durante muzzle, but any shelter in Mojave Creek was out of the question. Diggs guessed that Jerad had gotten the dog for nothing or bought him for next to nothing. The dog's previous home might have been a shelter. Until he and the dog arrived in Chandler, they would stay together.

Once they were back inside the motel room, Diggs turned his attention online. A quick internet search found a Walmart that promised two-hour delivery. He ordered a ten-pound package of dog food, a water bowl, a food bowl, and a bouncy red rubber ball. Diggs reached over and felt the dog's dirty collar and ragged leash—too many ugly memories. He added a new leash and collar to his cart and clicked send.

After he discarded the old leash and collar into the outdoor dumpster, he prepared to take a shower. The moment he shut the bathroom door, the dog began to whine and scratch at the door. Diggs finished up quickly and with a wet towel draped around his torso, took a seat on the floor against the bed. He reached to rub under the dog's chin and was greeted with several licks across his palm.

"I need to give you a name."

Diggs thought for a bit. He found the dog at an unusual party hosted by a somewhat strange man. His sister's disappearance was strange. He was caught in the middle of a strange case. Everything about Mojave Creek so far had been strange. He moved over to the desk with the dog following. A quick internet search confirmed that the title of the novel was *The Strange Case of Dr. Jekyll and Mr. Hyde*.

Diggs understood that the dog's calm nature and undeniable sweetness made Jekyll the more appropriate name of the two, but that made him Mr. Hyde, which as Swenson reminded him two days before, happened to be his reputation. Naming the dog after his reputation would be his inside joke, and Mr. Hyde was a cooler name than Jekyll anyway. Diggs spoke Mr. Hyde out loud several times in various cadences. He appreciated how the three beats rolled off his tongue. No matter how loud or soft or what tone he spoke, Mr. Hyde sounded respectful and mysterious, and if the dog was anything, he was mysterious.

Diggs sat on the floor beside the dog and scratched around his small, upturned ears. Looking into the dog's eyes, Diggs asked, "How does Mr. Hyde grab you?" The dog returned Diggs' smile with his tail wagging.

"I guess it's a done deal then."

Diggs moved over to the desk and typed into a browser, *Dogs with wrinkled faces*. There were nine breeds listed, but the photos made it obvious that Mr. Hyde was a Shar-Pei.

Diggs read out loud, "Intelligent and stubborn." He looked down at Mr. Hyde looking up at him. "You sound like all of my ex-girlfriends."

Diggs opened the Uber application on this phone and punched in the Sleeping Volcano's address. Only a driver named Cindy was available. Cindy wasn't going to help him find Rusty. He needed Noah. He didn't book the trip and punched in the address to Petey White's ranch. Cindy was again the driver who would pick him up and again Diggs didn't book the trip. Diggs entered the address of the Walmart from where he had placed the order. Once more, the only driver available was Cindy and once more he didn't book the trip.

Minutes later, the Walmart delivery truck arrived. While Mr. Hyde scarfed down his breakfast, Diggs opened the Uber app again. This time he punched in the address to the Geist murder house. Cindy's photo and profile again filled his screen. He gave up on finding Noah and accepted Cindy's ride, hoping that she might have a way to reach Noah.

In seemingly no time at all, Cindy's Ford Escape pulled into the Western Jewel Motel parking lot. From the front seat, she said through a welcoming smile, "Good morning, you have any bags I can help you with?"

"No, but do you mind if my dog comes along? I promise he won't be a problem."

She stuck her head partially out the window. "He's a cutie. No problem."

Diggs allowed Mr. Hyde to hop in first before piling in behind him.

"5990 Blackhorse Lane, right?"

"Yes."

The SUV pulled out of the parking lot. Cindy looked at Diggs through the rearview mirror. She asked, "Are you a true crime aficionado?"

"Not really. I chose the Geist address because the app required an address. The truth is I got into town yesterday and I'm trying to find a particular Uber driver."

"What's his name?"

"Noah. I don't know his last name. I'm really looking for his nephew and I thought I could find him through Noah."

She grinned into the rearview mirror. "This is getting complicated. I'm sorry to say that I don't know Noah. You want me to turn back?"

"No, we can go to the Geist house. I'd like to get a feel for the town anyway."

"I'm sorry to report that there isn't much to see in Mojave Creek. Not a lot happens around here—except for a triple murder. Just Mojave Creek's luck, right?"

"Did you know the Geists?"

A sharp shake of the head was followed by a tone that puffed mild annoyance. "I've had a lot of people ask me that. My mom and sister live in Boise. They both wanted to know if I knew the Geists. So did my best friend from college. She lives in Denver. I told them all the same thing. Mojave Creek is small, but it's not ten people."

"I see your point. Can I ask you one more dumb question?"

"Sure, go ahead."

"My sister lives in Mojave Creek. First name is Claire. Maiden name is Diggs. Ever hear of her?"

The SUV lurched as if she had inadvertently pressed the brake. An uncomfortable silence hung in the air.

"You're kidding, right?"

"No, why?"

"You're not kidding, are you?"

Diggs shrugged. "No, why would I?"

Cindy stiffened in her seat. "I hate to tell you, but Claire Diggs is public enemy number one around here."

Diggs stared befuddled at the angry eyes glaring at him from the rearview mirror. "I'm not sure if I shouldn't throw you out of the car right now."

Diggs raised his hands in surrender. "Hang on. Before you jump to any conclusions, I haven't seen Claire in at least twenty years. I'm on my way to Arizona. I saw the Mojave Creek exit. I thought I'd look her up."

Her eyes left the rearview mirror and back onto the road. "If you had the ability to lock her up, I'd give you a free ride."

"You mind telling me what she did?"

"Why don't I show you."

They continued along the bumpy and lightly traveled single-lane road, passing mostly sprawling swatches of empty desert land. Within two miles, she turned south onto a two-lane road. The traffic picked up and carpets of sand were replaced with locally owned retail shops and businesses. Soon they were in a full-fledged business district with chain establishments Diggs recognized. Mr. Hyde woke from a nap and pushed himself onto his hind legs.

The driver made a series of rights and lefts and soon they were in a suburban neighborhood with ranch-style and two-story homes. Diggs saw landscaped front yards. He saw basketball hoops attached to garages. He saw home after home cared for and kept up. He saw a pleasant, attractive neighborhood. The driver pointed to her left. "The Geists lived a few blocks over that way."

Not more than a minute later, Cindy pulled up in front of a one-story U-shaped building painted olive green. A sign in front read: *The Frederic Remington Academy for the Arts.* Homemade banners hung from windows:

WE SEE, WE CREATE, WE DEVOTE!
ART IS THE SOUL OF LIFE!
WE LOVE OUR SCHOOL!

Diggs noticed that the grounds were shabby. Plastic grocery bags flailed against a wall near the front entrance. A long line of flowers abutting the front of the building had died. There were no cars in the lot and there were no students in sight.

The driver asked, "So, tell me. What don't you see?"

"Students, teachers, any signs of life."

"And what month is it?"

"What happened?"

"Your sister bankrupted the school. Until the owners can replace the funds, it's closed."

Diggs stared into the rearview mirror. "How is that possible?"

Cindy put the SUV in park. She turned in her seat to face Diggs. Bitterness soaked her words. "Your sister had access to the owner's bank account. At some point, she began to siphon funds. The owners found out in September. By then virtually everything had been drained.

"Mr. and Mrs. Guthu are frantically seeking donations and are appealing to anyone who has money. I heard they've considered taking a mortgage out on their home. In the meantime, all of these wonderful, creative kids have had to put their lives on hold. Everyone was let go until a solution can be found."

"How much did she take?"

"I've heard well over a hundred thousand dollars."

Diggs sat silent, wrestling with his thoughts, considering a story that seemed impossible.

"My best friend's daughter is one of the casualties. Her parents spent a lot of money and she's talented. Needless to say, her heart is broken."

Diggs muttered, "I'm sorry."

"She's far from the only one. A lot of people have been devastated—teachers, parents, students. Mr. and Mrs. Guthu put their entire lives into this school. Because of your sister's pure selfish greed, it's all been taken away."

"Was Claire ever arrested?"

"No, she hasn't even been charged. She hired a bigshot lawyer from Las Vegas. His claim—surprise, surprise—is that several people had the means and the opportunity to have stolen the money. It's a crock of crap. We all know she did it."

"You said her attorney is in Las Vegas?"

"Yeah, he came down here for a day, made a bunch of silly claims, and flew back. That's not to say he isn't a very capable shyster. He threatened a lawsuit against the local newspaper, *The Westerner*. He vowed to sue if any stories directly accusing Claire of embezzling were printed. His argument is that she hasn't been charged or arrested and suggesting any guilt was, in his words, 'biased speculation' that would cause irreparable harm to her reputation." She rolled her eyes. "Oh, brother, she has no reputation to be harmed.

"Anyway, an attorney for the newspaper claimed that if the case never went to trial, it would be grounds for a libel suit, which they couldn't afford to fight. They agreed not to publish Claire Diggs' name unless she was charged or arrested. So far, the police have done nothing. They claim an investigation is ongoing. Woo-hoo. In the meantime, there is no school."

Diggs understood law enforcement's perspective. The victims naturally wanted to know everything the police were up to. Some didn't understand and others didn't care that revealing information could damage the investigation. As for *The Westerner,* Diggs assumed they were only following their attorney's advice, and in a society that was rampantly litigious, it was advice best not ignored.

"My guess is that your sister has that money hidden away in a foreign bank account. It'll never be found, and she'll never spend a day in jail. The school will close permanently. A lot of dedicated teachers will have to find new jobs. The Guthu's life's work will end, and a bunch of talented kids' dreams will die."

Diggs thought as she spoke. An accidental fire seemed a lot less likely while a vigilante justice angle with literally hundreds of suspects emerged.

"You mind waiting here for a few minutes? Mr. Hyde could probably use a bathroom break."

Smirking, she said, "Your dog's name is Mr. Hyde?"

Diggs' mind was too cluttered to waste any time explaining the backstory to her. "We'll be back in a few minutes."

Diggs and Mr. Hyde walked toward the front door entrance. Through smeared and dirty glass, Diggs gazed into a long dark, barren hallway. He and Mr. Hyde veered around to the back of the building to a pond filled with fish and shaded by four palm trees. The fish were plentiful and appeared healthy. Someone hadn't forgotten them.

Toward the edge of the building, a seven-foot-high pink-painted wooden arrow pointing toward the sky sprouted deflated white balloons. In a circle surrounding the arrow were hundreds of pink flowers.

On the arrow written in beautifully elaborate calligraphy was *XOXO Julia*. Covering all sides of the arrow beneath the calligraphy were fifty or so handwritten messages. Some of the messages were long and detailed while others paid their respects with a simple, *RIP Julia*. A Mr. Ortiz wrote that Julia was a gifted actress, an example that all young men and women should want to follow. A student named Liam had drawn an elaborate illustration of Julia's smiling face with a thin pale blue marker.

Within virtually every message was the symbol XOXO. Out of habit and almost subconsciously, Diggs snapped several photos of the shrine and the writings. When Diggs saw Mr. Hyde squatting in the middle of the dead flowers, he pulled him away and led him to nearby a sandy patch.

Cindy was reading something on her phone when Diggs opened the car door. She turned her head to him. "Does Noah Boyer sound right?"

"The Noah part does."

"That's the only Noah I could find. He works nights."

"It's important that I talk with him as soon as possible. You wouldn't be able to get his contact information, would you?"

"Sorry no, I tried."

"Was Julia Geist a student here?"

"Last year, I heard."

"You said the Guthus own the school?"

"Yes, Hal and Lilly Guthu. They're a wonderful, eccentric old couple. Seeing their whole life going up in flames has to be killing them."

Diggs made a mental note of her reference to flames and asked, "Do they live nearby?"

"Less than a mile from here. You should see their house. It's purple and yellow with all these crazy angles. It looks like something out of an animated movie."

Back at the Western Jewel, Diggs accessed *The Westerner* website and found it to be a painfully small-time offering filled with promotional stories that weren't much more than paid ads and a smattering of local news. Diggs typed Claire Diggs into a search field and came up with nothing. Next, he typed *Frederic Remington Academy for the Arts*. There were four stories regarding the theft of its funds. All four were generalized and sanitized with scarce details and no mention of Claire Diggs or any other suspects. Each of the four articles did include a quote or two from Sheriff Greg Potter. He expressed confidence that the guilty party would soon be brought to justice.

Diggs accessed the school's Twitter and Facebook accounts. Each had the same goodbye message and the same promise that school would be returning soon. Neither made any mention of Claire Diggs.

Diggs pushed himself away from the desk. The day before, Potter had given no indication that he knew anything about Claire Diggs and yet he must have known exactly who she was.

16

If anything, Cindy had downplayed the Guthu home. The dark purple exterior was expected, and the triangular-shaped garage and the circular room that jutted from the side of the house like a word bubble wasn't a surprise. The yellow-painted domed roof and the diamond-shaped windows fit right in. The lime-green driveway made Diggs' eyes hurt.

A couple dozen cactus formed a maze that led from the curb to the house. Diggs rang the bell and rather than a buzz or a chime, he heard several notes from what he thought might be from *West Side Story*. A moment later, a seventyish woman wearing a long purple dress, red high heels, and oversized sparkling earrings opened the door. Her hair was jet black and tied in a bun. Her blue eyes sparkled with excitement.

"Well now, I see a tall handsome stranger at my door with a beautiful dog. The possibilities for drama are endless."

Diggs wasn't sure whether to grin or offer her a breathalyzer test. "Are you Mrs. Guthu?"

"Yes, I am, and whom may I ask are you?"

"I'm with the police." She didn't immediately ask to see

his badge and before she had a chance, Diggs quickly added, "I'd like to talk about your school."

She lightly touched her chest. "Please, do come in."

Diggs nodded to Mr. Hyde. "May I?"

"He's not a bloodthirsty attack dog, is he?"

"No, he's quite harmless."

"Well then, he's welcome. Would you like me to bring him some water?"

"I think he's fine, but thank you."

Diggs followed her into a living room neatly cluttered with furniture that might have been antiques or just old. Several prints of Frederic Remington's work covered one wall. A collage of photos featuring young people Diggs assumed to be former or current students engaged in the creation of art covered another wall. A bamboo rod supported by brown twine hung over the furthest corner of the room. On the rod, two cockatoos paced and screeched. Below the cockatoos, open newspapers performed a thankless role.

The birds squawked, "Visitor, visitor."

Mrs. Guthu said, "Harold, the police are here."

A short man with a full head of thick brown hair peppered with gray hopped spryly off a well-worn creaky sofa and approached Diggs with his arm extended. As they shook hands, Diggs introduced himself as Detective Malcolm. Mr. Guthu enthusiastically said, "Call me Hal." He turned his head toward the rambunctious birds and yelled, "Lucy, Ethel, quiet!"

Mrs. Guthu told Diggs to take a seat. He did so on a zebra-striped chair while Hal and Mrs. Guthu sat across from him on the sofa. Hyde studied the cockatoos for a moment before lying at Diggs' feet.

Hal said, "You have a fine-looking hound."

Diggs thanked him and added, "I hope you don't mind me bringing him along. I'm on my way to the vet. He's friendly. He won't cause any problems."

Hal said, "Were you aware that dog spelled backwards is god?" He quickly added, "It makes you think, doesn't it?"

Diggs told him that it did. "I'm here to speak to you about the theft at your school. Forgive me if I ask questions you've answered before. I'm new and want to make sure I understand completely."

Mr. Guthu waved him off. "Not a problem in the slightest. We're thrilled to have you here. Needless to say, both Lilly and I are quite depressed over this matter. We're frantically trying to acquire funds. Many of the parents are working diligently to help us, but we can't ask everyone to pay again. A few have threatened to sue."

Mrs. Guthu added, "It's been an absolute nightmare. We're so glad you're here. We didn't think anybody cared."

Diggs wondered if the police had done anything at all. "My apologies. The Geist case has consumed most of the police resources."

Mrs. Guthu sighed. "A terrible tragedy about Julia and her family. She was once a student here. A very talented young lady."

Diggs asked why Julia left.

"The usual reason, I'm sorry to say. Money. Her family couldn't afford another year."

Hal added, "At least at first."

"Yes, at first. Julia came to us in mid-September and told us she could make the payments after all. We had to tell her it was too late. We can only take so many actresses and we had enough for that semester. We told her we'd save a place for her in the winter, or if someone dropped out, we'd contact her. She was agreeable, although she was strange about it."

Diggs asked, "How so?"

"Frankly, she seemed to be hiding something. We have her contact information on file, but she gave us a cell phone number we didn't have and told us to only contact her at that number. She was quite adamant about it. We've already told the police all of this."

Mr. Guthu spoke in a confidential tone. "Don't know if it means anything, but Claire was quite friendly with Julia."

Mrs. Guthu rolled her eyes and scoffed. "Harold, Claire was friendly with everyone, including the cleaning crew and the landscapers. Don't you get it? That was part of her criminal genius."

Diggs intercepted the burgeoning argument. "Let's talk about the embezzlement. How did it happen and who discovered it?"

Mr. Guthu took over. "We hired Claire as our bookkeeper just over a year ago. Her resume was excellent."

"Did she offer any references?"

"She did and I'm sorry to say we didn't check any of them. When we interviewed her, she was so impressive that she instantly won us over. She seemed perfect, and for a year, we had no regrets."

"Do you still have her reference list?"

"I wish we did. I searched for it after all this happened and I couldn't find it."

"How much did Claire steal?"

Mrs. Guthu glared at her husband. "Hal isn't certain that she stole anything."

Diggs turned to Mr. Guthu. "You believe Claire is innocent?"

"No, not anymore. At one point…" His voice faded. A moment later, he added, "I had questions is all."

"Hal believed our daughter stole 157,000 dollars from us. I assure you, she did not."

Mr. Guthu sighed before he spoke. "Unfortunately, Emily has had recurring substance abuse issues. I am ashamed to admit that she's taken money from us before without our knowledge."

"And she had access to your bank account?"

Mrs. Guthu forcefully interjected, "No, only Claire, me and Harold had access, and I know that neither of us stole it."

"If that's the case, why would you think your daughter might be responsible?"

"We had the password to our account taped to the computer in our bedroom. Emily was aware of it."

"Where's Emily now?"

"We haven't seen her since this all happened. I lost my temper and I lashed out. I was in a very agitated state. I made accusations I shouldn't have."

Diggs spoke to Mrs. Guthu. "If Emily had access to the password, what makes you believe she didn't take the money?"

"Other than I don't believe my daughter would attempt to ruin our academy, on our accountant's advice I changed the password every few weeks. The first unauthorized withdrawals began in July and picked up in August. Emily would have had to steal a new password at least three times. Emily doesn't live with us and she didn't visit us all that often. Claire was immediately made aware of every password change."

"Did Claire know your daughter wasn't here a lot?"

"At this point, we don't know what Claire knew. We assume everything."

Diggs assumed the same thing. "Does your daughter have a key to your house?"

"Of course."

Hal spoke with incredulity. "It's just so hard to believe. Claire completely supported what we were doing. She and I would have lunch together on the back patio. We talked about the theories of Uta Hagan, Barrymore's most outstanding stage performances. The very first day we met, she told me her all-time favorite painting was Remington's *Sun Fisher*. She regaled beautifully about her parents' stable and how peaceful she found riding a pony at dusk."

Diggs couldn't help grimacing. Their parents never owned a stable and the closest Claire ever came to riding a pony was watching reruns of *Mr. Ed* with him.

Looking sad, sounding resigned, Hal added, "I guess Claire probably is responsible. She won't answer my phone calls and she doesn't live at the address she claimed she did. I'm just so surprised. I used to tease her about her love of Norman Rockwell."

Diggs told them he knew where Claire lived and that her home had burned down two nights before.

Mr. Guthu cried out, "Oh no, was Claire hurt?" The force of his concern surprised Diggs.

Diggs answered, "No," although it wasn't what he believed. He decided against mentioning the volunteer fireman's account of smelling burnt flesh.

Mrs. Guthu asked, "Was it an accident?"

Diggs said he wouldn't know until the fire marshal issued his report.

"Can you tell me the make and model of Claire's car?"

The Guthus looked blankly at each other. Hal finally said, "It was a black four-door. Not a new car, but not terribly old. I think it was American made, but I'm not entirely certain. It's frustrating now that you ask. I saw her car dozens of times parked beside the school, but the make or model never really registered. If I had to guess I'd say it was a Chevrolet, but don't hold me to that."

Diggs hid his frustration. A make and model would make recanvassing the path between Claire's home and hospital palpable. He would have followed with a search of the hospital parking lot. A black four-door that might be but probably wasn't a Chevrolet offered nothing at all.

Mrs. Guthu added, "I'm afraid I can't offer any help either. Would it make sense to hypnotize us?"

Diggs said he'd pass on the suggestion.

"Do you have any opinions where Claire might have gone? Did she have a boyfriend, or a close girlfriend?"

They both shrugged ignorance. Hal began to speak, and the shame coloring his words was unmistakable. "I look back now and realize that I told Claire so many details about my life and she never really offered anything about herself. A few stories here and there, but the truth is, she's a complete mystery to me. It wasn't that long ago that I would have said that Claire and I were close friends."

Mrs. Guthu pleaded, "Find her soon, please. The longer she's free, the more opportunity she has to spend our money."

Diggs wondered if Claire had taken the job for the sole purpose of siphoning the institute's funds. The Guthus were sadly prime marks—older, trusting, too caught up in their own world, and with a significant amount of money to steal.

It angered him that he could do nothing to help. Grappling for anything, he said, "Have you thought about reaching out to Petey White? He seems to have a lot of money and he's an actor. Maybe he'd be willing to help out financially."

Mr. Guthu smiled politely. "We'd prefer not to be associated with Mr. White."

Diggs asked why.

Mrs. Guthu said, "It'd be the ultimate Faustian bargain. Petey White is an insufferable braggart. He doesn't seem to comprehend that he knows nothing about acting and that television program he continually boasts of is utter garbage. If we accept a donation from Petey White, rest assured he'd want to exploit it."

Her husband added, "He'd probably want to rename us the Emmy Award-Winning Petey White Institute of the Performing Arts, and frankly, we'd both rather die."

17

When an investigation frustrated Diggs, it usually meant he was getting ahead of himself. He needed to slow down and allow his brain to process the percolating jumble of facts, speculations, and likelihoods at their own pace. Diggs called it crockpot thinking. When it worked, a coherent line of thought emerged. It was then that Diggs could devise a strategy that might get him somewhere.

Silence was a necessity; it cleansed his mind and enriched his focus. With Mr. Hyde beside him, gnawing on the red ball, Diggs lay on his bed and silenced his phone's ringer. He began a slow, deep breathing pattern. In and out. In and out. He knew the intensity of the breaths would soon slow and his mind would close. Then he'd trust his subconscious to follow any direction it pleased.

Crockpot thinking wasn't a guarantee and sometimes it was a complete bust. Every now and then a stupid idea would get caught in his brain like hair in a backed-up drain. The beverage can that cooled itself was an example. Perfect for summer car trunks and the unforeseen beverage emergency.

Two years later, it remained rattling around in his head, an annoying song on an endless loop.

Diggs' memory drifted back to the day he first heard Claire moved to Mojave Creek to follow a boyfriend. He was at Arizona State. His grandmother told him over the phone, and she was not pleased. She never did mention the boyfriend's name, but she did call him a ninny and offhandedly said he was a mechanic. Diggs was certain that he and the ninny had met. He was in high school and his Camaro had broken down again. It was blocking Claire's Ford Escort and she was pissed.

Out of nowhere, a mechanic knocked on the front door. He was a non-descript guy with an impressively thick black mustache. After only a few minutes, he got the Camaro running. He slammed the hood and turned to Diggs. The conversation went something like this:

Mechanic: "I came out here on my day off. I'm going to have to charge you above my normal rate."

Diggs: "How much do you want?"

Mechanic: "How much you got?"

Diggs opened his wallet and counted out twelve ones. "Twelve dollars."

Mechanic: "That sounds about right."

Diggs figured he must have hesitated a bit, been a little slow relinquishing the twelve singles. Claire interjected, "Don't argue, Lenny. Pay the man."

Then to his surprise, Claire didn't get into her car, she got into his. She kissed the mechanic on the cheek and off they went. Diggs remembered calling them Bonny and Clyde. It was the last time he'd ever seen the mustached mechanic.

Diggs rolled off the bed and stepped to the desk. A Yelp search for Mojave Creek auto mechanics found eight potentials.

Diggs started at the bottom of the barrel—the shop with an average rating of one and a half stars: Gary Wagner Auto.

Complaints of dishonesty, deceptive billing, overbilling, incompetence, and outright lying were common. The most recent review, barely a week old, written by a woman in Sedona, accused Wagner of offering to cut her bill by twenty percent if she'd let him touch her foot.

A second review, written a day before, accused Wagner of siphoning his gas and altering his gauge. The reviewer made it to the freeway before his car stalled out. When he called Wagner Auto to complain, Wagner offered to discount the towing fee by ten percent.

Diggs scrolled though a long venomous list of dissatisfaction. Curiously, the earliest reviews were all five-star, relating an entirely different experience with Gary Wagner Auto:

Never had a mechanic as knowledgeable as Gary.
Gary is the best.
Gary can fix anything.
Gary will be my mechanic for life.
My car loves you, Gary. Keep up the GREAT work!

Diggs clicked over to Wagner's website. On the homepage was a photo of a dark-haired, mustached man standing in front of a gray-painted garage. Inside the garage, three clean-cut guys in blue coveralls were working on a red Mercedes Benz. Diggs was certain that Gary Wagner was the man who worked on his Camaro.

*   *   *

Wagner Auto Repair was located on a lonely side street at the far end of Mojave Creek's commercial district. Next door was a Long John Silver's. Across the street, a badly cracked concrete parking lot with chairs, stacked tables, and desks lined up like solders standing at attention. A sign written in thick black marker on a piece of cardboard read: *Everything Must Go!* Other than those testaments to American big business, the block was comprised of undeveloped vacant lots.

Diggs didn't see any clean-cut guys in blue coveralls working on expensive cars, nor did he see any customers. The garage door was pulled wide open revealing a car lift, an engine hoist, various tools hanging on a wall, and a few small machines that were entirely foreign to him.

Diggs and Mr. Hyde entered the customer area and waited a few moments before ringing a bell on a counter. Seconds later, a man wearing blue coveralls entered through a door that led from the garage. His hair was grayer, and his face tanned and sun-lined, but he still had the impressively thick mustache, albeit peppered with gray specks.

In a laid-back conversational voice, Diggs said, "Hi Gary, you remember me?"

"No, sir. Should I?"

"I'm Leonard Diggs. A long time ago you came to my sister Claire's house and got my Camaro running. You charged me twelve dollars."

He smiled apologetically. "Oh sure, I remember. If it means anything, the money went straight to Claire." Without any sense of wistfulness, he added, "Your sister was some piece of work."

His face brightened. "I followed you at Arizona State. I thought you had a chance."

"For a while, I thought I did too."

"That's the injury bug for you. It's messed up a lot of potential."

"I'm looking for Claire. I was hoping you could lead me to her."

"Sorry, I don't know where she's at." He looked down at Hyde. "That's a handsome dog." He bent to a knee and petted him. "He's a friendly guy. Look at his tail wagging. What's his name?"

"Mr. Hyde."

Wagner stood. "I like it. It's different. I haven't seen Claire in a long time. I can't help you."

"You heard about the art school embezzlement?"

"Sure."

"Then you probably heard that Claire is a suspect?"

He clapped his palms together and chuckled. "A suspect? That's a charitable way of putting it. She did it." Contempt edged into his voice. "Claire never learned there's more to life than money. Personally, I hope they throw the book at her."

His preachy, holier-than-thou posturing made Diggs want to roll his eyes. "Why so judgmental, Gary? It's not like you're a beacon of honesty." As soon as the words left his mouth, Diggs wanted to take them back. He had more questions to ask. Antagonizing Wagner served no purpose.

Wagner grinned bitterly. "Oh, you've read some reviews and now you're an expert. You have no clue, pal. Those reviews were written by your psycho sister."

"There are dozens from different accounts with different

profile photos. You might want to stop blaming Claire and take a long look in the mirror."

"Why don't you take a look at the other mechanics in Mojave Creek. You won't find more than five or six reviews for any of them. Last I counted, I had forty-seven."

"The quality of your service obviously stands out."

"You don't know shit. I know for a fact she wrote them because I've never met any of those people. Those reviews are pure fiction. When we broke up, Claire promised she was going to ruin me. Your sister is a dangerous nutcase and a world-class grudge-holder. I doubt that I'll ever be fully rid of her."

"Why the enmity? You do something to her?"

"Nothing that no other sane man would do, which is get the hell away from her. She'll suck your soul dry."

"Were you married?"

"No, and thank god, no kids."

"How long did you stay together?"

"Twelve very lousy years."

"That's a lot of soul sucking."

"Even in a war zone there are some decent days. Claire knew how to make money. Without her, I never get this shop."

Diggs remembered Claire's neighborhood. Rainmaker wasn't the first thing that came to mind. "What did Claire do for a living?"

He mockingly rubbed his chin pretending to be deep in thought. "Hm, let's see. She worked for an attorney. He died under mysterious circumstances and left Claire twenty grand. She worked for an insurance company. Got fired after a couple of months. Ran a few internet scams that brought in a decent income. Then she became an entrepreneur and that's when the money started to pour in."

Diggs asked what her business was. An idiot grin filled the bottom half of Wagner's face. "It was quite a colorful one. You ready?"

Diggs sighed. "Why don't you just tell me."

"She beat up men."

Diggs squinted his confusion.

"Surprised, huh? I was too, but it's true. Men would pay her a lot of money to be slapped around, kicked in the nuts. That kind of thing. She brought home three, four grand a week. A lot of times more."

Diggs had trouble picturing it in his head. The concept was too damn bizarre. He wasn't even sure he grasped what Wagner was trying to convey.

"Four thousand a week in Mojave Creek? That's hard to believe."

"Not just Mojave Creek, my friend. Claire had clients from all over. Imagine making that kind of money kicking weirdos in the balls. Only in America, right?"

"She had a website?"

"No."

And thus, no way to verify his claims.

"Claire said that once a website is up, it's always up, and when you take it down it's still up, which made no sense to me."

Diggs understood. "She was right."

"If you say so. She used Craigslist and then Backpage and the money rolled in."

"Is she still doing this?"

"Naw, she screwed it up."

Diggs asked what happened.

"She was too damn rough. For Claire, a slap in the face

wasn't enough. It had to be a right cross to the jaw. She broke three fingers on one guy. She tied a naked guy to some stakes in the backyard and left him out there all night. He wasn't too happy, and neither was I. Picture seeing that with your first cup of coffee. Most of them stopped coming back. One guy sued and she settled. A couple more threatened lawsuits. I know she paid the hospital bill for a guy from Phoenix. Shit, Claire was lucky no one got killed. It would have happened eventually."

"Did you know her place on Ocotillo burned down?"

Wagner shrugged indifferently. "I didn't and I don't care. A lot of bad memories there. Torched?"

"I haven't heard."

"All the enemies she's made, the school thing. Someone might have decided to give her what she deserves. But, if she needs money and if there's a big enough insurance payout, I can easily see her burning it down. Your sister is a scammer and a thief. There's nothing she's not capable of."

Diggs had grown tired of Wagner. He doubted he could be trusted, and he was having trouble believing anything he said. The fake reviews. The unapologetic grifter. The paid-for torturer. Wagner was drawing a comic book super-villain.

"Claire called me a few days ago. She said she had a fiancé. You know anything about that?"

"Nope, but I'd bet he has money. For now, anyway."

Diggs hid his disdain. He wasn't sure if he was entirely finished with Wagner. "Thank you, Mr. Wagner. You've been helpful."

"Hey, I've answered your questions. How about you answer one for me?"

"What?"

"You said Claire called you. What'd she want?"

"She read something. She called to congratulate me."

"She didn't want anything?"

"Sorry to disappoint you."

He let out a harsh laugh. "No offense, but if you believe Claire wasn't angling for something, you're as dumb as a bag of hammers."

"She's inside your head, Mr. Wagner. You might want to consider a therapist."

"Therapist, my ass. Let me tell you something. I lived with Claire for twelve years and she barely said a word about you, but when she did, it wasn't to start a damn fan club."

Diggs tugged on Mr. Hyde's leash. "Objectivity, Mr. Wagner. Objectivity."

Diggs and Hyde were at the door when Wagner called out, "If you do find Claire, don't leave her alone with your friend there. He's way too trusting. He'll be easy to kill."

Diggs turned to face him. "Why would she do that, Mr. Wagner?"

"You haven't been listening, have you?"

18

Diggs left Wagner's shop ruminating on the possibilities of arson while juggling Wagner's assertion that Claire always had a self-serving motive in her back pocket. He thought about Claire's non-existent pony and struggled mightily to believe she had any appreciation for Norman Rockwell. He wondered how long Claire had studied up on Uta Hagen before she convinced herself that she sounded credible.

Faulty wiring was a lot more common than arson, but the embezzlement and the tales of paid-for abuse offered an unknown number of potential suspects, and Gary Wagner, watching his prized business bleed to death, wasn't above suspicion either. An accidental fire was possible, but the truth seemed as simple as a Bob Dylan lyric—you don't need a weatherman to know which way the wind blows.

Diggs ruminated on the conversation he'd had with Claire. Peeling away the small talk and the friendly vibes, Claire's interest had been Brian Harper. What was he like? What were his motives? Diggs recalled the disappointment in her voice when he didn't have more to report.

If Claire was the true crime junkie she asserted, why hadn't she mentioned the Sidewalk Ghoul case? Diggs was nearly the Ghoul's eighth kill before shooting the Ghoul dead in a smack house. The Sidewalk Ghoul murders were compelling enough that Diggs was forced to relive the case on a two-hour primetime television program. Claire didn't seem to know the Ghoul existed, or that her brother nearly lost his life breaking the case. Diggs wondered if Claire's true crime fascination was nothing more than another pony story.

With the sheriff's office only five minutes away, Diggs decided to make a side trip with the hope that Potter had both the fire marshal's report and the make and model of Claire's car.

At the front desk, Diggs asked a woman in a police uniform with a jubilant smile to speak with the sheriff. She cheerfully told him that Sheriff Potter wouldn't be available until tomorrow at the earliest. As she spoke, another woman in a police uniform stepped behind her and gave the back of her neck a hug.

A palpable buzz hung in the air. Ten feet away, three smiling uniformed officers were standing at the entrance to an office in a tight circle speaking in hushed whispers. Diggs recognized the excitement.

He said, "Feels like something interesting is about to happen."

Through a sing-songy voice, the woman answered, "Could be."

"The Geist case?"

She raised both hands with her fingers crossed. "No comment."

"If the sheriff isn't available, can I speak with someone else? It's important."

The woman turned her head to the three uniformed officers huddled together. "Jason, can you help this gentleman out?"

An officer with wide shoulders and a crew cut walked over.

Diggs said, "I left Sheriff Potter a message this morning," and then explained to the officer that his sister Claire had likely been burned in the Ocotillo Road fire and he suspected that she had tried to drive to the hospital but never made it.

Diggs asked, "Have you found a car with a body inside?"

All along the officer had listened impassively, revealing no clues as to what he knew or didn't. His answer to Diggs, a quick, "I'm not at liberty to talk about that."

In an agitated tone, Diggs said, "Why not? I'm her brother and I'm a cop." He pulled his wallet from his back pocket and showed the officer his badge. The officer appeared disinterested in Diggs' arguments or the badge.

"Everything involving Claire Diggs goes through Sheriff Potter. You said you left a message with the sheriff. He'll be in touch. I'm sorry, that's all I can say."

Diggs felt a strong urge to continue arguing, with the goal of wearing him down, but he knew it would ultimately be futile. A rigid police hierarchy existed in every department and family or not, cop or not, investigations always operated on a need-to-know basis. Diggs turned away sharply without another word. He and Hyde headed back to the Western Jewel.

Once inside his room, he sat at his computer and logged into his Malcolm account. He typed out a message.

Billy T.

A few important matters have come up. Can we postpone our meeting for a day or so? Maybe Saturday or Sunday?

Definitely not backing out. Still want to purchase your collection. If you would like a down payment, I am happy to provide one. Let me know.

Malcolm

Diggs had walked Mr. Hyde around the motel in the morning. He walked him at the school. To burn off his excess energy, he took him out again. Twenty minutes in, Diggs groaned an obscenity. He cut the walk short and dropped Hyde off in their room.

The chime rang and the battleax paid it no attention. She was glued to the same seat, hollering to take box number two. Diggs stood and waited. At some point he had bought into the notion that it was his obligation to stand grounded at the front desk like a bearded totem pole until she decided to grant him her attention. He couldn't pinpoint when the rules between customer and merchant had flipped. He presumed at first slowly and then quickly. In whichever way it unfolded, the customer now served at the pleasure of the merchant. With the population growing and businesses constantly merging, and all the regulations being legalized out, excellent customer service was one more item to add to the ever lengthening remember-when list.

The show cut to commercial and she sauntered to the front desk. "I thought you skipped."

"And forfeit one more night at this palace, not a chance."

"One more night? What an honor. I thought you'd be off to the governor's mansion."

Diggs slid his credit card across the counter.

"You have a dog in your room. You didn't mention that when you checked in."

"He was unexpected."

"You're going to be charged an extra cleaning fee—fifty dollars per night—starting yesterday."

"Wouldn't have it any other way."

"Cute dog."

"He's a Shar-Pei."

"I know. When I was married, we had one. A couple thousand years ago, they were bred as fighting dogs. All those wrinkles were part of their defense."

She swiped the card on the imprinter. "What's his name?"

"Mr. Hyde."

"Did you come up with that all by yourself?"

Diggs nodded a yes.

She slid his card across the desk and in a comically exaggerated manner, patted her chest and cackled. "Mr. Hyde? Oh, brother."

"There's a backstory you wouldn't understand."

She waved him off. "Nuts to you. Have you ever known anyone who wasn't a blockhead give their dog two names?"

He remembered Stall telling him that he and his wife named their Sphynx cat Mary Poppins, but he was there to pay his bill, not to debate. "Don't project your personal hang-ups onto my dog. You got everything you need?"

"I certainly do. Please, send Mr. Hyde my best."

Diggs wished her the loveliest of days and headed back to his room. The moment he opened the door, Mr. Hyde began running in circles, wagging his tail at a rip-roaring pace. Diggs bent to one knee and the dog jumped into his chest, licking every part of Diggs that his tongue could reach.

"Calm down, I've only been gone three minutes."

He picked the red ball off the floor and bounced it off a

wall across the room. Hyde aggressively dashed after it and promptly brought it back. Diggs tossed it a few more times, but after a spilled drink and a nearly tipped over lamp, Diggs ended the rambunctiousness.

Diggs fed Hyde and ordered delivery from a sandwich shop. While he waited, he opened the CNN website, searching for news on the Geist case and finding nothing. He next tried *The Westerner*.

Anyone who got their news exclusively from *The Westerner* would believe that the world occasionally stopped for a day or two. The last update of any kind came two days before. Diggs laughed out loud when he discovered that Petey White Enterprises published the rag.

A soft whimpering drew his attention behind him to Hyde. His paws were frantically scratching at the bed covering. He was crying in his sleep. In a calm voice, Diggs said, "Mr. Hyde, Mr. Hyde, Mr. Hyde," while at the same time, tapping the side of the bed. Soon, Hyde startled himself out of sleep. Diggs sat beside him and gently rubbed his back. Soothingly, he whispered, "It's okay. It's okay."

The sandwich delivery driver arrived and while Diggs worked on his lunch, he dialed Stall's cell number. A professional sounding voice answered, "Good afternoon, Detective John Stall's office. Out of the womb and into the light."

Diggs remembered Stall making the same womb utterance outside of Brian Harper/Richard Reed's house. He thought it was gibberish then. Never had he envisioned it as any kind of campaign slogan, until he remembered that all campaign slogans dabbled in gibberish.

He asked, "Who is this?"

"My name is Diane. I am Detective Stall's liaison. Who is calling please?"

"I'm John's next-door neighbor. He's never had a liaison before. Just kind of surprised me."

"Detective Stall is an important member of Mayor Pelton's team, and his time is in very high demand. Please leave a message and I will make sure Detective Stall receives it."

Diggs spoke with concern. "Like I said, I'm John's neighbor. His cat Mary Poppins is sick. I want to take her to a vet. His wife isn't home and I'm not sure who they use. Can you have John call me back as soon as possible?"

"Aww, that's sad. I'll let him know right away. Your name and phone number?"

He gave her his number and hoped she wouldn't ask for his name.

"I'm sorry, and your name is?"

Stall had told him the names of most of his neighbors, but for the life of him, Diggs couldn't remember any of them. He knew one mowed his grass during *The Masked Singer* and another kept a bedroom light on during the day.

"Tell him Mr. Boss called."

Minutes later, the phone rang. A cry of pure anguish shrieked in Diggs' ear. "How is she? Is she okay? Can you put her up to the phone?"

"Stall, calm down. It's Diggs. Didn't you recognize my number? Mary Poppins is fine. I made that up. I thought Pelton might be trying to keep us apart."

"Thank you, Jesus. Thank you. When I heard Mary Poppins was sick, I lost it. Give me a second to catch my breath." Diggs listened to thirty seconds of heavy breathing before he interrupted. "Stall, can we talk?"

"Okay, boss, sure. Please don't ever do that again."

"Can you find the address on Reed's driver's license?"

"Okay, boss. I'll work on that."

"And while you're at it, ask if anything stood out. Anything that caught the investigator's attention. Anything they didn't expect to find."

"Like what?"

"I don't know. I'm not sure what I'm looking for."

"Okay, boss. I'll work on that."

"Thanks, Stall. Are they treating you alright over there?"

"I'm exhausted. I must have shaken hands with everyone in San Diego. I'll be glad when this is all over and we can get back to solving cases. Just so you know, I'm not sluffing off. Whenever I have any free time, I've been working on Huszer."

"Excellent. See you in a week."

Diggs lay next to Hyde and checked the Uber app. Noah wasn't on duty, but it was only a little after 5:00 p.m. Diggs could feel himself getting restless. He had made a mess at White's party and the heat would likely fall on Rusty, or maybe it already had.

Diggs opened a people-finding website. For a nominal fee, it allowed access to a wealth of public records. Diggs knew of these sites but had never had an occasion where he needed to call on one. The resources of the San Diego police department provided him all the public records information he would ever need.

He entered his credit card information and made the charge. In the search field, he typed Noah Boyer. There were over thirty in the United States but only one in Nevada. That Noah Boyer had three marriages and a bankruptcy. For eight years ending in 2014, he resided at the Nevada State correctional facility.

Boyer's most recent address was 2200 County Road 192 in Mojave Creek. A quick search in Google maps showed that address was ten minutes away from the Sleeping Volcano and fifteen minutes away from his motel.

Diggs was jotting down the address when he heard the same frightened whimpers coming from Hyde. As he did before, he sat beside Hyde and spoke in a smooth voice at a low volume. "Mr. Hyde, Mr. Hyde, come on, buddy. Wake up."

Hyde opened his eyes and immediately pivoted his head from left to right. Diggs again stroked his back. "Brother, I can relate. The Ghoul gave me plenty of nightmares."

He gave Hyde a moment to gather himself and then picked up the leash off the dresser.

"Come on, let's get out of here."

Hyde jumped off the bed and they were out the door to find Noah Boyer.

19

As dusk neared, the Sleeping Volcano's parking lot was three-quarters full. Customers were streaming in, and a wealth of diners ate and drank under the Volcano's long purple canopy. Diggs considered the possibility Rusty might be among the crowd but decided against making a side stop. The best place to start investigations was family and that was Noah Boyer.

At the Highway 23 entrance ramp, Diggs headed east. Two miles later, he exited at the Tomcat Trail off-ramp. After a quarter mile of badly cracked asphalt road, he met a T-shaped intersection that ran east and west—County Road 192. He turned west onto a ruler-straight road that paralleled the highway.

The setting sun casted a dull pale light against a sea of dark brown sand. Heavy gusts of wind blew clouds of dust across the single-lane road. Miles in the distance a red house sat near the top of a hill. Somewhere behind it, a thin plume of iron-colored smoke dispersed into the darkening sky. Diggs felt edgy and impatient. He glanced at Hyde on the passenger seat and then back to the rising smoke. He pressed the gas pedal and accelerated well past the fifty mile per hour speed limit.

In a matter of minutes, Diggs parked in front of a large, splintered sign. Its sun-faded black lettering read: *McCallum Trailer Park—Welcome Home!*

A gravel driveway snaked past the sign and onto the trailer grounds. Diggs pulled forward and stopped at a four-foot square metal box. Behind scratched plastic, he saw that N. Boyer lived on lot forty-two.

Diggs had been to quite a few trailer parks over the course of his career. Many were well thought out with wide roads and well-placed signs and a logical design. At McCallum Trailer Park, the road curved sharply in several places. There was no overhead lighting anywhere and no posted speed signs. It struck Diggs as both a burglar's paradise and liability nightmare.

Diggs came across a small graveled parking area. Seeing no signs that read *Tenants Only* or *Visitor Parking*, he took an empty slot and exited the car with Hyde.

They walked twenty yards, stopping five feet in front of Boyer's residence. Flower beds ran the length of the trailer. Under a canopy, a tomato garden had been planted near the front door. The layers of grime crusted on so many of the other trailers was absent. Through a window, Diggs saw a woman with dark hair standing over a kitchen sink. From behind him, a male voice said, "Who are you and what do you want?"

Diggs cursed himself for his lack of awareness. He was a stranger standing in the shadows and staring into a window like a voyeur. He stepped into the light emitting from inside the trailer. A man with a shaved head and long gray sideburns stood six feet away. He wore a dark-colored t-shirt and his stomach hung over his belt. Both arms were covered in tattoos. As the man stepped closer, Diggs could see swollen and bloodshot eyes.

Diggs loosened his body language and spoke in a non-threatening conversational voice. "Good evening, sir. I'm looking for Noah Boyer."

"That's me. Who are you and what do you want?"

"I'm a friend of Rusty's and…"

He furrowed his eyebrows. "You look pretty old to be any friend of Rusty's."

Continuing with the easy-come, easy-go façade, Diggs responded, "We became friends recently. We met at the Sleeping Volcano. He took me to Petey White's party."

Diggs could see tears begin to roll down Boyer's cheeks. He sniffled once and wiped his face with the back of his hand. He blurted, "You're too late. Rusty is dead."

Diggs felt his body go cold. An explosion of dizzying guilt thundered inside his head. For a moment he stood silent, browsing Noah Boyer's tear-streaked face. After several seconds of silence, Diggs said, "What happened?"

"Goddamn hit-and-run driver."

Diggs offered his condolences. "When?"

"This morning. He was going to Burger King. I found him myself. Off to the side of the road. He was mangled, like he'd been tossed in a meat grinder. To do that kind of damage it had to be one of those goddamn semis going way too goddamn fast."

"No witnesses?"

"They said nobody saw a damn thing, but it was early. Probably weren't any customers."

Hyde was staring up at Boyer with his tail wagging. Boyer dropped his eyes to Hyde. "He's a good-looking dog. What's his name?"

"Mr. Hyde."

"He looks pretty friendly to be named after a bad guy."

Diggs shrugged. "I appreciate the irony."

Boyer got to one knee and rubbed Hyde's head. "How you doin', Mr. Hyde?" Hyde started to sniff Boyer over, which brought a smile.

Boyer gave Hyde a smooth pet across the length of his back and stood. "A while back I did some time. My dog died while I was still inside. Broke my heart. Danny and I were inseparable, and I couldn't even be there to comfort him when he got sick."

Hyde edged to Diggs' leg. Boyer nodded at Hyde. "He loves you a lot. You must treat him well. A dog will look out for you if you look out for him. Rusty loved dogs, but he was allergic. Still worked at a shelter though."

"He did?"

"At least once a week."

"I had no idea," and that wasn't a surprise. Diggs knew very little about Rusty Boyer.

"Was Rusty going to meet anyone at the Burger King?"

"I doubt that. Rusty was a loner. He'd get up early and walk to get breakfast. I think he liked the peacefulness of the early morning. He'd bring it home and eat in his room."

"Can you tell me anything about Rusty's relationship with Petey White?"

Boyer pulled a pack of cigarettes from his back pocket. He held it out.

Diggs shook his head. "No, thanks."

Boyer put one in his mouth and lit up. He tilted his head back, taking a deep drag before exhaling toward the sky.

He dropped his eyes to Diggs. "No offense, but you sound like a cop."

"I am a cop but from San Diego. My name is Leonard

Diggs. I have no standing in Mojave Creek and I am not working with the Mojave Creek police department in any way. I'm here only because of Rusty. Anything we discuss is between you and me."

He stared silently, sizing Diggs up. "I can only give you a few minutes. Rusty's mom is barely holding up, and I'm not doing a whole lot better. We're trying to make preparations for a funeral. It's tough, man. Trust me."

Diggs blew air from his lips. "I believe you."

"Mr. White is good people. Sometimes I work for his construction business. Pays well and on time. Treats me fairer than any of the other places I've worked recently. There hasn't been much going on lately though, which is why I'm driving an Uber and doing other piddly-ass shit to make ends meet. Rusty was a busboy at Mr. White's diner. He seemed happy there."

"What about White's son Jerad? Did Rusty know him?"

He took another deep drag. "I don't know."

"How about a short Hispanic guy who works for White? His name is Johnny. Don't know his last name. Rusty made it very clear that he didn't like him."

Boyer shrugged his ignorance. "Sorry, wish I could help you."

"You know anything about a guy named Remy?"

"Oh, yeah, I know that fucking punk. Wannabe tough guy. Weak-ass bully. Can't stand him. When I first went looking for Rusty, I thought Remy might have beaten him up or something."

"Why would Remy do that?"

"Rusty got smart and finally dumped his ass. Told me a couple weeks ago that he'd had it with him. They weren't friends anymore. Rusty usually kept things to himself, but I guess he knew that would make me happy, so he told me."

"You're certain that was a couple weeks ago?"

Boyer thought for a moment. "Two weeks is high. It was more like ten days."

"What's Remy's last name?"

"Gomez."

"Know where he lives?"

"I wish I did. I'd go kick his ass."

Diggs asked how Rusty and Remy had met.

"At the White Buffet, Remy was a cook. The stupid fuck got caught trying to steal money from the manager's office. Got his ass fired."

"Thank you, Mr. Boyer. Again, my sincere condolences."

"Before you go, can I ask you a legal question?"

"I'm not a lawyer but go ahead."

"You said everything is between you and me, right?"

"Everything."

Boyer looked Diggs over for a couple of seconds, searching for something to convince him he was making the right decision. He glanced at Mr. Hyde and after another drag, he said, "I found some shit in Rusty's room. An expensive electronic thing under his bed. There was more hidden in a box in his closet. All Apple shit. Brand new, still wrapped in cellophane. He must have stolen it and planned on turning it. I meant to talk to him about it, but I never got the chance. I've been around long enough to know that something was up. I didn't want him making the same mistakes I did. You know what I mean?"

Diggs told him he did.

"After he died, I figured the cops would come by and I

didn't want his mom finding it. I took the box and put it in my trunk. Now, I don't know what the hell to do with it. Dump it in the desert? Fess up and tell the cops I found it? I've had problems with the law in the past and I don't need any more trouble, and Rusty's mom doesn't need to know about it."

"How much is there?"

"Phones, watches, other shit that I wouldn't have any idea how to use even if I wanted to."

Diggs asked him to show him. Boyer led him to the same graveled lot where he was parked.

"The sheriff came by this morning. He searched Rusty's bedroom. Didn't have a warrant, but I let him. I think he knew about the stuff."

"How so?"

"He wanted to know if Rusty had any computers. He specifically mentioned Apple. I was trying to protect Rusty's mom, so I lied. I admit it was a dumbass move, but the shock of Rusty's death made me want to protect him more than ever. I told the sheriff that Rusty had an old computer that he'd had since high school. I showed it to him and he took it away."

Noah stopped at an older-model SUV parked four cars away from Diggs. He popped the trunk and Diggs sorted through the box. There were five iPhones, four iPads, four watches, and one MacBook Pro. All were sealed except for a single iPad Mini out of its packaging. Diggs lifted it out of the box. The charging cord was attached.

"That's what I found under his bed."

Diggs looked it over. He tapped the screen and it remained black. He laid it beside the box. "I'm heading down to Phoenix. I'll drop this off at an Apple store. Tell them I found it by a dumpster. I'll show them my badge. They'll believe me."

"That's fine with me. I don't want any part of this."

"Do the cops have Rusty's cell phone?"

"I never thought to ask. I didn't see it in his room. Unless it got smashed by that fuck who killed Rusty, I guess they must."

"What else did the sheriff say?"

"Offered his condolences. Said he'd do his best. He didn't sound too hopeful. He said he'd check the Burger King for video."

"Had Rusty ever been arrested?"

"No, he was a good kid. A weird kid but a good one." He nodded toward the box in his trunk. "I'm surprised as shit about this."

"Thank you, Mr. Boyer. If you don't mind, do me a favor. If the police come back, keep our visit private."

Boyer made it abundantly clear that he would. He placed the box of electronics in Diggs' trunk. Diggs laid Rusty's iPad on the backseat. As he opened the passenger door for Hyde, he asked, "Before I go, I'd like to ask you a couple basic questions. I'll be tape recording you. Is that okay?"

"I guess."

Diggs turned on his phone's voice recorder. He asked Boyer the date of Rusty's birthday, the date of his mother's birthday, Rusty's high school graduation year, any lucky numbers, favorite football teams or players, Noah's date of birth.

"Any other important dates in Rusty's life?"

"None that I can think of. Why are you asking?"

"I'm hoping for a lucky break."

*   *   *

Diggs found the Burger King further west on County Road. He parked along the street, roughly where Boyer had said he found Rusty. He patrolled the side of the road and saw no skid marks or displaced sand. He saw nothing that made him believe that the vehicle had hit anything other than Rusty.

He also didn't find any shrines with colorful balloons or bouquets of flowers, but Diggs never expected that. Beautiful young teenagers with potential were granted shrines. Dead twenty-two-year-old misfits who worked as busboys rarely rated more than a sentence or two in the local newspaper.

The sun was shining on another part of the world and Diggs could feel the temperature dropping. Hyde's head stuck through the driver's side window. Semitrucks zoomed past, leaving behind a burst of air so strong that it could knock a child off his feet. Standing so close to the road without the light of the sun felt life-threatening. Even the best driver could lose focus for the briefest of moments, accidently veer over a line, and mow down a young man on his way to Burger King. It could happen so easily—it might have happened before—but that's not how Diggs figured it.

Diggs opened the car door and nudged Hyde to the passenger seat. As they sped toward the highway, Diggs thought about the red house on the hill with the plume of gray smoke drifting toward the heavens. It reminded him of a fuse attached to a bomb. He remembered what Noah Boyer had said. He thought he understood why Rusty wanted no part of White's party. He speculated on how Hyde might have found his way into the barn. Diggs reached across the seat and laid a hand on his friend chewing on a rubber ball.

Diggs pulled into a gas station and purchased four newspapers and a five-gallon plastic gasoline container. He filled the container with premium octane and continued to the highway entrance ramp. Rather than go east toward the Western Jewel, Diggs entered the ramp heading west.

Diggs was telling himself he hadn't decided, but his mind had been made up before he bought the gasoline. Claustrophobic cages. Cruel indifference. The exchange of cash for the entertainment of suffering.

Knowing the location of the barn made it easy to spot. A narrow dirt road cut off of Iguana and appeared to end somewhere near it.

Diggs turned onto the road. He stopped a hundred feet from the barn and maneuvered so that the hood of his car faced Iguana. Hyde couldn't sit still. He paced back and forth on the seat and whined. Diggs touched under his friend's jaw and looked him in the eye. "Don't worry, it's okay."

Diggs lifted the gasoline container and the newspapers from the backseat and jogged toward the barn with the container in his right hand and the newspapers under the crux of his arm. Cloud cover made the terrain darker than it had been the night before. His left hand held his phone, its flashlight pointed at the path in front of him.

Diggs stopped at the barn door. No light emitted from the inside. He pulled open the door to complete darkness. The steady shine of his flashlight made several paths across the walls. The dogs and the cages were gone. The chain-link fence cage remained, but the folding chairs had been stacked against a wall. Nobody was inside and there was no reason to abort.

Diggs poured gasoline at the base of three vertical wooden beams and covered each with newspaper. He poured the remaining gasoline against the interior walls. He lit what newspaper remained and placed it at the base of the gasoline-doused beam closest to the door. He dropped a lit match onto the newspaper. Hungry flames quickly rose. Thick suffocating smoke chased Diggs out of the barn.

*   *   *

Diggs approached the Highway 23 ramp at the legal rate of speed. The air rushing through the open windows erased the smoky scent from his clothing. Mr. Hyde sat in his seat, staring past Diggs, mesmerized by crazed orange flames dancing against the charcoal black sky.

20

In a blur of movement, Diggs raised his head from his pillow. Except for a sliver of daylight that had snuck between the curtains, the room was dark. Through foggy eyes, he searched for the iPad. It was laid on the desk exactly where he left it, its charging cord connected to an outlet. He slipped from under the sheets and off the bed. When he tapped the center of the iPad, the passcode screen lit up.

He nudged the iPad aside and opened his e-mail. At the top of his inbox, a response from Billy T. waited.

Hi Malcolm,

Sorry you won't be able to make it as scheduled. I can give you until Saturday, but after that I can't promise I can hold the magazines. Another buyer is very interested. Since we've been in contact for a while, you can still have first crack, but we have to get this done by Saturday at the latest. If you can't make it, I'm going to contact him. I hope you understand.

Billy T.

Diggs wrote a response promising that he would be at the storage facility on Saturday at 1:00 p.m. He unplugged the iPad and returned to bed.

Diggs propped pillows against the headboard and lay on his back, holding the iPad five inches from his chest. A six-digit numerical password or facial ID was required to unlock it. From his phone, he played back the numbers and dates Boyer had provided.

Rusty's date of birth didn't work. Nor did Noah's. Nor did Rusty's mother's. Nor did his graduation date. Rusty's lucky number was twenty-one. Diggs typed 2-1-2-1-2-1. That got him nowhere. He typed in Kurt Warner's uniform number three times. That didn't work. He tried 1-2-3-4-5-6 and then he tried 1-2-1-2-1-2. The iPad remained locked.

Diggs felt gloomy and doubtful. Even if he could break the code, the iPad might offer nothing more than a collection of music and games.

He returned to the desk and typed in a Google search for *Apple electronics store theft—Nevada*. He found nothing that fit the bill in Nevada, but a robbery had been committed in Utah three weeks before. An electronics store in St. George reported an armed robbery just before closing. A man described as very large and wearing a ski-mask entered the store. Armed with a knife, he made the lone employee open a locked cage that contained the store's inventory of Apple products. The employee was then forced to pile the merchandise into an SUV that had been reported stolen three hours before. Once the SUV was loaded, the robber punched the employee in the face, breaking his nose. The SUV was found three miles away abandoned in a mini mall parking lot. The estimated loss was 30,000 dollars.

Diggs made a rough guess at the cost of the merchandise in his trunk and estimated zero chance it was worth 30,000 dollars.

At the time the article was published, no suspect had been arrested. Diggs searched for follow-ups and found nothing. He mapped the distance between St. George and his location. A four-hour drive from the 15 freeway to the 93 to Mojave Creek.

The described robber couldn't have been Rusty but it sure could have been Remy. The size was right and punching a frightened man in the face sounded right up Remy's alley. The newspaper account never alluded to a second robber and the employee was made to load the electronics into the stolen SUV. A risky move—it took more time and it gave the employee a chance to escape. A robbery that was ideally a two-person job but committed by one.

Diggs figured that Rusty could have had a role that wasn't clear. Driving the getaway car back to Mojave Creek while Remy hid in the back seat would have been smart, but did Rusty even know how to drive? If Rusty played no role, why would Remy give him a few thousand dollars' worth of merchandise? To sell or fence? Diggs recalled Noah Boyer's claim that Rusty was no longer Remy's friend, but somewhere along the way they had made up. Was Rusty's stash a make-up gift?

Mr. Hyde stood on the bed staring at Diggs with somber eyes. Diggs grinned as he spoke. "Patience, my friend. I haven't forgotten."

As Hyde wolfed down his breakfast, Diggs opened Facebook and searched for Rusty Boyer. Other than being pleasantly surprised that Rusty had a Facebook account, there wasn't much reason for rejoicing. His account was an incomplete work of nothing more than a handful of superficial facts—a back-lot movie façade and nothing remotely close to what Diggs had hoped for.

Rusty had been born in Mojave Creek and graduated high school four years before. He enjoyed the *Pimp My Wheels* television show and Pearl Jam. His Friends section included zero entries.

Rusty's profile picture was the only image his page offered. He stood beside his Uncle Noah in front of a stadium with his arms held in a touchdown pose. They both wore broad, happy smiles. The caption read: *Big Win! Cardinals top the always tough Ravens 26 - 18!* A cross-check with the Cardinals website revealed that the game was played on October 26, 2015. Diggs typed 1-0-2-6-1-5 into the iPad. It remained locked.

If numbers weren't going to get him anywhere, Diggs hoped that words might. On the iPad lock screen were numbers one through nine in three rows. Centered below the bottom row was zero. Starting with the number two and ending with the number six, three alphabetized letters were assigned to each number. The number seven included four letters: P, Q, R, S. The number eight had the next three letters and nine had the last four letters: W, X, Y, Z.

Diggs tried to think of any six-letter words that might have held any special importance to Rusty. 7-8-7-8-9-2—RustyB—didn't work. Neither did his favorite Cardinal player, Warner—9-2-7-6-3-7—or his mother's name, LindaB—5-4-6-3-2-2.

Diggs considered calling Apple technical support, but it didn't take more than a moment for him to scratch that thought. The iPad had been stolen and the support tech would know the moment he typed in the serial number. Diggs searched the web for articles instructing how to break into an iPad and several products existed, but none could guarantee that the data wouldn't be wiped clean at the same time.

Diggs set the iPad aside and opened the same people-finding website that had led him to Noah Boyer. There were nineteen results for Gomez in Mojave Creek and none of them were named Remy.

He tried social media and was pleased to find that Remy Gomez took it seriously, or at least he did at one time. His Facebook profile picture showed a preening wannabe tough guy desperately trying to market a nasty attitude. Standing against a wall, wearing a blue jean jacket, his shoulders were slouched and his arms were crossed defiantly. He stared contemptuously into the camera lens. His hair was short and heavily gelled. He appeared at least ten pounds lighter than when they had tangled at the Sleeping Volcano.

Remy Gomez was as garrulous as an afternoon talk-show host. An enthusiast of MMA and John Wick movies, he also had a love for death metal, listing Cannibal Corpse, Death Angel, and Obituary as favorites. World War II documentaries, serial killers, and Martin Scorsese gangster movies thrilled him. He graduated from high school two years before Rusty. His Friends page included two females and three males, none of whom were Rusty Boyer.

Up until two weeks before, Remy Gomez posted to his timeline regularly, writing of faraway concerts he wished he could attend and opining on popular culture. He wrote of fights he'd participated in, and shockingly he always came away the victor. Never did Remy Gomez write of a having a job or girlfriend.

There were no signs of a father or any siblings, but there were several photos of Remy's mother Mary, a prim-looking, conservatively dressed woman with a delicate build and gray hair that was always tied in a tight bun. In several shots, Remy stood or sat beside her and most of the time he appeared happy. He announced her passing six months before. After her death, his postings became more irregular.

Gomez's October 18th posting was his last and his most peculiar—a photo with a mostly black background except for three blurred objects, each with a dot of red following one after the other. The caption read: *What's going on? Not my problem. Going back to bed.*

Diggs downloaded the photo and used an editing tool to play with the coloring. He dulled the background and brought out the colors. Soon, it became clear that he was looking at three police cruisers, shot from a high angle. The blurriness of the image had a jerky just-got-out-of-bed shaky-hand feel. The caption implied that the cruisers were loud enough to wake a sleeping man. That indicated to Diggs that the cruisers were responding to an urgent call. The date of the post was familiar. Diggs confirmed that October 18th was the day that the Geist family were found murdered in their home.

Diggs continued to adjust the colors in the photo. By adding light to everything except the cruisers, he made out a fat L-shaped object. He added some darker hues and lowered the contrast. He fiddled with colors like a recording engineer would play with a sound board. He figured out that the fat L was two houses set fairly close together. Remy Gomez lived in a two-story home across the street from a two-story beside a ranch house.

Not quite fifteen minutes later, Diggs and Hyde were cruising Blackhorse Lane barely above a slow crawl. A decidedly Midwest ambience surprised Diggs. Most of the homes had grass front yards rather than colored rocks and mani-cured sand. Large trees paralleled the length of the street. The news reports described the Geist's neighborhood as quiet and middle-class, and that was accurate.

The pattern of a two-story across the street from a two-story beside a ranch was more common than Diggs hoped. When he reached the Geist house, he stopped. It was a two-story gray-painted stucco. Light blue shutters framed a large front window. Yellow crime-scene tape made an X across the front door. A fresh lawnmower path was easily visible on the front lawn. Across the street were two side-by-side ranch homes.

Diggs circled the block with his window rolled down searching for someone to strike up a conversation with. He passed two joggers but kept on driving. At best, they'd only allow him a couple of seconds of their time, and they might be suspicious of a stranger meandering through their neigh-borhood. He might end up answering more questions than asking.

He was circling back toward the Geist home when he saw a man at the front of his house watering plants. A woman with two young children tossed a beach ball. Diggs parked a few houses away and got out of the car. He clipped on Hyde's leash and walked in the direction of the family.

When he reached the front of their house, he called out, "Good morning."

The two little girls squealed. "Look at the doggy!"

"He's very friendly. If your mom says it's okay, he'd be happy to meet you."

Both girls stared pleadingly at their mom. A nod sent them scampering towards Hyde.

For a moment, the little girls stood in awe. One said, "Look at his face!"

The other said, "All those wrinkles!"

"His name is Mr. Hyde. You can pet him if you want."

The girls fell to their knees, showering Hyde with attention.

The mom had caught up. She said, "He's a beautiful dog."

"Yes, he is."

The father walked over. He said, "Haven't noticed you before. You live around here?"

"My name is Leonard Diggs. I'm a detective from San Diego, working on a case." He showed him his badge and identification. "I was on my way to speak with someone who might be able to help me with a case, but I'm a little lost and he's not answering his texts. In the meantime, I thought I'd walk the dog."

"You're a long way from San Diego."

Diggs grinned. "Unfortunately, criminals know no boundaries."

"You always take your dog on cases?"

"If it's possible."

The man let that sit for a second and then nodded with an uneasy smile. "I'm Lionel Gutierrez. You mind if we talk over there?"

Diggs handed the leash to Gutierrez's wife and followed him to the plants he'd been watering.

"Does your case have anything to do with the Geists?"

"No, nothing at all. I read about it though. I bet it was quite a shock to the neighborhood."

"It sure was. I know everyone says it, but I never expected something like that to happen here. I went out and bought a gun."

"Were you friends?"

"I knew Bill a little bit, but I wouldn't say we were friends. Once in a while, we'd talk. My wife and I went to the vigil at the park—the Hugs and Kisses Celebration. I think most of Mojave Creek went to that one."

Diggs asked if anyone from the Mojave Creek police department had spoken with him.

"The sheriff came by. I couldn't help him. We were all in bed. None of us saw or heard a thing."

"You have any opinions as to why it happened?"

"There's been a lot of talk about drugs. To me that's far-fetched. Bill had his pot-smoking motorcycle buddies—bunch of space cadets, if you ask me. They called themselves the Weekend Warriors."

He rolled his eyes. Diggs smirked.

"Met a couple of the Weekend Warriors once or twice. Had no interest in hanging out with them. If any of those guys were big-time drug dealers, I'm El Chapo. The cops might want to look into Bill's gambling, but they probably already have and it's probably a waste of time anyway."

"Mr. Geist was a gambler?"

"Not as much as claimed. At least, I didn't believe him. He bragged about his system a couple of times. Said he always won big, which I didn't believe for a second. Said he won so much that he often thought about quitting his job. As far as I know, he never did."

"Did he gamble around here or in Las Vegas?"

"He told me Laughlin. Supposedly, he had some kind of inside information at one of the casinos."

Gutierrez glanced at his girls and his wife playing with Hyde. "You know what I think really happened?"

Diggs told him that he'd be interested to know.

"I don't think drugs or gambling money is behind any of this. I think the cops should take a hard look at Jerad White, but being that his father practically owns Mojave Creek, he's probably off limits."

"Why Jerad?"

"He assaulted Bill at a bar. According to Bill he did, anyway. Jerad was with a girl. Bill and the girl started chatting. Bill said that it was all totally innocent. He wasn't coming on to her. He said they were literally talking about the weather when all of a sudden she takes offense to something he said. He told me he had no idea what. Bill said he apologized, but the girl wouldn't let it go. An argument started and then Jerad got involved and punched him. Knocked a few teeth loose."

"I don't know about Nevada law, but in California, an assault like that will get you jail time."

"That's what Bill thought. I think he was looking for a settlement."

"When did this happen?"

"He told me about it a few weeks ago. I don't know the exact date that it happened."

"Was there a resolution?"

"That's what I'm saying. Bill never got the chance."

"You tell the police about this?

"Sure did."

Diggs guessed that Potter reacted the same way he would have. Unless Jerad was a straight-to-DVD psychopath, he wasn't going to viciously murder an entire family when his father could write a check and make the problem go away.

Diggs pulled his phone from his pocket. "Still no text. You wouldn't happen to know where Remy Gomez lives?"

Gutierrez called out to his wife, "Honey, who lives in that hellhole over on Maricopa? Is it Gomez?"

She yelled back, "That's him."

Gutierrez's shoulders collapsed in an exaggerated manner. "Can you please take him back to San Diego with you?"

Diggs smiled. "What's he done this time?"

"He's been doing a fine job of bringing down everyone's property values."

Diggs chose not to remind him that a triple murder six houses over wasn't going to help his property values either.

"Where's Maricopa?"

He pointed west. "Three streets over."

"What is he doing that's bringing down property values?"

"Take a look and you'll catch my drift. God only knows what it looks like inside."

They walked to the girls who were laughing and shrieking. Hyde was crawling over the chest of the smaller girl.

The other girl giggled. "We love your dog."

Diggs told them that unfortunately he and Hyde had to leave. The girls whined and made him promise that he'd bring Mr. Hyde back.

Once they were in the car, Diggs rubbed the top of Hyde's head. "Well played, my friend. First Boyer and now these folks. You are a becoming quite a valuable secret weapon."

Diggs found Maricopa and recognized Remy Gomez's home immediately. It was the two-story mess with a front yard of dead grass and deep skid marks. The eyesore with an oil-stained driveway and a battered ten-year-old Ford pickup parked in the front yard at a comically awkward angle. The once nice middle-class home that now had an aura of a dead carcass and a future as bright as a skid-row drug den. And directly across the street from this nightmare was a two-story home beside a ranch home.

Diggs parked two houses away. The car's thermometer read seventy-one. Long, thin white clouds were doing an adequate job of blocking the sun. Diggs opened all four windows a third of the way.

His gun was hidden under the front seat and for a moment, he considered bringing it along, but he wasn't in Mojave Creek as a cop. He had no jurisdiction or any benefit of the doubt. A gun invited problems and Diggs figured that unless he was fully prepared to use it, he was better off without it. A gun hadn't been necessary the first time, and he had no interest being involved in any kind of fracas anyway. He was there to offer Remy condolences or, if necessary, break the news and then ask his questions. If a worst-case scenario broke out, he'd find a way to handle it, but because violence remained a possibility, Diggs decided that Hyde would sit this one out.

Hyde stood on his seat, ready for another walk. Diggs looked into his eyes and touched under his muzzle. "Sorry, I promise I won't be long."

He left the car and walked directly to Gomez's front door, his body language carefree, his arms swinging loosely at his sides. If Remy was watching, he wanted to appear as non-threatening as possible. He rang the doorbell and took an immediate two steps backwards in case Remy wasn't adept at reading friendly body language. Fifteen seconds later he rang the doorbell again. Out of the corner of his eye, he watched the closed drapes for movement. He wasn't catching anything, and the door wasn't being answered.

He headed round to the back of the house for no reason

other than he didn't want to leave until he was certain that no one was home.

The backyard was a case of negligence over chaos. A square plot of uneven yellow grass and aggressive weeds was surrounded by chain-link fencing. A broken outdoor lounge chair and a filthy grill took up most of a small cement patio. A single stair led from the patio to a sliding glass door without any blinds or shades.

Diggs edged to the door. He peered through dirty glass and there was Remy wearing a white-t-shirt, sitting on a chair at a dining room table. Diggs took three quick steps backwards. He had his words ready: Rusty was dead and he was a cop. If that didn't assuage him, another brawl was probably on the way.

Ten seconds had passed and the sliding glass door hadn't opened. Remy hadn't even stepped up to the glass. Once more, Diggs approached the door.

Remy was sitting exactly how he had been the first time around. His hands were resting on his lap and his head was in a slightly tilted position, as if he was watching something intellectually fascinating on television. Diggs raised a hand and snapped his fingers. No reaction. He placed his nose to the glass. He saw a thin taut wire connected from Remy's neck to the base of a light fixture.

Diggs pulled a tissue from his pocket. He tugged on the door. It slid open and he stepped inside.

21

An electronic ringing that Diggs immediately recognized echoed. Quickly, he scanned the kitchen counters and surrounding area for an AI device. Seeing none, he turned his attention to a very dead Remy Gomez. His face was shaded blue and his eyes were bulging from their sockets. His hair was tangled and messy, and the wire connecting his neck to the fixture was as taut as a guitar string. There were no blood drippings on his white t-shirt or on his bare legs, nor were there any streaks running down his neck.

The lack of blood didn't make sense until Diggs saw the needle protruding as straight as a skyscraper from Remy's left forearm. On the dining table, a note along with a pile of unopened mail, a syringe, a razor knife, and an open black 35mm film canister lay on its side. A quarter-inch line of white powder trailed from its opening. Two possible modes of death. Remy was determined not to screw up. The note had been handwritten on a sheet of plain white, letter-sized paper.

I murdered the Geists. I murdered Julia. I am evil. I am a coward. I deserve a painful merciless death.

Diggs' skin began to crawl. The constant beats of the

computerized clang were adding to the creepy aura that seemed to exist in every suicide house Diggs had ever stepped into. A stillness that cried out. A home missing its soul.

Diggs searched Remy's arms for track marks or any telltale scars of a longtime addict and found nothing. He thought back to Remy's Facebook page. Fights were often bragged about. Tales of drunkenness were fairly common. Diggs recalled not a single mention of drug use.

The small amount of blood around Remy's neck indicated that the needle had finished him off before the wire could. Diggs figured that Remy overdosed and at near death, gravity began to slowly pull his body downwards, allowing the ligature to saw into his flesh.

Diggs flicked the top of the needle with his index finger and it didn't budge. Rigor had set in. Remy had been dead for at least two hours.

Diggs went back to the suicide note. Remy's handwriting had a disjointed start-and-stop quality that struck Diggs as curious. The stem of the "d" in "deserve" broke off making it look like an "o" beside an "l." The stem in the "J" in "Julia" also broke off, making it appear like a "u" and an "i." A two-letter gap between the "c" and the "i" in "merciless" made Diggs wonder if Remy had injected the drugs into his arm before beginning the letter. As his mind drifted further and further into the void, his writing got sloppier and his pauses longer. Diggs eyed the table looking for any other samples of Remy's writing or any blank sheets of white letter-sized paper and found nothing.

The perpetual electronic ringing had become twenty-first century Chinese water torture. Diggs stepped into the kitchen and searched. Behind a mass of balled-up plastic grocery bags he found the AI device pulsating an orange glow.

Diggs had the same device at home. He spoke clearly: "How long was the timer set for?"

The device answered, "Your twenty-one-minute timer is ringing, and no other timer is set."

The top of the stove was nearly spotless, and in that filthy kitchen, it stood out. Diggs pulled opened the oven door with his tissue. The inside of the oven was room temperature and with the exception of several old pieces of charred food, it was empty. Plenty of dirty dishes were stacked in the sink and several used drinking glasses were set about here and there, but Diggs saw nothing that required a timer.

He found a trashcan under the sink. Floating at the top, an empty bag of potato chips and beneath it, nothing that would have needed a twenty-one-minute timer.

Diggs scoured the immediate area trying to figure out why a twenty-one-minute timer had been set, but saw nothing that provided an answer. He glanced at his phone. He had been inside the house for just over five minutes and on the property for an additional three. He needed to get out soon.

He stepped into the dining room to take a closer look at the connection of wire to fixture. A square knot. Common enough and secure but tricky with thin, sharp wire. He bent to a knee and looked at Remy's fingers. Not a single cut. His eyes searched the table and then the floor. There were enough crumbs to feed a colony of ants for years but no gloves.

Diggs noticed a dark red circle around Remy's right ankle. Over mild bruising, frayed skin rose like shag carpeting. It appeared to be a ligature mark. Remy's left ankle showed nothing unusual. After snapping a photo of the strange marking, he read the suicide letter again. He found it interesting that Julia Geist had received her own sentence. He took a photo of the letter.

The smell of Remy's urine and feces had become noxious. Soon, the entire house would be consumed with the reek of death. Diggs glided from dining room to living room, stepping along a narrow path abutted on both sides by worn socks, video games, Amazon boxes, used paper plates, soda, and beer cans. Diggs stepped on the edge of a fast-food wrapper, which oozed out a portion of a burrito. Remy had been living at the bottom of a polluted river. Diggs half-expected to come across a worn-out tire.

Diggs hurried upstairs over badly stained orange carpeting. A peek inside the bathroom revealed a disgusting disarray that he fully expected. Like everything he had seen so far, Remy's bedroom was a disaster area. Diggs dodged balled-up clothes and random shoes. He nicked his hip on a dresser drawer left hanging open. In the corner of the room, a stack of sealed iPads, iMacs, iPhones, Apple Watches, and MacBook Pros were propped against a wall. Diggs guessed there was at least three times as much as he had in his trunk.

Diggs looked out a window onto the street. He saw a two-story home beside a ranch home. Without question it was the same window that Remy had shot the blurry photo of speeding police cruisers.

Using the tissue, Diggs opened a door that led to the second bedroom. In comparison to everything else he had seen, it was the VIP suite at a luxury hotel. The pillows were fluffed and placed side by side. The floral bedspread didn't show a single crease. Tiny porcelain religious figurines adorned the top of a dresser that should have been caked with dust but was polished and clean. Nothing was on the floor and the carpeting showed vacuum markings. Diggs left the room believing that Remy must have loved his mother very much.

His phone indicated that twelve minutes had passed. He rushed down the stairs and out the sliding glass door.

A plastic garbage bin at the side of the house caught his attention. Diggs lifted the bin's lid with the tissue. Resting on top of several trash bags was a frozen pizza box. Crushed and crumbled inside was a pizza that had spent some time in an oven. Slices of pepperoni had burn marks, and the cheese was melted and smeared. Diggs snapped a photo of the box and the pizza. He closed the bin and casually walked to his car.

An enthusiastic welcome awaited. Mr. Hyde danced in tiny circles and licked at Diggs' face like a camel slurping out of a bucket of water. It was sloppy and exhausting but after what Diggs had just witnessed, Hyde's genuine love felt very much welcomed.

Diggs drove from one end of Maricopa to the other. He hadn't noticed anyone sitting idly behind a steering wheel when he arrived, and he didn't see anyone on his way out.

Several miles away, he stopped at a convenience store and purchased dog treats and a burner phone. He parked along one of the countless lonely roads and dialed 911. Loosely covering his mouth with a hand and the radio turned up, he anonymously reported a dead body at the Gomez address.

Suspicions and dark thoughts raced through Diggs' investigative mind. He didn't believe Remy Gomez took his own life and if that were true, Rusty Boyer was likely not a gruesome accident caused by an inattentive trucker.

Diggs turned down the radio, switched off his phone, and began an aimless nowhere drive. Long bouts of random driving often worked as medicine to clear his head. Due to the daunting Southern California traffic, most of his reset drives were held late in the evening, or in the early morning hours. In Mojave Creek, a fifty-mile road trip might see twenty cars.

The open windows allowed an exhilarating cross-breeze of clean and damp air. Mr. Hyde lay on the passenger seat engaged in a ritual in which he'd poke his paw at the rubber ball. He'd watch the ball roll for a few moments and then he'd pick it up with his jaws. For several seconds, he'd sit patiently with the ball in his mouth and then, for reasons known only to him, he'd drop it and start all over again.

Diggs made a right and then a left and then two rights, all for the purpose of getting further nowhere. After a half hour or so of driving, he came upon a large park with a baseball diamond. Without a second thought, Diggs sailed into the entrance.

There were no other vehicles. No one was walking their dogs or jogging. The ten or so picnic tables were all empty. Nobody was strolling the park or sitting in the grass or on a bench. By all appearances, he and Mr. Hyde had the park all to themselves. Diggs cut the engine and exited. Ignoring Hyde's leash on the floor, he opened the passenger door and grabbed the ball from between Hyde's paws.

"I trust you. Let's go."

Together they jogged side by side. When they reached the home plate, Diggs bounced the ball twice before holding it in his open palm, allowing Hyde to stare it down lustfully.

Diggs cocked his arm back and hurled the ball into center field. Hyde immediately dashed after it like a hungry leopard chasing down an antelope. As Diggs rubbed his bicep, he watched with delight. Hyde caught up with the ball and sniffed at it for several seconds. Once he was satisfied with whatever he was sniffing for, he picked it up and trotted back.

Diggs took the ball from Hyde's mouth and looked in his eyes. "You ready, you crazy bastard?"

Diggs pivoted his body toward first base. He bent his knees slightly and counted out loud. At three, he ran toward first base with Hyde trotting alongside him. As he rounded second base, he hoped to pick up speed, but the forty-four-year-old tank was already low.

Mr. Hyde bounded along, keeping up as if it were no more than a leisurely stroll. By third base, Diggs could feel his lungs burning. He was running too fast and in the wrong shoes, but with only ninety feet to go, he accelerated into a dead sprint.

He made a perfect slide into home, but his body felt the pain of crashing to the hard dirt. He lay still on the ground with his arms extended and Hyde's nose sniffing his face. Staring at clouds rolling across the sky, he reached up with the ball in his hand.

"Here."

Hyde snatched it and lay next to him.

Watching the heavy clouds turn the dark blue sky into an ominous gray, Diggs marveled at how rapidly the years had fallen past. Once upon a time, the baseball diamond had been his sanctuary and for two glorious years, all had gone according to plan. He had his scholarship, and scouts from several big-league teams were interested, but then catastrophe struck during the first inning of the first game of his junior season.

Diggs lined a fastball between the center and right fielder. Diggs saw that the right fielder was fumbling with the ball. Certain that if he picked up speed the triple was his, he burst into another gear. As he turned his head from the outfield to the basepath, he saw the shortstop standing directly in front of him, his attention fully on the right fielder. Diggs tried a last-second dodge but they crashed. The shortstop got back to his feet with barely a scratch, while Diggs lay between second and third base, his knee ripped apart and his right hip fractured.

For the next year, Diggs rehabbed through setback after setback. After the first surgery, the hip wasn't healing properly. A second surgery was ordered and then a third. When Diggs thought his knee was improving, the tendons would begin to swell again. After a year, it was still painful to walk and impossible to run. Swinging a bat and moving his hips made him feel like a machine turned on for the first time in a hundred years.

Diggs tried to stay positive. He followed his doctor's advice to the letter and for fourteen months rehabbing became his full-time job. At some point, he realized that all the rehabbing in the world wasn't going to save the career he'd fantasized about since he was seven. Rather than admit that he gave up, he chose the route of many athletes with vanishing dreams. His physical therapy sessions got less frequent. Video sessions went from seven days a week to five and then to three and then none at all. At around the same time, he stopped watching practices. Then he quit going to games. In his mind, he knew it was over when his coaches stopped expecting anything from him. They allowed him to fade away at his own pace because they knew it would be less painful.

Giving up on the game and pursuing a career in law enforcement had been his first important decision as an adult. Over the next several years, all the choices that mapped out a life came one after another. At forty-four, his job was set. His habits had been established. His life was what it would pretty much always be. What he had left, or at least what he hoped he had left, were the pleasant surprises. The tiny twists and turns that would improve upon what had become a dependable and predictable existence.

He lifted himself into a sitting position and watched Mr. Hyde chew into his archenemy. Hyde was going to be one of those pleasant surprises. He wasn't going to spend a minute in a Phoenix shelter or a San Diego shelter, or any shelter at all. Mr. Hyde wasn't going anywhere. They were going to be a forever deal.

Diggs limped to the car with Hyde bopping beside him. He hurried back to the Western Jewel to catch the local news at six. Taped to his motel room door was a handwritten note. He was told to come to the office immediately. Diggs pulled the note off the door and laid it on top of the television.

As Diggs waited for the news to begin, he fed Hyde and then opened the *San Diego Union-Tribune* website. A headline story reported that Wackerly's one-time six-point lead had turned to a two-point deficit and Stall was receiving most of the credit for the turnaround. A poll conducted by the *Union-Tribune* ranked Stall as the most trusted man in San Diego.

A photo accompanying the article showed Stall in a football blocking pose, clearing the path for little Glen Palmer who was cradling the pigskin tightly under his tiny arm. It was as corny as anything Diggs had ever seen, but the childlike-hero role worked perfectly for Stall, and the elation on Glen Palmer's face was entirely authentic.

Diggs lay on the bed trying not to feel the aches in his muscles. A minute later, dramatic theme music followed by an anchorman's dire tone opened the newscast.

"Mojave Creek Sheriff Greg Potter has convened a news conference at City Hall. We now go there live."

While cameramen jockeyed for position, Potter stood

confidently behind a podium. A handful of well-dressed men and women made a half-circle behind him. The sheriff began to speak.

"Thank you for coming. After a thorough and exhaustive investigation encompassing thousands of manpower hours, I am happy to report that the murderer of William Geist, Farrah Geist, and Julia Geist has been identified. His name is Richard Edward Michael Gomez."

An angry pounding on the door vibrated the room. Hyde barked. Diggs bounced off the bed and peered between the curtains. It was the battleax. Her face was puffy and bruised.

22

A black bulge swelled to an ugly purple and black under her left eye. Before Diggs had a chance to say anything, her clipped voice said, "I want you to check out, now."

Diggs raised his hands in a calming gesture. "Hold on, what happened?"

Her inflections wavered between venom and despair. A tear fell from her damaged eye. "Here's what happened. Some little shit with a greasy smile and bandages on the side of his head came looking for you. I told him you already checked out. I have no interest involving myself in other people's business." She looked down at Mr. Hyde staring up at her from beside Diggs' leg. "But I like dogs and you have one who seems to be loyal to you.

"He called you Malcolm, but he described you to a tee. Even described your dog. When I told him you weren't here, he warned me to never lie to him and swatted me across the face like I was a house fly. Then he walked away whistling like a damn fool. Can you imagine that?"

"He was alone?"

"He came in alone. Someone was in his SUV."

"A large guy?"

"I didn't see him other than his head and shoulders. He had bandages on his face too, only a lot worse. He looked like the Invisible Man. They both looked like they escaped from the loony bin."

"Was the guy who hit you a paunchy Latino?"

"Sounds like him. Beady eyes, yellow teeth, smelled like cheap cigars. A real piece of garbage. Beats up a sixty-three-year-old woman for no reason. You have to leave."

Diggs backed away and reached for his wallet on the dresser. "I'm a cop." He showed her his badge and identification. He pointed over to his gun lying on the nightstand. "I can protect you."

Her voice rose, mockingly, she said, "How wonderful, a cop from San Diego. How exactly does that help me? And before you suggest we make a report with the local police, don't. That'll go nowhere."

Diggs could offer no acceptable response. Once he left Mojave Creek, his offer of protection would be as useful as his thoughts and prayers. The best he could do was offer an honest opinion. "He won't be back. He's not that ambitious. By now, he figures I've left town."

Diggs wrote his cell phone number on a sheet of Western Jewel-stamped notepad paper. Contradicting himself, he held it out. "If he comes back, here's my cell number."

She scowled at the phone number before raising her eyes to glare at him. She tried to work up a steely voice, but mostly she sounded terrified. "The license plate was taped over. They're pros."

"What color was the SUV?"

"Black and shiny and as big as a tank. The damn thing probably cost more than my house. You have to go."

Abruptly, she marched away. Diggs closed the door and sat on the edge of his bed. He thought about Johnny and man waiting for him in the expensive SUV.

By the time Diggs turned his attention to the television, the broadcast had moved from the press conference to the weather. Clouds and rain were predicted for the next several days.

Diggs found the press conference video on the Mojave Creek Sheriff Department website. He watched the conference from the beginning.

Potter revealed that Gomez became a serious suspect when an eyewitness claimed he saw Gomez at least twice after midnight sitting in his car watching the Geist home. A partial fingerprint from Gomez's right hand was found on the headboard of Julia Geist's bed. Before police could arrest Gomez for the murders of Julia, Farrah, and William Geist, he had taken his own life. A handwritten suicide note admitting to the murders was found beside his body.

Potter refused comment on Gomez's motive until a later date, nor would he confirm or deny if Julia Geist or Farrah Geist had been sexually assaulted. When Potter was asked if Gomez had accomplices, he said that only Gomez's DNA had been found at the scene. Potter refused to elaborate as to why Gomez chose the Geist family, but he assured that more details were forthcoming. Potter ended the press conference with words of inspiration.

"A beautiful family is now in the hands of God. A murderous predator has been taken off the streets and prepares to enter the gates of Hell. The citizens of Mojave Creek should say a prayer for Julia, Farrah, and William Geist."

Diggs took Hyde on his last walk of the night. Menacing black clouds marched over the horizon like an advancing army. Diggs was estimating when the storm would hit when his phone rang.

"Stall, good to hear from you," and it was.

"Sorry it took me so long to get back to you. Flores has been watching me like a hawk. It's frustrating. He keeps telling me he wants me to be myself but then he tells me exactly what I should say."

"So, what do you do?"

"I usually forget what he tells me anyway, so I just wing it. It's not all bad. They're treating Phoebe real well. She's made a lot of new friends. We both have. Glen and I have been spending time together, but I'll be glad when the election is over."

Diggs said, "Me too. Got something interesting?"

"You asked me to find the address on Harper or Reed, or whatever his name is. I did, and talk about a coincidence. He lived in Mojave Creek. That's where your sister lives, isn't it?"

Diggs told him it was.

"You think she knows him?"

"You never know, Stall. You never know. What's the address?"

"It was already checked out. A UPS store."

"Any forwarding address?"

"Yep, where we found Glen."

"Thanks, Stall. Anything else?"

"You wanted me to ask around for anything unusual. I think I have something."

Stall had already broken the bank with the news that Reed

had lived in Mojave Creek, but Diggs had no problem being greedy.

"Tell me."

"The autopsy results showed a ton of scars on Reed's body. He looked like something out of a Syrian torture camp. The investigators thought he might have been a prisoner of war. As far as I know, they haven't found any record of him serving, and the scars are too recent anyway. The coroner estimates them to be not even a year old."

"Anything else?"

"There's one more thing and this is top secret, boss. I need you to promise that you'll never tell anybody."

"Between you and me only."

There was a moment's pause. Diggs could picture Stall with narrowed eyes hunching his shoulders guardedly, craning his head in every direction until he was satisfied that no one was eavesdropping.

In a whisper, he said, "Reed did not sexually assault Glen."

It was terrific news that also seemed unfathomable. With no ransom angle, Diggs assumed Reed's motives must have been sexual. Diggs asked Stall how he knew.

"Glen said they watched DVDs all day. He said he slept a lot and the sedatives found in his system backed that up. He said that Reed never entered the room we found him in. Glen said Reed never forced himself on him or exposed himself or did anything remotely sexual. Glen has been adamant about that since day one. The doctor who examined him found nothing that would indicate otherwise. Glen spent several hours with a psychologist and she believes nothing sexual happened. The detectives in charge of the case are still skeptical. They think Glen is too traumatized to admit anything."

Everyone who followed the local news knew that Stall and Palmer had formed a tight friendship. Diggs asked, "What do you think?"

"I believe Glen one hundred and twenty percent. If something happened, he would have told me."

"Unless the abuse occurred while he was drugged."

"Like I said, the doctor that examined him found nothing to indicate any abuse. The psychologist asked Glen if he ever woke up with his clothes put on differently and he said no. Glen said that he took a shower every other day. Reed kept the door closed and he never entered."

"No peep holes?"

"They tore that place apart. Reed wasn't watching him. He wasn't filming him. He didn't own a camera. Not even a cell phone."

"Any trafficking angles?"

"He was a total loner."

"Has anyone determined Reed's motive?"

"No, and I don't know that we ever will. Glen's parents don't want him involved anymore. They don't think it's healthy for him, and I agree. Pelton is happy with the way things are. So is the chief. They want to let it go."

"There should be an inventory of items found in Reed's house. Can you email that list?"

"You want a list of the items found in Richard Reed's home? You mean, the residence on San Marcos that we found Glen at?"

Diggs wasn't sure what he had heard. He squinted into the phone. "Hold on, are you saying Reed had a second residence?"

"What! He does? Did you tell anybody?"

Diggs ran his fingers through his hair. "No, no, Stall. I

misunderstood you. There's no second residence. Let's go back to the beginning. Can you find the Reed file?"

"Yep, got it on my screen."

"Okay, find the pages that itemize what was found in his home. It's in there somewhere."

After several seconds of listening to Stall hum a catchy and frustratingly familiar tune that Diggs couldn't quite place, Stall said, "Got it right here. Do you want the apology letter too?"

"I don't know. What is it?"

"You should take a look. They found it in Reed's bedroom. I think it proves what Glen has been saying. It's more than that though. It's strange. I can't put my finger on it. I wish I had more time. I bet it would lead to something important."

Diggs was pleasantly shocked that Stall had formed opinions based on real evidence. "Stall, you're thinking like a detective. I'm proud of you. Send it along."

23

Attached to Stall's e-mail were two PDFs. The first was labelled *Inventory* and the second *A-Letter*. Diggs opened *Inventory* first. At the top of the page a heading read: *Reed, Richard Inventory List.* Below an underlined subheading read: *Living Room.* Beneath *Living Room,* a detailed single-spaced list ran a page and a half. On the third page, the inventory of the kitchen. On the fourth, the inventory found in Reed's bedroom., and on the fifth, the inventory of the room where Glen Palmer had been discovered.

The living room inventory included a sofa, side table, lamp, television, and various other items Diggs remembered seeing but that held no interest. The cardboard box beside the television was more intriguing. It contained twenty-six DVDs. The titles were virtually all Western-themed movies and television series from the 1950s and 60s—*Shane, The Virginian, Gunsmoke, The Searchers, High Noon, Rawhide,* amongst others. The lone non-Western: *Rev and Roll—The Complete Series.*

Reed had lived in Mojave Creek, he and Petey White were about the same age, and Reed had the *Rev and Roll* DVD in his possession. Diggs believed there was a better than average chance that Reed and White knew each other, but the three connections—location, age, and the DVD—were not nearly enough to conclusively tie them together.

Diggs accessed Petey White's IMDB page and clicked the *Rev and Roll* entry. The cast list stretched long with names Diggs vaguely recognized—Dack Rambo, Mary Crosby, Adrian Zmed—and others that went on to bigger careers—Melanie Griffith, Tom Selleck, Danny DeVito. Amongst the close to two hundred names, Diggs found no Richard Reed. Diggs typed Richard Reed into the IMDB database and found a few Richard Reeds, including two actors that were both too young to be his Richard Reed. Diggs searched Google using the phrase *Richard Reed—actor* and found nothing of value. He tried the same with Brian Harper and found nothing. He leaned back in his chair, disappointed that his theory had so far been foiled.

Diggs thought of other possibilities and gave it another go. He typed *Richard Reed—Petey White*, and came up blank. He typed *Richard Reed—Mojave Creek*, and missed again. He typed *Richard Reed—Rev and Roll*, and got a hit.

Two years earlier, *The Westerner* ran an article celebrating the thirty-seventh anniversary of the premiere of *Rev and Roll*. In the article, a Richard Reed who was identified as a "well-respected Hollywood producer" reflected on the pure artistic joy of working with Petey White. He made three asides to an episode titled *Murder is a Four-Letter Word*. Apparently, it was White's single directorial outing. Reed waxed on the significance of *Murder is a Four-Letter Word* as if he were pondering Orson Welles and *Citizen Kane*.

Diggs rechecked IMDB, focusing only on the *Murder is a Four-Letter Word* episode. Petey White was credited as the director. Richard Reed was not listed as a member of the production staff or as a producer.

In the article, Reed went on to say that he first met Petey White on the set of *Gunsmoke*. Reed joked that he had one line while White was an extra. In the next sentence, he backtracked as if White was standing over him, frowning displeasure. Reed claimed that White would have easily won the role, but he had a terrible cold the day of shooting and the director was a germaphobe. Even though White was far better suited for the role, the director offered it to Reed so that he wouldn't have to be near White's sniffling nose. Reed called White the most charismatic man he'd ever met and went on to claim that his mother worked with Jean Harlow on an early talkie. She told him that Harlow was the most charismatic performer she'd ever worked with. Reed mused that White and Harlow would have been a Hollywood dream pairing of the likes of Bogart and Bacall.

Diggs looked up *Gunsmoke* on IMDB. There had to be at least a thousand cast credits, but a search revealed no Richard Reed or Petey White. If White was an extra, it would make sense that he wasn't listed, but if Reed uttered any dialog, he should have been included.

Diggs scrolled through the credits. The stars always came first. James Arness was at the top of the list. Next came the series regulars and after that, cast members who had large enough roles that their character had a name. At the bottom were the uncredited actors. The ones who played the role of Townsman or Party Guest or Man on Horse. Being that Reed claimed to have only one line, Diggs suspected that if he was anywhere, he would be amongst the uncredited actors, but since Richard Reed wasn't in the general search, Diggs wasn't going to find him with the uncredited actors. He scrolled absentmindedly through the list, staring at black and white faces of performers, most of whom were long dead, while he tried to figure out his next move.

Near the bottom of the list, directly below an actor who played the role of Card Cheat, was a face that leapt from the screen and practically grabbed Diggs by the throat. The actor was a strangely handsome young man. In the photo, he looked no older than twenty. His soft somewhat effeminate facial features and his model-high cheekbones could have typecast him as the safe and non-threatening leading man, or the critically ill young husband, or the crusading junior attorney teamed with an older more experienced barrister, but his wild eyes would probably make that impossible. Large and round like an owl's, as dark and mysterious as a black hole, as unpredictable as untreated bi-polar disorder. A twinkle from his eye might mean he saved a young girl's life, or he strangled her and threw her under a train. His eyes would typecast him as a dangerous psychopath, a sympathetic nutcase, or somewhere in-between. The name beside the photo took Diggs' breath away. He whispered in awe at the screen. "You've got to be kidding."

He clicked the link beside the name and he was taken to Ricky Racine's IMDB page. Eight years after his appearance on *Gunsmoke*, Racine would co-star with Petey White in *Rev and Roll* as Rev Davis, Howard Roll's lunatic partner.

Racine's IMDB page included only five photos, all from *Rev and Roll*. Diggs opened the photo that offered the best shot of Racine's face—a black and white cast shot from its second season.

Racine sat on a desk at a make-believe police precinct. His hair was long and blonde, his shirt unbuttoned to the navel.

Tight blue jeans and black boots that nobody would ever dare to run in completed the hackneyed Southern California cop ensemble. Petey White stood to Racine's right in a starched three-piece suit, his face consumed with agitation.

Diggs enlarged the photo. Racine's thin face was reminiscent of the man who falsely identified himself as Brian Harper. Like Harper, Racine's legs were long. His rear end sat squarely on the center of the desk and his feet still touched the floor.

When Diggs watched *Rev and Roll*, he never got the sense that the height difference between Racine and White was significant, but back then he wasn't a particularly sophisticated viewer. White could have been standing on a crate of bananas for all he knew.

Diggs thought back to the Harper interrogation. The jagged scars under Harper's eyes had been noticeable enough to catch his attention. At some point, had Racine attempted cosmetic surgery, perhaps to escape unwanted typecasting? Diggs clicked on Racine's bio.

Ricky Racine was born on October 31, 1950 in Sparrow, Oklahoma, USA. He is an actor, known for Rev and Roll (1975–1979). He attended Langston University on a basketball scholarship. Racine's mother Florence Racine was an actress who worked with Jean Harlow on The Secret Six.

Jean Harlow clinched it. Richard Miller aka Brian Harper aka Richard Reed was in reality Ricky Racine, the eccentric co-star of *Rev and Roll* who left Hollywood to join a cult in Northern California.

Diggs next opened the PDF file labelled *A-Letter*. It had

been handwritten on the kind of spiral notebook paper sold just about anywhere.

Mr. P. I'm so very sorry. I've done some terrible things. I tried to be an honorable man, but I failed. My only excuse is that I faced devils and I weakly submitted. That was in the past. It will never happen again. I'm a changed man, I've proven that. From here on out, I'll be the friend you can always trust. Please forgive me.

Love,

Your faithful amigo

Diggs didn't know for certain why the letter hadn't been sent other than it could have been a draft and maybe a different version had been sent, or Racine and Mr. P. could have communicated in another way, making the letter unnecessary. Only Mr. P. would know for sure, which raised the question: who was Mr. P?

It seemed obvious that Mr. P. was Petey White, but Diggs wanted conclusive proof, and he thought he'd seen it. The confirmation came in the twelfth paragraph of the *Rev and Roll* thirty-seventh anniversary article.

Racine said, "That shows you what a tremendous actor Petey was. He won an Emmy playing a shy and conservative character—the kind of man who spent New Year's Eve baking cookies with his mom. In his real life, Mr. P. had as much fun as anyone in Hollywood."

Diggs took Hyde for one last walk around the motel. Four empty cars, three with out-of-state plates and a beat-up in-state Accord scattered about the lot. No sign of a shiny black SUV.

Diggs reread the apology letter in his head. Something Harper had said in custody didn't jibe. He walked across the courtyard and peered through the glass doors into the motel lobby. A young guy sat behind the front desk staring into his phone. Diggs and Hyde stepped inside. Immediately his attention turned to the front entrance.

"Good evening, is Esther around?"

"She goes home at ten."

"Quiet tonight."

"So far. I hope it stays that way."

Diggs wished him a good night and returned to his room. He was pulling the bedspread over his shoulder when his phone rang. Diggs read the number and picked up immediately.

"Sheriff Potter, I'm glad you called."

"Sorry it had to be so late. I've been meaning to get back to you, but as you probably heard, it's been busy around here."

Potter's voice was loud and full of energy, even a little tipsy. Nearly shouting, he said, "I have news that will interest you."

Diggs was suspicious enough of Potter that whatever he had to say would be taken with skepticism. Before Diggs could respond, Potter added, "I found your sister."

Then he added a qualifier as big as Mojave Creek. "She's in Texas."

"How do you know?"

"She made a purchase at a grocery store in San Antonio. That was yesterday. Nothing today."

"Has she been arrested?"

"No."

"Any other charges before the grocery store?"

"Quite a few. A couple days before a charge at a Hampton Inn in Kirby. A Comfort Inn a day later. A gas station in Austin. Let's see… Two convenience stores. A car wash in Fredericksburg. A number of restaurants in the same general Texas area."

"Any video proving Claire made the purchases?"

"I'm working on that."

Diggs frowned and mouthed into the phone, "Sure you are."

"Why all the effort? A couple days ago, you acted like you didn't know who Claire was, when obviously you did."

"Of course I knew who Claire was. I didn't know who you were. Your sister is devious. Before I could be straight with you, I needed to know your story."

"You still don't know my story."

"Yes, I do. I've had a chance to do some checking up. You have the reputation of being kind of a jerk but extremely proficient."

"Did you get my message about the fireman smelling burnt flesh at Claire's home?"

"I was told."

"And?"

"And nothing. I don't believe him. Detective, you're not familiar with the local personalities. To put it kindly, Robby is an obsessive storyteller who desperately wants to be seen as important. He's applied to the police department twice already and as long as I'm here, he won't be considered."

"You didn't check the route between her house and the hospital?"

"I didn't believe there was any point, and I was right. If you want to find your sister, take a drive to San Antonio."

Potter was full of shit, but for the time being, Diggs kept it to himself. "You going to have her arrested?"

"Soon. I'll have to spend taxpayer money to get her back here. Why don't you do me a favor and bring her back for us. I'll promise you a key to the city."

Diggs ignored Potter's over-the-top chortle. "You ever find the cause of the fire at her house?"

"Arson. I suspect Claire knew several charges were coming. She torched her place, probably to destroy evidence."

"Any proof of that?"

"No, speculating is all."

"You say you haven't seen any video of Claire making these alleged purchases in San Antonio?"

"Not yet, I'm working on that."

"Any idea what evidence Claire was trying to destroy?"

"We'll probably never know for certain."

Up to that point, Diggs had forced himself to be cordial with Potter to make things easier for himself, but he no longer cared.

"I assume you've heard of identity theft?"

Potter sighed into the phone. "Yes, Detective, I'm familiar with identity theft."

Diggs snarled, "Then before you make sweeping assumptions, make sure you know what the hell you're talking about."

"Thanks for the advice. Have a safe trip back to San Diego." The line went dead, and Diggs knew he'd never hear from Sheriff Greg Potter again.

Diggs glanced out the window. The same four cars were in the lot. The vacancy sign shined white above the lobby door. The green neon cactus stood tall and bright under the cloudy night sky and his doubts about Sheriff Potter were mushrooming. Diggs laid his head on a pillow and closed his eyes just as large drops of rain began to pelt the window.

24

Rain battered against the window and crashing thunder occasionally jarred Diggs out of sleep. When he awoke for good, it was to a silence he wasn't expecting. He got out of bed and peered between the curtains. Droplets of rain streaked the window. The courtyard had become a minefield of puddles, and the sky hung heavy with steel-colored clouds as thick as a milkshake, but the rain had ceased.

Nothing seemed out of the ordinary. A quiet early morning with an apocalyptic sky that promised a deluge of rain at any moment.

While Hyde slept on the bed, Diggs sat at the desk in the gray-sky-lit room, attempting to assemble the pieces of his sister's complicated life.

His and Claire's first conversation in twenty years seemed solely motivated by a personal interest in Brian Harper/Richard Reed/Ricky Racine. As much as Diggs hated to admit it, he believed Claire's former live-in Gary Wagner portrayed Claire somewhat accurately. The Guthus offered additional first-person testimony that Claire was fully willing and capable of dispensing misery.

Diggs thought the scars on Racine's back probably came from Claire, but he didn't believe they were the result of paid-for kink. Stall never mentioned any other bizarre markings on Racine's body, and there wasn't any evidence Diggs saw at 3215 San Marcos Boulevard and nothing he heard afterwards that pointed toward a hardcore masochistic lifestyle, and nobody does that to their body on a whim. Diggs suspected that Racine, with the help of Claire, was practicing behavior modification at its most bizarre.

Diggs read the apology letter again. The takeaway he chose to accept was Racine had been waging a war against his sexual deviance, and he had called upon Claire to use her unique skill set to aid him in keeping his monstrous desires at bay. His motive: to please Petey White. The Palmer boy had been his final exam, his proof to White that he was indeed the changed man he claimed to be on the apology letter.

Diggs knew that if he had called it right, it placed Claire squarely in Petey White's orbit, and how tempting for her that must that have been. A prolific and clever thief with direct access to Mojave Creek's wealthiest resident. For a world-class scammer, what could be more thrilling than to pull one over on a rich, ego-maniacal, beloved local celebrity?

Diggs had to admit that his scenario had unfolded so easily and so logically that it was hard to believe it wasn't true, even without any direct evidence that White had been blackmailed, extorted, or scammed.

Diggs understood that he might be inventing a crime, but someone burned down Claire's house. A revenge-crazed parent or teacher, or even an unbalanced student couldn't be discounted, nor could one of Claire's former customers or Gary Wagner, but if Claire had performed her magic on

White, Diggs didn't figure him the type to call on the police or consult an attorney. Torching her house seemed more suited to his personality.

Potter claimed Claire had fled to Texas, and with an attempt on her life, that made a semblance of sense, but Claire was in Mojave Creek. Claire had been burned in the fire just as the volunteer fireman had told him. A record of a hospital stay didn't exist because that isn't where Claire went.

Petey White ran Mojave Creek. The moment Claire admitted herself, White would find out and as soon as she was discharged, White would have someone waiting. Claire chose her only option: refuge at the home of her fiancé—the creep he had beaten up in a barn, the lowlife who blackened Esther's eye, the overly friendly party-greeter Rusty referred to as a "fucking piece-of-shit asshole". Her face heavily bandaged, it was Claire who had been seated in the passenger seat of the shiny black SUV. Claire's fiancé was Johnny, and she was the Invisible Man.

Diggs understood that for his theory to hold water, White could not be aware that Johnny and Claire were a couple, and he didn't believe that to be even slightly farfetched. It was entirely plausible that Claire was imploring Johnny to keep their relationship a secret for reasons that somehow made sense to Johnny, all the while bleeding him for information. It wasn't impossible to believe that Johnny was a willing accomplice, resentful at his role as the White family's faithful grunt, or it might be as simple as Johnny's greed yanking him in a dangerous direction.

It was 7:00 a.m. and Hyde was wide awake and getting restless. Diggs fed him breakfast and afterwards they meandered around the motel for nearly a half hour. All the while, Diggs picked apart his premise, searching for holes and not finding any that convinced him to change his thinking. His theories made sense, but ultimately, he had a car with no engine. If Claire attempted to extort White, what did she have on him? If she already scammed him, how much did she get?

Threatening to reveal Petey White's best friend as a pedophile didn't seem like enough. Diggs found no evidence that White went out of his way to protect Racine. The apology letter could easily argue that White hadn't a clue. There was no evidence that White was aware Racine had kidnapped Glen Palmer.

If Claire had leverage, it would have to be something that seized White's attention and gripped like a vice. Shady business deals were always a possibility, and White's lavish parties were a marvelous means to launder money. The possibility couldn't be entirely discounted, but it didn't feel quite right, nor did any money scam.

Everyone cared about money, but keeping the tank filled didn't seem to consume Petey White's life. Noah Boyer, who had likely scammed and been scammed throughout his life, called White "good people" and claimed White treated him more fairly than anyone.

Petey White clearly had access to money, but he didn't seem to be about money. He was about respect and ego and his Emmy Award. The only price to attend White's extravagant parties was bowing to him as if he were a king and admiring his Emmy as if it were a dead head of state. White promised, and Diggs fully believed, that had he damaged the Emmy, he would have been taken far out into the desert and buried.

Diggs recalled a headline to a comment on the *Rev and Roll* IMDB page. Once he and Hyde returned to their room, he opened IMDB. The headline read: *One of the Great Upsets in Emmy History!*

The commenter identified himself as K.D. and listed his location as Bel Air, California, which seemed a little unusual in itself. Why would a rich guy be commenting on *Rev and Roll?* Diggs answered his own question with, why not? The wealthy had bad taste too and just because a pair of initials claimed to reside in Bel Air, didn't make it true.

K.D. made a case that White beat out a bevy of A-list actors on programs that were all fondly remembered. He argued that *Rev and Roll* had been tripe from its very first episode and nobody cared when it was cancelled. K.D. ended with: *Everyone in the industry knew that White's Emmy win never should have happened and I'll leave it at that.* Diggs read through the nine other comments and found nothing as provocative.

Diggs searched the internet for bloggers who wrote about television and found more than he would have imagined. He settled on the three that sounded the most promising: 70s Cop Heroes, The Television Guru, and Book Em' Danno. He sent each an e-mail identifying himself as a detective in San Diego and wrote that he had questions about a TV series called *Rev and Roll* and its lead Petey White. Diggs included his phone number and stressed that what he was working on was an urgent matter.

His stay at the Western Jewel had ended. He and Hyde headed to the lobby to check out. Esther stood at the counter glaring at the entrance as if she were guarding the Alamo and waiting for the inevitable.

At the sight of Diggs, her frightened vigilance turned into predictable disdain.

"Oh, it's you."

"I'm checking out."

"I'll remember you fondly. Have a wonderful life."

"Can I ask you one more question about the man who hit you?"

"If you must."

"When he went back to his car, did you see anything that might suggest the other person was a woman?"

She grimaced. "I don't know. I'm trying to forget." She sighed. "Let me think."

Several moments later, she said, "The only thing I can think of is that the lowlife in the passenger seat touched his face."

"In a feminine way?"

"I don't know, maybe. I think it was the tops of his fingers, kind of streaked his face like he was brushing something off. I guess it could have been a woman."

"Okay, anything else?"

"No."

"Make sure to keep my phone number."

"Why? You're off to California. You can't help me."

Diggs could offer no argument. He had to go. Billy T. and his storage locker were beckoning.

For the first time since he entered, she gave Diggs her full attention. "Just so you know, I don't entirely blame you. Other lowlifes have come here bent on causing trouble. I've learned from experience that you can't back down. You have to let them know who's in charge. He caught me by surprise. I'll be ready for him next time." She reached under the counter and showed Diggs a .22 semi-automatic, tiny enough to conceal in his fist.

A .22 could be an effective weapon, but this one's size and weight would affect its accuracy, particularly if she was a novice shooter. Diggs suspected that Johnny would know that and doubted the gun in her hands would put much of a scare into him.

"If you sense any trouble, call 911—they're there to help." Diggs heard his voice trailing off. It was all he could think to say, and it wasn't enough.

In her stern teacher demeanor, she said, "You take care of Mr. Hyde. He'll give you a lifetime of happiness."

Diggs told her he would and left the lobby without a good-bye. He pulled out of the parking lot hoping the best for Esther and blaming himself.

25

The interstate that would lead Diggs south toward Arizona was approaching and except for nagging curiosity and a deteriorating residue of sibling loyalty, nothing was stopping him from merging onto the ramp and leaving Mojave Creek forever.

Diggs felt like he was standing over a cliff watching a boulder roll away. There was nothing he could do to save his sister. She had made her choices and by every account, he'd heard she had no regrets.

But as awful as the stories and his own suspicions were, Diggs couldn't completely write Claire off as a lost cause. All of her malfeasances had been related by people with agendas. Gary Wagner was a bitter ex-boyfriend. The Uber driver, although rightfully angry, spoke in hearsay. The Guthus were almost certainly right about Claire, but absolute conclusive proof had not yet been established. Anything Potter said about Claire couldn't be trusted.

The remaining fragments of the ballplayer implored Diggs not to judge the fastball until he had watched it cross the plate. He needed Claire to directly confront the allegations against her. As hackneyed as it sounded, she deserved her day in court. Diggs knew that if he left Mojave Creek with holes in his thinking, any misreads would metastasize into misjudgments. Eventually they would age into a truth he would carry to his grave. For Diggs, it was as simple as: she was his sister and he didn't want to be wrong.

His meeting with Billy T. was still a little more than twenty-four hours away. He had more than half of that to locate Claire. Considering he had spent the last two and a half days searching with no success, he decided to swap roles and allow her to find him.

Diggs pulled over to the side of the road and checked his phone for nearby hotels and motels. In Mojave Creek's commercial district, there were eight. A well-traveled business district on a Friday morning seemed as good a starting point as any.

He drove along the main road, passing by shops and restaurants, places to lodge and gas up. All the while, his eyes seesawed from the road to the rearview mirror, hoping that Johnny's expensive black SUV would suddenly drop in behind him.

He pulled into the Walmart, driving up and down the rows of cars and around the perimeter of the vast lot, setting himself up for a slow pursuit. When that didn't happen, he drove across the street to a Smart & Final and parked in a slot facing the main drag. A handful of black SUVs cruised by, but none with Johnny's bandaged face in the driver's seat and none with the Invisible Man riding shotgun.

The watching and waiting had a Great Pumpkin feel to it, and soon Diggs suspected that his window of opportunity had closed the day before. There were only so many places to search in Mojave Creek. Johnny had likely either given up or had better things to do on a Friday morning.

Diggs meandered through mild traffic, veering into a fast-food drive-thru. He bought Mr. Hyde a hamburger and a Diet

Coke for himself. He made one more drive around the block, sipping on the beverage and listening to Hyde lick his chops for a lot longer than the ten seconds it took him to devour the burger. Nearly an hour of patiently seeking attention and five thousand glances into his rearview mirror was enough.

Diggs considered finding a concealed spot near White's ranch and try to catch Johnny leaving. If he got lucky, perhaps Johnny would lead him to Claire. Diggs glanced at the time on his dashboard. It wasn't even noon. Assuming Johnny was at the ranch, he likely wouldn't be heading home for several hours. While Diggs considered the pluses and minuses of spending his last afternoon in Mojave Creek on a gamble that was far from sure, he drove toward Remy Gomez's neighborhood to scratch an itch he'd had since he'd found Remy's body.

Under a rain cloud covered sky, Diggs arrived at Remy's house, finding it very different from the day before. A seven-foot-tall chain-link fence caged the property. The beat-up Ford and all the junk in the front yard had been expunged. A construction company notice announced that the house was scheduled for a complete tear down in a week.

Diggs turned on his navigation and plugged in the address of the Geist residence, wanting the shortest possible route. He cruised the three-quarters of a mile searching front porches and garages, scanning for video cameras that pointed toward the street. He saw four for certain and guessed there had to be at least as many doorbell cams.

It took less than three minutes to reach his destination. A small shrine had been erected at the Geist's front door. Bouquets of pink and white flowers lay on the porch. On the front window, a white sign with pink lettering read: *XOXO Julia, Farrah, Bill.*

Diggs took a long moment to stare at the sign. The XOXO sentiment had been prevalent at the school. Gutierrez mentioned that the Geist vigil was called the Hugs and Kisses Celebration. XOXO obviously held some special meaning for Julia Geist. Diggs remembered that Remy's suicide note had given Julia Geist her own sentence. Rusty didn't admit to knowing Julia, but he stated that she was "nice".

Diggs dug thorough his luggage and retrieved the iPad. With Hyde's muzzle hanging over his forearm, he pushed the start button and waited for it to power up. When the keypad appeared, he typed in 969696—XOXOXO. The iPad remained locked. He tried 969654—XOXOJG. The keypad faded to black, and the home screen appeared. Diggs jutted his fist forward and gave Mr. Hyde a playful rub across his body.

The home screen had never been customized. All the standard applications were in their factory-sealed positions. Diggs pressed the Photos application and the first signs of life came in the form of eighty-eight photos, seemingly taken from a variety of sources. Some appeared to have come from yearbooks, the majority had likely been downloaded from social media, and Julia Geist was the star of every shot.

Julia as a cheerleader, captured in mid-air, her pom poms waving. A gleeful Julia seated at a cafeteria table, blowing a kiss to the photographer. Julia in a peasant costume, performing on stage. Julia in the stands of a football game. Julia with her family at a barbecue. Julia at the mall with friends. Julia at what looked like a Game of Thrones-themed party. Julia and her friends standing in front of lockers making the XOXO declaration with their thumbs and index fingers. XOXO—the symbol of Julia Geist's young life.

Scanning through the photos, Diggs observed the amazing

physical progression of Julia Geist. In one shot, she was a cute teenager with frizzy dark hair and a bubbly tom-boyish grin. In other shots, she was the face of a future homecoming queen—a black-haired beauty with a welcoming smile and kind expressive eyes. As he watched the young life of Julia Geist advance through photos, a magical charisma blossomed. By the last shots, her considerable beauty had become magnetic. Julia Geist had become a young woman born to be seen. In a world where physical presence opened countless doors, Diggs couldn't help believing that Julia Geist would have led a life to be envied.

Behind the video tab, Diggs found five. The first video was dated October 10th—eight days before Julia Geist and her family were murdered. It had been shot just after midnight. Diggs pressed the play button. The initial image was dark and shaky. Quickly, the video stabilized. Rusty held the iPad in front of his face in a tight close-up. The lack of light made the shot grainy and claustrophobic. Wearing a poker face that Diggs remembered vividly, Rusty said, "Hello, out there."

After a second of camera jiggling, the image switched from selfie to the front of a house. A half-circle of light cast onto the front porch. It was the porch of the Geist home, no more than fifteen steps from where Diggs was parked. Rusty turned his head and said something that Diggs couldn't decipher. Abruptly, the video ended.

Diggs tapped play on the next video. It had been shot on October 11th at three minutes after midnight. The camera shook nervously as a car pulled halfway into a driveway. Diggs paused the video and examined the car. It appeared to be a newer model Acura. The angle made the driver impossible to see. Diggs resumed the video.

In a low but clear voice, Rusty asked, "Who's that?"

A calm and unemotional voice answered, "I don't know. Never saw it before." Diggs guessed the voice belonged to Remy Gomez.

The brake lights turned off. Moments later, the driver opened the car door. Diggs could tell it was a man. He walked briskly to the front porch of the darkened Geist house. A sliver of light escaped as the figure quickly stepped inside. The iPad remained focused on the porch for twenty-eight seconds before the video ended.

The third video had been taken on October 13th at 1:45 a.m. The iPad focused on the Geist house but from a different angle—on the opposite side of the street three houses away and pointed south.

A car with its headlights off parked on the opposite side of the street in front of the Geist home. Rusty said, "That car again. What's going on?"

The second voice sounded perplexed. "I have no fucking idea."

After several seconds, Rusty said, "This worries me."

The camera watched the man get out of the shadow of the car and followed him to the Geist's front porch and through the barely opened front door without ever breaking stride.

The video ended.

A lamppost positioned at the same corner indicated that the penultimate video had been shot at about the same spot as the previous. The timestamp read 12:16 a.m. and it was dated October 16th—two days before the Geists were murdered.

For fifteen seconds, the camera bounced in jarring movements, seemingly focusing on nothing. Remy called out, "Look, look, look." The camera immediately sliced to the Geist front porch. It held still on two figures leaving the house and walking across the front yard and into a car.

The taller figure opened the passenger door for the smaller. He hurried around the hood and into the driver's seat. The headlights illuminated and the car headed toward the camera.

"Get down!"

The camera slid downwards as if Rusty had tried to hide himself under the dashboard.

"Shit, they're pulling over."

A moment later, Remy's frantic voice called out, "Oh my god. Get this. Get this."

The camera peeked over the window. After seconds of bouncing, the lens found the car double parked no more than ten feet away. The camera zoomed in on the driver's face. He was leaning back in his seat, his head lay against the head rest, and his eyes were closed.

"Jesus Christ, Rusty. She's fucking blowing him."

The camera watched the man's face for eight seconds, plenty of time for Diggs to recognize him. The passenger lifted her head. Only her eyes, her forehead, and portions of her long dark hair avoided the shadows, but it was enough for Diggs to confirm that it was Julia Geist.

Remy let out an irritating cackle that made Diggs wish he could reach into the screen and pound Remy's head into the dashboard. Gleefully, he said, "Shit, we have it made."

The video ended.

The final video was listed at twenty-two minutes and seventeen seconds. It had been shot on October 18th at 3:22 a.m. The night of the murders. A grueling marathon awaited. After a deep breath, Diggs started the video.

The beam of a flashlight shone steadily against a wall. For

a split second, it caught the arm of a sofa and then the edge of a coffee table. Diggs imagined Rusty sweating profusely, holding the iPad tight enough to squeeze like an accordion. Up to that point no one had said anything.

A voice whispered, "Upstairs."

The beam of light turned upwards and started to bounce. The backside of Remy's large upper body filled most of the screen. Diggs heard low breathing on the verge of hyperventilating. The light shone along a wall before stopping at a door. The iPad tilted downward to a gloved hand turning a doorknob. The door pushed open. The camera focused on a bed. A light shone on Mr. Geist's face. He opened his eyes and groggily sat up. A clenched-teeth voice said, "Get the fuck up. Keep your hands where we can see them."

"What? Who are you?"

The camera swung to the left. Mrs. Geist sat up on the bed, holding covers at her chest. In a terrified squeal, she said, "Take whatever you want. Don't…"

Mr. Geist interrupted, "Hey, no problem. No problem at all. It's cool. Whatever you want is yours."

The clenched-teeth voice said, "We want everything in the safe. You, get up and stay quiet. If you do as we say, your daughter will never know we were here."

Mr. Geist kicked the bedcovers away. "There's nothing in the safe. Literally. There is nothing in the safe. I got other stuff though. Valuable stuff. You can have all of it."

"Bullshit. Watch her. If she causes any problems, stab her face."

Mr. Geist sat at the edge of the bed. "Okay, okay, I'll show you. I got money in my wallet. You can have my credit cards. Anything you want."

A confused female voice said, "Mom, Dad?"

The iPad swept toward to the right and stopped at Julia Geist standing in pajamas. The clenched voice said, "Get your ass in here."

Mrs. Geist screamed. The iPad fell to the floor. The screen went black. Muffled grunts and ear-splitting screams continued on and off for seventeen seconds.

Without warning, the room turned quiet. Several moments later, Remy spoke, out of breath. His clenched-teeth voice had left him. "Take them to her room."

Mrs. Geist began to sob. She said, "Please. Please. No. Take what you want."

"Shut the fuck up. Dumb fuck did it to himself."

For fourteen minutes and forty-seven seconds the picture remained black. Diggs increased the volume to the max. Between mostly dead air, he heard dull thuds and distant voices that were impossible to decipher. At the 21:15 mark, the camera was lifted from the floor. Where the lens was pointed was unclear. Remy said, "You wiped everything, right?"

A pause later, he said, "She's yours, buddy. Have at her."

The anguish in Rusty's voice made Diggs cringe. "No, let's just leave."

"What the fuck is wrong with you? This is your chance to fulfill a lifelong dream."

"No, let's go." Rusty's voice had a force behind it that Diggs had a hard time imagining.

"Well, it's too late. We have to finish the job. It's your fault. She knows who you are."

Like the howl of a dying animal, Rusty screamed to leave her alone.

"Fine, if you don't have the balls, I do."

Rusty began to sob. "Don't. Don't. Don't."

The video ran black for twenty-one seconds before it ended.

Diggs laid the iPad on the backseat, feeling exhausted and sick. He needed to clear his head. He needed something to wash away the stench of human cruelty at its worst. He snapped on Hyde's leash and they walked along the street for several blocks until they reached a front yard with a Weeping Yoshino Cherry tree. Diggs sat on the curb. Wet pink blooms floated onto his shoulders as he petted his dog. He looked into Hyde's friendly brown eyes and tucked his body against his.

He opened his phone and pulled up the photos he shot at the Remington Academy shrine. He looked at each, enlarging them, attempting to read the written sentiments. He focused on the gaps between the messages. He wanted to read the ones that were furthest away from the rest, where the outsiders and the misfits would reside. It didn't take long to find what he was searching for. At the base of the arrow, written in black marker: *I really liked you, Julia. You were always nice to me. Rusty.*

Diggs put his phone in his pocket and rubbed between the folds on Hyde's face. "We'd better go."

Once inside the car, Diggs phoned Sheriff Potter's office. The voice said, "Sorry, the sheriff is out for the rest of the day. May I take a message?"

Diggs hung up. He opened the people-finding service, and in less than five minutes, he knew the address of Julia Geist's boyfriend and the killer of Remy Gomez and Rusty Boyer. He switched off his phone's ringer. He needed to think without any distractions.

26

Sheriff Greg Potter lived in a quiet enclave with the quaint name of Indian Springs. With curving roads and manmade hills, professional landscaping, and a private park with a small pretty lake, Diggs suspected that Indian Springs was Mojave Creek's version of wealthy seclusion.

Potter's home was a brick ranch style, not excessive or showy like of some of the flamboyant mini-mansions Diggs had passed, but comfortable and well cared for—the type of house Diggs could picture himself living in. A light glowed from behind a drawn curtain at the front of the house.

Diggs approached with Hyde on his leash. Under his jacket, the Glock was clipped to his belt. He rang the bell and thirty seconds later, Potter hadn't answered. Diggs could feel a growing concern begin to take hold. The setting began to feel eerily reminiscent of his visit the day before to Remy Gomez's home.

Suddenly, the door swung open, and Potter was standing in the doorway. He wore loose-fitting jeans, a white shirt, and brown slippers splotched with paint stains. For a moment, Potter stared at Diggs with bewilderment.

Diggs broke the silence with a cheerful, "Good evening, Sheriff."

Through an uncomfortable smile, Potter said, "How did you know where I lived?"

Diggs shrugged with an affable grin. "I'm a detective, remember? Pretty neighborhood. It would be a great place to walk Mr. Hyde."

Potter's left hand gripped the frame of the door. Diggs noticed that he wore no wedding ring.

"What would you expect? I'm the sheriff—it's my neighborhood."

Diggs faked a chuckle before nodding down at Hyde. "Can we come in?"

Potter exhaled heavily. "I'm a little busy but okay." Diggs and Hyde stepped past Potter and into his home.

"You found me through the internet, right?"

Diggs waited for Potter to close the door. "Guilty. It can be a blessing and a curse."

Potter led Diggs into the family room of a renaissance man. Two tall stacks of books lay on a heavy wooden coffee table. A book on labor unions of the 1950s topped one stack, a poetry anthology the other. A plugged-in electric guitar was propped against the back of a red painted chair. A Tupac Shakur song played on an old-school vinyl turntable. The walls were adorned with paintings, but not the kind bought from a catalog or at a frame shop. They were originals. Some were oils, most were watercolors. None of them particularly impressive, but all were lightyears better than anything Diggs could ever hope to accomplish.

A watercolor above the fireplace caught Diggs' eye. It was the largest of the paintings and its frame was carved from thick dark wood and stenciled with an elaborate design. The subject was a young woman sitting on a hardback chair. She wore a black dress, and her bare legs were crossed at the knee. A red high-heel shoe dangled from the toe of her right foot. The painting had a deliberately playful quality. Her red lips were parted in a campy smile and the tip of her index finger pressed against her chin as if she were pondering something frivolous. On a small table beside her, a bowl held two goldfish. The impish young woman looked a lot like Julia Geist.

Diggs didn't pay it as much attention as he would have liked. Julia Geist would come later. He slowly gazed around the room pretending to admire the walls of paintings, but his interests were guns first and AI devices second.

Diggs gushed, "Wow, did you do all of these?"

Potter answered with a flat, "Yes."

Diggs lied, "They're incredible." He almost added, "You should open your own exhibit," but decided that was too rich. To the right of the kitchen was an outdoor patio—a convenient place to separate Potter from any hidden firearms.

"You mind if we sit on the patio? Probably be best for Hyde."

Potter shrugged. "Sure."

Potter led Diggs across the family room, past a spacious kitchen that didn't appear to have an AI device. They exited through a sliding glass door and to the patio. On the center of a terracotta tiled patio was the white circular aluminum table and four outdoor chairs that Diggs had seen from the living room. What hadn't been visible was a piece of white cardboard spattered with blue paint on an easel.

"Oh, so this is where the creativity begins."

As he spoke, he noticed that the door had been left open. Potter smiled stiffly. "It's a hobby more than anything."

Diggs took a seat closest to the opened door. Hyde lay at his feet. Potter sat on the chair directly to his left.

"Any influences? Inspirations?"

"I doubt that you sought me out to talk about painters. Why don't we get down to business?"

"Okay, fair enough. Let's start with the mistakes you made."

Potter let out a grunt of confusion. Mild agitation colored his words. "I have no idea what you're talking about."

"You should already be in jail."

Potter lifted his arms just below his shoulders and let them collapse on his thighs. "What are you talking about?"

"You killed Remy Gomez and Rusty Boyer and despite your attempts to cover it up, you're going down for it."

Potter's exasperation erupted into anger. "Are you fucking kidding me? You're accusing me of murder? I should throw you out on your ass."

Hyde lifted his head and began to growl. Diggs touched him and whispered a soothing word. Hyde calmed down and Diggs turned his attention to Potter. "But you won't until you hear me out. You'll want to figure out your options. You'll want to know if you need to worry about the state police."

Potter's twisted face transformed into an almost believable amused grin.

"This is ridiculous, but I'm all ears. Go ahead and tell me how I murdered a hit-and-run one day and a suicide the next day, but make it quick, my paint is drying."

"No way Gomez would have taken his life because of the Geists. They meant nothing to him. After he murdered them, I doubt that he gave them a second thought."

Potter shrugged. "We'll never know."

"No one was watching Gomez's house. He was your main suspect for a triple murder, and there wasn't any surveillance. I'd think you'd want to be damn certain you didn't lose him. Of course, there'd be no need if you knew he was already dead."

"How do you know nobody was watching his house?"

"Because I was watching his house, and no one was around."

"I personally watched Gomez, okay? Maybe not every second of every minute, but I knew where he was at all times."

"A number of Gomez's neighbors have video cameras facing the street. If you were around Gomez's home late last night or very early this morning, a camera somewhere will have picked it up."

Potter shrugged disinterest. "So what? A camera will see me in Gomez's neighborhood at all hours of the day. It was all part of the investigation. You're wasting my time, Detective. Gomez left a note. He admitted killing the Geists."

"That must have been a dilemma. You couldn't imitate Gomez's handwriting, but you needed a letter. You decided your best bet was to make it appear like Remy had scrawled one out in a drug haze. An independent examiner won't be able to authenticate Gomez wrote it, so it won't prove anything."

"Hold on. You saw the note? You were in Gomez's house?"

"Let's talk about the frozen pizza."

Potter placed his elbow on the table and rested his chin into a palm. "You lost me."

"When you entered Gomez's house, he must have just put a pizza in the oven. An AI device had been set for twenty-one minutes. It was behind a bunch of empty grocery bags, so you probably didn't see it. Had it gone off before you left, you would have unplugged it or taken it with you, and no one would have been the wiser. No one would have thought to look in the trash bin at the side of the house. Why would Gomez take a pizza out of the oven before it had fully cooked and throw it away, not in his messy kitchen but outside, and then come back inside and kill himself?

"Some time last night, or early this morning, you entered Gomez's house. I didn't see any signs of forced entry so maybe he let you in. You subdued him, probably with a stun-gun. He's too heavy and bulky to lug around, so you attached something to his ankle and dragged him into the dining room and propped him on the chair. You overdosed him and hung him.

"If the body is examined closely, the ME will find stun-gun marks. He'll find bruising on his body and maybe even a broken bone or two."

Through a tight smile, Potter said, "An elaborate theory without an ounce of proof."

"Has Gomez been cremated?"

Potter glanced at his watch. "As we're speaking."

"That's okay. There's plenty of other evidence."

"If there is, I haven't heard it."

"I saw the videos. You shouldn't have killed Rusty until you either found his iPad or were damn sure no one else would."

Potter's face began to turn an unhealthy shade of white.

"You avenged Julia's death and at the same time saved your job and your reputation. Kind of heroic and cowardly at the same time."

Potter's hands gripped onto the chair arms. He appeared to be leveraging himself for an attack. Diggs casually adjusted his body. If a blitz was imminent, he wanted the best angle to kick Potter in the stomach.

"Either Gomez or Boyer told you that they had you on an

iPad in your car with Julia. Maybe Gomez let out that Boyer had it or maybe you figured that on your own. I know that after you murdered Boyer, you went to his house looking for it. Had you found it, maybe you wouldn't have murdered Gomez, but you didn't find it. So instead of arresting Gomez, he had to die too. I'm giving you the benefit of the doubt on that one. Since Gomez knew about you and Julia, you were probably going to murder him regardless."

Potter appeared to have calmed himself. He sat back in his chair and waved dismissively. "If you have this iPad, prove it. Show it to me. Show me the video."

"You don't want to see the video. They filmed not only you and Julia. They filmed the murders."

Potter let out a gasp. For a moment, he sat silent, seeming to let the horror set in his mind. "I need to see that video, now."

"I sent it to the state police. They'll have it by tomorrow afternoon. It's going to prove that Gomez did kill the Geist family and Boyer was there. It will also show that you were having an inappropriate relationship with Julia Geist. Someone will take an interest. They'll catch you."

Potter dropped his hands onto his lap. He spoke gently and patiently like a high school guidance counselor. "For the record, Detective, nothing about my relationship with Julia was inappropriate. We were going to get married."

His eyes were sorrowful, searching for sympathy. He shook his head and whispered, "You two think alike."

"You tried to pay Julia's tuition, didn't you?"

"Acting meant so much to her and she was talented. How could I turn her down?"

"How was Julia killed?"

Potter's voice broke. "Her neck was snapped."

For several moments, Diggs felt the dull silence of waiting. Tears were streaming down Potter's reddened face. Although Potter appeared broken and docile, Diggs remained vigilant. A cornered man could turn savage in a heartbeat. If Potter had violence on his mind, it would be coming at any moment.

Potter wiped the tears from his face. "I don't believe you sent the iPad to the state police. If you show it to me, I have an offer that I know will interest you."

The offer. Throughout his career, Diggs had heard more offers than a staff of car salesmen over a hundred Memorial Day weekends. The offer always came from men in handcuffs or in interrogation rooms. They were usually ridiculous and always desperate. On rare occasions, an agreement might be struck, but not for a cop who murdered twice. No deal could save that guy. No arrangement was ever going to happen.

"I'm listening."

Potter rubbed his palms greedily together. A giddy glint sparkled in his eyes. Fantasies of an eleventh-hour reprieve were building in his head. Before he made his pitch, he needed to soften up the buyer. He spoke with an exaggerated cadence. "You know as well as I do those two were scumbags. They got exactly what they deserved. The state would have killed them anyway."

Diggs glanced at Hyde sleeping peacefully and envied him. "The offer, Sheriff."

"How's this? Not only can I take you to your sister, I can save your sister."

"Save her how?"

"I have all the evidence I need to arrest her for embezzlement. Getting close to finding the money too. Let me tell you,

Detective, your sister is not a sympathetic woman. Her crime was appalling. Stealing from gifted kids. Putting teachers out of work. Destroying a local institution. She'll get somewhere between ten and fifteen years. Closer to fifteen."

"I thought she was in Texas?"

"She is, but I'll get her back here."

"Did you ever find any video proving Claire was in Texas? I shouldn't have to keep explaining this to you. It doesn't matter anyway because you're lying. Claire isn't in Texas. Never was."

Potter barked, "Oh, fuck you. Your Sherlock Holmes bullshit makes me want to puke. The biggest case of your life was finding the Palmer kid and you were a tagalong. You got lucky is all. You found the goddamn iPad before I did." His words dripping with sarcasm, he added, "Great work, you arrogant asshole."

Diggs edged forward in his chair ready to leave.

"You know why those two monsters did it? Gomez convinced himself that being a murderer would make him famous. His plan was to steal Bill Geist's huge gambling winnings that didn't exist and use the money to finance a cross-country killing spree. He was going to bring along Boyer and create all the mayhem he could until they went down in a blaze of glory."

"Gomez told you this?"

"No, Boyer did. Being Dylan Klebold to Gomez's Eric Harris didn't sound as exciting to him as it did to Gomez. Boyer had no interest in ending his life in a hail of bullets. He was ratting out his best friend while trying to cover his ass. Gomez must have gotten to Boyer because he changed his story. He said he lied because he was mad at Gomez.

"You give me the iPad and your sister wins and Gomez loses. Nobody needs to know anything about Gomez. You know how the internet is. Tens of thousands of morons will glorify his sorry carcass. He shouldn't get an ounce of fame. He's an atrocity. His memory should disappear off the face of the earth."

"You two think alike."

"What?"

"You said to me, 'You two think alike.' You were talking about Claire. She knows about you and Julia. When Julia was a student, Claire was working as the bookkeeper and somehow, she found out. Maybe Julia let it slip. Claire's been blackmailing you. With Julia gone, so is most of her leverage, but Claire can still be a problem. Now that Julia's dead maybe you think it's time to settle that score. You've killed twice already, what's one more, right?"

Potter shook his head and whispered, "Don't blame Julia, she never said a word." He began to plead. "Detective, just cut me some slack. Please. If you have the iPad, destroy it. Forget about Boyer and Gomez. They got what they deserved. I'll retire. I'll never wear a badge again."

He looked past Diggs into his home. Diggs followed his eyes until they landed on the painting of the girl beside the goldfish bowl. A wistful smile filled his face, and for a moment, he closed his eyes, seeming to gather his thoughts.

He and Diggs met eyes. "Detective, your sister is going to be arrested eventually. If not by me, by whoever replaces me. I can promise you that whoever comes next won't do her any favors. If you let me handle it, your sister walks. I can convince the Guthus to drop the charges if Claire gives the money back. I've been in contact with Claire's attorney. She's agreeable to returning it."

"Why?"

"Because your sister isn't as clever as she thought, and she doesn't want to go to prison. The money isn't necessary anyway. She found herself a rich sucker. She's engaged to Petey White's son."

"Jerad? You mean Johnny."

"No, Jerad. Since the fire, she's been staying at White's ranch. They're a couple."

Diggs felt flabbergasted. "I don't believe you."

"It's true. I swear it on Julia's grave."

"Did you burn down Claire's house?"

"Of course not, I was working twenty hours a day searching for Julia's killer. Even if I wanted to, I had no time to plan and commit an arson, but I can help her out on that. I found out about an insurance claim she made. If we can make a deal, I'll tell the agent that she had nothing to do with the arson. Once that's done, it'll be next to impossible to prosecute her even if she did torch it. I can also put her under so much suspicion that she'll never see a dime."

All delusion as far as Diggs was concerned. Once the state police began an investigation, Potter wouldn't have the pull to influence a neighborhood crime stoppers program.

"Thank you for your time, Sheriff." Diggs got out of his chair. "Let's go, Hyde."

Potter remained seated. His voice was hopeful. "Do we have a deal?"

Diggs looked at him contemptuously. "What do you think?"

Diggs led Hyde to a gate along the side of the house. Never again did he want to see the Julia Geist watercolor. The calamity of her young life lost and the horror of the iPad video were cajoling him to make decisions that he wouldn't be able to live with.

Once Diggs got Hyde safely inside the car, he watched the gate and the front door, not exactly sure what he was waiting for. A gun fight? Potter to beg him on his hands and knees? Seconds passed and Potter hadn't followed him out, and the front door never budged.

Diggs regretted letting it go as far as it had. He regretted being at Potter's house at all. The Geist case wasn't his and Mojave Creek wasn't his jurisdiction. Potter had called it right. He was an arrogant asshole.

Diggs drove to the lake and parked along the shore. He and Hyde stood on a narrow pier overlooking the water while a fine mist blew in five directions at once. Diggs inhaled deeply and exhaled it all out. From his first day out of the academy, he had promised himself that fairness and competency would be his aspirations. Inconvenient laws would never be ignored, nor would he rationalize away crimes or be a part of any good ole boy networks. Whether it be a small-time thief or a death row candidate, he would treat them without prejudice and exactly as the law required. On Potter's back patio, he had been at the precipice of breaking his pact, and it left him shaken.

Potter was absolutely correct. Gomez would have received all the media attention he desired along with love letters from women who imagined they saw a brightness inside of him that didn't exist. Rusty would have been forever anchored to anguish and regret, discarded into an oppressive system where he would spend the rest of his life struggling to survive. Potter dispensed a justice that saved Rusty from a Hell on Earth and stole Remy's cherished infamy.

Had he agreed to Potter's deal, the first step to the end of his career would have commenced. Diggs watched the angry waves crash against the pier and blew a wisp of air from his lips. He was kidding himself; his consideration had been the first step. Diggs spoke a prayer into the wind and walked Mr. Hyde back to the car just as the rain began to pour.

27

Jazz always sounded better in a storm. Slow and wandering horn solos felt more authentic under clouds. A soft bluesy guitar when done right could play off a steady rain as if it were an expert percussionist. The best jazz could soften the downpours in life and offer hope without forgetting the sadness.

Diggs was soothed by the music and comforted by his friend in the passenger seat. Hyde watched on curiously as Diggs maneuvered along narrow, winding roads. Once they departed Indian Springs, the road turned straight, and the pretty scenery fell away to lower-income homes and scattered mom and pop businesses.

As Diggs soaked in a melody, he considered Potter's confessions. If Potter was to be believed, it seemed more likely that Jerad along with Claire was shafting Petey White rather than Johnny and Claire taking on the entire the White family.

If it was a team effort with Jerad, Johnny, and Claire all working in concert to bleed away Petey White's fortune, Diggs assumed Claire was the brains and Jerad provided the access. Where did Johnny fit in? What exactly did he bring to the table?

The music faded and the entertainment console beneath his dashboard lit up, identifying a phone call coming from Los Angeles.

Diggs' finger was an inch away from the red decline button. After a resigned grunt of responsibility, he swayed his finger an inch to the left and pressed the green button. Through an annoyed edge, he said, "Who's calling?" The voice on the other end identified himself as David Walgreen, the author of The Television Guru blog.

Diggs reined in his hostility and thanked him for calling.

"You were asking questions about Petey White. That's a name I haven't thought of in forever."

Diggs told the guru that he was interested in the backstory behind White's Emmy, adding, "I read that it's the greatest upset in Emmy history."

Although Diggs had already read Walgreen's credentials and chose him because they were impressive, the guru insisted on rehashing.

"I was a publicist from 1972 to 1993. I knew everyone at the networks. Went to all the industry parties. The household names were my friends. I was in David Soul's wedding party. I was privy to countless behind-the-scenes stories. Have you read my book? *Confessions of a Television Guru*. It's on Amazon."

Diggs muttered that he hadn't.

"If you're interested in the television industry, the celebrities and the power struggles behind the scenes, it's a page turner."

Diggs tried to work up some polite enthusiasm. The best he could muster was, "Mm, I'm sure it is."

"So, Petey White and his Emmy." He laughed. "Simply put, he cheated."

"How so?"

"In one regard, White and his people were way ahead of their time. A few months before the Emmys—I don't remember exactly when—ads promoting White appeared every day in both *Variety* and *The Hollywood Reporter*. In 1977, it had a big effect. Of course, it later became common practice."

"How is buying ads cheating?"

"It's not. It's cheesy, but no, it's not cheating. It's bribing academy members that's cheating."

"Any proof of that? It sounds expensive and hard to do."

"Petey comes from a wealthy background. His father was a patent whore, mostly for the auto industry. I don't know anything about cars, so don't ask me what patents he held. All I can tell you is that they made him millions. You don't have to buy everyone, just one or two influential members. In Hollywood, favors are currency and handing out an undeserved Emmy isn't exactly the crime of the century. Back then, the Golden Globes were well known for dubious winners. To a large degree they still are. Remember *Butterfly*?"

Diggs told him he didn't. "If White cheated, why wouldn't the other networks raise a stink?"

"Before White won, CBS and NBC had no idea what was in the works. If Silverman at ABC knew, he probably would have kept quiet. He had enough to worry about trying to lead ABC out of the third place. An Emmy for any of his shows, even one as bad as *Rev and Roll*, was a feather in his cap."

"The actors White beat out didn't care that he cheated?"

"There was never a smoking gun. No one ever admitted anything and for an actor to openly complain would cross a line. Kind of like honest cops turning in crooked cops, and to tell you the truth, I doubt that they cared all that much. White beat out Peter Falk and Jimmy Garner. Michael Douglas and Jack Klugman. All of them had won before. Klugman had won multiple times. Jimmy, Michael, and Peter all had their eye on the movies, and they had a sense of humor. I have no doubt that between them, Petey White was the butt of a lot of jokes."

"You said that it wasn't proven for certain that White stole the Emmy. What are the chances that he won it legitimately?"

Walgreen howled. "Have you ever watched *Rev and Roll?*"

He never gave Diggs a chance to answer. Lost in his own remembrances, Walgreen's voice became animated. "I was at that Emmy ceremony. I'll never forget it. When White was announced as Best Actor in a Drama Series the audience openly gasped."

Diggs asked Walgreen if he'd ever met White.

"Oh, yes, several times. I liked him. He had a lot of charisma. No one would ever call him a great talent, but he had something interesting going for him. You and I can laugh at *Rev and Roll*, but how many thousands of wannabe actors have come to Hollywood with plans and big dreams and went home the same way? White had an enviable career."

Diggs thanked Walgreen for his information.

"If I may ask, why are you interested in Petey White? Before I looked at his IMDB page this afternoon, I assumed he was dead."

"No, he's alive, although he never made it out of 1977."

"For Petey, I imagine that's as good a place as any."

The rain had eased, but dark clouds brought an early nightfall to Mojave Creek. While keeping one eye on the time, Diggs stopped at a Subway and shared a turkey and cheese sandwich with Hyde.

Once he left Mojave Creek, Diggs knew that he wasn't coming back. A three-minute phone call would be the last contact he and Claire would ever have. What he knew now about Claire was all he'd ever know.

Diggs thought back to what Lionel Gutierrez had told him about the bar fight that knocked William Geist's teeth loose. Diggs wondered if Geist had described the woman to Gutierrez. If he had, it might confirm or disprove the identity of Claire's fiancé. He was about to search for Gutierrez's phone number when he saw a red number one glowing over the phone's green icon. A call arrived thirty-three minutes before, and an eight-second voicemail had been left. The call came about the time he was standing in front of Potter's house with the phone's ringer turned off.

Diggs pressed play. Immediately, a terrified voice screamed, "They're here! Oh my god, they're back," before the message ended. Her tone and her words, and the length of the message all spelled out an unmistakable narrative. Diggs pressed the ignition button and bulleted out of the parking lot.

*   *   *

The smell of smoke was inescapable. The eight-foot-tall lizard wasn't glowing, and the neon white vacancy sign was dark. Yellow crime-scene tape surrounded the property. The back portion of the building that once roomed Diggs was fire gutted. Three squad cars blocked the street. Diggs approached a uniformed officer wearing a jacket wet with drizzle.

Sounding weary and frustrated, he said, "May I help you, sir?"

"Good evening, Officer. I'm a detective from San Diego." He gave the officer a long look at his badge and his identification. "I'm a friend of Greg's. Is he around?"

"No, sir."

"What happened here?"

"A lot. A woman was shot and killed." He pointed toward the burned-out section of the motel. "We found her in there."

Diggs breathed in deeply. "What was her name?"

"Esther Bosko. Apparently, she owned the place."

Diggs could barely hide his fury. "Has the shooter been caught?"

"We don't know. There's also a dead male. He's over there." The officer pointed to a black SUV partially hidden behind a squad car. "His head was bandaged up. It's pretty clear he took two behind the ear. Whether he was involved in Bosko's murder or something else, we don't know."

"Was he carrying his driver's license?"

"Yeah, Johnny Morales. I've seen him before."

"At Petey White's parties?"

"That's right. He was the greeter guy."

"Anyone speak to White yet?"

"That's the sheriff's call, but I'm sure he will."

"Is he on his way?"

"So far, we haven't been able to reach him. When we do, I'm sure he'll be here."

Diggs turned away from the officer without another word. The murders forced Diggs to once again adjust his theory. This one featured Claire as a solo act and Johnny's murder the commencement of an everyone-must-go game plan.

Diggs assembled the pieces in his head. Claire's embezzlement scheme had backfired badly. She tried to frame the Guthu's daughter, and it hadn't worked. She had been exposed and at least one attempt had been made on her life.

Any leverage over Potter died with Julia Geist and Potter

called it right—she was not a sympathetic character. A long prison stretch loomed in her future.

If Claire cut herself away from the art school embezzlement albatross, she could flee Mojave Creek, and if she got far enough away, she'd probably be safe. If the Guthu's money was returned, the Mojave Creek police might not want to spend untold amounts of resources chasing her across the globe, but before she gave back anything, she needed to replenish the kitty. If Claire could frame Jerad for a couple murders before killing him off, she might be able to disappear into the wind with perhaps a nice chunk of the White fortune.

Johnny had been the first to go and Diggs had no doubt that more bodies were on the way. Next in line was easy to guess.

28

Diggs parked on the same narrow dirt road he had two days before. All that remained of the barn were three vertical beams quivering in the wind, standing over bumpy piles of charred wreckage.

Hyde appeared calm. Diggs touched under his chin. "I'm sorry, we won't be here long. I promise, I'll be back soon."

Diggs shut the door behind him and for several moments, stood beside his car with specks of wet sand blowing against the back of his neck. Plunging from soupy dark clouds came a bolt of lightning and seconds later thunder that seemed to shake the sky. In the distance, a dot of white light beaconed Petey White's castle.

Diggs jogged slowly, getting a feel for the blend of uneven dirt and loose sand under his feet. As he got more comfortable, his focus narrowed, and his legs moved with more confidence. The wind gusted behind him and before long he picked up speed. In what seemed like not much more than a minute, he was standing in Petey White's backyard, his adrenaline as high as the stars above the clouds. With the last remnants of the party surrounding him like islands scattered across an ocean of wet sand, he waited a few moments for his breathing to slow and his mind to calm.

Outdoor furniture had been wrangled together and covered with plastic sheets at the edge of the house. Picnic tables and benches were stacked next to a U-Pack. Near the sliding glass door that Diggs had once excitedly exited and later warily entered were the grills and the vats that once held baked beans and potato salad.

Diggs positioned himself between two rectangles of light emanating from inside the house. He watched with an open mind, waiting for nothing in particular but hoping that something he could act on would present itself.

A steady rain started, and nothing was materializing. Diggs approached the only window that was both dark and free from any covering. Inside he could see an unmade queen-sized bed and a large television on a dresser. The room's opened door looked out to a dim light against a wall.

Diggs considered turning on his phone's flashlight to get a better look inside, but he decided the opened door made it too risky. A moment later, he was popping off the screen, pushing up the window frame, and climbing inside the house. Sometimes Diggs didn't understand himself.

He landed on a high-heel shoe, which didn't help his ankle any. Shaking off the pain, he glanced around the room. On the bed, a laptop computer partially covered a bra, and draped over a chair were blue jeans way too small for Jerad. Beside the television were several packages of medical grade burn dressing, some opened, others not.

Diggs listened carefully and heard nothing. No voices conversing or arguing or laughing or singing. No television or music. No footsteps, cupboards shutting, toilets flushing, a sneeze, or a cough. Absolutely nothing. It didn't appear that anybody was home.

He stepped out of the bedroom into a long hallway lined with framed photos. The nearest to the door had Petey White seated on a beanbag chair next to Hugh Hefner, a chess board between them, a cluster of big-busted bunnies surrounding them. Both men held deadly serious expressions.

Two feet from Hefner was a shot of White standing in a make-believe cornfield, surrounded by a fat male hillbilly stereotype, a fat female hillbilly stereotype, and a skinny guy missing several teeth. All were in mid-hysterics.

In long careful steps, Diggs continued into the heart of the house. The first door he came upon was closed. From inside came a ratty string of coughing. For several moments, Diggs stood against the door and listened for other voices. After nearly a minute of nothing but hacking and guttural throat clearing between silence, Diggs cracked open the door to a darkened room. Light from the hallway touched a bony white leg. Diggs made out a nightstand by a bed. He took four steps into the room and flicked on a table lamp.

Petey White lay sprawled in his underwear. His skinny arms were at his sides. His palms lay flat against the bed. His hair was tangled, and his eyes were shut. The old man looked like a corpse that had been thrown from a four-story window.

On the nightstand, a pill holder the size of a dinner plate was deluged with a rainbow of colorful pills. Diggs didn't see a cell phone, but that meant nothing. It could have been buried beneath the mountain of used tissue beside the pill holder or hidden in the ball of tangled bedsheets.

White's head sprung from his pillow as sudden as a jack-in-the-box. In deathly fear, he cried out, "Who are you?"

Diggs raised his palms in surrender. "Don't be frightened, Mr. White. It's me, Malcolm. I'm not here to harm you."

His fearful suspicion remained for several seconds. Diggs could tell he was raking his memory trying to remember who Malcolm was.

"I wanted to tell you that the Gumshoes were incredible the other night."

White smiled with teeth as white as ivory and as straight as an orthodontist's favorite son. "Thank you, Malcolm. I was pleased with our performance."

Diggs stepped over to a window beside White's bed. He pulled open a thick brown curtain that looked out into the backyard. He unlocked the window and raised it six inches. In a worst-case scenario, a quick escape hatch might save him from a bullet.

"Mr. White, I hope you don't mind me opening this just a crack. It's kind of stuffy in here."

"That's fine. I don't mind. To what do I owe the pleasure of your visit?"

White's eyes were puffy and bloodshot, and there were enough used tissues on the nightstand to fill a garbage bag.

"Are you okay, Mr. White?"

He sniffled and wiped snot away from his nostrils. "I've been better."

"Is there anything I can help you with?"

His skinny arm pointed to a dresser across from his bed. "If you could get her for me, I'd appreciate it."

Diggs turned toward the dresser and saw the Emmy broken into two pieces. Diggs looked into White's heartbroken eyes. "What happened?"

"I fell, and I damaged her."

Diggs lifted the pieces of the Emmy off the dresser. The statue's tiny hands were broken away from the globe.

"I wouldn't worry, Mr. White. A little glue and she'll be as good as new."

The old man's eyes brightened. "Could you fix her for me? I would so much appreciate that. There's a junk drawer in the kitchen. There should be glue in there."

Diggs groaned to himself. He'd already put himself in a precarious situation. Wandering through the house without a quick escape could result in the kind of misadventure that either left him dead or haunted.

"If you don't mind, I'd like to ask you about Jerad's fiancé."

"I'd really appreciate if you could fix her."

"There's no glue anywhere in here?"

"No, I already told you. In the kitchen."

"I'm not familiar with your home, Mr. White. Is there anyone in the house that I can talk to?"

"They left me here alone."

"Where'd they go?"

"The kitchen is easy to find. Take a left out of here and a left at the end of the hall. Two lefts. You can't miss it."

"What's Jerad's fiancé's name?"

A shaky index finger pointed at the door. "The glue. Go get the glue."

Diggs didn't trust Petey White, but his plans didn't include roughing up a seventy-seven-year-old man for answers, and he didn't want to take any more time quarrelling. If he were going to get anything from White, he'd have to schlep for him first.

Diggs held the Emmy in front of him, pretending to examine it carefully—a subtle reminder that he had the Emmy in his possession and any double cross could prove disastrous for the copper lady's future.

"I'll be right back with her and the glue."

White offered no protest, which made Diggs more confident that no surprises were waiting. His gun in his right hand, the pieces of the Emmy in his left, Diggs moved furtively toward the kitchen.

On a kitchen counter were two clean dishes and two sets of unused silverware on paper towels. A pot half-filled with beef stew simmered on a stove. Diggs wondered what had so abruptly interrupted dinner.

He pulled open three drawers before he found the right one. He pushed aside two pairs of scissors, a roll of transparent tape, several pads of paper, about fifty pens, a tape measure, a screwdriver, and finally, in the very back, found a two-pack of super glue with one tube unopened.

Diggs returned to White's bedroom. He was greeted with a hopeful, "Did you find the glue?"

"I did."

As Diggs dotted the copper arm with a pinpoint of glue, White never blinked. His breathing was slow and heavy, the equivalent of Hyde watching the red ball tossed in the air. Thunder shuddered the room just as Diggs lined up the hands with the globe. He waited a second for the thunder to roll past before successfully connecting the two pieces. For thirty seconds, he firmly held them together. He examined the statue for any overflow of glue, saw none, and handed the statue to White, who greedily snatched it away. Through a smile of contentment, he said, "Thank you, Malcolm. I appreciate this from the bottom of my heart."

"May I ask you a few questions, Mr. White?"

"Why of course."

"What is Jerad's girlfriend's name?"

In a confidential tone, he said, "He doesn't call her anything nice, I can tell you that. That boy is a mess. I love him dearly, but I can't figure him out. I see nothing on God's green earth that tells me that either of them wants anything to do with the other. I know a lot about love, Malcolm. In the summer of 1974, Gladys Knight and I were passionately in love. I couldn't breathe without thinking about her. She'd sing to me while I showered. She couldn't keep her hands off me." With silly grin and a wink, he added, "And believe me, I didn't mind that at all."

"Is her name Claire?"

He answered through a mischievous grin. "Lately, I've been calling her The Mummy."

Diggs smiled with him. "That's very clever."

White's grin was replaced with fearful eyes meant to warn. "She's a mean dog, Malcolm. I know what she did to that school. Jerad insists that she's being railroaded. That's hogwash. I have a lot of connections, Malcolm. Not a soul believes that polecat is innocent."

"Did you burn down her house?"

White's eyes narrowed. "I am not a criminal, Malcolm. I have no idea who burned down her house. She came here after it happened. Her face was red, blistering all over. A horrible mess. She begged me to call my doctor and I did. He came right over and bandaged her up. Even then, I knew I was making a mistake. I should have turned her away. Told her flat out that we weren't a hospital. Now that she's here, how am I going to get her out? How am I going to get my son back?"

Diggs had been half-listening for any ambient noises, and

up to that point, he had heard nothing. "Ricky Racine used to live with you. Why did you make him leave?"

White lifted his arms an inch from the mattress, his palms facing the ceiling. He spoke with befuddled discouragement. "Ricky left on his own. He never told me why. Have you seen him?"

Diggs lied that he hadn't.

White's face turned sour with disappointment. "Ricky is my best friend. He's like a second father to Jerad. I wish he'd come back. We all miss him here."

Diggs stood completely dumbfounded. "Ricky never sent you an apology letter?"

"Apology letter? For what? He just up and left. I haven't seen or heard from him since. Have you seen him?"

Diggs again told him he hadn't.

He remembered Racine in the interrogation room, quietly offering an apology to his "little amigo". Diggs assumed it had been meant for Glen Palmer, but there had never been any indication that Racine tried to ingratiate himself to Palmer. The Palmer boy had been a challenge to abstinence and nothing more. Diggs was miffed that he so easily bought into a narrative that never made much sense. He now understood Claire's scheme and it disgusted him.

White lifted the Emmy off his thin grass of white chest hair. "You know, a lot of people don't think I deserved her."

Diggs feigned disbelief. "Why would anyone say that?"

White raised his palm as if he were taking an oath. "That's the God's honest truth. The headline in *Variety* read: *White Showed His Might, But It Can't Be Right!*

"Everyone was certain that Silverman put in some kind of fix. All nonsense. I met Silverman only once before. We weren't friends. He never made it to the set. He almost cancelled us after the first year."

Diggs pulled his phone halfway out of his pocket and read the time. He had been in White's bedroom for almost ten minutes. Lightning brightened the sky and crashes of thunder had become routine. Petey White was safe for the moment and Diggs had given up on Claire. She was a murderer and a lost cause beyond redemption. It was time to get back to Hyde and allow the state police to take over.

White's whispering words interrupted his thoughts. "Can you keep a secret, Malcolm? Before I say anything, you have to promise. It's as big a secret as you'll ever hear."

Diggs answered, "I'll guard it with my life," as he began to lift the windowpane.

White took a moment's pause, heightening the drama for his audience. "There are times I think my father might have intervened on my behalf."

Diggs turned away from the opened window, and he wasn't sure why. Anything regarding Petey White and his Emmy held zero interest but something about White, his strange charisma, the urgency in his voice, made Diggs want to hear more.

"Are you saying the Emmy was fixed?"

"My daddy was thrilled when I chose to become an actor. He loved television. Loved Milton Berle. Loved *Highway Patrol.* Daddy was always proud of me. He was the only one who truly believed in me."

White pulled the Emmy toward him and gave it a tender kiss. "That's why I cherish her like I do. If I won fair and square, I was the best actor in a drama series. If Daddy pulled a string or two, it's a testament to how much he loved me."

"Your father was a very special man. Mine was too."

White smiled kindly. "Yes, he was, and I'm happy to hear yours was. I pity any son who doesn't have a father in his corner. Makes all the difference in the world."

"I'm going to leave now, Mr. White, but before I do, listen to me carefully. Jerad's fiancé, The Mummy, is planning something that could be very dangerous to you and Jerad. I want you to promise me that you'll reach out to one of your friends. Have them take you away from here—tonight. I'm going to contact the state police. They'll be in touch. Can you call a friend to come get you?"

White squinted his confusion. "Malcolm, I don't know what you're talking about."

"I'm serious, Mr. White. Give me a name and a phone number. We can call right now."

An ear-splitting blast knocked Diggs sideways. The bottom of the window frame shattered and a shard of wood bit into Diggs' wrist. Petey White's chest had become a bloody crater. Behind the muzzle of a rifle was a head tightly wrapped in white bandages.

29

Diggs flipped the nightstand, crashing the lamp to the floor. The bedroom in darkness, he threw himself against a wall as he pulled his weapon.

Somewhere inside the house, he heard a noise. Footsteps, he guessed. A second shooter looking to trap him in the room like a rat in a cage.

Diggs fired two quick shots at the window and bolted toward the door. He escaped into the hallway without any bullets following him. No one was waiting to gun him down, but his disadvantage remained severe. Claire knew the layout of the house. She knew where to set up an ambush. Tilting the odds in his favor meant losing himself in the desert.

Diggs carefully maneuvered through the house, searching for exits and shooters. No one revealed a presence and the footsteps he thought he heard had gone silent. At the front door, Diggs stepped outside to a constant rain and a dazzling parade of lightning strikes. Twenty feet away was the iron gate that, had it been open, would have led onto the street.

He ran to the side of the house. A gate within the vinyl fencing was swaying in the wind. Diggs immediately burst though the breach with his eyes focused on the desert blackness in front of him. As he ran, a jagged bolt of lightning lit up the sky. At precisely the same moment, a metal folding chair flew into his path, crashing into his knees and planting him face first into the dirt.

Seconds passed. Diggs lay on his back staring at the sky, his body aching and his head woozy. The cascading rain drenching his face made him feel like a bar of soap on a shower floor. He could feel the heat of a figure approaching. The lips were visible, but the eyes were partially hidden behind black slits. Diggs shut his eyes and silently began to count, waiting for the inevitable. When he reached six, he slowly opened his eyes. The rifle's muzzle dangled over his throat.

"Get up, Lenny. I don't have all day."

Her voice was thick and muggy like a Florida swamp. Her words stuck together a quarter of a beat longer than they should. Diggs suspected he was hearing her through a concussion.

"Oh, and before you get up, toss your phone and your gun."

*   *   *

Over wavy mounds of wet sand, Diggs pushed a wheelbarrow toward a bright light near where the barn had burned. His sister walked six paces behind him, perfectly silent, pointing the rifle at his shoulder blades. If it weren't for the gusting wind puffing her raincoat like a tarp in a hurricane, Diggs wouldn't have known she was there.

"What's with the wheelbarrow?"

"To keep your hands where I can see them. Later on, we'll see." Her voice held no edge or regret. It was flat as a dime and as unemotional as a cardboard box.

"You're looking fine, Claire."

"Ha, ha. Shut up, Lenny."

Diggs slowed his pushing and turned his head, attempting eye contact. She held the rifle with arms as straight as a two-by-four. He guessed she was inexperienced with rifles, or her intentions were making her anxious.

"You're having second thoughts, aren't you, Claire?"

"About what?"

"Killing me."

"No, I'm not."

Diggs needed to stretch out this death march. He hoped Claire's arms would get tired and then he'd have a chance. He counted on the lifeblood of the narcissist.

"I was impressed how you ingratiated yourself to the Guthus. A pony at dusk? I laughed out loud at that one."

"I wish the Guthus no harm."

"Did your attorney give you the bad news that you're getting jail time even if you give the money back?"

She offered no reply.

"I understand why you had to kill Johnny, but the motel clerk seemed gratuitous. Was she planned or collateral damage?"

"Run your mouth if that makes you happy, Lenny."

Diggs craned his neck backwards. "Come on, Claire. At least tell me how you got Julia to spill her guts about Potter. I can't stand Potter so it would be fun to know."

A triumphant voice called out. "Okay, stop for a second. I get all the credit. Julia didn't tell me anything. It was all set up by me and only me." Diggs turned to face her. She was a bizarre sight. Her long black trench coat flapping in the wind, her white bandaged head floating in the rain. She took two steps backwards. The rifle dipped slightly.

"I'm really proud of that one. I'd been wanting to get something on Potter forever. Last year his wife of twenty-something years died, and a brilliant idea came to me.

"I knew Julia from the institute. We weren't friends. Actually, I found her kind of annoying, but she was a perfect lure—gorgeous and wonderfully gullible. I had a friend of mine accidentally run into her and convince her that he was working on a reality TV show that Petey White was financing."

"Let me guess. Ricky Racine."

"Bravo, Lenny. Ricky had a wonderful gift of gab. He had Julia and her father come here while Jerad was running errands with Petey. Julia and her dopey father sat with Ricky in Petey's living room listening to me over a speaker, supposedly in Hollywood." After a rollicking laugh, she added, "I was talking into one of those voice-altering gizmos while I cooked spaghetti in my kitchen."

Diggs thought back to the apology letter. Racine had written that he weakly submitted to "devils". Diggs had already figured out the first devil. He was pretty sure he'd found a second.

"Ricky seemed to know me."

"He saw you on TV."

"He was aggressive toward me at first, but he later denied he had any problem with me. It was you he loathed, wasn't it?"

"You want to hear the story or not?"

"Go ahead."

"Once Julia's father approved, I took over. I offered Julia a job as my eyes and ears in Mojave Creek. I told her to keep our relationship confidential because if anyone found out, the element of surprise would be gone, and the show crashes and burns. By the way, it was called *Back in Love*. It was about lonely people who tragically lose their mates and want to fall in love again. Sweet, right?"

"Sounds dumb."

"Quit judging, Lenny. It wasn't even real."

She lifted the rifle to Diggs' face. "Let's get going. I'm tired of getting wet."

"You're wearing a raincoat."

"Quit stalling and start pushing."

Diggs pushed as she proudly rattled on. After a few steps, he pretended he couldn't hear her. She moved in a little closer.

"I tell Julia that I heard about a kind-hearted widowed sheriff. He's just the type I'm looking for. A good man who deserves another chance at love. I tell Julia to run into him when he's alone. She does and makes the pitch. He politely tells her no thanks. She reports back to me and I'm disappointed with her. I talk about pulling out of Mojave Creek, which means she's stuck here. She really wanted to move to LA. Her goal in life was to become a famous actress or a television entertainment reporter. Kind of pathetic, don't you think?"

Diggs turned his head toward Claire and smiled. "I've heard worse."

"I'm not interested in your editorializing, Lenny."

"Couldn't help myself."

"Get moving."

Diggs did, but at a slower pace. Engrossed in reliving her conquest, Claire didn't seem to notice.

"I tell her to try Potter again. She must have really turned on the charm because he told her he'd consider it. A day later, Potter calls her. Says he wants to talk about it. I make reservations for her and Potter at a romantic outdoor restaurant with a fantastic vantage point from the street. While they're laughing and smiling, I'm shooting photos of the two of them.

"To make a long story short, for some reason they connected. They start an incognito relationship and I got him."

Diggs stopped. Speaking over his shoulder, he said, "Hold on a second. What if Potter isn't interested in a seventeen-year-old girl or what if Julia tells him no thanks?"

"It doesn't matter. I just need them together at as many romantic places as possible. After that first night, I set them up for a second night at that pretty park where all the weddings are held. I take more photos. Then I set them up at Pike's Ridge. Julia was the handsy type. Always touching. It worked beautifully.

"The more I can get them together, the worse it looks. Potter's wife hasn't been dead a year and he's running around with a teenager. By the time Potter realizes he's been scammed, *Back in Love* has disappeared off the face of the earth. Ricky is nowhere to be found. My Los Angeles phone number is disconnected, and Julia has no idea that I was the Hollywood producer. Petey will deny financing any TV show and everyone will believe him. Wholesome Julia Geist looks like a slut and Potter is a letch. Take it from me, Lenny. When it's perception versus reality, always bet on perception, especially if it's negative.

"But what the hell, it worked out better than I could have ever imagined. She actually fell for the loser."

"I assume Jerad knew nothing about this?"

"Nope."

"Have you killed him yet?"

"Why not wait and see?"

"Petey must keep a lot of cash in the house."

She giggled. "Oh, yes, for sure. A bottomless pit."

"It's not hard to see what you're up to, Claire. I figured it out, others will too. Petey has loyal friends. You'll be running for the rest of your life."

"Lenny, you don't think I've considered all the possibilities? I'm pretty good at this sort of thing."

"Apparently, not as good as you think. Can't you see how this is spiraling out of control? You've killed Johnny, the motel clerk, White, Jerad, and now you're going to kill your own brother?"

"If it means anything, I don't hold any grudge against you. I appreciate that you stayed out of my life for so long. But now you haven't. It's not my fault that you've become a problem."

Diggs could see that the illumination ahead came from an SUV's headlights. He slowed his pace. Twice she got close enough that a strike appeared feasible, but she'd catch herself and take a step or two backwards.

As the wheelbarrow bumped and grinded through the sand, Diggs stopped to pretend to catch his breath. He wanted her closer, but she stopped the moment he did.

"By the way, we found your car. We found the dog too. Kind of ironic. That dog caused so many problems and he's back like a bad penny."

Diggs was fully prepared to swing the wheelbarrow toward her and take his chances. He wiped the rain from his face and glanced over his shoulder. Even with his best effort, it might land a foot in front of her.

"What happened to you Claire?"

"What?"

"You're a grifter. You're a thief. You're a murderer. What happened to you?"

"I'm a survivor, Lenny."

"That translates that you're afraid of something. What are you afraid of, Claire?"

Approximately fifty feet away, Diggs saw a silhouette with a shovel in his hand removing ground from the earth. The size and shape made it obvious that it was Jerad. Diggs was surprised he hadn't been murdered yet.

"Lenny, I don't have the time to get into this, but let me tell you that after Dad died, it was a lot different for me than it was for you."

He stopped pushing and turned to face her. "Tell me how it was different, Claire. I want to know. I really do."

The bandages covered any clues her face might reveal, but the sorrow in her voice was unmistakable. "You wouldn't understand. You're one of them. Start pushing or I will shoot you right now."

Diggs began to push the wheelbarrow slowly before gradually picking up speed. The rain had made the ground harder, but it was still unstable, making it nearly impossible to keep the wheelbarrow completely under control. Diggs could feel her behind him. She had to be walking briskly to keep the pace. She hollered at him to slow down. He accelerated.

She hollered, "Lenny, don't make me shoot you."

Diggs immediately stopped. Claire's momentum got her close enough that Diggs took a swipe at her. She turned her body away to protect herself and fired. Diggs spun around her and ran into the black. Keeping his head low, he zigged and zagged across the wet sand. At the explosion of two rapid shots, he dove to the ground.

Jerad rushed toward Claire, which gave Diggs the opportunity to circle around to the SUV. Hyde's leash was tied to the bumper. At the sight of Diggs, he barked and jumped with delight. A few feet away, Sheriff Potter lay dead in a wheelbarrow, his arms and legs hanging loosely over its sides. A shovel stood tall in the loose dirt.

Diggs searched the SUV for keys. They weren't in the ignition, but on the front seat he found a gun. Diggs grabbed it and tucked himself with Hyde behind the SUV.

He shouted into darkness. "Jerad, take the rifle away. She killed your father. Take it from her. You're free from her. She can't harm you anymore."

The rain had picked up. Diggs' entire body felt like a sponge. The flashes of lightning had become irregular, but thunder continued at a constant rumble.

"Your father is dead. Claire killed him. You and I are supposed to be next."

Raised voices that were animated and emotional drifted from the blackness. Diggs continued to shout, "What happened between you and Ricky wasn't your fault. You were a kid, he betrayed you. Your father and I talked about it. He didn't blame you. He would have told you himself, but Claire murdered him. She can't harm you anymore, and she knows it. That's why she's going to kill you. She's going to prison otherwise. The new sheriff won't cut her any slack. She's going to jail unless she disappears."

Seconds passed before Jerad shouted, "My dad is really dead? No joke, right?"

Diggs could hear his grief. "I'm sorry, Jerad. He is. I'm sorry. He loved you. He believed you. He told me so."

For several moments, Diggs heard only the whistling wind. For a passing second, a bolt of lightning illuminated Claire and Jerad. He had the muzzle of the rifle pressed against her chest.

A shout and then two gunshots one right after the other, followed by a deafening boom of thunder made Diggs flinch just as he felt something brush against his leg. Hyde was darting into the desert, his leash straggling behind him like a banner attached to an airplane. Diggs stood in horror as the rainy night stole Mr. Hyde away.

30

Diggs abandoned the protection of the SUV and sprinted after Hyde, frantically calling out his name. In near pitch-black darkness with no idea which direction to follow, stone cold panic began to set in. Diggs fell to his knees and pounded his fist into the wet sand.

"Damn it. Damn it. Damn it."

Soaked to the skin and sweating with fear, Diggs' chin dripped rainwater and his hair matted to his skull like black algae on a drenched rock. Over and over, he admonished himself to get himself composed. He needed a plan that had a chance of succeeding. More light and a way to quickly maneuver through the desert were the first steps. Diggs looked out toward the SUV. Its long rectangular headlights were still illuminating the partially dug hole.

Diggs hadn't seen the keys the first time, but the interior was black, and he only had time to check the ignition and glance across the front seats. If the SUV wasn't going to work out, he still had his own keys. A Prius wasn't ideal for muddy and sandy terrain, but it had headlights, and anything was better than searching on foot.

Diggs got to his feet and ran toward the SUV. Twenty paces away, he slowed to a standstill. Potter remained in the wheelbarrow and the shovel still pierced the ground. There was no sign of Jerad, and that's when Diggs recalled not one but two shots.

Diggs made a straight arrow dash toward the SUV. Steps away from the driver's side door he caught a blur moving at his left. As he turned, he was grinning from cheek to cheek. He slid to the ground as Hyde jumped against his chest. Their reunion celebration was brief. A figure wearing a cowboy hat walked steadily toward them in a slow and deliberate stride.

Diggs grabbed Hyde's leash and picked the gun off the dirt. Eight feet away, Jerad stopped. His eyes were puffy. His jacket was smeared with blood.

"You found him."

Diggs answered, "Yes, thank god."

"You can take him with you. Anyone who is willing to risk being shot to chase after a dog in this weather must care about him a lot."

"I do. Where'd you find him?"

"Claire wanted a specific breed and Johnny got him. I think he knew someone at a shelter."

"She was going to annihilate him."

For a fleeting moment, Jerad glanced at Hyde staring up at him. Quickly, he averted his eyes to Diggs. "I found that out later. Had I known, I would have let you take him at Dad's party."

"Is she dead?"

"Yeah."

"What are you going to do about her?"

"I don't know. I was going to ask you the same question. She's your sister."

"And your fiancé."

"We were never going to get married. I hated her. I was willing to stick to her story until I found a way to get rid of her or Dad passed."

As he spoke, he held a strange vacant stare. His breathing was becoming labored. Diggs stood still holding Hyde's leash and said nothing. After several moments, Jerad appeared to have gathered himself. His eyes met Diggs' eyes. Calmly he asked, "How did Dad find out?"

"After Ricky killed himself, we found a copy of a letter he wrote. Your father confirmed the same letter was sent to him."

Part of Diggs felt shoddy for making up stories, but he couldn't convince himself that he was making the wrong decision. Diggs believed that half of the falsehoods ever told were for the better, and listening to Jerad's heartbroken words, it was impossible to argue that he wasn't seeing one more example.

"Ricky killed himself? When?"

"About a week ago, while he was in custody."

"In custody for what?"

"Shoplifting."

A sad smirk laid bare on Jerad's face. "No kidding? Shoplifting. All the terrible shit he did and he gets busted for shoplifting."

"It was more than that. He kidnapped a boy."

"Huh, I hope he's alright."

"He is. He's with his family."

"I'm glad. Ricky sent me a letter too. His little amigo."

"Don't blame yourself, Jerad."

"I try not to, but it's kind of hard. He was Dad's best

friend. His partner in *Rev and Roll*. You probably have a pretty good idea how Dad felt about *Rev and Roll*. How do you explain what his partner on TV, his best friend in real life, had done? I don't know that he would have believed me. He would have been mad as hell, but I'm not sure at whom."

"He would have believed you. He told me so. He knew it wasn't your fault. He wasn't angry with you."

"I wish I could have heard him say it. You know, Dad would have done anything for Ricky. He'd tell me that there was never an episode where either Rev Davis or Howard Roll did dirty to the other. Through all the adventures, they were always loyal. Somehow, Dad believed that would naturally extend to real life. Crazy, huh?"

"Maybe *Rev and Roll* meant too much to your dad, but he was an honorable man."

Jerad reached into a pocket of his trench coat and pulled out Diggs' Glock and his cell phone. "Claire had these. I assume they're yours?"

Diggs took them from Jerad's wet fingers and stuck them in his pocket.

"Why did Ricky go to such length to hide his identity?"

"What'd you mean?"

"I first met him as Richard Miller. Then he claimed he was Brian Harper. Then Richard Reed. He had an ID for all three."

"You forgot his cult name, Lofis Sky."

Jerad smiled weakly. Diggs couldn't even manage that.

"I always called him Uncle Ricky. Dad sometimes called him Ricky. Most of the time it was Rev. I don't think Ricky wanted to be Ricky Racine, and who can blame him?"

"I'm going to ask you a question and I need you to be truthful with me."

Jerad nodded. "Alright."

"Who killed Potter?"

"Claire."

Diggs asked how it happened.

"I was in Dad's room getting him ready for dinner when the doorbell rang. A minute later, maybe less, I heard Claire. Her voice was loud. I came out to see what was going on and Potter was lying on the floor."

"How'd she kill him?"

He pointed at the wheelbarrow. "There's a statue under his body. She hit him with it."

"Whose idea was it to bury him out here?"

"Claire's."

"Where's Potter's car?"

"In the garage."

"What are you going to do?"

"I don't know yet. What do you think I should do?"

"Call the police and tell them what you just told me. Admit that you shot Claire because she was about to kill you. I'll back you up on that. Tell them I witnessed Claire murder your father."

"You'd do that for me? She was your sister."

"A long time ago, she was my sister. She became something else."

The wind blew in circles, but the rain had softened to a drizzle. Diggs noticed a hint of a smile across Jerad's face. He shook his head.

"Not entirely. Blood is forever. Claire could have killed you in the house. She could have killed you out here. The truth was she didn't want to kill you. Blood is forever, and it's the only reason you're alive."

"Where is she?"

He pointed behind him. "Over there. You going to call the police?"

"I will if you don't."

"I'll do it."

"Okay. I'm trusting you. I have to meet someone. If I don't hear from the police soon, I'll contact them."

"Okay, fair enough."

Diggs and Hyde walked toward Claire's body. Ahead of them, a hole had burst through the clouds. The stars hadn't gone anywhere, and the universe remained a mystery. When Diggs found his sister, she was lying face up. Her bandages were soaked and peeling. Her eyes were closed, and her mouth was opened in an anguished scream.

Headlights grazed Diggs and Hyde. Jerad's SUV headed toward the house. Diggs stood under breaking clouds thinking about the last conversation with his sister. She said he was one of them, it was different for her. More riddles. Another mystery. Diggs tugged on Hyde's leash and they headed back to the car.

A few miles into Arizona, Diggs stopped at an interstate traveler's town along the highway. At a Wendy's, he bought Hyde a burger and shared a small order of fries. They checked into a hotel near the entrance ramp. Diggs pushed a remote button, bringing the television's slate face to life. He prepared himself for a shower while Hyde lay on the bed over towels Diggs had heated with a blow dryer.

Diggs had already changed into sleeping clothes when he saw a reporter standing in front of San Diego's City Hall. He stepped toward the television and adjusted the volume.

"Margo, there's a fascinating election shaping up in San

Diego. And it's not because the two candidates are in a neck and neck race, or the race has been contentious or ugly. In fact, all indications are that this election is going to be a big win for incumbent Randy Pelton. It's the backstory that is so captivating. It's the manner in which Pelton seized victory that is so astonishing. It's a story that has everybody in San Diego talking."

John Stall was the story that had everybody in San Diego talking. He had been credited as the difference maker, the life preserver that allowed Pelton's reelection to stay afloat and eventually win. The secret weapon that in a mere ten days had turned a six-point Wackerly lead into a three-point deficit and an almost certain loss.

Diggs turned out the lights and went to bed. An hour later, he remained wide awake. Images of darkened bedrooms, a terrified family, Petey White's bloody chest, Claire's dark eyes staring at him through her bandaged face refused to let him rest. Diggs switched on the television just to drown out the silence. His eyes were half open when a news report out of Gilbert, Arizona caught his attention and left him in stunned silence.

Diggs spent the rest of the night with his arm over Hyde listening to him snore and weighing the pros of unfairness and cons of decency. He tried to talk himself out of the obvious right for the selfish wrong.

As hard as he tried, he couldn't convince himself that being a loathsome creep was all that terrible. Goofus always seemed happy, and Gallant almost certainly endured a miserable life chained to his morals and his rules. Diggs imagined how Claire would have giggled at his dilemma.

He stared at the ceiling resigning himself that he had been Hyde's caretaker. The middle reliever who didn't win the game or get the save but played his role effectively before heading to the shower.

*   *   *

At sunrise, Diggs drove Hyde to a park. For a while, he threw the rubber ball into an open field and watched Hyde chase it down. From there, they ate at an outdoor restaurant. Hyde's last meal was a hamburger patty, carrot slices, and a third of a banana for dessert.

At 9:00 a.m., Diggs was sitting on the edge of the motel room bed talking into the phone. The person at the television station excitedly told him that he'd be getting a callback. Less than ten minutes later, his phone rang.

Heidi Wage was on the line. He recognized her soft voice from the news report. Diggs knew it was a lost cause, but he needed his own confirmation. "What did you say his name was?"

After she told him, Diggs spoke a silent prayer before calling out, "Kato, Kato."

A resting Hyde immediately raised his head. His tail swayed like a magic wand.

Diggs spoke into the phone, "It's him."

On the other end of the line, Diggs heard screeches of joy.

"I'm on my way to Chandler. Gilbert is pretty close. I'll drop him off."

She thanked him with gratitude that crackled with emotion. The call ended and Diggs fell back on the bed. Hyde crawled beside him, and Diggs raised himself to one elbow and began to stroke the top of Hyde's head. "I guess I'll be calling you by Kato from now on."

Diggs tried to convince himself that Kato was heading for a better life. The Wage family offered stability and routine. All he could offer was a workaholic consumed with solving murders.

Diggs talked himself into believing that, in the end, nothing had changed. His life's work would continue. He would speak for the victims and bring justice to grieving families. He would continue the daily grind of perseverance.

31

Hyde paid no attention to the red ball rolling across the rubber floormat. His paws were pressed against the passenger side door, his attention on the well-tended homes that made up the suburban Gilbert, Arizona neighborhood. When Diggs neared the address and slowed the car, he saw Mrs. Wage sitting beside her son Luke on the front porch of a small blue home. By the time Diggs turned into the driveway, Kato was barking wildly and the boy was bolting toward them with his mom following in a brisk walk.

They were waiting at the edge of the driveway when Diggs turned off the ignition. A grinning Mrs. Wage held a hand on the boy's shoulder while he beamed a euphoria Diggs wished every child across the world could experience at least once.

Diggs reached around Kato and unlocked the passenger door. The boy yanked it open and Kato leapt into his chest, knocking him backward.

Mrs. Wage was how he remembered her from the television news story. Shoulder-length blonde hair parted on the left, porcelain skin, blue eyes, pretty face. Diggs took a step toward her with an arm extended for a handshake. She stepped through it and embraced him.

"Mr. Diggs, thank you so much."

Diggs wrapped his arms loosely around her waist. "It's Lenny. I'm happy I could help."

She saw the sadness in Diggs' face that he was trying very hard to hide. "Are you going to be okay?"

"I'm fine. I'm going to miss him is all. We had a lot of fun together."

She placed a hand on Diggs' shoulder. "You're a hero. You should be proud of yourself. You gave a boy back his best friend."

"Your husband is the real hero. It's a tragedy what happened. My sincere condolences."

Diggs looked closely at her face. Her pale blue eyes glowed with kindness. Her smile was warm and compassionate. He needed to leave before emotion took over and he embarrassed himself. He took a step backwards. I'm glad it worked out."

She reached into her front blouse pocket. In her hand were several neatly folded bills. "It's Heidi, and let me give you your reward."

Diggs raised his hands in a no-thank-you gesture. "I don't want a reward for taking care of Kato. He helped me solve a case."

An enchanting, quizzical smile brightened her face.

"I'm a detective with the San Diego police department. He was a big help."

"He was? How so?"

"People respond well to him."

Diggs' eyes left Mrs. Wage and turned to Luke and Kato playfully roughhousing. A happier pair, he couldn't imagine.

Speaking to Heidi, Diggs said, "He's where he belongs. By the way, he likes Wendy's hamburgers. Plain but with the bun."

Her smile turned into a silly grin. "I think Kato likes everything, but I'll keep that in mind."

"I should be going now. I'm due in Chandler in an hour."

"Would you mind giving me your business card?"

Diggs reached in his wallet. "Sure. If you don't mind me asking, why?"

"You'll be getting Christmas cards from us for the rest of your life."

Diggs handed her his card. "That's very thoughtful of you."

She called Luke over. For the first time, he noticed the boy was wearing a tshirt with a Diamondbacks logo.

"You a fan of the Diamondbacks?"

"Yes, sir."

"I think they have a chance this year."

"I hope so." He reached out his hand and they shook. "Thank you, Mr. Diggs. I really appreciate you bringing Kato back."

Diggs bent to a knee and with both hands caressed Kato's oversized muzzle. As Kato licked his hands, Diggs said, "Take care of yourself, buddy. I couldn't have made it through without you."

He kissed Kato on the top of the head and said to the boy. "Take good care of him. If you look out for him, he'll look out for you."

Mrs. Wage and her son watched Diggs pull out of the driveway. He drove slowly, keeping an eye on the rearview mirror, entranced with the reunited family. Mrs. Wade had joined her son and was playing with Kato in their front yard. A car came from the opposite direction and, for a moment, blocked his view. By the time it had passed, Heidi Wage, her son, and Kato were out of his sightline.

On the floorboard of the passenger seat, Kato's ball rolled back and forth to the movement of the car. Diggs stopped and lifted the ball off the floor. It was littered with teeth marks and sticky with dry slobber. He dropped it in his glove compartment and put the car in drive. Minutes later, he was on the interstate that would take him to Chandler, Arizona.

32

Diggs pulled up to the gate of Wee Store It All feeling a sense of déjà vu. Over the years he had been called to his share of storage facilities. Sometimes a dead body beckoned but usually it was the motive in the form of contraband: drugs, guns, once a locker full of stolen catalytic converters. Another time, sports memorabilia.

Diggs punched in the code Billy T. had provided. A motor roused and the gate haltingly rolled from right to left. While Diggs waited, he kept his eyes on two men leaning against a Pathfinder smoking cigarettes and felt a buzz of adrenaline. The weariness from the sleepless night and the long drive was put aside and the sorrow of losing Hyde had been sufficiently compartmentalized. His mind was clear. He was prepared for anything.

Large black lettering clearly marked four individual buildings. The Pathfinder sat parked in front of building A— precisely his destination. Diggs pulled his car a space away from the SUV as the two men watched on silently. Diggs entered the building. Almost immediately to his right, the end of the rainbow—unit A-6.

The two men followed behind him. The one in front wore a Brigham Young University cap. Prominent lines etched his clean-shaven face.

"Malcolm?"

"Yes, Billy T?"

Billy held out his hand and they shook. Through an irreverent grin, he said, "Welcome to your one-stop bondage smut shop. Glad to meet you. Seems like we've been e-mailing each other forever."

Billy turned and nodded to the second man standing two steps behind. Faded blue jeans, blue jean jacket, and black boots gave him an urban cowboy aura. A prominent handlebar mustache covered much of the center of his face. The cowboy nodded at Diggs.

"My husband, Paul. He's my muscle. I take him everywhere." Paul narrowed his eyes playfully.

Diggs smiled and shook the cowboy's hand. After the social rituals, Billy's face turned serious. He said, "Unless you have any questions, I guess we might as well get started."

Diggs nodded. "Let's go."

Billy pulled a key from his pocket and stuck it into a thick padlock. At the click, Paul stepped around him and pulled a painfully screeching steel door upwards. Dim hallway light seeped into a locker that was no more than a narrow closet. Against every wall, white banker boxes were stacked four high.

His hands on his hips, Billy said, "Ahh, the memories. I haven't been in here in what?" A pause later, he answered his question. "At least ten years."

Paul added, "It's a time capsule."

Billy said, "Indeed."

Diggs stepped inside the unit. Black writing labelled each box with a code: BBF 1-60, BP 1-110, IK 1-19.

Behind him, Billy said, "There you have it. All nice and neat. If you don't mind, let's take care of the business part."

Diggs pulled a white envelope from his jacket pocket and handed it to Billy.

"Two thousand in hundred-dollar bills."

As Billy counted the bills, he said, "That'll work."

Diggs blew out a puff of air. "Wow, I never thought there would be so much."

"There's a lot a duplication. You'll find three, four, five copies of some titles. Silk never did have the heart to throw anything out. If you want, you can take over the locker. I won't be needing it anymore."

The mention of Silk's name immediately caught Diggs' attention.

Ungently, he asked, "You knew Silk Hemmingway?"

Billy raised his eyebrows comically. "Whoops, slip of the tongue. No harm in telling you, I guess. I worked for Silk. What you have here was Silk's private stash."

"Silk is dead?"

"Afraid so, I got all of this by default. Should have gotten rid of it a long time ago. You know how it is with storage lockers."

Paul interjected, "You rent 'em and you forget 'em."

Billy smiled at him. "Exactly."

Diggs said, "The codes written on each box. What do they mean?"

"It's the series. For instance, BP is *Bondage Possibilities*. BH is *Bondage Heroines*. IK is *Irving Klaw*. It'll make sense after you sort through a few boxes."

"I'll be honest with you. I'm mostly interested in a couple models."

"Which models?"

"The first is Jennifer Page."

Billy's eyes narrowed. He spoke with an angry edge. "I thought you were a collector. That's how you represented your-self. If you're looking to exploit a tragedy or have some ghoulish interest in murdered women, you won't be getting any help from me." He yanked the envelope from his pocket and held it out. "Here, you can have this back. I have another buyer."

Diggs raised his hands defensively. "No, that's not it. I'm Jennifer's son. Malcolm is an alias. My real name is Leonard Diggs. I'm a detective in San Diego. My father was accused of her murder. I think he's innocent."

Billy's offended tone hadn't changed. "You believe that some sleazy pornographer killed Jennifer?"

"No, no. That's not it either. I'm just searching for new leads. My mom kept her modeling life secret. I know she made at least one friend. The model named Libby Grace. I'm hoping my mom told Libby something of value. They drove from Oceanside to LA to get to the shoots. I want to know what they talked about. Libby is my last shot. I have no other leads to follow."

Billy let the silence sit for a moment.

"What was Jennifer's real name?"

"Sylvia Wright."

"Why is your last name Diggs?"

"After my father died, my sister and I moved in with my grandmother from my mom's side. She believed my father was guilty, so she legally changed our last name to my mother's maiden name."

"Well, you're right about Libby. She and your mom were friends. There's a coffee shop not too far away. It's close enough that we can walk. Paul, while we're gone, could please you find the Jennifer Page box? It's in there somewhere."

As Diggs and Billy made the short hike to Jenny's Coffee and Bagels, Billy rattled off questions that Diggs guessed were meant as a final hurdle to assuage any lingering doubts.

"I remember Sylvia saying that there was a certain day she was able to work because her husband was home to take care of the kids."

"My father had Wednesday and Sunday off."

"Sylvia complained about her car. I guess it broke down all the time."

"The Grenada?"

"I think so. It was blue, right?"

"No, white."

"You have any siblings?"

"A sister, Claire."

"How's she doing?"

"Not so well."

Billy T. and Diggs sat across from each other in a red plastic booth. Billy nibbled on a croissant while Diggs waited patiently with a glass of water. Diggs believed the best approach was slow and easy. Let Billy breathe, allow his memories to focus.

"Your mother was a nice lady. I liked her."

"You were at the shoots?"

"Sometimes, usually I worked in the mailroom. The shoots were in a room above me. The mailroom bathroom was a second changing area. Your mom and I got to talking between scenes. She said you were a budding baseball star. She was proud of you."

Diggs took a drink of water to battle his urge to choke up. Two beats after swallowing, he asked Billy how he got involved with Silk Hemmingway.

"Silk and I met at Brigham Young University. He ended up working in Los Angeles for one of the studios as a marketing guy while I drifted a little bit. He gave me maintenance jobs around his house, helped me get some carpentry work. I was Silk's first and only employee. I did a little bit of everything: working mailroom, stuffing brochures into envelopes, sometimes I shot the photos. Silk was a good friend. Helped me out more times than I can count."

"When did Silk pass away?"

"About fifteen years ago." Billy shook his head sadly. "Tragic. Shot and killed in his driveway. An attempted carjacking. No one was ever arrested. He willed me some money and that storage unit of old magazines and VHS tapes that no one has the equipment to play anymore."

Diggs asked Silk's real name.

"Tim."

"His last name?"

"I'd rather not get into that."

After so much time, Diggs didn't understand Billy's reluctance unless he had been correct that Hemmingway or his family somehow remained relevant. For the time being, he let it slide.

"Tim was a smart, smart man. He was a history buff. He was married and divorced three times. He was colorful as all hell and a bit of an operator—exactly the type of person who would start a bondage company."

"Was bondage a personal interest?"

"He stuck to his story that he was searching for a niche.

According to Tim, all of his motives were financial." Through a grin, he added, "And owning an adult company was an easy way to meet free-spirited, pretty young women."

Like the turning of a coin, the emotion left Billy's face and he went silent. Diggs watched him pick at the croissant. After several seconds, he began to speak forlornly.

"Tim knew he messed it up. He never forgave himself for what happened to your mom."

Diggs felt uneasy pushing this stranger who wasn't a criminal, who was trying to be helpful, who was being generous with his time but was also speaking in riddles. Diggs had spent most of his life guessing and speculating. He wanted the facts spelled out in black and white.

He tried a well-worn interrogation tactic. He leaned in slightly over the tabletop for emphasis and spoke low and decisive. "I need to know, Billy. How did Tim mess up?"

"I'm sorry, I'd rather not discuss it."

Diggs let out a frustrated sigh. "Can we talk about Libby Grace?"

Billy smiled wistfully. "I miss her. In my opinion, she was the most beautiful woman we ever worked with."

"Can you help me find her?"

"I haven't seen Libby since Tim's funeral. My gosh, she gave a lovely eulogy. Had me and everybody else in tears. I can try to reach out to her, but I won't make any promises. If she's not interested in speaking with you, there's nothing more I will do."

It wasn't the answer Diggs wanted, but even an hour before it was more than he could have dreamed for, and he appreciated learning that Libby and Tim were close enough that she'd speak at his funeral. Diggs took his winnings gratefully. "That's fair. Thank you."

Billy abruptly pushed himself to the edge of the booth, leaving behind most of the croissant. "Paul should have found the box by now. For obvious reasons, Tim kept your mom's material separate."

When they returned to the storage unit, Paul was leaning against the hood of the Pathfinder, smoking a cigarette. A brown-edged white banker's box lay at his feet.

"Well now, Paul. That was beautiful work." He kissed him on the cheek. "Thank you, dear."

Diggs' eyes were focused on the holy grail. "May I?"

"You paid for it."

Diggs knelt to a knee.

"While you're looking through it, Paul and I will be at the office to start the paperwork. Once you sign, the locker is all yours."

"That'll be fine."

Diggs touched the top of the box. Scrutinizing what his mother never would have wanted him to see made him feel like a peeping tom approaching a dimly lighted window. Diggs had always rationalized that seeing the photos was vital to finding her killer. With Libby Grace within reach, the priorities had shifted. The magazines no longer held the same relevancy.

Diggs lifted the box and placed it on the backseat of his car. He vowed that he would find Libby Grace and they would speak, and it would be soon.

33

The first homicide detective Diggs passed on his first day back at work stopped him to comment on Stall's breathtaking ascent.

"Worst detective Homicide ever had."

Diggs growled, "Not as long as you're still here," before brushing past him. He passed Swenson's office door. A booming voice called out, "Diggs, my office."

Diggs made a U-turn and waited under the door frame while Swenson chortled into his phone. After five seconds, Diggs flicked the overhead lights off and on several times. Swenson glared at him before abruptly ending the call.

"What the hell was that?"

"I don't have all day."

Swenson's face turned from angry to quizzical. "Alright, I'll make it quick. You got your wish. You have a new partner. How do you feel about Regio?"

Diggs shook his head dismissively. "That's not going to work. Regio was Sarducci's best friend. Sarducci blamed me for his relapsing. He's convinced that I got him fired. Remember when they escorted him out of the building? He tried to mace me. Regio and I haven't spoken since. He won't trust me, and I won't trust him."

Swenson shrugged. "Ancient history. You're both pros. You'll make it work."

"Sir, it's not going to. I'm telling you…"

Swenson interrupted. "We can talk about it later. I got a meeting at City Hall that I can't be late to."

"If you see Stall, give him my best."

Swenson sighed gloomily. "One of these days, we're all going to be working for that nitwit."

All that was left at Stall's cubicle was a computer monitor caked with gunk and a battlefield of crumbs captured in balls of dust strewn across his desk. On Diggs' chair was a handwritten letter taped to the Huszer murder book.

Boss, this is as far as I got with Huszer. Call me if you have any questions.

Michelle Huszer's half-brother, Bobby Vacca, came up a couple times—pages six and eleven. I was able to track Vacca down through public records. At the time of the murder, he lived in Grand Junction, Colorado.

Vacca remembered that Michelle Huszer's boyfriend at the time of her husband's murder was a guy named Duane Earls. Vacca described Earls as a "scary dude" who was "always in trouble." Since he was always in trouble, I checked the system and there he was. He is serving twenty to life at the Colorado State Penitentiary for murdering his father (must have been some family!).

I located Earls' one-time wife, Trinity. She lives in Delta, Colorado. Over the phone she stated that Earls admitted to murdering Huszer for stiffing him over a drug debt. She claimed that he often bragged about it. She also said that Huszer's wife Michelle was "messing around" with Earls for a long time before Huszer was killed. If you want to call Trinity, she said that she would be willing to sit for an interview.

I located the former Michelle Huszer. She is now Michelle Jahn and is living in Chatsworth, CA. I spoke with her, but she hung up after less than a minute. She made it abundantly clear that she hates cops. Maybe you want to give her a try? I haven't contacted Chatsworth PD.

I won't be working in Homicide any longer. I wanted to thank you for everything you've done for me. I know I'm not anywhere near the detective that you are, but that would be impossible because you're the best.

I'm not sure where I am going to end up. During the campaign, Pelton talked about the chief position. It would be a great opportunity, but I don't know that I'm ready for that. Maybe if you were second in command? Wherever I end up, I bet it won't be as exciting as working with you.

Eternally grateful,

Stall

Diggs sat in his chair unable to keep the grin off of his face. He leafed through the Huszer murder book past several pages stained with large droplets of fresh tomato sauce to the envelope of photos.

He laid the one perfect shot of Huszer on his desk. No longer did Huszer's chest resonate. Kill or be killed had become a rallying cry for futility. All or nothing, all the time. Even with a lot more wins than losses, it was a barely livable philosophy.

Diggs turned over the stolen Apple products to the Robbery division. A concocted story about finding the electronics at a rest stop along the 10 freeway elicited shrugs and no promises to return anything.

At lunch, Diggs opened the *Mojave Creek Westerner* website. A search for Sheriff Greg Potter led to an article reporting that he had been found dead two days earlier on a trail near his home from an apparent biking accident. The article did not state if foul play was suspected.

A search for the arson on Ocotillo Road led to an article in which an unnamed seventeen-year-old confessed to setting the fire. No motive was given. Claire's name did not appear within the article.

After closing the browser, Diggs began to check over Stall's work. He found no significant inaccuracies or missteps. Amongst his notes under the heading *Hates Cops*, Stall noted two reasons Michelle Jahn hated cops. The first was that her brother was doing time on trumped up drug charges and the second was that her mother-in-law's death had been ruled as an accident. Diggs wasn't certain which mother-in-law Michelle Jahn was referring to, but if it was Huszer's mother, the Avon lady, it was the first he had ever heard that she had died prematurely.

Diggs searched death reports and found that Rose Huszer had been found deceased in 1986 at the bottom of a ravine a few miles from Diggs' home. The cause of death was ruled an accident. The exact time and date were unknown but based on the date she was reported missing and the condition of her body, it would have been within days of his mother's murder.

Diggs placed a call to Chatsworth PD and two days later Michelle Jahn was brought in for an interview. She admitted to the Chatsworth police that she was present when Earls pulled the trigger on her husband but insisted that she was merely an innocent bystander. Extradition to San Diego was to be completed within the week.

His search for Libby Grace had begun on the day he returned home. An article culled from the *Los Angeles Times* archive section dated November 23rd, 2004 was pinned to his cubicle wall.

Valley Village Man Murdered in His Driveway

A Valley Village man was shot dead as he waited for his garage door to open. Tim Fitzgerald, aged sixty-eight, was pronounced deceased at the scene. According to police, a lone gunman approached Mr. Fitzgerald's automobile at approximately 10:58 p.m. in the four thousand block of Radford Avenue.

The gunman fired into the driver's side window, killing Mr. Fitzgerald instantly before fleeing on foot.

Police ask that anyone with information to please contact the Los Angeles Police Department, Van Nuys division.

Diggs placed a call to the Van Nuys division. He spoke with detective Charlotte Alanis who was unfamiliar with the case. Diggs laid out what he needed, and the detective told him she'd get back as soon as she could. Three days later, she did.

"Sorry, it took me a few days. I wanted to get a better idea of what was going on before we spoke."

Diggs told her that he appreciated her looking into it.

"The first thing I can tell you is that a lot of work went into this case. A shame it went cold."

Alanis spoke casually, often pausing a second or so after each sentence.

"Neighbors reported hearing gunshots at around 10:58 p.m. The first 911 call came in at 11:01 p.m. By 11:04, a unit was at the home. Paramedics arrived at 11:07. Fitzgerald was ruled deceased at 11:10. It appeared to be a targeting. Fitzgerald's wallet was in his back pocket. Nothing was taken from the car."

Diggs asked if Fitzgerald was any kind of public official or if his family held any local importance, in particular in San Diego.

"I never saw anything like that. At the time of his death, Fitzgerald was retired. His last job was at a wealth management brokerage. Before that, he was self-employed—a house flipper. Before that he built swimming pools. There was nothing I saw that indicated he came from money or anyone in his family held any powerful positions or had any local notoriety. At the time of his death, his portfolio had him worth about three million dollars, but the detectives believed he accumulated that on his own."

Dixon and Pace's refusal to identify Silk Hemmingway as Tim Fitzgerald in the murder book remained a mystery. Diggs quickly filed his disappointment and turned his attention back to Alanis.

"Fitzgerald was married and divorced three times and his exes all had alibis. No children and no stepchildren that he had any kind of relationship with. He didn't owe anybody money. Nobody owed him money."

"Who got his money?"

"William Thompson received four hundred and fifty thousand. Some went to charities. His first two wives didn't get anything. His third wife took the grand prize, which probably put her at the top of the suspect list."

"How much?"

"Let's see. Um, one million, nine hundred and fifty thousand. Warms my heart to know that not all relationships end bitterly."

"Anything in the investigation held back?"

"Uh-huh, the weapon was a .22. Four rounds were fired. The shooter made no attempt to retrieve the shell casings. The weapon was never recovered. This is interesting. The shooter might have been a woman and possibly from out of state."

Diggs leaned forward in his seat. "A woman. How so?"

"A cross trainer named Brad Loch lived a block over from Fitzgerald. He reported seeing a figure in dark clothing running to a black four-door automobile, possibly a Sentra, shortly after the shots. He estimated the figure to be about five foot two to five foot seven. He said the figure ran like an unathletic woman. The detectives asked him to clarify and he claimed that he trained a lot of housewives trying to get in shape. Besides being a cross trainer, he was a licensed physical trainer. He claimed to understand very well how a female's body moved compared to a man.

"A couple minutes later, two blocks away on Addison, a dog walker said that he saw a person in dark clothing get out of a dark-colored car, maybe a Sentra, and pull cardboard off both the front and back license plates. He thought that was suspicious, so he stopped walking and watched. He wasn't wearing his glasses so he couldn't make out the plate number, but he was fairly certain it wasn't a California plate, at least not the most common ones. It could have been some kind of special edition thing, but they brought him in and showed him a catalog of license plates from California and then from all fifty states. He ended up picking four possibilities. The most promising was Nevada because that was the only state within easy driving distance to California. It didn't lead anywhere.

"The investigators considered the possibility that an out of towner had been hired by an ex-wife or someone who might have a beef, but that never went anywhere."

With a pen in his hand and a notebook in front of him, Diggs asked, "What were the wives' names?"

"His first wife was Angela Markel. They divorced in 1971. The second, Elizabeth Trasanski. They were divorced in 1978. The third, Carlotta Labotta, divorced him in 1999. Being that she was the last, got all the money, and was quite a bit younger than Fitzgerald, she was the most promising, but she had a solid alibi."

"How much younger and how long?"

"Married for just under five years. She was thirty-six when they divorced. He was sixty-three. Not surprisingly, she was described as quite a looker. No pictures unfortunately but in the notes it says she was close to six feet tall. Long dark hair, perfect makeup. She claimed her profession as an actress and model. You probably know the type. She spoke with a noticeable southern accent. Says here she was originally from Alabama, so I guess that explains the accent."

"Can you spell her name."

Alanis spelled it out as if she were in a spelling bee. "C-A-R-L-O-T-T-A LA-B-O-T-T-A. Interesting alliteration. Bet she got teased a lot as a kid. It's still better than her middle name.

Her parents must have had a bizarre sense of humor. Liberty. Liberty Labotta."

Diggs felt his heart pounding. "Or Libby."

"Maybe Libby. That wouldn't be quite as bad."

Diggs refocused. "Any address?"

"Let me take a look."

The line went silent for a few moments. "At the time of Fitzgerald's death, she was living at 1367 Livingston Way in Sherman Oaks. Only a couple miles from where Fitzgerald was shot. Her alibi eliminated her. She was in San Diego with her family for Thanksgiving."

"Any other suspects?"

"If you assume the shooter was a woman, no. Fitzgerald wasn't dating anyone when he was killed. He didn't have any female business partners or any work colleagues or former girlfriends that had a motive. If you discount the cross trainer's opinion, there were two males, but they were eventually cleared. That longtime friend, William Thompson, and a buddy from the wealth management firm."

Diggs asked if he could have access to the files.

"I can't send you anything. If you come to Van Nuys, I can arrange to get you in a room with the murder book and any evidence you want to see."

"I may do that, Charlotte. I'll let you know."

The call ended. Diggs leaned back in his chair and spoke to the *Times* article. "Tell me, Claire, how did you find Silk fourteen years before I did?"

34

A DMV search revealed that Carlotta Labotta lived in Sherman Oaks at the same address Alanis had provided. She was now Carlotta Daut, but her DMV photo confirmed she was also Libby Grace. Her license listed her as fifty-six years old, five foot ten, and one hundred and thirty pounds. Her black hair still flowed to her shoulders and like thirty years before, her large expressive eyes titillated.

Diggs took a day off and set out for Los Angeles just before 10:00 a.m. Under a shining sun on a cloudless mid-seventies fall morning all was smooth sailing until he reached the perimeter of LAX. For the next twenty-two miles, heat radiated off the slow-moving metal of an endless stream of stop and go traffic. A fog of exhaust fumes forced Diggs to roll up his windows.

At 1:35 p.m., Diggs turned onto pretty, tree-lined Livingston Way. Carlotta Labotta lived in a Spanish bungalow with an orange stucco roof and wind chimes that hung over a small square front porch. Colorful Mexican pottery flanked both sides of a red painted front door. The front drapes were wide open, and a recent model Land Rover was parked in the driveway.

Diggs maneuvered into a tight parking slot four houses away. At the center of her front door, a six-inch square opening protected by a panel and a black iron cross watched over the porch. Diggs rang the doorbell expecting to see a pair of eyes peering out at him at any moment.

Instead, the door flung open, and Diggs was standing eye to eye with Libby Grace. Expert touches of makeup hid any wrinkles and made her look years younger than any mid-fifties woman Diggs had ever met. Behind a long white dress, her figure was obviously lean and fit. She wore flat stylish sandals, and her nails were painted robin egg blue. She was a perfect picture of femininity and, in Diggs' mind, as desirable as any woman half her age.

She gazed at him curiously.

"May I help you?"

Diggs heard the same sweet and distinctly southern voice that had once called him "Sunshine". Memories flooded back to the day he first laid eyes on her.

"Good afternoon, Ms. Daut. My name is Leonard Diggs. Billy Thompson might have mentioned me. I'm Sylvia Wright's son."

She lightly touched her chest. "I'm so sorry. I planned on phoning you, but I hadn't quite determined what I was going to say."

"I'm just looking for the truth, Ms. Daut."

"Call me Carly, and please come in."

Diggs followed her over rust-colored Spanish tiles into her living room. Soft new age music drifted from speakers hidden in black ceiling beams. A rolled-up yoga mat was propped against a fireplace. She tucked herself into an overstuffed chair under an olive-green circular chandelier. Diggs sat three feet away on a leather sofa. She kicked off her sandals and slipped her bare feet under her bottom. After she adjusted her dress, she said, "You have a strong resemblance to Sylvia."

Diggs thanked her. "I'm sorry that I didn't wait for your call, but I've been searching for you for a long time. I'm hoping you could shed some light on my mother's mindset before she was killed."

She gently rubbed her hands and gripped her palms together. "Well, she was very worried. So was I."

"About what exactly?"

"It will take some time to explain. To an outsider, it will seem strange."

"I'm not an outsider."

"Billy told me you purchased all of Tim's magazines. Have you had a chance to look through any of them?"

"No, I decided to speak to you first, but I'm familiar with the content."

She nodded thoughtfully. "What exactly would you like to know? Your mother and I were friends. Not best friends, but we enjoyed each other's company."

"Let's start at the beginning. How did my mother get involved with Tim?"

"She needed money I suppose. She saw one of Tim's ads in one of the beach newspapers and sent Tim some photos. Tim thought your mother was very pretty. He liked that she had wholesome California blonde appeal. He asked her to come to his office in Van Nuys. Before she would agree to make the trip, she wanted more details. Tim intentionally tried to be vague in his ads. He had an easier time convincing the girls in person. Sylvia had told Tim that she lived in Oceanside and my mother didn't live very far away. Tim asked me to meet

Sylvia. By then, I had worked for Tim several times. I could vouch for him and his company. I could tell Sylvia that she would be safe."

She rolled her eyes dismissively. "Tim believed that physically attractive women naturally listened to other attractive women. 'The theory of feminine equality' Tim called it. In this case, maybe he was right. Sylvia and I hit it off, and she agreed to do a shoot as long as it were with me."

"How many shoots did my mother do in total?"

"In a perfect world, Tim would have gotten her several times. But it only turned out to be one. A second shoot was planned, but it didn't work out."

"What happened?"

"A horrible idea gone very wrong and ultimately why I suppose you're here."

Diggs listened carefully while watching her face and studying her body language. He searched for any hints of falsehoods while at the same time, gazing upon her stunning beauty.

"Billy told me that Tim never forgave himself for something, but he wouldn't elaborate. Was this second shoot what he was referring to?"

She nodded. "Yes, almost certainly. Tim was sorry and terrified. I was too."

Diggs asked her what happened.

"Since you know all about Tim's business, I'll just add that it was doing very well. He was making more money than he ever imagined. With success comes hubris. It certainly did for Tim, which if you knew him, wouldn't surprise you at all. Would you like something to drink?"

"No, thank you."

"Would you mind if I got myself a glass of wine?"

Diggs said he didn't. She lifted herself from the chair and Diggs watched her walk barefoot into her kitchen.

Moments later, Diggs heard the pop of a cork. Minutes later, she returned with a tall wine glass three-quarters filled. She sat on the sofa a foot away from Diggs.

Again, she tucked her feet under her bottom. Her upper body tilted slightly toward his. After a sip of wine, she said, "This is difficult to talk about, and to be honest, I never thought I would have to. Both Billy and I were surprised that you were investigating Sylvia's death." She gazed at Diggs with an interested smile. "And now this development."

"Tell me what happened, Carly."

"Tim came up with the idea of allowing customers to watch the photo shoots. One customer at a time. At a steep price. As I recall, Tim charged five hundred dollars for a couple hours of gawking. He paid the models one hundred and fifty. Tim adored being paid for creating the content and a second time selling it."

"So, it was popular?"

"Tim was convinced it would have been. He didn't do it for very long. I did two shoots and your mother was supposed to do one, but as I said, it went badly. After that, Tim never tried another."

She scooted in closer. Her knee brushed against Diggs' leg. Her lips were eight inches from his. She held out the glass of wine. "Would you like a sip?"

Diggs wanted to reach out and touch her cheek. He wanted to run his fingers through her hair. He wanted to taste the wine on her exquisite red lips.

"No."

"Before I go any further, let me assure you that Tim was

careful. Before setting up a shoot, he'd speak to the potential customer over the telephone and if he passed Tim's tests, he'd meet him in person. If at any point Tim thought the customer was a creep, he'd move on. Tim's goal was to corral a handful of regulars he could trust.

"The first one I did wasn't any problem at all. The customer was very polite. He even brought me flowers. At that point, it was going better than Tim expected and he was getting overconfident. A customer offered Tim a thousand dollars to watch a shoot with me and your mother. He insisted that it be me and Sylvia. No one else would do. That wasn't necessarily concerning. Fetish customers seem to be very particular. Tim spoke with him and decided to set it up."

For a moment, she closed her eyes. She took a sip of wine and gazed tenderly at Diggs. "Your mother had reservations. She said she had fun at the first shoot but didn't want to do any more."

"Why not?"

"She was almost ten years older than me. I think that made her a little self-conscious, but mostly, she was worried you or your sister would find out. Tim asked me to meet with her and try to convince her."

"She wasn't intimidated by the material?"

"No, she thought it was silly. She didn't understand why anyone would pay money for it. Many of the models felt the same way. That's how I felt, but it was easy and if Tim deemed you marketable enough, he wouldn't insist on any nudity. I never took off my clothes and neither did Sylvia. I saw it as just another modeling job." She smiled beautifully. "Albeit more unusual than most."

"You were able to convince my mother to do the second shoot?"

"Yes, I told Sylvia that Tim would pay her double and she agreed."

Diggs asked her if she was driving a red Mustang the day she approached his mother with Tim's offer.

She made a face and spoke with surprise. "How did you know?"

"We passed each other on the sidewalk. You said, 'Good morning, Sunshine.'"

She dazzled him with another brilliant smile. Diggs wanted to leave the room. Desires that had been pent up for decades were raging.

"I don't remember that. I do remember seeing your sister."

"You saw Claire?"

"Yes, I was talking with your mom and she peeked from around a corner. I saw her and she ducked away. I was afraid she might have heard something she shouldn't have. I hope not. Sylvia never told me she did."

Diggs thought back and guessed that Claire probably had been home that morning. A knock at the door and a pretty and unfamiliar voice would draw the attention of any curious thirteen-year-old. Claire had never said a word about it to him and he had never told her about the beautiful woman in the red Mustang.

"Did my father know?"

"Sylvia was debating whether to tell him. I don't know if she ever did or not."

The scent of her floral perfume was wafting into his nostrils. "Back to that last shoot. Something went wrong?"

"Yes, very wrong. The customer was acting up. Making

lewd comments. Wanting to do more than watch, if you know what I mean. The customer and Tim started to argue. Sylvia and I had already been tied. We couldn't do anything. The customer claimed he had a gun in his car.

"Thankfully, Billy was there. Back then, he was the type you didn't want to mess with. He got in the customer's face and he backed off. He left and Tim cancelled the shoot. He paid Sylvia what he promised, and I drove her home. She told me that she would never model again.

"Soon afterwards, Sylvia told me she kept seeing the same tan Ford slowly drive by her house. Sometimes two or three times a day. She got a look at his face. She was certain it was the customer. I told Tim. He couldn't figure out how he had found her. He hadn't given out Sylvia's personal information. At the shoot, he always called her by her model name, just as he did with me. The shoot was in Van Nuys and Sylvia lived in Oceanside. It was very worrisome for everyone."

"My mother didn't want to call the police because her modeling might be exposed?"

Carly finished her wine with a final sip and nodded. "Yes, as far as I know, but she could only take so much. She was afraid he might try to harm you or your sister. She decided she had no choice. She had his license plate number. She told me she was going to report him to the police. Not long after that, she was killed."

"Carly, who was he?"

She began to gently stroke his leg. Diggs' desire for her wouldn't allow him to ask her to stop. He wanted to see her perfect body. He wanted to lay beside her in her bed. He wanted to release himself into her.

"I didn't know his name until I saw him on television. He worked on your mother's case. His name was Scotty Dixon."

Diggs felt his shoulders tighten. Dixon was a name he thought about thousands of times, but only as an over-vigilant, narrow-minded publicity seeker. Diggs was furious with himself. He had always been suspicious of Dixon, but they had been the wrong suspicions.

Diggs' rage seeped into his words. "Why didn't you tell the police what you knew?"

She placed the wine glass on the floor and reached for his hand. He allowed her to hold it. "I was wrong. Tim was wrong. To be fair to us, we didn't know for certain that your father wasn't guilty."

Diggs squeezed her hand tightly and then pulled it away. "No, that's not it. Dixon got together with Tim and they cut a deal. Tim didn't want any publicity and neither did you."

Her fingers rested on Diggs' bicep. "Your father did take his own life. That seemed convincing. Had Tim known for certain that Detective Dixon had murdered Sylvia, he would have said something. I would have too. Tim saw no reason to get involved. I was up for a part on *Santa Barbara*. They couldn't find out."

She leaned into him and placed one palm on his chest and her fingers at his belt. Her perfume, the red wine on her lips, her dark, mesmerizing eyes, that perfect face, and her breathtaking body. She was an irresistible force that had likely gotten her every man she ever wanted. She whispered, "Do whatever you want with me."

Diggs pushed her away. "My father wasn't guilty."

In her sweet southern voice, she said, "I was wrong. I'm sorry."

Diggs stood and stared down at his lifelong fantasy.

"I don't know why you'd be sorry. It's who you are. You were very fortunate you were out of town the week Tim was murdered."

"Why is that?"

"Take my word for it. You were."

Diggs left her house with his anger rising and his thoughts swirling.

35

Retired homicide detective Roy Fares sat across from Diggs at a family-themed restaurant at an Encinitas mini mall. Diggs had known about Fares for years. Diggs knew the names of all the detectives whose time in Homicide overlapped Dixon and Pace. He had never spoken with Fares because he had no role in Sylvia Wright's murder investigation. Thirty-four years after Silvia Wright was found dead, Fares was the only detective still alive who worked homicide at the same time as Scotty Dixon and Chuck Pace.

Fares had sounded lucid over the phone and claimed that he and Dixon were closer friends than Diggs suspected they really were. Diggs gave Fares credit for being wily enough to get him interested and then insist that he take him out to lunch.

The former detective didn't have a car and had no interest in a cell phone. Diggs used his Uber account to gather the detective at his condo and transport him to the restaurant.

Fares couldn't have weighed more than a hundred and thirty pounds. His arms were as thin as the branches of a newly planted tree, and his face was scarily gaunt. Specks of burgundy blemishes sprouted under strands of thin white hair. Diggs ordered a cup of coffee. Fares wanted french fries and a vanilla milkshake.

"Thank you for meeting me, Detective. How did you enjoy the Uber ride? Your first, I assume?"

His voice was clear and firm. "Drove a little slow, but he seemed like a friendly guy."

Diggs smiled. "I'm glad to hear that. I'll get to the point. As we discussed over the phone, I want to talk about Scotty Dixon."

"Right. You're looking at one of his cases."

The server delivered the fries and the shake but forgot to bring the coffee. Diggs let it slide. He was perfectly content to sip from a glass of water.

"Do you remember the Nathen Wright case? Wright's wife Sylvia was murdered. She had posed for some adult-themed photos. Dixon thought her husband was good for the murder, but he killed himself before he was arrested."

Fares sucked the straw with as much force as his breath could muster. The frozen sugar concoction begrudgingly rose upwards.

He was panting when he said, "Sure, I remember that. You guys are reopening it?"

"Just looking into a few inconsistencies. We'll see where it leads. Did you ever believe that Wright might be innocent?"

He dunked a fry in a pool of ketchup. "I thought he was guilty as hell."

"Why?"

"He killed himself, didn't he? That was enough for me. I'm surprised this is being reopened. Scotty was a hell of a detective. Kind of a cowboy, did some unorthodox things, but I can't imagine him screwing that one up. Once he found the smut, it was a slam dunk."

Diggs felt like he was swallowing a pair of scissors. "He was a hell of a detective alright. Did he do anything unorthodox on that case?"

"Considering his reputation, probably a lot of things. I know he interviewed the kids by himself. No parents. No psychologist. No audio or video recording. That was all against protocol, but he insisted and he got his way."

Diggs thought he must have misunderstood. "What kids?"

Fares' face twisted. "What do you mean what kids? You think I'm talking about the Jackson 5? The Wright woman's kids."

Diggs felt bowled over. He had never been interviewed by Scotty Dixon. The day after his father's death, he spoke with a police psychologist. Claire did the same. Nothing after that, for him anyway.

Fares poured a portion of the milkshake onto the fries. He picked one up with a fork and left half of it sticking out of his mouth like a cigar. "You married, Detective?"

Diggs told him he wasn't.

"You better start thinking about it. How old are you?"

"Forty-four."

"Don't get too caught up in the crime-fighting life. You'll never eradicate the world of criminals. New ones being born every day and you only got so many good years. I'm eighty-four, but I might as well be dead. Everyone I care about is gone. I'm the last man standing. All those people who talk about living forever are always young. Wait till they get to be my age. We'll see how enthusiastic they are then. Get yourself a wife and hope you die first."

"I'll keep that under consideration. Is Scotty's wife alive?"

"I dunno. She might be. Did you check the retirement homes? Don't think it matters. Debra's not going to talk to you for all the tea in China."

Diggs asked why.

"She was very protective of Scotty. If it's the same Debra, she won't like that you're looking into one of his cases. She's also pissed at the police in general. She was unhappy that Scotty had been determined an accident pretty much out of the gate."

"She thought Dixon was murdered?"

"I think she was embarrassed. There was no official reason for Scotty to be in Las Vegas. She didn't know he was in Vegas until we told her. He was having fun without her. Scotty liked to drink. He liked the girls. When they found him, his blood-alcohol level was over the limit. He lost control of his car and he crashed. Simple as that. To please her, we opened an investigation with the San Bernardino police. There was nothing there."

"The accident was on the 15?"

"Just over the California border. Two-lane highways out there. Everyone goin' a hundred miles an hour. Have too many drinks in you, it can be over before you know it."

Diggs asked Fares to tell him what he could remember about the Dixon investigation.

"Not much to tell. It happened in the early morning hours. A witness said he saw the car on the side of the road. No cell phones back then and no gas stations until Baker. He called the highway patrol from there."

"If the accident happened just over the California border,

he could have turned back and called from Primm. It would have been a lot faster."

Fares shrugged. "Guess he didn't think of that."

"Did your investigation satisfy Mrs. Dixon?"

"Not at first. Debra was a very bright woman. Scotty shared his cases with her. I guess she could be pretty helpful. She insisted on seeing all the evidence. She kept asking why there were no skid marks on the road, and she didn't believe the sand was disturbed enough for him to be going very fast. The thing they tried to explain to her was that Scotty wasn't wearing a seatbelt. His head hit the dashboard. He could have been going fifty and it probably wouldn't have mattered. She saw the light pretty fast. I think she also began to understand that the more of a fuss she made, the more likely Scotty's inner hound dog would come to light."

"Do you remember the witness's name?"

He waved dismissively. "No, no. It's been way too long. I do remember him being an auto mechanic."

The name fell hard out of Diggs' mouth. "Gary Wagner?"

"Can't tell you for sure."

"Did he live in Mojave Creek?"

Fares' eyes widened. "He did! I remembered wondering where the hell Mojave Creek was."

A grim smile crossed Diggs' lips. Claire had Wagner on an accessory to murder rap, and for a cop no less. She owned him for the rest of his life, and he knew it. Wagner said he was afraid he'd never be rid of her, and he was almost right.

"Do you remember anything about the Wright case?"

"It wasn't my case. I didn't spend any time on it."

"Besides Scotty interviewing the kids, nothing else you heard that went against the rules?"

"Not that I can think of but with Scotty, who knows."

"Is anyone alive who might have worked with Dixon on the case?"

"Chuck Pace was his partner. He would have been the one to ask. He can't help you though. He died a long time ago."

Fares put a dwarf fry in his mouth. A pink stain was spreading across his plate.

"You ready to go? I'll drive you home."

He pointed a crooked finger at the tall glass. In a rankled voice, he said, "I still have some milkshake left."

Diggs was halfway out of the booth. "You can get a to-go cup at the cash register. Let's go."

36

Shaded by two massive Eucalyptus trees on a quiet residential street, Diggs sat in his car and searched his phone for retirement homes. With the name Debra Dixon in his head and a long list of homes on his phone screen, next came the tedious chore of matching the two, assuming Debra Dixon was alive to be matched.

The winner was number seventeen on the list—The Happy Grandma and Grandpa Retirement Village in Vista. Diggs asked if Debra Dixon was a resident and the cheerful voice on the phone answered, "Yes, Debra is part of our family."

Diggs asked the visiting hours and the sunny voice answered, "Really anytime you want, but if Debra is sleeping, we won't wake her up unless it's an emergency."

"Is Debra awake now?"

"Let me find out."

Several minutes later, her voice was back on the line. "I am told that yes, Debra is awake."

Diggs' foot pressed heavy on the gas. A sense of fatalism admonished him to get to the retirement home before Debra Dixon died.

The retirement village was located on a heavily traveled road amongst concrete edifices and chain businesses. Across the street was a pretty park with a pond and a family of quacking ducks that must have been a godsend for the website and the promo brochures. The retirement village itself was two stories of coral-painted cinderblock with a passable street ambience. Diggs guessed it was middle of the pack for those kinds of places. If you were wealthy, you wouldn't give it a sniff.

Diggs approached a woman in blue hospital scrubs sitting at a desk in a large open lobby. Behind her, an aquarium was built into the wall.

"I'm here to visit Debra Dixon."

Through a smile she said, "Oh, yes. You called earlier. Your name again please?"

"Leonard Malcolm, but she might not remember me. I was a friend of her husband."

"Debra hasn't had anyone come by in a while. I'm sure she'll be happy to see you. Please follow me."

Diggs was led into a large screened in room and told to have a seat. Two ceiling fans quietly circulated room temperature air. An old woman sat silently in a wheelchair with her chin nearly touching her chest. Two old men sat at a table, a chess board between them. Diggs noticed that all four rooks stood side by side and every piece remained in play.

While Diggs waited and thought about Roy Fares' words of wisdom, one of the old men took himself away from the chess board and approached. Separating Diggs from visions of a somber future, he said, "Excuse me, sir. Were you in the War of 1812?"

Diggs smiled kindly. "What was that?"

"The War of 1812. Did you fight? You look very familiar."

"Sorry, you're mistaking me with someone else."

"Do you have a brother? A twin maybe. You sure look like a gentleman I knew during the war."

Diggs nodded knowingly. "As a matter of fact, I do. He lives in Delaware. He sells used muskets. I'll send him your best."

"I would appreciate that and thank you for your service." He saluted Diggs and returned to the board. Diggs waited another ten minutes before an aide dressed in slacks and a white blouse pushed in an old woman in a wheelchair.

In annoying baby-talk, the aide said, "Here he is, sweetie pie. His name is Leonard. He was a friend of Scotty. Remember Scotty, sweetie pie? Leonard was a friend."

The old woman glared fury at the aide but said nothing. Dropping the baby-talk, the aide said, "I'll be over there."

Her body was compact and shriveled and her hair white and matted. She looked like a frail ninety-year-old woman, except for her eyes. They were like tiny lasers beaming from a hostile country—cold, sharp, and tenacious.

Her eyes worried Diggs enough that he switched tactics. He was too young to have known Scotty Dixon and he feared she'd pick up on that immediately. He wasn't there to answer her questions.

Diggs pulled his chair closer. In a friendly voice, Diggs introduced himself as Detective Malcolm. "I'm Chuck Pace's nephew. Detective Pace worked with your husband."

She smiled. "Oh, yes, Chuck was a fine man."

"Yes, he was. He's ultimately why I became a policeman. I work for the San Diego police department." He gave her a long look at his badge but not his identification. Diggs was relieved but not especially surprised that she didn't ask to see it. At that point, she had no reason not to believe him.

"Your husband was one of the best. A legend." He pulled his badge from under her nose and stuck it into his jacket pocket. "I've heard so many great stories about him."

Looking pleased, she nodded in agreement.

Diggs' tone turned serious. "Do you remember a woman by the name of Claire Wright? She would have been about thirteen when your husband first met her."

Her eyes widened. "Yes, I do remember Claire."

"She lives in San Diego now. I'm investigating some things she's done that I can't get into. Over the course of my investigation, and I'm very sorry to break this to you, but you need to know..." Diggs paused a moment before adding, "I've found evidence that makes me believe that Claire killed your husband."

Without any emotion, she said, "I'm not surprised."

Her response jolted him, but his bogus compassionate face remained intact. He closed the space between them. "Why are you not surprised, Mrs. Dixon?"

"I don't know."

"Mrs. Dixon, that doesn't make sense. If you're not surprised that Claire murdered your husband, you must have a reason."

She stared blankly, seemingly disinterested in elaborating on her suspicions.

"Don't worry about it, Mrs. Dixon. It doesn't matter anyway. I already know what Claire did. Can you keep what I say between us? If you can't, I'm going to have to leave."

She spoke flatly, barely above a whisper, "Yes, of course I can."

"I want to put Claire in a cage for life. Not just a few years. For life without the possibility of parole. I need your help to do that."

"Alright."

"Let me lay my cards on the table. This is the most confidential part of everything I'm going to say. You cannot, I repeat you cannot ever discuss what I'm about to tell you. Is that understood?"

"Yes, I understand."

"I think Claire Wright's motive for killing your husband was revenge. Let me make this perfectly clear. I don't care what your husband did. I know all about Sylvia Wright's smutty past. A hundred of her isn't worth one Scotty Dixon. I have no intention in dragging your husband's reputation through the mud. All I want is for Claire Diggs to pay for killing a cop. It's as simple as that. I am willing to do whatever it takes to make that possible."

Diggs didn't see a hint of curiosity on her face. She already knew what her husband had done.

"Mrs. Dixon, I'm going to pin a murder on Claire. Not your husband's murder, a different one. She got away with killing your husband, but she's still going to pay. I'm going to get her for a murder that she didn't do, if you understand what I'm getting at."

She stared at Diggs silently. He could hear her slow methodical breathing.

"Can you help me, Mrs. Dixon? You know how it works. Cops protect each other. It doesn't matter if they're living or deceased. My uncle cared very much for Scotty. I'm doing this for my uncle. I'm doing this for Detective Dixon. I'm doing this for you, if you'll let me."

"What do you want from me?"

"I have to know everything before I move forward. It's the only way that I'll feel safe. I mean everything. I need to know exactly why Scotty had to take care of Mrs. Wright. I know he must have had a very good reason. He was a great man. I just need to know what his reason was."

"Couldn't you find an easier way?"

"Like what?"

"Couldn't she just disappear?"

Diggs lowered his voice to not much above a whisper. "Believe me, I've considered that, but it gets a lot more complicated. The best option is to send her away. Make her stew for decades. Make the rest of her life miserable."

Her head bobbed slightly. "I see."

"Then help me make this right."

"You already know what Scotty did. Why are his reasons important?"

"Scotty murdered Sylvia Wright?"

"Yes, both of them."

"Both of them?"

"The woman and her husband."

Diggs stared into her eyes looking for delusion but saw only an icy glow.

"Why both?"

"She was going to lie about Scotty. Her husband was too."

"What was she going to lie about?"

"It had to do with some pictures. They were going to make Scotty look bad. It was so unseemly."

"How do you know this?"

"Claire told Scotty things. That whole family was nasty.

Scotty tried to be generous to her. Gave her money. Bought her things. She was not a grateful child."

"You're doing very well, Mrs. Dixon. Did you help your husband?"

"Of course not."

"Are you sure? Remember, I need to know everything. Scotty never called on you for help. Any kind of help?"

"No."

"Mrs. Wright was afraid of Scotty. Somehow, he lured her to a vacant field. Did you help Scotty get her there?"

Her eyes narrowed suspiciously. She raised her arm and wiggled her wrist. The aide immediately left her seat. Debra Dixon took her own version of the fifth. She lawyered up the only way she could. She said to the aide, "I'm tired. Take me to my room."

Diggs raised an index finger. He said to the aide, "Just one more second."

The aide stepped away and Diggs positioned himself between her and Debra Dixon. He bent over and spoke into her ear, "You fucking cunt, I'm Sylvia Wright's son. I'm glad Claire murdered your corrupt piece-of-shit husband. Too bad she didn't murder you too."

He turned to the aide and smiled cheerfully. "You have a blessed day."

37

By the time Michelle Jahn was placed in a San Diego jail cell, she had hired an attorney and had completely clammed up. Diggs had her brought to an interrogation room anyway.

Rivers of deep lines ran across the former Mrs. Huszer's sun-damaged face. Her eyelids drooped and her mouth carried a permanent sneer. Scar tissue covering the length of her arm made it appear that she had spent many years dieting on a drug habit.

"I don't know why I'm here. My lawyer told me not to say anything to any fucking cops."

Diggs spoke in a calming voice. "I'm not here to ask you any questions about your ex-husband, or about any charges pending against you. I'd like to know about Jesse's mother, Rose. The way I understand it, you don't believe she died from an accident."

She stared suspiciously at Diggs and said nothing. Diggs waited, his patient expression never changing.

"About time someone took an interest."

"I'm very interested."

"Like I told the cops thirty years ago, Rose told me she saw someone casing her neighborhood. She sold cosmetics to a lot of the homes around there. She was always hustling, trying to make a buck. I respected that."

So far, so good. Diggs remembered regularly seeing Rose Huszer around the neighborhood. His mother had been an occasional customer and some of his friends' mothers were customers.

"Rose had never seen the car or the driver before. She thought he might be a pedophile scoping for kids. Women's intuition, she said, and Rose had a lot of nerve anyway. She pulled her car right alongside his. Asked him what he was doing. He didn't even look at her, just drove off. Not five minutes later, Rose notices that he's following her. A couple days later, she's dead."

"What did the man in the car look like?"

"Fuck, it's been thirty years. He was a middle-aged white guy. I can tell you that."

"Did he have any facial hair?"

"Yeah, Rose said he had a goatee."

"Make or model of his car?"

"Rose said it was a brown Ford, four-door."

"Did she get a plate number?"

"I'm sure she did."

"And you told the police about all of this?"

"I did, and they didn't do shit."

*   *   *

The sun had dipped below the horizon. Diggs sat on a bench in front of the merry-go-round with an opened box of popcorn on his lap. Yellow bulbs drooped from overhead wires. *Walk Like an Egyptian* blared from a speaker. Teenagers giggled and flirted. Children with fudgesicle-stained faces bopped from booth to booth while their young parents attentively watched on. For the first time since the fall of 1985, seven months before his mother and father were murdered, Diggs was in the middle of an island of colorful, carefree happiness—the Oceanside High School carnival.

He had been with his family that night in 1985. He'd won a purple stuffed panda for hitting the bullseye on a tin plate with an old scarred up baseball. Claire stood beside him, jumping up and down, far more excited for his win than he was. As the carny handed over the panda, Claire sweet talked him into exchanging it for a catcher's mitt. Diggs remembered the drive home that night. He and Claire were in the back seat of the Grenada, the mitt was on his lap. He remembered being glad that she was his sister.

Diggs thought back to what she'd told him in the desert, while her rifle was pointed at his back. "After Dad died, it was a lot different for me than it was for you."

Diggs again attempted to decode her words and he came up with the same answers he had every time before. He believed Roy Fares: Dixon had interviewed Claire alone. He believed Carly Labotta: Claire had overheard a private discussion between her mother and Carly. Diggs believed Debra Dixon: Claire heard something from that conversation and relayed it to Scotty Dixon.

Whether Claire's information helped Dixon or not, she believed, or was led to believe, that it had been vital. She had been a snitch. Dixon had convinced her, or she had convinced herself, that she contributed to her father's suicide. The gifts Mrs. Dixon alluded too made her a Judas. It was different for her. What could she ever do that would be worse than what she had already done?

Claire told him that he wouldn't understand, that he was one of them. Diggs guessed she meant a cop. Maybe not a Scotty Dixon, but he was a member of the fraternity. A fraternity that failed to protect his thirteen-year-old sister from psychological annihilation. A fraternity complicit in covering up the murder of his mother. A fraternity that likely covered up the murder of his father.

Diggs was part of that fraternity and from his first day out of the academy, he never doubted that he was one of the good guys. Year after year he worked countless hours righting wrongs, bringing justice to the living and speaking for the dead. Claire viewed him as bowing before an entity that had destroyed her and their family.

As a child, Claire had been fooled into becoming a traitor. As an adult, Diggs became a traitor on his own volition.

38

The manager of the Long Beach State Dirtbags was on the other end of the line. He said, "I think you should do what makes you happiest. As for that second part, let me make a few phone calls. They've already told me that they'd be thrilled to have you. I'll tell you though, we'll miss you."

The call ended and Diggs walked out to his balcony. The last sliver of a radiant orange sun had dipped below the navy blue horizon. Red and white Christmas lights decorated the shopping plaza across the street. At the entrance to the grocery store, a Santa Claus waved a bell.

Diggs stepped back inside and clicked around the internet. A front-page story on *The Westerner* website from nine days before reported that Petey White had died in his home from natural causes. Diggs wasn't surprised that Jerad opted for an alternative narrative. Diggs wasn't surprised that Jerad never contacted the police, nor was Diggs surprised that he never carried out any of his threats, nor was he surprised that he had no interest in tipping off the Mojave Creek police.

Despite Jerad's musings that blood was forever, Diggs had no illusions that Claire had every intention to murder him. She was leading him toward a shallow grave with a rifle pointed at his back. With three cold-blooded kills in less than two hours, the heat of a murder frenzy had consumed her. She fired at him twice as he ran into the desert, and nothing had led him to believe she wasn't aiming for a kill.

Murderers sometimes get murdered and those who travel sordid lives seeped in treachery normally don't receive a bouquet of flowers on their way off the mothership. The fact was, Claire had chosen a life that led to a somewhat predictable ending.

Diggs scanned through edition after edition and never once found a reference to his sister. He did find an article reporting that the money stolen from The Frederic Remington Academy for the Arts had been recovered and the funds would be in the hands of Mr. and Mrs. Guthu by Christmas. The satisfying news brought a welcomed smile that momentarily cooled Diggs' expanding case of burnout.

His mother's murder solved, Diggs figured that it might be time to travel another road. Too many murders and too much darkness were leading him down a path that offered nothing but regrets.

The monitor screen had fallen asleep. Diggs turned on the desk lamp and considered a thought that had been bouncing inside his head for weeks. The satisfaction of making one bold decision built his confidence to make a second and, at that moment, Diggs felt like he had nothing to lose. He lifted his phone and scrolled through the numbers he had received until he found hers. He placed the call, and she picked up. Her sunny response to his introduction made him believe he had made the right choice.

"How's Kato?"

She laughed. "Probably feeling a little claustrophobic. Luke never lets him out of his sight."

Diggs thought he heard a hint of melancholy. "How are you doing? Are you and Luke okay?"

"To be honest, it's been tough. It's our first holiday since Mark passed. Luke is not having an easy time. We'll get through it. It's going to take some time is all."

Her voice brightened. "I read an article about you finding that kidnapped boy. What you did was amazing."

Diggs didn't understand. Stall had always gotten the media credit for finding Palmer.

"You did?"

"There's an article on Yahoo. Your old partner was interviewed. He detailed the whole investigation. He said that the only reason the boy was found was because of you."

"I'll have to look for it."

"Can I be honest with you?"

"Sure."

"After reading the article, I looked you up on the internet and saw that you were once a baseball player."

"A long time ago I was a baseball player."

"You're still a lot more of an expert than I'll ever be. Can I ask you a baseball question?"

"Of course."

"I want to buy Luke a glove for Christmas. Are all gloves the same? It doesn't look like they are."

"No, not at all. What position is he interested in?"

"I don't know. Sports are confusing to me."

"Ask him what position he wants to play. Or, if you don't want to be that direct, find out who his favorite player is. That will give you a clue. Once you find out, let me know and we'll go from there."

His words came out in a flurry. "Maybe we could get together after Thanksgiving. I plan to be in Tempe for a while. We could have lunch and buy a glove? I'd love to see Kato again."

Diggs listened for hesitation and heard none. "That sounds like fun. Maybe the second week of December? Luke will be spending the week at his grandparents. I work during the day, but maybe I can get a day off or if you're working, we could get together afterwards. There's a restaurant out here that allows customers to bring their dogs. Believe it or not, the food isn't bad."

"Sounds great. It's a deal."

They spoke for another thirty minutes. Diggs got the impression that she didn't want the call to end, and he was happy to stay on the line as long as she desired. She wished him a happy Thanksgiving and told him to call her early the following week when she'd have a better idea of what was going on. Diggs hung up feeling like doing a jig on his balcony, and so he did.

*   *   *

It was just after 9:00 a.m. on a mid-December morning. The air was crisp and cool. Snow topped the mountains like marshmallow coating over a chocolate ice cream cone. The satellite radio station Diggs normally listened to was having technical issues. He was punching around the dial searching for something that wouldn't give him a headache when he heard a song he liked. After it ended, an obnoxious clown show took over. The DJs were loud rather than funny, and they laughed at everything they said. Diggs was ready to switch stations when one of them said, "Here's a new dead has-been to celebrate. Petey White. Anyone know who he is?"

A woman said, "I'm totally stumped."

A man said, "Umm... Is he Walter White and Betty White's son?"

"No, he was a television actor from the 1970s. He won an Emmy Award for a show called *Rev and Roll.* Anyone ever seen it?"

The man said, "Seen it? I've never heard of it."

The woman added, "Not even once."

"Petey White, a true has-been. God bless you, Mr. White, whomever you are."

The three idiots began to howl like banshees. Diggs offered his middle finger to the radio before flicking it off. He dialed Stall's number, expecting to have to deal with the liaison, but he picked up.

"Stall, it's Diggs."

"Hey boss, Merry Christmas. Give me a second. Let me get into my office." From a desk in Juvenile Crimes to a cubicle in Homicide to an office at City Hall. Almost certainly a corner office with floor to ceiling windows overlooking both the city and the ocean. Diggs still couldn't quite believe it. A moment later, Stall was back on the line.

"I didn't screw up a case, did I?"

"Hardly, you did a hell of a job with Huszer. His wife is in jail thanks to you."

"Oh, man. That's fantastic. That makes my day."

Diggs heard the same elation he used to feel after he solved a case. "I called because I wanted you to hear it from me first. After the holidays, I'm going to take a leave of absence."

"You're kidding. For how long?"

"As long as the union will allow and probably more than that. I need a break."

"Boss, you're not the type to sit around the house. After two days, you'll go crazy."

"I'll be doing volunteer work at Arizona State. With the baseball team."

"I didn't know you liked baseball. You always struck me as a bowling kind of guy."

Diggs smiled into the phone. "Take care of yourself, John."

""Boss, before you hang up, I want to let you know that after the new year, I'll be starting a new job. Assistant to the chief."

"Congratulations. What'll you be doing?"

"It's going to be open-ended. I'll be working with media relations. Sometimes I'll be assisting detectives. The chief promised me I could be involved with the big cases. The ones like Glen's. Why don't you come back then? I've learned so much from you, but I know I've only touched the tip of the iceberg. I'm sure the chief would let us work together."

Diggs felt oddly moved. "I certainly appreciate the offer. How about if I take some time to think about it?"

"Sure thing, boss. You know how to find me. I hope you'll say yes. We need you. Pelton wants to make the department the best in the world."

Diggs grinned into the phone. "Not the universe?"

Stall laughed. "For now, he's settling for the world. He wants ideas from me. I have one I like a lot. Can I run it by you?"

"Of course."

"Glen and I came up with it. We call it the Children's Commission. The idea is to have a cross-section of kids ten to thirteen years old suggest ideas that will make the department better. Kids are going to tell it like it is. I think they deserve to be heard. It's their city too."

"Mm, that's an interesting idea. If you're going for the best department in the world, you have to think outside the box."

"My thoughts exactly. Make sure to keep in touch, boss. My office is always open to you."

They ended the call. The exit to Gilbert was a mile away. Diggs reached a hand over to the passenger seat and grabbed hold of a brand new red rubber ball. He kept his eyes open for a Wendy's.

ACKNOWLEDGMENTS

This book could not have been written without the help of Robert Eversz who pointed out the flaws while offering nothing but encouragement. Bryan Smith was a great friend in reading the next version whenever I asked. Brilliant authors like Willy Vlautin and Dan Chaon were my aspirations. This book came to fruition because of very happy two-year period when I was able to see my canine best friend regularly while also enjoying the company of his human mom. Wonderful days indeed.